DUEL OF SORCERY

Her Noris stands high on the mountain, black boots ankle deep in cold stone, his narrow elegant form a darkness half obscured by swirls of snow and mist—cold, cold, so cold. Pale hands reach for her, sad eyes plead with her. "Help me, Serroi," he whispers, and the words are splinters of ice tearing into her flesh—cold, cold, so cold.

Stone creeps around his knees while below, far below, the valley stretches out in golden splendor. "Help me," he pleads. Grey and relentless the stone rises past his waist—cold, so cold.

"Come to me, daughter, come to me." The stone closes around his neck.

"Let me be, father, let me be, teacher," she whispers and sees before the stone closes over his head the agony in his eyes, an agony without measure as the pain in her is without measure—cold, so terribly cold.

JO CLAYTON

MOONGATHER (#1: The Duel of Sorcery)

MOONSCATTER (#2: The Duel of Sorcery)

CHANGER'S MOON (#3: The Duel of Sorcery)

DIADEM FROM THE STARS

LAMARCHOS (Diadem #2)

IRSUD (Diadem #3)

MAEVE (Diadem #4)

STAR HUNTERS (Diadem #5)

THE NOWHERE HUNT (Diadem #6)

GHOSTHUNT (Diadem #7)

THE SNARES OF IBEX (Diadem #8)

A BAIT OF DREAMS

MOONSCATTER

by

Jo Clayton

DAW BOOKS, INC.

DONALD A. WOLLHEIM, PUBLISHER

1633 Broadway, New York, NY 10019

FIRST PRINTING, FEBRUARY 1983

5 6 7 8 9

PRINTED IN U.S.A.

MOONSCATTER

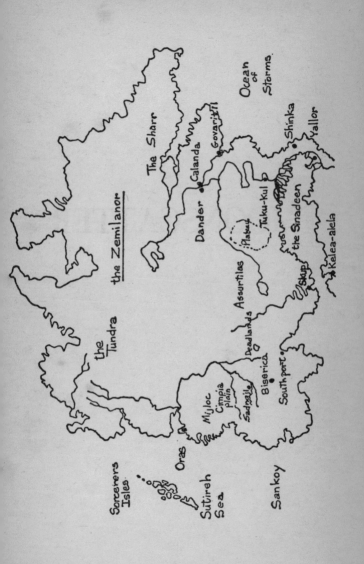

the Zemilanor

the Tundra

The Sharr

Ocean
of
Storms

Sorcerers
Isles

Sutireh
Sea

Oras

Mijloc
Cimpia
plain

Sadgeji

Deadlands

Bisérica

Southport

Sankoy

Assurtlas

Dander

Calanda

Govar'ill

Plateau

Tuku-kul

the Snadeen

Skup

Kelea-alela

Shinka

Yallor

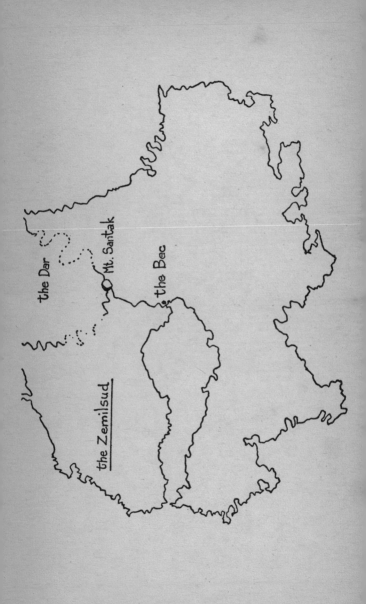

the Dar

Mt. Santak

the Bec

the Zemilsud

Once upon a time a sorcerer soured on life and challenged it to a duel—in other words, this is

WHAT HAS GONE BEFORE

A master of many sorceries secured for himself what amounted to immortality—a cessation of the processes of growth and decay within his body—and in so doing, promoted himself to the rank of noris. For several centuries he enjoyed himself collecting knowledge, honing his skills, dueling with other adepts. But as time passed he grew bored, monumentally, disastrously bored.

After fretting and starting to feel old and useless, he realized that he could beat his boredom by extending his control of change and decay beyond the narrow confines of his body and imposing it on the world beyond the Sorcerers Isles. He could make for himself a new game. To make the game worth playing, he needed an opponent worth playing against. He found his opponent in She whom men called variously Maiden, Matron and Hag, She who was implicit in the alternation of death and birth, in the cycling of the seasons, the complex circling of the moons, She who was phoenix continually reborn from her own ashes, She who sometimes used as a vessel of her presence Reiki, janja to a tribe of the pehiir.

In *Moongather,* the challenge is issued, the pieces are selected, the game is begun.

THE PIECES
(who act without knowing they are pawns in a power game)

SERROI
used by both players—Ser Noris and Reiki janja.
misborn of the windrunners, preserved from death by burn-

ing by Ser Noris, taken to his Tower, raised and taught by
him, her gifts used by him until she is twelve.

abandoned in a desert east of the mijloc when she becomes
useless to him.

walks out of the desert to a tribe of pehiir whose wise
woman is Reiki janja, spends several months with her.

makes her way finally to the Biserica, where she lives in
peace for a number of years, studying and learning the skills
of a meie. On her second ward—this time a guard to the
women's quarters of the Plaz and the Domnor's wives,
Floarin and Lobori, and his assorted concubines—she and
her shieldmate learn of a plot against the Domnor; her
shieldmate is killed and she runs.

when her panic dissipates, she returns to Oras, acquiring a
companion called Dinafar, meeting the Gradin family on the
way.

(She is disguised as Dinafar's brother.)

played in the game as Reiki janja's piece, she thwarts the plot
against the Domnor, though only partially because he is
driven from power by his wife, Floarin, with the aid of a
norit and forced to flee for his life.

she returns to the Biserica, taking the Domnor and Dinafar
with her.

HERN HESLIN
Fourth Domnor in the Heslin line since the original Heslin
united the mijloc.

is nearly yanked out of his skin and replaced by a demon at
the Moongather, but Serroi and a poison knife along with a
small horde of rats and roaches introduce a little healthy
havoc to the scene, and he escapes with her after a sword
fight and some spectacular magic.

his role in the game seems minimal at first but gradually
grows in importance.

MINOR PIECES
Moved by Ser Noris: the plotters who think they're the insti-
gators of the plot, assorted Sleykynin, Plaz guards, demons, a
temple keeper of some importance and others.

Moved by Reiki janja: creata shurin (small brown intelligent
teddy bears, sort of), Coperic, rogue and spy for the Biserica,
the fisherfolk, the Gradin family, and others.

In *Moonscatter*, the game continues, shifting into a new
phase. Ser Noris applies pressure wherever he can put his
thumb. Reiki janja seems to be losing, though she is fighting
hard, but there are small things that begin to disturb the
noris.

SOME WORDS

AGLI
A norid with religious aspirations, a taste for sniffing tidra
and for watching folk make fools of themselves.

BISERICA
An idea.
A structure at the north end of the Valley of Women.
Training school for shrine keepers, meien, healwomen.
Refuge for girls who find it painful or impossible to live
within the bounds of their cultures.

> Girls everywhere, a flood of girls, girls chattering, laugh-
> ing, impatient, sullen, cheerful, glowing, lazy, bubbling
> with nervous energy. Tie girls, tarom's daughters, city
> girls from Sel-ma-carth and Oras, girls from distant
> peoples whose names and locations would be a catalog
> of the countries of the world. A culling of girls, the re-
> bellious, the restless, the pleasure-loving, the pious, some
> fleeing repression, some seeking whatever it was the
> Biserica seemed to offer.

Sometimes the refuge is temporary, sometimes permanent. An
ancient order whose origins are lost in misty before-time.

FOLLOWERS OF THE FLAME
Those dissatisfied with Maiden worship, those who find much
more support for self-worth in a male image with aspects of
control, strength, order, power, those who want to make sure
everyone acts in a way they consider proper.

HOUSE OF REPENTANCE
Brainwashing bureau.

MAIDEN
Aspect of Her honored in the mijloc.

MEIE
Weaponwoman.
Sent out from the Biserica on three-year wards.

Fees are paid to the Biserica for the services of a meie pair and these are given an additional fee for themselves.

Generally serve as bodyguards, guards of womens quarters, escorts for women traveling in caravans or on board ships, as aides to merchants and in other miscellaneous duties that require integrity, intelligence, agility, skill with assorted weapons.

Up to the present, meien were welcomed and respected everywhere but in Assurtilas.

NEARGA NOR
1. All sorcerers currently living.
2. The council of adepts.
3. Ser Noris (since the most powerful adepts left alive jump when he says hop).

NOR
General term for sorcerers when rank is not in question.

NORID
Lowest rank of sorcerers, little more than tricksters performing in the streets.

NORIT
The classy types. Not a lot of them around, perhaps a thousand scattered about the world. Their abilities and power are limited when compared to the great nor, but much beyond those of the rather pitiful norids.

NORIS
The highest rank. The immortals. The survivors. Four left, one of whom is Ser Noris.

SHAWAR (The Silent Ones)
The heart of the Biserica. A circle of women Elders who are greatly talented in magic and whose gifts are devoted to the service of the Maiden and the forces of life. Very little is known about them beyond the above.

SLEYKYN
Weaponmen.
They hire out to provide services; fees are paid both to the individual and the order.

They serve as bodyguards, assassins, torturers, muscle for ambitious lordlings, raiders, spies.

SOÄREH
Lord of light, his aspects are reason, logic, control, power, force, order.
He is eternal and unchanging.

STENDA
Mountain dwellers whose holds are united by a common culture and a great deal of intermarriage.
Very loosely affiliated with the mijloc, nominally under the rule of the Domnor.
Independent, arrogant, rigid in their interpretation of custom, xenophobic, deadly fighters, terrible soldiers.

TAR
A big chunk of land held by one family, a glorified farm.

TAROM
Owner of a tar, head of a family.

TAROMATE
Landowner's council, more or less runs things in its area. Usually organized about a town or a village.

TIE
A person born on a tar, not legally bound to the land, but in practice that's what it amounts to.
As taroms inherit land, ties inherit jobs.

TILUN
Combination prayer meeting and orgy.

TORMA
Tarom's wife.

The Belly of the Lune (an interlude)

A tic fluttering beside his mouth, long pale fingers tapping a ragged rhythm on his knee, he squatted before the board, slitted obsidian eyes flitting across the pebble patterns where black was advancing in a somber wave to encircle all that remained of white.

She knelt on an ancient hide, the coarse wool cloth of her skirt falling across the rounds of her thighs in stiff, hieratic folds. Sweat crawled down her calm unsmiling face, down gullies worn in her weathered flesh by time and pain.

The gameboard sat on a granite slab that thrust through shag and soil like a bone through broken flesh and fell away a stride or two behind the squatting man, a thousand feet straight down to the valley floor where the earth lay groaning under the weight of its own abundance, where even in the breathless autumn heat black midges swarmed across the land, scything and sheaving the grains, stripping a golden rain from fruit trees in the orchards, stooping along plant rows in the fields.

The sun struck bloody glitters off the ruby teardrop dangling from one nostril as he leaned forward and placed a black pebble on a point, closing a black circle about a lone white straggler. He smiled, a quick lift and fall of his lips, plucked the pebble from the circle and held it pinched between two fingers. "Give it up, Reiki janja. The game is mine. Or soon will be."

The clear brown-green of water in a shady tarn, her luminous eyes turned sad as she watched him rise, flick the pebble aside and walk to the cliff edge where he stood gazing hungrily down into the valley, hands clasped behind him, paperwhite against the dull black of his robe. "No," she said. The word hung heavy in the hot, still air. "You started it. End it."

A film of sweat on his pale face, he kicked restlessly at bits of stone, unable to match her response, his irritation all the greater for this. After a moment's strained silence, he turned his gaze on her, his black eyes flat and cold. "End it—why? Hern? Or the meie?" He jabbed his forefinger at the

14

many-courted edifice below. "They're impotent as long as they sit down there and in my hands if they come out. When I'm ready, I'll sweep them off the board." He swung his arm in a slashing arc. "The mijloc is mine already, janja, in all the ways that count. I gather strength every day. You retreat."

"Perhaps." Getting heavily to her feet Reiki edged around the gameboard, shaking her skirt down as she went, pulling hot fat braids like ropes of yellowed ivory forward over her shoulders. She stood beside him at the cliff edge, touching the single gold chain about her neck, stroking its pendant coins, smiling as she did so at the memories it evoked. Once she'd worn a double-dozen chains, but these she gave away—all save the one—on a tranquil summer night long ago. "She'll surprise you, our little misborn meie. The change in her has begun; you force her growth by everything you do, my friend. Yes, our Serroi will surprise you again and yet again." He winced as if the words were stones she flung at him. Sighing, she brushed her hands together then rested them on the gathers of her skirt while she watched the bustle far below. "Harvest," she said softly. "Winter comes on its heels. Your army won't march through snow."

"Winter comes when I will it, not before." His voice was harsh, his skin drawn taut across his facebones (she saw him for a moment as a black viper cocked to strike). He spoke again (she heard rage that didn't quite conceal an unacknowledged pain), "Serroi feels my hand on her every night, janja. If she changes, she grows to me. She'll come to me soon enough when she sees the sun burning hotter each day, when the waterways go dry and the deepest wells spit dust. The vanguard of my army, janja—a furnace wind and a sucking sun."

"So you say. We'll see . . . we'll see." She used both hands to shade her eyes as she gazed intently at the massive double gates in the great wall that cut across the Valley's narrow northern end, watching a pair of riders pass through the gates and ride up the rough road toward the mountains. "So the blocked pieces get back in the game." Carefully not looking at Ser Noris, she returned to the gameboard, settled herself on the soft old leather where she'd been before and contemplated the pebble pattern. "My move, I think."

CHAPTER I:

THE MIJLOC

Tuli sat up, shoved the quilts back, annoyed at being sent to bed so early. *Like I was a baby still.* She ran her fingers through her tangled hair, sniffed with disgust as she glared at the primly neat covers on her oldest sister's bed. *Hunh! If I was a snitch like Nilis. . . .* She wrinkled her nose at the empty bed. . . . . *I'd go running off to Da 'nd tell him how she's out panting after that horrid Agli when she's s'posed to be up here with us.* She eyed the covers thoughtfully, sighed, stifled an impulse to gather them up and toss them out the window. Wasn't worth the fuss Nilis would create. She drew her legs up, wrapped her arms around them and sat listening to the night sounds coming through the unglazed, unshuttered windows and watching as the rising moons painted a ghost image of the window on the polished planks of the floor.

When she thought the time was right, she crawled to the end of the bed, flounced out flat and fished about in the space beneath the webbing that supported the mattress until she found her hunting clothes, a tunic and trousers discarded by her twin. She wriggled off the mattress, whipped off her sleeping smock, threw it at her pillow, scrambled hastily into her trousers, shivering as she did so. She dragged the tunic over her head, tugged it down, resenting the changes in her body that signaled a corresponding change—a depressing change—in the things she would be allowed to do. She tied her short brown hair back off her face with a crumpled ribbon, her eyes on her second oldest sister placidly asleep in the third bed pushed up against the wall under one of the windows. Sanani's face was a blurred oval in the strengthening moonlight, eyelashes dark furry crescents against the pallor of her skin, her breathing easy, undisturbed.

Satisfied that her sister wouldn't wake and miss her, Tuli went to the window and leaned out. Nijilic TheDom was clear of the mountains, running in and out of clouds that were the remnants of the afternoon's storm. The Scatterstorms were subsiding—none too soon. It was going to be a bad wintering. Tuli folded her arms on the windowsill and looked past the moonglow tree at the dark bulk of the storebarn. Her back still ached from the hurried gleaning after the scythemen—everyone, man woman child, in the fields to get the grain in before the rain spoiled yet more of it. With all that effort the grain bins in the barn were only half full—and Sanani said Gradintar was one of the luckiest. And the fruit on the trees was thin. And the tubers, podplants, earthnuts were swarming with gatherpests or going black and soft with mold. And there wasn't enough fodder for the hauhaus and the macain and they'd have to be culled. She shivered at the thought then shoved it resolutely aside and pulled herself onto the sill so she sat with her legs dangling, her bare heels kicking against the side of the house. She drew in a long breath, joying in the pungency of the night smells drifting to her on the brisk night breeze—straw dust from the fields, the sour stench of manure from the hauhau pens where the blocky beasts waited for dawn milking, the sickly sweet perfume from the wings of the white moths clinging to the sweetbuds of the moonglow tree. Grabbing at the sides of the window, she tilted out farther and looked along the house toward the room where her two brothers slept.

Teras thrust his shaggy head out, grinned at her, his teeth shining in his sun-dark face. He pointed down, then swung out and descended rapidly to wait for her in the walled garden below.

Tuli wriggled around until she was belly-balanced on the sill, felt about for the sigil stones set in the plaster. Once she was set, she went down almost as nimbly as her brother, though the tightness of the tunic hindered her a little. At about her own height from the ground she jumped, landing with bent knees, her bare feet hitting the turf with a soft thud. She straightened and turned to face her brother, fists on her narrow hips, her head tilted to look up at him. Two years ago when they were twelve she'd been eye to eye with him. This was another change she resented. She scowled at him. "Well?"

"Shh." He pointed to the lines of light around the shutters half a stride along the wall. "Come on." He ran to the moonglow tree, jumped and caught hold of the lowest limb, shaking loose a flutter of moths and a cloud of powerfully sweet perfume.

Tuli followed him over the wall. "What's happening?" she

whispered. "When you signaled me at supper. . . ." She glanced at the dark bulk of the house rising above the garden wall. "Nilis?"

"Uh-huh." He squinted up at the flickering moons. "TheDom's rising. Plenty of light tonight." He started toward the barns, Tuli running beside him. "Nilis was sucking up to that Agli down by the riverroad a bit after the noon meal." He kicked at a pebble, watched it bound across the straw-littered earth. "She caught me watching and chased me, yelling I was a sneak and a snoop and she'd tell Da on me." He snorted. "Follow her, hunh! Maiden's toes, why'd I follow her?" He dragged his feet through straw and clumps of dry grass as they rounded one of the barns and started past a hauhau pen. Tuli slapped her fingers against the poles until several of the cranky beasts *whee-hooed* mournfully at her. Teras pulled her away. "You want to get caught?"

"Course not." She freed herself. "You haven't told me where we're going or why."

"Nilis and the Agli they were talking about a special tilun, something big. That was just before she saw me and yelled at me so I don't know what. She sneaked off yet?"

Tuli nodded. "Her bed's empty."

Teras grinned. "We're going to go, too."

"Huh?" She grabbed at his arm, pulling him to a stop. "Nilis will have our heads, 'specially mine."

"No. Listen. Hars and me, we were looking over the home macain to get ready for the cull. I got to talking with him about tiluns 'nd things, Nilis being on my mind, you know, and about the Followers 'nd everything and he said there's some big cracks in the shutters, they put the wood up green and the Scatterstorms warped th' zhag out of 'em. Anyone looking in from outside could see just about everything going on." He grinned again, skipped backward ahead of her, hands clasped behind his head. "I think he watched them the last time he took off to Jango's, anyway he said they get real wound up, roll on the floor, confess their sins 'nd everything." Pupils dilated until his pale irids were only thin rings, his eyes gleamed like polished jet. "Maybe Nilis will be confessing tonight." His foot snagged suddenly on a clump of grass; he tottered, giggling, then caught his balance.

"What a chinj she is." Tuli mimed the popping of a small-life bloodsucker as she ran past him laughing. She swung up the poles of the corral, rested her stomach on the top pole, balancing herself there, her hands tight about it as she

watched the macain heave onto their feet and amble lazily
toward her.

Teras climbed the fence and sat on the top pole, knees
bent, bare heels propped on a lower one. "Remember the
time when ol' spottyface was courting Nilis and we made the
mudhole in the lane and covered it with sticks and grass?"

Tuli grinned. "Da whaled us good for that one. It was
worth it. She was so mad she near baked that mud solid."
Teetering precariously, she reached out and stroked the warty
nose of the nearest macai. "I wonder what she could find to
confess, she's so perfect, according to her." The macai
moaned with pleasure and lifted his head so she could dig her
fingers into the loose folds under his chin. "Which one's
this?"

"Labby." Teras stood up, wobbling a little, arms outstretched; when he had his balance, he jumped lightly to the
macai's back, startling a grunt from the beast. "There's a halter over there by the barn, get it, will you?"

Cymbank was dark except for Jango's tavern and even
there the shutters were closed; only the burning torch caged
above the door showed the place was still open. The streets
and the square were deserted, no players or peddlers, no one
camped out on the green or restless in the spotty moonlight
to catch the twins in their prowl, not even stray guards from
the double decset quartered in the Center for the last tenday.

Tuli rested her cheek against her brother's back, wondering
mildly what she was going to see. The Followers of Soäreh
the Flame had been around the mijloc awhile, a ragtag sect
no one paid much attention to, though there were rumors
enough about the tiluns, whispers of orgies and black magic,
other whispers about their priests who called themselves
Aglim though everyone knew they were only stupid little
norids who couldn't light a match without sweating. Still,
there did seem to be a lot more Followers and an Agli here in
Cymbank and she'd heard of others in other villages along
RiverCym. Not long after the Great Gather when the Domnor vanished somehow and Floarin took over as regent for her
unborn child, not very long after that, orders came down
from Oras and the Doamna-regent for the Taromates of the
South to provide land and roof for the Followers and their
Aglim, orders backed by a Decsel and his ten guards. The
Taromate of RiverCym had grumbled and done the least they
could, giving the Agli a long abandoned granary that was, by

mischance, directly across from the Maiden Shrine. The location made the people of Cymbank very unhappy and the taroms weren't too pleased with it but no one had anything better to offer and the thing was done. That was near a year ago now and folks were used to it, ignored it mostly.

The walls of the granary, though crumbling a little on the outside, were solid enough and the roof reasonably intact. The Agli had looked it over and accepted it, though Tesc told Annic in the hearing of the twins that he didn't like the look in that viper's eyes and he prayed that he never got his teeth in any of them.

Teras turned Labby toward the back of the Maiden Shrine. "Almost there," he whispered. She could feel the muscles tighten in his back, hear the tension in his voice. He pulled the macai to a stop, tapped his sister's hands, and when she loosed her grip on him, swung down. As she slid after him, he knotted the halter rope to one of the rings on the hitching post then waited for Tuli to take the lead.

His night sight was only adequate; he didn't stumble around, but saw few things sharply once the sun went down. His realm was daylight while the night belonged to Tuli. Everything about her expanded when the moons rose; she ran faster, heard, smelled, tasted far more intensely, read the shifts of the air like print—and most of all, saw with dream-like clarity everything about her, saw night scenes as if they were fine black-and-white etchings, detailed to the smallest leaf. No night hunter (no hovering kanka passar or prowling fayar) could track its prey more surely. She loved her night rambles nearly as much as she loved her twin, loved both with a jealous passion and refused to acknowledge that she'd be wed in a few years and shut away from both these loves, from her brother and the night. "Through the shrine?" she whispered.

"For a look first," Teras murmured. His hand brushed across his eyes, a betrayal of his anxiety, then he grinned at her, gave her a little push. "Get on with it or we'll miss everything."

Tuli nodded. She circled the small schoolroom where she and Teras had learned to read and figure, had memorized the Maiden chants, moved past the Sanctuary and the Shrine fountain, stepped into the columned court. As she passed the vine-wreathed posts with their maiden faces, moon-caught, smiling through the leaves, Tuli relaxed. There was a gentle goodness about the court that always reached deep in her and smoothed away the knots of anger and spite that gathered in her like burrs and pricked at her until she burst out with ugly words and hateful acts whose violence often frightened her. Sometimes after Nilis or one of the tie-girls had driven her to distraction she ran away to this court for help in subduing her fury when, staying, she might have half-killed the other. Night or day, the Maiden gave her back her calm, gave her the strength to live with herself and with others no matter how irritating. This night she felt the peace again, forgot why she was here until Teras tapped at her arm and urged her to hurry.

She stopped in the shadow by the shrine gate; Teras pressed against her as they both examined the bulky cylinder of the old granary. He stirred after a moment, itchy with the need for action. "See anything?" There was trouble in his voice. He had a sense she lacked. It was like a silent gong, he told her, if you can imagine such a thing, like a great dinner gong vibrating madly that you couldn't hear only feel. It didn't sound often but when it did, it meant get the hell out, if it was really loud, or sometimes just watch where you put your feet, there's danger about.

"Gong?"

"A rattle."

Tuli nodded. Leaning against the gatepost, she narrowed her eyes and probed the shadows across the street. At first she saw nothing more than the wide, low cylinder with its conical roof, then in the deeply recessed doorway she felt more than saw a faint movement, as if the air the watcher stirred slipped across the street and pressed against her face. The watcher moved; she saw a darkness pass across a streak of red-gold light. She scanned the building with slow care for one last time then let out the breath she was holding. "Guard in the doorway. That's all. If we go out the back here, circle round and come down the riverbank, we can climb over the court wall and get to those windows Hars told you 'bout." She frowned. "He must 've got over the wall himself without getting caught, but maybe there's a guard there now."

Teras shrugged. "Won't know till we look. Come on."

Tuli loped easily along behind the shops that lined the main street, Teras behind her; in a kind of litany she named them under her breath—cobbler, saddlemaker, turner, mercer, hardware seller, blacksmith, coper, candy maker—a litany of the familiar, the comfortable, the unchanging, only she would change, though she'd hold back that change if she could. They circled kitchen gardens and macai sheds, ducked past moonglow groves and swung round the empty corrals where macai dealers auctioned off their wares at the Rising Fair. She felt a bubbling in her blood; her face was hot and tight in spite of the chill in the air blowing against it; she was breathing fast, not from the running, her heart knocking in her throat with excitement. Before, when she was still a child, running wild at night was worth a licking if she was caught at it, now she'd started her menses the danger was far greater. *I might be cast out of the family, utterly disowned, left to find my living however I could, poor, starved, beaten, maybe I'd even end up in the back rooms at Jango's.* She swallowed a giggle, luxuriating in imaginings, knowing all the while that Tesc, her father, loved her far too much to do any of these dire things to her.

She led Teras back along the riverbank until she came to a clattering stand of dried-out bastocane directly behind the granary. She scanned as much as she could see of the walls of the square back court, then nudged her brother. "Gong?"

"Not a squeak." He came around her, trotted silent as a wraith across dry grass and debris to the crumbling mud brick wall. He turned and waited for her, propping his shoulders against the wall, his eyes glistening with mischief. Tuli grinned at him, kicked at the mud, jerked her thumb up. He nodded and started climbing, feeling for cracks with feet and fingers, knocking down loose fragments that pattered softly beside her. She watched his head rise over the top, saw him swing across the drop without hesitation. Following as quickly as she could, she pulled herself over the wall and let herself down beside her twin. She heard a macai honk in a shed at the back of the court, heard the wail of a kanka passar in swoop close by, the buzz of night flying bugs, but that was all, no guard, nothing to worry about.

Thin streaks of red-gold light outlined a series of double shutters that covered what once had been grain chutes but now were, presumably, windows set into the thick wall. The shutter nearest the courtwall had a long narrow triangle of wood broken off one edge. Light spilled copiously from the opening and gilded the ground beneath. Teras touched Tuli's shoulder, pointed, then moved swiftly, silently, to the broken shutter.

Belly cold with a vague foreboding far less definite than her brother's gong and somehow more disturbing, Tuli hesitated. Teras swung away from the crack and beckoned impatiently. She shook off her anxiety and crossed to him to kneel by the bottom of the crack while Teras leaned over her, his eye to the opening. Sighing, Tuli looked inside.

The room was round with one flat side, taking up most of the ground-level space within the granary. Tuli was surprised how much she could see from her vantage place, the curve of the wall giving her an unexpectedly wide angle of view. Half the room was filled with silent seated figures uncertainly visible in the murky light from oil-wood torches stuck up on the walls. On a low dais a four-foot cylinder supported a broad shallow basin filled with flames that had a misty aura about them like a river fog about a late strayer's lanthorn. She sniffed cautiously, picked up a faint oily sweetness that tickled her nose until she feared she'd have to sneeze. Eyes watering, she pinched her nostrils together until the need faded, then began to examine the faces more closely, recognizing some, too many for her comfort. Some were neighbors, some their own people, members of families that had lived on Gradin lands and worked for Gradin Heirs for as long as the Taromate had existed. She must have made a slight sound. Her brother's hand came down on her shoulder, squeezed it lightly, both warning and comfort.

Nilis sat among the foremost, an exalted look on her pinched face, a passion in her staring eyes that startled Tuli; she'd seen Nilis fussing and angry but never like this. *We've missed some,* she thought, seeing weariness as well as exaltation in her sister's face. *Wonder what's going to happen now?* She looked up, met her brother's eyes. His lips formed the word *chinj*. She tried to answer his smile, swallowed and once again set her eyes to the crack.

The Followers were sitting very erect, as if they had rods rammed down their spines. Two dark figures, heads hidden in black hoods, stood before the fire-filled basin. Long narrow robes covered their bodies chin to toe, long narrow sleeves covered their arms, even their hands, and fell half an arm's length beyond their fingertips. Muffled hands moved, swaying slowly back and forth, the dangling sleeves passing through clouds of droplets spraying out from the flames. A moan blew through the seated figures, grew in volume. The Followers shook as if a strong wind stirred them.

"Light." One of the dark figures intoned the word, his voice a clear sweet tenor.

"Light." The response was a beast moan, a deep groan.

"Father of light." The tenor rang with tender power. It was not possible to tell which of the dark ones spoke.

"Father of Light," the beast groaned. The smell of the incense grew stronger as it pressed out past Tuli's face, turning her light-headed though she got not one-tenth the dose the Followers inhaled.

"Bright one, pure one."

"Bright one, PURE one." A moan of ecstasy.

"Burn us clean."

Outside in the darkness Tuli felt the pull of the chant, felt the heated intensity of the many-throated beast, her disgust weakened by drifts of drugged incense. Over and over the phrases were intoned and responded until they wore a groove in her mind, until she found herself breathing with the beast, mouthing the words with it, until her heart was beating with it. Alarmed when she realized what was happening, she wrenched her face away from the crack and laid her cheek against the splintery wood, breathing deeply the chill night air. It smelled of manure and musty grain, of damp earth and stagnant water, of unwashed macain and rotting fish—and she savored all these smells; they were real and sane and redolent of life itself, a powerful barrier against the insanity happening inside the granary. She became aware that the chanting had stopped, replaced by the rattle of small drums. Unable to resist the pricking of curiosity, she set her eye once more to the crack.

A third dark figure (she wrinkled her nose as she recognized him) stood before the basin; his wrists were crossed over his heart, fingers splayed out like white wings. The acolytes knelt, one to the right the other to the left, like black bookends (she swallowed a giggle at the thought) tapping at small drums, their fingers hidden in the too-long sleeves.

"Agli. Agli. Agli," the Followers chanted as the acolytes beat the rhythm faster and faster, pushing at them, forcing them harder and faster until the massive old granary seemed to rock about the serene magnetic figure of the Agli.

Tuli watched with horror as people she knew, some she'd counted almost friends, her sister, all of them howled, beat at themselves, tore at their hair, screamed wild hoarse cries that seemed to tear from bloody throats, rocked wildly on their buttocks, even fell over and rolled about on the floor.

The drums stopped. The moaning died away. One by one the Followers regained control of their bodies and sat again rigidly erect.

The Agli spread his hands wide, wide sleeves falling from his arms like black wings. The acolytes set their drums aside and each brought hidden hands together, palm to palm, in the center of his chest, sitting like an ebony orant as the Agli spoke.

"Think on your sins, o sons of evil." He spoke softly, his rich warm voice caressing them. "Think on your sins." This time the words came louder. "Think on your sins!" Now the sonorous tones filled the room. The Followers moaned and writhed with shame. He wheeled suddenly, turning his back to them, rejecting them, one hand stretched dramatically toward the flame, the other lifted high above his head. "Look on this light, o you with darkness in your soul." He whipped around, his face stern, a forefinger jabbing in accusation at them. "Look on the Light and know yourselves filled with darkness. Soäreh of the Flame is light, is purity, is all that is good and true and worthy. Soäreh is your Father is the flame that cleanses. Be you clean, you who call yourselves the followers of Soäreh. Burn the filth from your sodden souls, you sons of evil. Cast that filth into the outer darkness, cast out the hag who fouls you."

Tuli shivered, fear so strong in her she was sick with it. He was talking about the Maiden, how could he say such things, how could they bear to listen? And how could Floarin doamna-regent sponsor such . . . such . . . she couldn't find the words. Grimly she watched what was happening, determined to know the worst.

The Agli was winding up to a climax, his voice hammering at the Followers. They stared at him, eyes glazed, unfocused, faces idiot-blank, surrendering will and intellect utterly to him. "Follow the hag and you will be cast into the outer darkness, foul to foul, eaten by worms." He flung his arms out again, black wings silhouetted against the red and gold and dancing blue of the flames. "Do you renounce the sins that taint you?"

"We do." At first the answer was ragged, uncertain, then the Followers found their voices again. "We do renounce them."

"Do you renounce the dark hag?"

"We do." A full-throated roar.

"Confess your sins, oh sons of evil. Confess. Set your hands in the fire and confess.

Nilis staggered to her feet and stumbled forward, arms outstretched.

Tuli shuddered. Teras and she had laughed at the idea but the reality was not funny at all.

Nilis stopped before the Agli, her face shining with an eagerness that Tuli found obscene. The Agli laid his hands on hers, then he stepped aside. Without hesitation she plunged her arms to the elbows into the flames. She stepped back a moment later, raised her arms high, small tongues of fire racing up them to curve into a crackling arc above her head. "Blessed Soäreh Father, I have sinned." Her voice was triumphant, no hint of shame, a thin harsh whine that grated on Tuli's ears.

The two acolytes began tapping out a simple rhythm. "Fire cleanses," the tenor sang. Again Tuli had no idea which of them spoke.

"Fire cleanses," the Followers answered him.

"I accuse myself, I dwell with evil."

"The light is pure."

"Pure is the light."

"I accuse Tesc and Annic Gradin."

"Blessed be the light."

"The Light be blessed."

"They plot against the light. They plot against our blessed patron Doamna Floarin. They plot to withhold the grain share owed to the blessed of the Light."

"The Flame will purify."

"Be purified in the Flame."

"Tesc Gradin, my father, called the Taromate of River Cym together to plot treason. All of them will hide in secret cellars a portion of the harvest from the Servants of the Light when they come to take the Doamna's tithe."

Tuli bit her lower lip to keep from crying out in blind fury. She pounded her fists on her thighs and couldn't even feel them; she wept and didn't know she wept. She heard as from a great distance her brother's muttered curse. When her eyes cleared, the first thing she saw was Nilis looking smug and self-righteous. To control her rage she swallowed and swallowed again. *How can she do this to her own? How can she?*

"The light be blessed."

"Blessed be the light." There was a greedy pleasure in the Followers' response, a stench of malice.

Tuli searched the faces of some she knew, seeing in them hunger and spite, greed and hate. Chark—three healthy older brothers who stood between him and any chance at his own land, a father who despised him, a sickly stooped body; his eyes glistened with spite as he chanted. Nilis—a cursed woman, her single suitor a stuttering second son courting her only because no one else would have him and even so only lukewarm in his pursuit while her sister Sanani, two years younger, was promised already and happy in it. Kumper— only son of Digger Havin, a good old man; Tesc endured Kumper's whines and complaints and slovenly work for his father's sake, but two seasons ago, when he found him tormenting a macai, he threw him off the Tar, telling him not to come back ever.

"The Taromate has named Tesc Gradin spokesman. He leaves tomorrow early for Oras to protest the tithe."

"Cursed be those who deny the light."

"Be they cursed."

"I live because I have to among the followers of the dark hag. I am tainted with their evil. Purge me, Soäreh. Be Father and family to me."

"Fire burns clean, the Light cleanses all."

"Blessed be the light."

"Father, mother, sisters, brothers, all refuse the light. I sin because of them. I give in to anger. I doubt the right. They are the roots of my sin. I renounce them, Soäreh, my Father. I renounce them." Her glowing eyes were fixed on the arc of flame above her head.

"Blessed be the light that burns away the darkness."

"Blessed be the light."

"Let my soul be a transparent glory, let the light shine in me." With this final outburst, Nilis lowered her hands and thrust her arms back in the fire, crying out after a moment, a wild hoarse wail of a pleasure too much for her slight body to hold.

As Nilis swayed back to her place and another of the Followers stumbled to the fire, Tuli slapped at her brother's leg, then wriggled away from the window. Without waiting for him, she clawed her way up the wall and dropped to the ground outside.

Teras thudded down beside her. "How could she do that?" There was anguish in his voice. His usual control stripped away, he slammed a hand against the mud bricks. "Traitor!"

Fighting with her own anger, Tuli caught his hand in hers, held it tight, his need the one thing that could cool her heat. "What are we going to do?"

He tugged his hand free, rubbed it hard across his face.

"Tell Da first, that's one thing." His voice was hoarse. "We have to, he has to know what she did." He kicked at the wall, stared away from her, blinking tears he was ashamed of from his eyes. "I can't believe she did it, Tuli. Why'd she do it? Why?"

"She's Nilis, I s'pose that's all." Tuli touched his arm. "What can *we* do?"

"I don't know." He struck the wall with the flat of his hand, then raced along it toward the street.

Tuli ran after him, caught hold of his arm, stopping him. "The watcher," she breathed.

He pressed his back against the crumbling brick. Eyes closed, head back, he stood, breathing raggedly. In the light of Nijilic TheDom, directly overhead now, clear for that moment of clouds, he looked far older than his fourteen years. Tuli shivered, chilled by a sense of loss—then he opened his eyes, grinned at her and the world was right again. She grinned back, pointed down the street, started loping through the shadows of the overhanging storefronts, moving with the stealth of a prowling fayar. Several shops down she cut across the street then circled around behind the Maiden Shrine toward patient Labby slumping half-asleep against the post.

They rode in silence, Tuli's arms around her brother's waist, her cheek pressed against his back. Neither spoke until the barns of Gradin-Tar loomed ahead and the great black bulk of the watchtower, then Teras brought Labby to a halt. He twisted around, his face grave. "You better get back up the wall 'fore I go in. Da 'ud skin you alive if he knew you were out."

"Yah." She relaxed her hold, shifted back until she was sitting on the macai's rump. "Think he'll believe you?" With a small grunt, she swung a leg up and over, slid off and stood looking up at him.

"Why shouldn't he?" He clucked to Labby, started him walking again in a slow amble. "If he doesn't, I'll have to tell him you were with me and heard the same things."

Tuli grimaced, touched a buttock. "My backside will heal faster than what Nilis is doing to us. Teras. . . ."

"Huh?"

"Make sure Da knows that if he still is going to go, he should leave right now, not wait for morning. And he should be careful, real careful."

"Hah! You think I didn't think of that?" He leaned forward, squinted at the moonlit area in front of the house; the macain tied there earlier were gone. "The meeting must be over."

Tuli sniffed. "Course it is, you heard Nilis."

"Hunh!" He slid off the macai's back. "Get up that wall, you, before Da wears out your bottom." He led Labby toward the corral. "Girls."

CHAPTER II:

THE QUEST

Her Noris stands high on the mountain, black boots ankle deep in cold stone, his narrow elegant form a darkness half obscured by swirls of snow and mist—cold, cold, so cold. Pale hands reach for her, sad eyes plead with her. He touches her, catches her hands in his—cold, so cold.

"Help me, Serroi," he whispers and the words are splinters of ice tearing into her flesh—cold, cold, so cold.

"Come to me, dearest one," he cries to her. Stone creeps around his knees while below, far below, the valley stretches out in golden splendor, golden warmth. "Help me," he pleads. Gray and relentless, the stone rises past his waist—cold, so cold. His hands reach to her again. She feels feather touches on her face—cold, cold, so cold.

"Come to me, daughter, come to me, my child." The stone closes around his neck; the yearning in his eyes touches the long-denied yearning frozen deep within her—oh cold, so cold.

"Let me be, father, let me be, teacher," she whispers and sees before the stone closes over his head the agony in his eyes, an agony without measure as the pain in her is without measure—cold, so terribly cold.

Moonlight slanted silver through the window, painting an oblong of broken silver on Serroi's body. She turned and turned in her troubled sleep, side and back and stomach, caught in dreams she could neither banish nor wake from.

Her Noris reclines on black velvet before a crackling fire. She is a small girl, comfortable and happy beside his divan, half-sitting, half-lying on piled-up pillows, silken pillows glowing silver, crimson, amber, azure, violet, emerald, midnight blue. His hand drops, strokes her hair, begins pulling soft curls through his fingers. The fire is no warmer than the quiet happiness between them.

"No!" Serroi jerked up from her sweat-sodden pillow, leaped from her bed and reached the door before she woke sufficiently to remember she was home, home and safe, safe in the Valley where Ser Noris could not come. Once, long ago, he'd tried using her as a key to unlock the Biserica defenses for him. She pressed her face against the door's polished wood, squeezing back tears she refused to shed. *Now I'm no key, I'm a lever and you're using me to force an opening for you. It won't work, won't, can't work. I would have done anything for you once, but not now.* "Not now," she whispered.

Still trembling, she tumbled back to the bed and sat wearily on its edge, dropping her head into her hands. "Maiden bless, I'm tired. Let me sleep, will you? Please. Please, let me be." Her eyes burned. She rubbed them then lifted her head to gaze out the window toward the shadowy granite cliff across the valley. "You're up there now, aren't you? Wanting all this not for what it is, wanting it because you can't have it, wanting it though it would turn to dust and ashes at your touch." She shivered in spite of the night's warmth at the thought of that touch, feeling a painful mixture of revulsion and desire. Her lips curved tiredly up then fell to a bitter line. "If only you knew, my Noris, you betray yourself with every dream you send to torment me. You show your own weakness, not mine . . . ah, Maiden bless, that's a lie. My weakness too, too much mine." She turned her eyes from the cliff but found no ease for her spirit, not when the only other thing she had to look at was the empty bed across the cell. Even in the cloud-mottled moonlight she could see the precision of the blanket folds, the crispness of the white pillow. Tayyan had never in her life left a bed like that, not without a lump here, a sag there, a wrinkle or two that her greatest effort couldn't eliminate. A knocking at the door broke her from her brooding. She lifted her legs onto her bed, crossed her ankles and tugged her sleeping smock over her knees. "Come."

Yael-mri pulled the door open and stood in the dark rectangle, the candle she held stiffly before her painting inky shadow into the hollows and lines of her strong face. "The Silent Ones sent to tell me you were dreaming again."

Serroi's hand trembled on her knee. "Yes."

The flame wavered as Yael-mri sighed, licked at a raised edge sending a liquid slide down one side of the candle. The smell of hot wax was suddenly strong in the small room. Absently Yael-mri straightened her arm, holding the candle farther from her. "The Shawar are troubled by these sendings. Their meditations are disturbed, and what's worse, several makings have collapsed."

Serroi licked dry lips. When she met Yael-mri's compassionate gaze, she stopped breathing, then tried to smile, but the twisting of her mouth felt more like a grimace so she let the smile die. "I'll have to leave the Valley."

"I'm afraid so. Come to the prieti-varou when the bell sounds treilea. We'll talk. I have some suggestions I want to make about your destination once you set out."

"I hear." Serroi drew shaking fingers across her eyespot, trying to counter its painful throbbing. She grimaced. "At least I'll be doing something, not just sitting around watching the rocks grow."

"You do a great deal more than that."

Serroi shrugged. "Other people's work."

Yael-mri watched her a moment, frowning thoughtfully. "Do you want someone to stay with you the rest of the night? Or should I send one of the healwomen?"

"No." As Yael-mri still hesitated in the doorway, Serroi lifted her head, stared coldly at her. "Don't worry, I won't sleep again. There won't be any dreams."

The door clicked shut, footfalls moved crisply away, fading as the thick walls cut off the sound. Serroi pulled the quilt off her bed and wrapped it around her shoulders. She touched her eyespot again, traced its outline, a long oval with its major axis parallel to the line of her brows, a dark green oval almost black against the bright olive of her skin, remembering other fingers that had touched her there, slim white fingers of surpassing beauty when she was a child and, later, the love touches of tan fingers rough with calluses from swordhilts and macai halters, thin and a little bony and very dear. *Tayyan, lover and swordmate. Tayyan, abandoned on a street in Oras to bleed to death, her body tossed outside the walls for demons to eat.* She pressed the heels of her hands against her eyes, then let her hands fall into her lap. The days had dribbled like quicksilver through her fingers, days unnumbered, one much like the other. Time. Too much time. Her grief was blunted, her guilt lost in fear as her Noris fought to reclaim her. She leaned against the wall, her eyes on the window as she watched the shifting clouds, the shadows dappling the mountainside. *Find me something hard to do, Yael-mri, hunt out an impossible quest and I'll hug it to me like it was my only child.* Her lips twitched. *Foolishness. Still—anything would be better than this wretched drifting.*

She spent the morning cleaning out one of the stables and washing down trailworn macain brought in by meien who came home dismissed from their wards, some of them running ahead of hostile mobs. The mindless labor brought quiet to her spirit until she was calm and ready to face whatever Yael-mri had in mind for her.

When she heard the dalea bell, she swiped at the dusty sweat on her face and carried her tools to their shed. The stable-pria looked up from a macai's slashed leg as Serroi came from the stable; she was an old meie, mountain bred, better with animals than people though time had taught her to read her fellows nearly as accurately as she did her beasts. She was Yael-mri's closest friend and unofficial adviser, wise beyond her years, wiser perhaps even than the most venerable of the Shawar because she'd suffered more. She came to the fence. With wordless sympathy she held out a lean, callused hand. Serroi smiled as the rough fingers closed around hers. "It's nothing so bad, pria Melit."

Melit nodded. "Not life or death, it will pass. Later, after the talk is done, come see me."

Serroi nodded, warming to the warmth offered her. "I will."

By the time she'd washed away the grime of the stable and pulled on clean leathers, the bell was ringing treilea. She stood still a moment, fingers opening and closing, then walked quietly out with no backward glance at the room that had been hers for half her life.

Before the aste-varou, the ascetic waiting room—more like a stunted corridor—outside Yael-mri's office, Serroi hesitated, brushed nervously at her sorrel curls, straightened her shoulders, then pushed the door open.

Dom Hern glanced at her as she stepped inside. He stood at one of the windows that marched along the north wall of the narrow room. His eyebrows rising, he left the window and crossed to settle himself on the hard wooden bench backed against the south wall. "You too?"

Serroi hitched her weapon belt up and dropped onto the bench. "Too?"

"Summoned." His light grey eyes mocked her.

"Yes." Her curt monosyllable seemed to amuse him even more than her presence here. She swung around and ran cool eyes over his pudgy body. She hadn't seen him since he'd moved into the gatehouse, though she'd certainly heard enough about him. She grinned at him, willing, for no reason she could think of, to share his amusement. "We're being kicked out, Dom."

"Thought so." He rubbed at his nose, then bounced to his feet, his mood changing suddenly from amusement to an irritated frustration. He stared out the window at the drying flowers and listless vegetation, tilted his head back to gaze at the mountains rising to the north. She remembered then the other things that occupied his time (besides riding, play with sword and staff and endless loveplay), the hours in the Biserica library pouring over maps and searching through reports, the time he spent with meien new come from the mijloc, probing into Floarin's words and deeds, into the words and deeds of the Followers and their Aglim. She watched the strong square hands clasped behind his back. *He wouldn't have stayed here much longer anyway. But why did she send for him now?*

When Yael-mri opened the door to her varou, Hern swung around, Serroi rose to her feet. Yael-mri smiled at Serroi. "Sorry to keep you waiting so long, but I had a visitor I didn't expect." Her lips compressed to a thin line, her face stern and disapproving, she turned to Hern. "Dom."

"Prieti-meien." He bowed, graceful in spite of his bulky body, but when he took a step toward the door, Yael-mri stiffened; anger flashed in her light brown eyes. To depress his presumption, she stopped him with a chopping gesture and beckoned to Serroi. "Come, meie." She stepped aside and let Serroi move past her into the varou. As soon as she saw her seated, she waved Hern in.

Ignoring his affronted scowl, she walked calmly to a wide table and arranged herself in the high-backed chair behind it. "If you will sit, Dom Hern, I wish to discuss something with the two of you." She leaned back, her hands resting palm down on the age-smoothed arms of her chair, brown eyes shifting from Hern to Serroi and back, the flecks of gold in the brown catching the light, lending the commonplace color an odd unstable quality. Between the two of you, life in the

Valley is becoming impossible." She tapped long thumbs against the chairarms. "You, Dom Hern, are getting to be more than a nuisance. Two knife dances yesterday alone and a hair-pulling brawl." She snorted. "You needn't look smug, Dom. It's no compliment to say you have the sexual habits of a yepa in heat. What my meien do off-duty is no business of mine. Keeping the peace most certainly is. I won't have this nonsense disrupting our defenses, not when we're threatened as we've never been before." She scowled, leaned forward, slapping her hand on the table, looking—in spite of this vigorous action—drawn and weary. "I think it will be no surprise to either of you that I require your absence." She twisted around, reached a long arm to a taboret beside the table, took a small silver box from it, straightened, turned the box over in her hands then set it on the table and slid it toward Serroi. "You'll remember this."

Serroi lifted the box, drew her thumbnail along the smooth metal. "The tajicho?"

"Yes. Don't open the box here." She leaned forward to fix disapproving eyes on Hern. "What are your intentions toward the mijloc?"

Serroi bent slowly, slipped the box into the top of her boot. As she tucked it away, some of her anxiety flowed out of her. Slumping back in the chair, eyes unfocused, smiling a little, she drifted away from Yael-mri's inquisition of Dom Hern into memory of that stormy night when she turned aside from her return to Oras (duty and penance) to defend the small furry creasta-shurin from the hideous great worm that was eating them into extinction. When the Nyok'chui fell to her arrows, she remembered old tales from the books in the tower of the Noris, cut the third eye from the Nyok's skull and called down lightning to form the crystal that could deflect the farsight of sorcerers and seers, that could turn spells back on the spieler. Once it was out of the shielding silver and touching her, hers again, no one could take it from her. It turned aside men's eyes like a shuri's fur turned water. And the Noris would have to let her be, stay out of her dreams if she couldn't force him from her memory.

"Meie."

Serroi blinked and sat up.

Yael-mri tapped her thumbs on the tabletop, her eyes flicking once more between her visitors. "You'll be leaving the valley this afternoon, both of you. The Biserica will provide mounts and supplies and a little gold. Not much, I'm afraid.

Dom Hern, you have named half a dozen possible destinations but you don't seem much committed to any of these."

He smiled amiably and said nothing.

Yael-mri sighed. "You don't make it easy." She pinched at an earlobe, lifted her eyes to the carving above the door—a striding macai. "I have a quest for the pair of you if you choose to accept it."

Hern continued to look bland, heavy lids drooping over his pale eyes. "Quest?" he murmured.

"Perhaps an ally for you, Hern." Yael-mri's voice was dry; her mouth drew momentarily into a small pursed smile. "You don't have many of those."

Serroi saw a muscle twitch at the corner of Hern's mouth; he didn't like being reminded of how isolated he was or how bad his chances were of doing anything at all about Floarin's usurpation.

"I'm listening." His mask in place again, he looked sleepy and a little stupid.

Yael-mri looked grim. She splayed her fingers out on the table, stared down at them, watching them tremble, forcing them still, obviously reluctant to continue. There was a strained silence in the office for several minutes, then she spoke. "There exists a being of very uncertain nature but great power who calls himself Coyote." She rubbed her long thumbs across the glossy wood. "He . . . ummm . . . pronouns are a difficulty. Coyote is neither male nor female nor . . . I'm blathering. Dom Hern, Coyote is capable of disrupting anything the Nearga-nor do. In . . . well, let it be his . . . in his own way, he is greater than the Nearga-nor and the Biserica combined. But he's capricious and inclined more to mischief than constructive aid to either side in this battle of ours. Coyote . . . he picked up that name in his travels *elsewhere;* Maiden alone knows what he means by it, but he told me it fitted him more nearly than any other he tried on . . . Coyote is capricious, as I said; he is also intensely sentimental, intensely curious, inclined to poke his finger into events just to see what happens and inclined also to weep copiously over the havoc he creates. And he pays his debts, though more often than not with disastrous results. Remember that, Dom, as you decide. However, if you can find him, if you can coax him into letting you look into his mirror, if you can make the right choice among the choices he offers you, then you will have the best chance you'll ever get to take back the mijloc. In doing this you will be, in effect, defending us in the Valley, so. . . ." She contemplated Hern, shook her head. *Impossible to tell what he was thinking, to know if he was thinking at all,* Serroi thought. She watched them both, amused at the antagonism between them—two dominants maneuvering for points like sicamars jousting for a hunting range—and startled at the embarrassment both obvious and incongruous on Yael-mri's face each time she mentioned the oddly named character. *Coyote. A strange word, I wonder where he picked that one up, I wonder if I'll ever know.* She scratched thoughtfully at the side of her nose.

Hern opened his eyes, raised his brows.

Yael-mri's tight smile wavered. "Coyote owes me a favor." A faint color strained her face, the tip of her nose reddened. "As the defense of the Biserica is involved you may use my name once you find him. This might catch his interest long enough to gain you a hearing. As I said, he pays his debts. I promise nothing, but I do swear to you, Dom Hern, that there is no other way that offers any comparable chance of defeating the Nearga-nor. I can tell you where he sometimes shows his . . . um . . . face when he's not elsewhere; what you make of him will be up to you."

Hern blinked lazily. "Both of us, you said. The meie is coming with me?"

Yael-mri stiffened. "If she so chooses," she said after a moment, each word edged with ice. "The meie is free to accept or reject the quest as she wishes. She most certainly will not be *with* you in the sense you mean, not subordinated to you in any way."

"We'll work that out." He smiled at her with practiced charm, then sat up, his lazy mask dissolved. He dropped his hands on his thighs, leaned forward, intent grey eyes hard on her face. "Details, please."

CHAPTER III:

THE MIJLOC

When the sun was only a promise in the east, hands shook Tuli gently awake. She blinked up into an unsmiling face whose features were side-lit by the pale red glow of the dawn. Hearing the soft breathing of her sisters, she sat up, scrubbed at burning eyes, still dazed with sleep, vaguely wondering why her mother had waked her so early. Then she remembered.

With a hiss of pure rage she shoved at her mother's encircling arms, pushed with knees and elbows at her mother's bending body as she fought to kick free of the quilts and launch herself at Nilis who lay deep asleep with no remorse or fear troubling her in the bed by the two windows, her traitorous mouth slack, the breath issuing in small snores through her long nose. Mama Annic grasped Tuli round the waist, lifted her kicking and struggling from the tangled quilts, somehow got a hand free and clapped it over her mouth, muffling the animal whines and squeals she made, somehow half-carried, half dragged her from the room, by a miracle waking neither Nilis nor Sanani.

Annic edged the door shut with her toe; breathing hard with emotion and exertion, she hauled Tuli down the hall to the carved and painted linen chest by the head of the stairs and dropped onto it with a puffing sigh of relief, then tugged at Tuli until she collapsed onto her lap. She held her tight, patting her shoulders, rocking her until the fit of rage passed off. "I know, bebe," she murmured. "I know, my little firehead, it's not easy, not easy at all. It's my curse too and I gave it to you. It will get better, I promise you, it will get better." Annic continued to hold Tuli until she felt the sobbing and shaking stop.

Tuli hiccoughed herself at last into an exhausted calm. She lifted her head from the damp folds of her mother's robe, hot with shame that she, almost a woman, sat like a baby in her mother's lap, feeling all elbows and knees as she tried to wriggle loose from her mother's hold. Annic smiled and shifted Tuli off her knees onto the chest beside her. "I thought I'd better wake you early."

"She. . . ."

Annic's hand closed tight on her shoulder, stopping her. "I know, Tuli. Your father left not long after you got home. I thought you'd want to know."

Tuli's hands moved restlessly on her sleeping smock. She stared at them, blinking, then curled the fingers under to hide the black crescents under the nails, dirt picked up from climbing about walls and digging into the earth outside the granary window. "What's going to happen, Mama?" She twisted her hands into the thin cloth, shifted restlessly on the chest lid.

Annic sat silent for what felt like a long time, her eyes fixed on the far side of the hall though she didn't seem to see the wall tiles. "I don't know." She sighed, ruffled Tuli's short brown hair. "Stay away from Nilis, bebe. Your father will deal with her when he gets back. The orchard needs work and it's far enough off to keep you out of her hair." She sighed again. "I wish I could keep her out of mine." With a quick vigorous push of her legs, she got to her feet. "Chop away at those weeds and suckers, firehead, till the rage is small enough to hold in the palm of your hand." She laughed softly, bent and patted the backs of Tuli's hands, then went quickly and gracefully down the stairs.

Tuli hacked furiously at suckers growing like green whips from the roots of the chays tree. When she had them all slain, each one Nilis for her, she tossed the sharp-edged trowel aside, gathered the suckers and cast them into the aisle between the rows of fruit trees where someone else would chop them into the soil.

The orchard was some distance from the house, planted in the wide curve of a stream that wandered through the Tar before heading for RiverCym—a dozen rows of trees, most of them long mature, though a few saplings replaced the storm-lost. Malat for their crisp red fruit and the cider that warmed many a winter evening. Chays trees, chewy golden chays to be pitted and strung on grass twine after drying and hung in loops from kitchen rafters, chays—sweet and tart at once, best of all on cold stormy nights with long glasses of hot

spiced cider. Pleche and rechedd, chorem and lorrim, burst-
ing with juice, small round fruits, translucent garnet skin over
golden flesh, long twisted oval fruits with blue-purple skins
and red-black flesh, small green rounds growing in tight-
packed bunches, red-cheeked waxy green fruits with hard tart
flesh, fruit for drying, winter sweets, fruits for jams and jel-
lies, fruit to ferment for wine. And all of it thin upon the
branches. Shadows flickering across her face, Tuli sat back on
her heels, wiped at her forehead with the back of an earth-
stained hand, scratched at her nose. Nilis blew up storms
whenever Tuli slipped out of the house and went to work in
the fields. Man's work, she said. Not proper for a daughter of
the house, she said, scolding Mama for permitting this. Tuli
snorted, wiped her hands on her skirt. Not proper, never
mind that Tuli hated being shut inside, that she was useless at
any kind of sewing, that she couldn't clean anything without
leaving streaks no matter how she tried. Not proper, Maiden
bless, from a daughter of the house who just might've con-
demned her own father to prison or death—if he couldn't
talk his way free. Tuli had great faith in her father's nimble
tongue, if only she got a chance to wag it. She caught up the
spading fork and dug vigorously around the roots, each stab
a stab into her sister's disloyal heart, easing still more the
simmer of anger and frustration inside her.

Mama was right, keep away from Nilis. She grinned and
dug with energy and force, clearing away clumps of
leechweed, working leaf castings and storm-stripped nubbins
into the sticky black earth, working slowly around the tree
until it stood in a ring of glistening umber. She sat back on
her heels, sniffing happily at the pungent odors circulating
about her (the clean green of the suckers, the chays-smell
thick as jam dropping down from the ripening fruit, the
damp brown earth smell, fugitive violet and lace perfumes
from the late-blooming autumn flowers hiding between
clumps of grass); the tranquility of the crisp, bright morning
brought her some of the same calm she found in the Maiden
Shrine. She was disturbed by the violence of her waking rage;
she hadn't been so bad for a long time; even last night, even
when she was actually seeing Nilis babble, she hadn't been so
lost in blind fury; if Mama hadn't been there she might've
really hurt Nilis and however much she might deserve it, Tuli
didn't want to have that memory nagging at her. She wiped
her hands on the worn patched workskirt, wishing for the

thousandth time she could wear her night-running trousers
while she worked. It wasn't possible, it would only scandalize
the ties and make her life a misery. Not worth the fuss.

She looked back along the tidy row of trees, sighing with
tired satisfaction. *Not bad for a couple hours' work.* She
spread her fingers out and frowned at the dirt staining her
palms and packed beneath her nails. *I'll have to scrub with
pumice.* With a grunt of effort she pushed onto her feet,
stretched. She twisted loose a leaf and stripped away all but
the center spine, used this to dig at the dirt under her nails.
*Mama was right. I feel lots better. Won't bite Nilis when I
see her next.* She giggled, patted her stomach. "I could eat an
oadat, fur and all." She stretched again, yawned, filled with a
vast lassitude, too tired and too hungry to fuss about Nilis
any longer. "Won't bite Nilis. Poison to the bone." Giggles
bubbling out of her, she scooped up the trowel and spading
fork, started back toward the house, humming a bouncy tune,
singing a song in her head sometimes, aloud sometimes.
*Won't bite Nilis. Won't see Nilis. Won't talk to Nilis. Won't,
won't, won't bite Nilis.* "Nilis is a slimy snake, Nilis is a toad,
toad, toad, Nilis is a nobody." *Nobody, nobody, nobo, nobo,
nobodaddy.*

Chanting under her breath, alternating her chants with
giggles, she circled the tie-village, sauntered past the barns
and corrals, her song dying away as she saw the hauhaus still
waiting in them, though they should have been on their way
to the pasture an hour since. She stopped and looked around,
suddenly aware of what she'd seen but hadn't taken note of
before. There was no one about. The tie-village usually had
kids playing around the houses, noisy packs of boys or girls
busy at their games or fighting with each other. She remembered empty lanes. It was washday but no ties crowded
the heavy grey stones of the laundry court, stoking the fires
under the kettles, stirring the clothes in the boiling water,
talking all the while at top speed. And no ties were taking
bread to the beehive oven. Nobody at all in sight, not even
Hars who was always puttering about, doing something or
other around the barns. Her jubilation evaporating, she
frowned at the trowel and spading fork, then hurried toward
the toolshed. After a last worried glance about, she pulled the
door open and stepped inside.

Teras was there, waiting for her. "Been pulling weeds with
your teeth?" He reached out, brushed at her cheek and nose.
"You all right?"

"I'm cool." She thunked the fork and trowel between their holding pegs. "What's happening? How come you're here, not with everyone else wherever that is?"

"Wanted to talk to you before you went in." He dug with his boot heel into the hard-packed dirt floor. "There's a Decsel and his Ten inside." He balled his hands into fists and shoved them in the side pockets of his tunic, then shouldered the door open. "Don't want to talk here."

She followed him out, pointed at the garden wall ahead. "Over there?"

"Uh-uh, not yet anyway." He scuffed ahead of her through dry tufts of grass, kicking angrily at small pebbles not caring where they landed.

"Where we going then?"

"Haymow."

A loaded wain was drawn up before the haybarn; overhead the loading fork swung gently from its pulley. Teras caught hold of the fork rope and began wriggling up it, climbing with a bumpy ease that Tuli watched with jealousy biting at her. She kicked at her skirt and went through a small side door into the barn.

The interior was dark and dusty except for the bright yellow light thronged with dancing motes that streamed down from the high haywindow where she saw Teras loom higher and higher, an ebon shade with opaline edges, until he stood upright in the window. With a sudden bright laugh he used the rope to send the fork trolly rumbling inward along its track, then pushed off from the window and rode the rope across the open space to drop into the high-piled hay. A moment later his head appeared over the binding stakes. "Come on up, Tuli. They'll be out looking for us sooner'n we want."

"Hold your hair on, I'm coming." She tucked the hem of her skirt into her waistband and started up the ladder nailed to the side of the interior mow. At the top she pulled her skirt loose, then crawled across the slippery straw to her brother and stretched out on her stomach at his side. She started to ask him about the Decsel then changed her mind. "Mama said Da was gone off."

Teras worked a stem from the hay and chewed on it a moment, his eyes squinted to cracks, the misty light igniting the sun-bleached ends of his light brown hair into a shimmering glow about his head. "He was getting ready for bed." He looked down at the straw, then tossed it away. "He looked so

damn tired and worried, Tuli. Ahh, Tuli . . . how he looked
. . . I could . . ." His hands closed tight on the hay making
it squeak a little and his face was strained and tense. "It was
hard to tell him, Tuli, worst thing I had to do since Hars
made me tell him I was the one who let the hauhaus get into
the grainfield and mess up half the crop." He sighed, shifted
onto his back and lay picking bits of straw off his tunic. "He
threatened to tear the hide off my behind if I ever did anything like that again, specially taking you along, I had to tell
him you were with me but he knew before, I think."

"Ummm." She rubbed at her nose. "What did he say about
Nilis?"

"He said to leave her be, he'd see to her when he got
back."

Tuli sighed, pulled lengths of straw from under her, tied
the ends together and began twisting them into a crinkled
braid. After a moment she narrowed her eyes, turned her
head, gave him a long questioning look. "You haven't said
anything about the Decsel. And where are the ties?"

"In the house, even the kids. Nilis. It's all Nilis. Soon as
the Decsel showed up she sent her pet viper Averine out and
ordered them in, said Mama wanted them, but I don't think
so. I was out with Hars in the pasture so Averine missed me
first time. Not the second, oh no, but Hars told him to get
away or he'd break off one of his skinny arms and feed it to
him. He ran out of there like we'd set fire to. . . ." He broke
off, his nose and ears suddenly purple-red. "Hars told me I
should get hold of you and warn you what's up," he
mumbled.

Tuli closed her eyes, dropped her head until it rested on
crossed forearms and she was inhaling the scratchy sweet
smell of the straw. After a few breaths she exploded up, too
restless to sit still any longer. Feet sinking deep into the loose
straw, she lurched about the top of the stack. "I'd like to
switch Nilis all the way up the steps to the top of the watchtower 'nd shove her off 'nd see if she can fly."

"Me too, but that wouldn't help Da. Or Mama."

"Would me." She staggered to the stakes, wrapped her
hands about one and stared through the haywindow.
"Teras. . . ."

"What?"

"Maybe we should just go off after Da. Not go in at all."

"You know what he'd do." He got to his feet and floundered over beside her. "Running off and leaving Mama to face that Decsel all alone."

"She wouldn't be alone, there's Sanani and the ties and the baby and . . . well, and the cousins and Uncle Kimor and Aunt Salah."

"You know what I mean."

She held up a hand, turned it around in the mote-filled light. "I better change then and wash." She sniffed, made a face. "You too, twin. You stink like macai-shit."

"You shouldn't say that." He sounded shocked and disapproving.

"Hah, you turning into Nilis?" She eyed the fork rope, shook her head, gritted her teeth and waded back to the ladder. As she swung herself over, she muttered every bad word she'd gathered from her years of night running, listening with and without Teras to the patrons of Jango's tavern and to the herders around their night fires when they didn't know she was there. She stormed out of the barn, thinking she wouldn't wait for Teras, but she stopped anyway and waited.

Teras dropped beside her, spat on his palms, wiped them on his tunic. "You should go for a meie," he said, then dodged back, laughing as she swung at him. "See?"

"Brothers, hah!"

He started walking backwards a few paces in front of her as she strode for the place in the wall where the mortar had crumbled, leaving cavities that made easy climbing. "I was just teasing, Tuli," he said, "but I really mean it; I think you'd be a good meie, or maybe a healwoman." He grinned and pointed as she kicked impatiently at the damp heavy skirt. "You wouldn't have to wear those long skirts no more."

She didn't answer until they reached the wall, then she set her back against it and folded her arms over her small breasts. "I don't know," she said slowly. "When things get . . . get too shut in, I think about it. And then I think I'd like kids sometimes. And I know Fayd likes me and we laugh a lot at the same things and he doesn't mind that I'm no good at housework."

"Not now, maybe, but in a couple years?" Teras scowled; he never liked it when she talked about things she couldn't share with him. He didn't bother with girls and couldn't see why she should be any different. He snapped his fingers absently, again and again. "So he's fun now," he burst out. "But you know what his Da's like. And Tuli, I thought I saw him at the tilun, Fayd's Da, I mean."

She squeezed her eyes shut, whispered, "Oh Teras, why does everything have to change, why can't it stay like it always has been?"

The assembly hall that occupied the greater part of the House's ground floor was filled with people. To the right, a clutch of ties in Follower black (silvergilt circled-flame badges pinned to chests male and female), unnaturally quiet children herded behind them, stood in rigid ranks, smug smiles on their faces, knowing glitters in their eyes. To the left, the other tie-families waited together, nervous and uncertain, hushing their children when the noise got too loud, talking quietly among themselves or looking around with a growing apprehension in their faces. As Tuli came slowly down the stairs, she saw the tide of black washed up to her right and wanted to spit on them. Trembling, she reached out. Teras took her hand, held it hard. In the strength and hurting of his fingers, she felt his anger and fear and knew it matched hers. They came down the rest of the stairs together and stopped just behind Annic and Sanani. Annic turned her head when she heard them, nodded unsmiling and turned back to face the armed men separating the two groups of ties. "All my children are here now, Decsel. Unless you want me to have the baby brought, he's all of four years old. I'm sure he'd find you very impressive."

Hars stood a little apart from the other ties, his worn sundark face blank, his wiry body held very straight. A slight smile touched his face at Annic's speech. When he saw the twins, the smile widened very briefly, then his face was as blank as before, a mask carved from seasoned hardwood. Teras took a step toward him, but Tuli caught his arm. "Not now," she whispered. She heard a sound behind her and turned.

Nilis was coming down the stairs, chin high, triumph in her squeezed smile, her shining eyes. (Tuli remembered her mother's words: *all my children are here,* and felt a momentary sadness for her mother and even for Nilis who didn't know what she'd lost.) Her sister's eyes swept over Tuli as if she were less than a spot on the polished floor. Tuli forgot sadness and started for her.

Teras caught her shoulder and pulled her roughly against him, whispered in her ear, "Not now. Let Mama handle her."

Tuli leaned against her brother and drew on his calm. She

needed it when she saw the Agli move from behind the massive, scarred Decsel, a hard-faced woman beside him, and cross the flags to greet Nilis. She chewed on her lower lip and held onto her temper as she saw the Agli flick a slender white hand at the Decsel.

The big man nodded, then stomped with a martial rattle of his accoutrements across the intervening space to confront Annic. In spite of his military bearing (*exaggerated somewhat, perhaps in disgust at his present duty,* Tuli thought, then wondered if she was reading her own feelings into that scarred mask), he seemed a little uneasy as if he caught a hint of how ridiculous he looked in his metal and leather, his iron-banded gloves and boots, his sword swinging with the shift of long meaty legs, marching to face down a smallish woman with grey-streaked brown hair and brown-gold eyes that often twinkled with amused appreciation of the world's absurdities or a comic exasperation when one of her children played the fool. Tuli saw her mother's cheek twitch, saw blood rush to darken the already dark face of the Decsel and felt a bit sorry for him. She knew only too well that glint in her mother's eyes, that twitch of the lips that said without words: Don't you know how foolish you look? Come, laugh at this with me and be sensible next time. *Poor man,* she thought. *After all, he's just doing his job; at least he's not enjoying this, not like THEM.* She scowled at Nilis, the Agli, the strange woman.

The Decsel cleared his throat, pulled a parchment roll from under his arm.

Annic didn't wait for him to speak. "You come into this house unasked, Decsel." Her voice was pleasant but there was a touch of steel in it. Across the Hall Nilis stirred, started to speak, Annic stared her into silence then continued, "On Gradin land you walk by leave of Gradin tarom or Gradin Heir and only by their leave. That is both law and custom. You have the leave of neither. I must ask that you get out of this House and off this land. Or are you Outlaw, Decsel?"

Nilis scowled, started to speak again, but fell silent at the touch of the Agli's bone-white fingers. Tuli felt Teras laughing under his breath behind her; in spite of her growing apprehension she found herself smiling. Nilis was rapidly working up a major snit; this business wasn't going the way she obviously thought it would; she wasn't the center of attention, wasn't the avenging flame of Soäreh.

The Decsel waited until Annic stopped speaking then he opened out the parchment roll. "Torma, this warrant of arrest and seizure arrived an hour ago, bird-flown from Oras, sealed with the seal of the Doamna-regent. In it the Agli Urith is appointed conservator of the Gradin holdings until the Gradin Heir is of an age to hold the Tar." He spoke in a monotone, gabbling the words as if he wanted this over soon as possible. "Tesc Gradin uran-tarom is proscribed rebel and traitor. He will be arrested and tried as soon as he reaches Oras for conspiracy to deprive Floarin Doamna-regent of her just tithe by secret concealment and open conspiracy."

Tuli held her face as still as she could; she knew her hands shook, she felt her twin's hands close hard on her shoulders, but she wouldn't let Nilis or any of those others see how afraid she was. *We have to warn Da*, she thought. *I was right before, we should've took off already after him.* She looked up when she heard the Decsel clear his throat.

"There's more, torma." He looked down at the scroll and read in a dull voice. " 'Because the Maiden cult has fostered treachery and rebellion and an immoral, unregulated populace, we, Floarin Doamna-regent of the mijloc and Oras—' " there was a growing disturbance among the loyal ties that the Decsel ignored, leaving their quieting to his men—"who must always cherish the well-being of the people of the mijloc, do hereby declare the cult of the so-called Maiden Outlaw an Anathema. All artifacts of that cult are to be purged from the homes of the people, the shrines in the towns and villages are to be closed and dismantled, the shrine-keepers are to be reeducated in the nearest House of Repentance. To facilitate the redemption of the populace, Houses of Repentance will be established in each of the larger towns of the Plain. Be these edicts announced to the recalcitrant and posted in the public squares of all towns. I say it who am Floarin Doamna regent of Oras and the Plains.' "

Annic held up a hand, quieting the ties on her left (to her right the Follower-ties were smirking or piously raising their eyes to the ceiling.) "I have heard you, Decsel." She stressed the *heard*. With a brisk flourish he handed her the parchment.

She read the scroll, her hands quite steady, her face calm. She read slowly, deliberately, ignoring the Agli's growing impatience, and Nilis's nervous dance from foot to foot. When at last she finished she rolled it back into a tight cylinder, held it at arm's length and dropped it with quiet contempt to rattle and roll on the stone flags. Still ignoring the Agli, she walked briskly across to Nilis (one heel coming down on the end of the parchment roll). She stopped in front of Nilis, eyed her for a moment until Nilis looked down, unable to endure the accusation in her mother's gaze. With a soft expulsion of air, not even a sigh, she slapped Nilis hard across the face, hard enough to send her stumbling against the Agli, the loud splat of hand against face lost almost immediately in the explosion of cheers and stamping from the loyal ties. Annic walked with quiet dignity to the stairs. When she'd gone up several steps she turned and stood with one hand resting lightly on the banister. In the sudden silence her quiet voice rang out more clearly and strongly than any shout. "Decsel, do what you must, but I call on you to search your conscience and restrain the excesses of your masters. To you who are still my friends, I say, do what you must to live but never serve with willing hearts or willing hands. For you, I ask the Maiden's Blessing and pray that you will see better times. To you who have sold yourself body and soul to this abomination, I pray that you get exactly what you wish, no more no less." She watched them without further words, her light brown eyes filled with contempt, then she turned and continued up the stairs.

For several moments there was only the sound of breathing in the great hall and the scraping of booted feet on the stone flags. The tableau held until they heard a door close above, then the Agli touched Nilis's arm, led her across the room to the Highseat where Tesc adjudicated disputes and awarded prizes and oversaw the celebrations of the seasonal festivals. Tuli sucked in a shocked breath as Nilis mounted the steps and took her father's place. Nilis heard, glared at her, then smoothed her face into a smile as she looked up at the Agli who had mounted the steps to stand at her shoulder. He snapped his fingers.

The Decsel bowed his head very slightly as if his neck were stiff, again evidencing distaste for what he was doing. But he would do it, being a man who left moral judgments and strategy to those who gave him his orders, a man who circumscribed his honor in duty well performed. He called one of his Ten, pointed to the scroll on the floor. The guard scooped it up, brought it to his leader, saluted smartly and stepped back to his line. The Decsel popped out the place where Annic's foot had flattened it and stood tapping it against his thigh. "By order from Oras the entire harvest of this Tar is forfeit to the Doamna-regent." His voice had the same dull lack of resonance. "Gradin-ties who wish to remain on the land must apply to the Agli Urith or Nilis new-torma Gradin-daughter for food and other necessaries. Who will receive and who must leave will be theirs to judge." The loyal ties stirred. Tuli heard muttered protests, saw people who'd been her friends glance furtively or openly at the three of them, Sanani, her and Teras. She couldn't help them; she couldn't help herself. Though they oppressed her spirit and irritated her mightily at times, the ties were her folk, she was Gradin and bound to them as strongly as they were bound to the land, bound by blood and custom and law, yet she couldn't stop what she saw happening. Some would leave, she saw it in their faces, knew they'd never bend knee to Nilis or the Agli; some would stay, awhile at least and be miserable with it. *A culling,* she thought. *They're culling the ties. They'll keep the weak and send the strong off to starve.*

The Decsel was still speaking, she'd missed some of what he'd said, but now she heard, ". . . return to your houses and cast out everything proscribed, every book or picture or other artifact touching on the Anathema. When this is completed the Agli and the new-torma will inspect your dwellings. Any objects concealed will be burned and that tie responsible will be sent to join the Gradin-born in the House of Repentance where he will learn to recognize error. After the noon meal all objects discarded by the free will of the ties will be burnt before the House for the purification of the House."

So fast, Tuli thought. *How can this be happening so fast?*

Her face troubled, Sanani turned to follow Annic up the stairs. She put one hand on the finial of the newel post, then spun around. "No," she said, her voice shaking with the anger that had been building in her, her shyness momentarily overwhelmed by that anger. "How dare you do this, you . . . you. . . ." She jabbed a forefinger at the Agli. "Get out of this House and take your toad with you." She brought her hand down, wiped it against the front of her blouse as if just pointing at the Agli had soiled it. "And you, Nilis, sister-not-sister, I hope you dream about drinking kinblood; kinslayer, I pray the Maiden sets her Scorpions on you; dream about them crawling over you. You aren't Gradin. You're nothing." She raised her chin, turned her back on Nilis. "Tuli, Teras, come," she commanded and marched up the stairs, her head high, her back militantly erect. Still holding hands, the twins followed her. In the thick, strained silence behind them they heard Nilis say bitterly, "When was I ever your sister, Soni? When was I ever treated like a Gradin-born?"

CHAPTER IV:

THE QUEST

Where the road twisted in a last switchback high on the side of the mountain Serroi whispered the macai to a halt and swung around to gaze with a valedictory fondness at the Valley, whose gold and green and brown sublimed into the blue of distance. The harvest was coming in well enough, many of the grain fields had only dry stubble left and leaves drifted into heaps in the orchard aisles as apprentices stood on ladders and dropped ripe fruit into canvas sacks. Wind like ovenbreath whistled up the slope while overhead the sky was cloudless with a coppery shimmer about the bloated sun as if the air itself had been compressed into a great burning lens that magnified the orb until it seemed three times its usual size. Wisps of hair, sweat-dampened, clung to her temples, collecting and loosing salt droplets down her face, into her eyes, into the corners of her mouth. She brushed impatiently at the trickles, moved her shoulders, uncomfortably aware that she was developing a rash under her arms where the sleeveholes of her tunic rubbed against her skin. She stared up at the sun, remembering all too vividly a small girl sitting and sweating on a pile of blankets in the empty animal pens of her Noris's hold as the stones of the island itself threatened to melt beneath her while her Noris fought and slew two others of the great Nor.

The macai moaned his displeasure as the wind blew grit and heat into his eyes and nostrils. He bent his limber neck, drawing his head around behind the bulk of his body until he was nuzzling her leg. She patted his shoulder, strained to see the top of the great cliff across the valley. The stone wavered like water behind the heat-haze, but after some minutes she thought she saw him by the cliff edge (he liked to stand a totter away from disaster, it seemed to please something in him), a ragged line like a brief stroke of a writing brush on ill-made paper; she couldn't even be sure she saw him, the air was too filled with windborn dust and fragments from the

52

partially denuded fields below, too unsteady as heat climbed from the valley floor to that burning lens above. Her eyespot throbbed painfully. She touched it, sighed. Behind her, she heard Dom Hern curse and call her name, heard the impatient scratching of his macai's claws against the stony rutted road. He sounded snappish already, give him half a chance, he'd start ordering her about. She ignored him and continued to gaze at the cliff and the bit of blackness there. "Watching me still," she whipsered. "You drove me out of my sanctuary. What now?"

Abruptly she bent, slipped her fingers into her boot top and drew out the silver box. She held it a moment, her fingers closed tight around it, the corners digging into her palm. "Maiden give you rest, my Noris, though I suppose you wouldn't want such a blessing." She forced her thumbnail under the tight-fitting lid and shoved it up. The thing inside seemed little more than one of those dull grey pebbles, water-polished to a flattish egg shape, found so plentifully in mountain streams.

Before she could lift it out, she heard the scrabble of macai claws and felt rather than saw Hern looming beside her. "What's that thing?" There was an arrogant demand in his voice. She knew it was bred in him too deep for simple warnings to eradicate, still it irritated her.

"Tajicho," she said curtly. "A near impenetrable shield against magic." She took it from the box, closed her fingers about it as it came awake, taking its power form—a clear crystal with fire at its heart. Light leaked through her fingers, through the flesh itself, turning it redly translucent until, for a moment only, she could see the bone shadows in each finger. "Good-bye, my Noris," she whispered as that first effulgence faded.

With the tajicho humming gently against her palm, she turned to Hern, intending to explain further the properties of the shield, but he'd already started to swing his macai about, having forgotten the thing in her hand. *The tajicho takes care of itself,* she thought, *turns men's eyes away*. Even if they saw it they soon found urgent reasons for turning away from it, some overriding concern to replace wonder about the glowing stone which they forgot as soon as they looked away.

Serroi bent again, slipped the tajicho into its boot pocket; she held the box a moment, intending at first to toss it into the rubble by the roadside. Surrendering to second thoughts, she tucked it into her other boot.

Hern looked back. "Two days over the mountains," he yelled at her, his words caught and whirled back at his face by the oven-wind. She raised her brows. After resettling herself in the saddle with slow care, she scratched at her complaining mount's neck, smiled one last time at the Valley though she saw little more than a shining blur. When she felt she'd dawdled enough to make her point, she turned the macai around. Holding him at a fast walk, she rode past the fuming man, ignoring him still, knowing with some satisfaction that plumes of red dirt and bits of rock were raining down on him as she climbed the steep slope. A touch of malice lighting her eyes, she heard the whomp-grunt of Hern's mount, then he was riding beside her; there was room for that now though the road was little more than a rough track winding through the peaks.

As long as the steep grade persisted, neither spoke, though Serroi found herself growing very aware of him. The unwelcome heat rising in her brought back with sudden vividness last year's escape from the Plaz. She remembered running through the passage in the wall, Hern at her heels, remembered the sudden stop, Hern caroming into her, knocking her down, pulling her up again, holding her tight against him, his mouth close to her ear:

"What is it?"

"Man ahead, sleykyn it smells like."

"One?" She could feel his breath warm against her ear, teasing at her hair; she could feel the judder of his heart against her breasts. Her breathing was ragged, her mind distract.

"Yes." She trembled in a way that had little to do with the danger ahead or the danger they'd just escaped. He laughed; she felt quick puffs of air caressing her cheek. He caught her chin, turned her face up to him, kissed her slowly, sensuously, until she sagged against him.

The road flattened a little as they reached the saddle of the pass. The afternoon was far gone, the sky behind them darker, the unnatural coppery tinge more evident than before. Serroi scraped sweat from her forehead, wiped her hand on her tunic, rubbed the tip of her finger along her lower lip as she frowned thoughtfully at Hern. "Dark soon."

He glanced toward her but his mind was apparently on other things; she saw that he heard the sound of her voice but didn't take in what she said.

"There's a track branching off from the road about two hours down from the saddle. Heads east, the way we want to go. With a spring near the turn-off and a meadow. We can camp there and in the morning get a good start to the Grey-bones Gate."

"No."

"What do you mean no?"

"We'll spend the morrow night in Sadnaji." His lips curved into an anticipatory smile. "At Braddon's Inn."

At first she wanted to argue with him, tell him what a fool he was even to think of setting foot anywhere on the Plain. He knew as well as she that meien were no longer welcome in the mijloc, he knew a breath of suspicion about him would raise powerful forces against them both and wreck the quest before it really began. She touched her graceblade, ran her fingertips up and down the wooden hilt she'd shaped so carefully to her grip, drawing comfort from the familiar feel, the satin-smooth wood oiled by her hands till she and it were linked as close as mother and child. She slid her hand along her weaponbelt, touched the coils of fine grey rope, seaspider silk braided thinner than her little finger and strong enough to bind an angry macai. She touched the small pockets in her belt, the worn comfortable leather that rested on her hips, as she wondered if this partnership was going to be possible at all. She wasn't about to let him take charge either of her or of the quest. She glanced quickly at him, lips compressed as she saw that he was calm again with no sign of the irritation that had pricked at him earlier. *He doesn't have the least idea what a bastard he can be. Sadnaji? Idiocy!* She sighed. *He's not stupid,* she told herself, *just pandering to that gut of his and his need to dominate. Calm reason, that's the thing.* "Even if we start early it will be very late, probably after midnight, before we get there."

He shrugged. "TheDom's rising full. The Road will be clear enough."

"Dom, neither of us will find any welcome on the Plain."

"Like you said, it'll be dark. The town will be sleeping."

"It won't be dark inside the inn." She thrust a hand at him, the green of her skin darker in the heavy light of the lingering day. "To know me takes one look and you're not the most nondescript of men."

He grunted, impatient with her for prolonging an argument he considered closed. "Braddon's a good man. He sees a lot in that inn of his." Without waiting for an answer he urged his macai past her, his pudgy body surprisingly graceful in the saddle. *He's definitely fatter.* She took a sour pleasure in the thought. *Damn him, one old tavernkeeper's words mean more to him than all the reports of mere females even though they're meien all of them.* She snorted. *But that's only an excuse. All he wants is to get his teeth into Braddon's fare.*

She smiled reluctantly. Old Braddon was a good man, he was right about that. Braddon's Inn was a prosperous happy place, one with a reputation for splendid food and fine wines that obviously reached all the way to Oras. A friend of hers, too. The Aglim were condemning all the pleasures of the flesh but surely Braddon would be safe from them, he had too many friends. She wrinkled her nose at the broad back in front of her. *I'd wager my right arm his mouth is already watering.* She considered letting him go down and get himself netted while she continued the quest alone. Alone. She closed her eyes. Alone. No. Later, perhaps, if they couldn't work out some accommodation of their temperaments, she could hunt out another companion. Right now the thought of leaving him turned her cold and hollow inside. His powerful sensuality disturbed her, his arrogance infuriated her, his blindspots frightened her, but with all this he was a distraction that chased away the loneliness that threatened to break her will and send her whimpering back to the Noris. She watched the flutter of his grey-streaked hair, the roll of his body. He radiated strength, she could lean on that now and then, when the battle got too much for her—if they could work out that accommodation. Sadnaji might tame the sicamar in him and teach him necessary things about his limits; he still had to learn what it meant to move about as an ordinary man without the trappings of power, to learn what it meant to depend solely on his own wit and his own strength. She moved her shoulders, eased herself in the saddle, disgusted at being sore and tired so soon into the journey. *Too bad Southport is closed to us, leaving there would have saved a lot of riding.*

Yael-mri unrolled the map, set a book on one end and a small carving on the other to hold it flat. "Here." She tapped a point just above the center of the southern continent. "You'll have to cross the Sinadeen somehow. Too bad Southport had to be closed. Something has stirred the Kry from their sandhills; they're swarming so thick on the ground we had to take the Southport folk behind the Wall. A shame, really. It would be much simpler to get passage there so you

wouldn't have to deal with the Minarka. That's always a du-
bious undertaking." She tapped the map. "Unless you think
Oras is open. . . ." She smiled at Hern's snort. "That leaves
Skup." Scowling, she clicked her fingernail on the small dark
blotch jutting into the bright blue of the sea. "Too bad if
your Noris has been busy there too, Serroi. Maiden bite him,
he's stirring up everything he can poke a finger in. Even the
Plain isn't safe any more." She slapped her hand down on the
map, suddenly very angry. "Meien are actually in danger
there. I never thought I'd see the day when the Plain was
more dangerous for us than Assurtilas." She drew her hand
across her nose, sniffed. "We keep getting girls running to us
every day from the tars and the ties and the hills. Much more
and we'll have to drive the Kry off and reopen Southport so
we can bring in supplies from Kelea-alela and the Zemilsud,
though where we'll get the gold to pay for. . . ." She broke
off. "My problems you don't need. Well. The Deadlands."
Her nail clicked across the map, stopped to tap nervously on
an irregular splotch painted blue. "Ghostwater. Don't drink
it. They say even the dust is bad there, make you sicker than
you want. There's a track of sorts and TheDom's rising.
Maiden bless, it's only a five-hour ride from Greybones Gate
to the Viper's Gullet." Her finger traced a line that skirted
the edge of the water, stopped at a series of small blue
circles. "The Cisterns. Wash yourselves down there, the macain too. Take a good long rest at the Cisterns so you won't
have to stop in the Vale. Keep to the road and don't try talking to the Minarka. They're. . . ." She smiled suddenly,
briefly. "They're terminally xenophobic. Comes of living next
to Assurtilas. Baby Sleykynin use them for training raids.
Strangers are not welcome. Don't—I repeat don't—try riding
at night in the Vale of the Minar. If you start down the
mountain before dawn, you should be able to reach Skup by
sundown. Serroi, you and Tayyan sistered Chak-may the first
year she was here. I'm sure she told you more than enough
about Skup. Hern, that's a treacherous place. The High Minarka grow madder every year. A false step, a whim of some
dweller on the High Ledges, and you're dead, both of you.
You'll need luck, Maiden grant it, but there's no way to the
port except through the city. One good thing—according to
the last ships into Southport, the High Minarka aren't mad
enough to touch the Traders. This time of year there should
be several ships in for minarkan preserves and fine cloth. You
should be able to get passage there for the Zemilsud." She

folded her hands on the map and looked gravely at Serroi
and Hern. "Kelea-alela. The Bec. Yallor-on-the-Neck." She
said the names slowly with heavy stress on all syllables. After
a moment's silence she unlaced her hands and moved a finger
south over the long blue sausage of the Sinadeen to a point
on the coast of the Zemilsud.

Serroi leaned back, letting her eyes droop half closed,
smiling a little, amused by both of them. Hern was enduring
Yael-mri's lecture with highly evident patience and politeness.
Yael-mri yielded with no struggle at all to her antagonism to
Hern and to her propensity to lecture to her listeners whether
or not they knew much of what she was saying.

"Kelea-alela. A Gather ago—before the Gather before this
last one—Kelea-alela was the capital of a Minark colony but
it broke away when the storms of the Gather kept Minark
ships off the Sinadeen. The locals slaughtered the Minark
Governor and any of the High Minarks they could get their
hands on—a well-deserved fate from all I've heard." She
smiled sweetly at Hern; Serroi suppressed a chuckle. "They
fortified the town. By the time the storms let up they were
firmly enough in place that the Minarkan war galleys couldn't
pry them out. We've got friends there still and it's the closest
of the three, that's why I'd prefer your starting inland from
that point. Kelea-alela, the Bec, Yallor-on-the-Neck, you can
start from any one of those and reach the Mirror. I'd better
tell you about all the routes, no knowing what will happen
once you leave the Valley.

"The Bec." A long gourd-shaped intrusion of the sea thrust
deep into the land mass of the southern continent. At the
base of the gourd was a sprawling black blotch that marked
the site of the ancient city called the Bec. "Becarnish are
friendly enough. They've never seen much reason to leave
their city but they admit that not all foreigners have their ad-
vantages so they tolerate their intrusions—and manage to find
use for whatever trade goods these foreigners bring with
them. You can't insult them, they'll just laugh at your ignorance." Her mouth twisted into a rueful half-smile. "An outsider's stomach will go sour after a tenday's residence there.
But never mind that. The RiverBernbec rises on Mount Santac. Here. It's a dormant volcano with a reflecting lake in the
crater. The Mirror. Though not the one you'll look in if he
lets you. It's a wild river, more trouble to the mile. . . ." Her
voice died away as she traced the jagged line from the Bec
up into the mountains and tapped thoughtfully at the small

blue circle. "Falls and rapids, underground segments. A stiff climb, but it's clean water all the way, no fever pools." She frowned at Hern, her eyes resting on the paunch that was emphasized by the way he was sitting. "The mountain tribes will give you trouble if you choose to go that way. They hold the upper reaches of the river sacred and do their accomplished best to slaughter any outsider coming up there.

"The best way starts at Kalea-alela and goes inland along RiverFalele. The only problem you would face are the Niyonius Marshes, a maze of dead-end channels. No guides available. But if you manage to keep to the main channel, the river will take you straight to the lake.

"Yallor-on-the-Neck." She moved her finger to the far end of the Sinadeen where a narrow strip of land separated the sea from the Ocean of Storms. "RiverYam. Starts from LowYallor here." Her nail clicked lightly on the spot. "You've got a narrow strip of farmland, some ragged hills, then the Dar. Flat country, not a pimple for hundreds of miles, reeds growing in great clumps, broad sheets of shallow water. Most days a strong sweep of wind inland, you could use a sail to propel you rather than depending on poles or oars. A thousand kinds of bloodsuckers, fliers and swimmers. Darmen. They're small." She grinned at Serroi. "The tallest won't stand past your brows, little one."

Serroi made a face at her. Hern grinned, leaned back in his chair, his fingers laced over his middle.

Yael-mri rubbed at her eyes. "They're shy folk, not hostile. If they don't like you, you won't see them, if they take to you, they'll keep you in fresh food and guide you around dead ends. I can't offer you any help with them, it's been twenty years since I passed that way." She set her hands on the table, fingers curved, nails touching lightly the map's tough paper. "Whatever way you go—and that's up to you— I imagine you'll be cursing me half a hundred times before this quest is done."

Nijilic Thedom hung heavy in the east, sitting on the points of the Vachhorns, the bleached bare peaks rising about the Deadlands. The macai's pads boomed hollowly on the plank bridge thrown across CreekSajin, a noisy, self-important stream not quite large enough to earn the name of river. Moth-sprites flickered over the water in elaborate patterns, their small lights thicker than she'd seen them any autumn she could remember. She stopped to watch the elaborate dance, shimmering lace woven from the tiny silver sparks, caught and recaught in the broken water. She smiled with affection at the sprites, pre-pubescent girl-children carved from moonglow, no larger than the first joint of her smallest finger. After several minutes, though, it seemed to her that the dance was less complex, less free, than she remembered, less exuberant and more precise as if the forms they made had become more important to them than their joy in the making. She watched until she could bear the sadness no longer, then she hurried after Hern.

Almost swallowed by the stronger white light of TheDom, a tiny glow touched Hern's back just above the high curve of the cantle. When she came up with him she saw a single sprite clinging desperately to a fold of his tunic, a disconsolate flicker of light gradually dimming as they left the stream behind. He wasn't aware of it and wouldn't have cared much if she told him, but she felt a little sick. Sprites were part magic, part natural, all too open to the corrupting and too-skillful touch of her Noris. As once she'd wept to see her beasts corrupt, now she ached to see a bit of autumn's ancient beauty turned away from the world of joy it once knew to fit itself into the rigid patterns required by Nor mindsets and to act against its light as a Nor-tool. Forgetting in her pain the tajicho and its effect on magic, she reached out to brush the sprite off Hern's back.

The sprite ruptured at her touch, whiffling into a lifeless husk that rolled down Hern's thigh to be trampled into the cold dust of the road. Feeling twenty times a murderer, she closed her eyes but could not weep.

Hern swung around and stared at her. "What was that for?"

She brushed at her eyes, sighed. "You were marked."

"What?"

"A sprite settled on you to mark you for the Nearga-nor. Going into Sadnaji is a fool's move and you know it, Hern. They're warned and waiting for us."

"Gloom and doom." Hern laughed. "A Norit behind every tree. All this over a damn silly little sprite?" Still chuckling, he urged his tired mount into a faster shuffle and drew ahead of her again, leaving her to wonder where his wits had got or if her Noris had somehow worked on his head to blind him to reason.

She reached up and drew a forefinger gently around the edge of her eyespot. Fifteen years ago, no, more like twenty

now, her Noris had learned how to manipulate her—with her
eager help and the eyespot as gate. She shook off a touch of
panic then stiffened. *I'm like the sprites*, she thought. *Not all
natural.* She bent down, touched her fingertips to the warm
stone in the boot pocket. *You unmake magic. I wonder if one
day you'll unmake me.* She shivered at the thought,
straightened, glanced at the moons. *Nearly there.* She shook
out the cloak bundled behind the saddle and pulled it around
her shoulders, knotting the ties with trembling fingers. *Magic,
Maiden bless, I hate it. Hate it.* She jerked the hood up over
her head. *I should never have been conceived, let alone born.*

The Longwind blew night and day across the Tundra at
the heart of Winterdeep, a ram of air so cold a moment's ex-
posure would freeze to the bone. Prey and predator alike
slept the long dark away while the windrunners and their
herds went inland to the Burning Mountains and the Place of
Boiling Water where the herds could find graze and shelter
from that wind of death. The Place was a long chain of val-
leys scooped from the black stone, tradition-tied to the various clans among the Windrunners.

By custom and by law no woman could lie with any man
there on pain of outcasting should the sin be known. And
known it would be if there was fruit of the coupling—all
babes so conceived were misborn, marked in one way or another. Misborn, their mothers outcast, had their bodies given
to the Cleansing Fire, their spirits sent home to the Great Hag
on that last day of Celebration before the clans separated in
the spring to follow their herds in the age-old paths down the
Tundra. Serroi was conceived on a drunken night near the
end of the wintering. Too much mead and too much dancing,
too much warmth and too much dark and afterward too
much guilt and fear even though her birthtime was no betrayal since she stayed overlong in the womb yet was born
much smaller than most. And she was born perfect, rosy and
well-shaped, bright, lively, a lovely babe. For two years her
mother thought herself safe from outcasting but in Serroi's
third year pale green splotches like old bruises darkened her
small body though her hands and face were left clear. By the
end of the third Wintering the splotches spread to her face
and the eyespot began to take shape between her brows. Her
mother watched her with a sadness and despair Serroi
couldn't understand; her brothers and sisters either shunned

her or played cruel tricks on her—that, too, she didn't understand.

In the spring of her fourth year The Noris came and took her away—saved her life, she knew later. Come next Winterdeep she'd be marked and given to the fire, her mother driven away to survive how she could on her own. But the Noris came before that could happen, took her away and loved her a little maybe and used her to dig into places otherwise blocked off from him.

The road looped across gently rolling land, winding soon between the high thorn hedges marking tar boundaries, past groves of brellim, spikuls and moonglows, past rattling clumps of bastocane. Loud whooshing grunts from the tired macai, macai pads thudding softly on the dust, sleepy twitters drifting sometimes from tree or hedge, chini howling in the distance at the moon, a few barks and rustles from the grass and brush at the side of the road—all familiar, even comforting, night sounds, yet Serroi felt a spreading coldness within. The air seemed to hang poised around her, though a vigorous breeze danced leaves about over her head; she felt eyes on her though she knew this had to be her own foolishness because the tajicho protected her most effectively from all spirit eyes.

She followed Hern around a last grove of brellim and moonglows and saw Sadnaji loom before them, a dark bulk with no light showing except the caged torch sputtering toward exhaustion above the Inn's door. It was still bright enough to show her the empty court beyond the broad low arch in the Inn's wall. Hern swung around, grinned at her. The flash of his teeth said without words: I told you so. She gritted her own teeth, fighting down an urge to tear off his arm and beat him over the head with it.

The silence was thick between them as they covered the last few yards to the welcoming arch. She bit down hard on her lower lip to hold back a last and probably futile plea, sighed and followed Hern into the Inn court.

A bent and tattered figure shuffled from the stables backed up against the Northwall of the court. Serroi swallowed hard as she recognized him in spite of the fifteen years since they'd met, fifteen years that had added more layers of dirt and malice to his withered face. The old hostler stopped in front of Hern, lifted his wrinkled evil face, peered up at him from red-rimmed eyes, exuding a powerful aroma of ancient sweat,

stale urine and bad wine. Serroi tugged nervously at her
hood, then wished she hadn't because the movement caught
the hostler's eye. He stared at her, blinked slowly, rubbed at
his nose with the back of a filthy hand. "Yer out late, c'taj."
His whine was filled with senile insolence. "Shouldna be pis-
sin' round in d' dark. I gotta go fer d'Agli 'nd tell." He
giggled then, breathy whistling hoots that propelled his foul
breath into Hern's face.

Serroi cursed under her breath as Hern went rigid. She
edged her mount closer to his and dropped a hand on his
arm, not daring to speak, hoping her interference wouldn't
provoke the explosion she was trying to avert. He glanced
around at her and she was startled to see laughter instead of
anger dancing in his pale eyes.

"Needs must," he said with smiling geniality and flipped a
silver coin at the hostler. "Stable these beasts and grain 'em,
they worked hard today, there's something considerable of me
to haul about." He slid off the macai, circled around the
gaping old man, strolled unhurriedly toward the main door of
the Inn. Serroi watched the hostler, his mouth still hanging
open, look down at the coin in his hand. Shaking her head,
she dismounted and walked quickly after Hern, feeling
slightly disoriented, as if a cooing macai foal had suddenly
sunk its teeth in her hand.

When she pushed through the door he was hauling on a
bell-pull dangling beside the stairwell. She looked around the
room surprised to find it so empty. Fear congealed in a cold
lump under her ribs. *This is wrong, all wrong. Where's Braddon?* She fidgeted with the hood of her cloak, uneasily
remembering Hern's orders to the hostler. If that old viper
took the macain to the stable and stripped them of their gear,
that cut off any quick retreat. Almost better to hope he left
the macain standing and hurried off to fetch the Agli, as he'd
threatened. A single lamp burned behind the bar, leaving
most of the room in heavy shadow. Hern pulled the bellcord
again, swearing under his breath with a growing impatience.
They did it after all, she thought. *They've taken away his
trade in spite of his friends.* She couldn't remember a single
night, no matter how bad the weather, when this room didn't
have a traveler or two, feet stretched to the fire, drinking and
swapping lies long after midnight with local folk come to sup
Braddon's beer and crunch down the extras he offered free.
She looked down at the table beside her, tapped fingers
lightly on the wood. Dry and shining clean. Not a crumb or

even a waterstain left. She frowned down at her fingers. *We left the Valley on Vara thirty. This is Gorduu two, Maiden bless, this is the middle of Gorduufest. This place should be packed and wet to near flooding. Where are the pole lights in the square, the straw maids blessed by the shrine keeper? The green should be filled with dancers, ringed with roast-fires.* She remembered the rigid patterns of the sprite dances and the sadness she felt watching them. This room, this whole Inn breathed a sadness that near choked her. She crossed to Hern, put her hand on his arm. "Let's get out of here."

"I begin to think you're right," he said softly. He passed a hand over his tousled grey-streaked hair, started for the door, then turned with Serroi to face the stairwell as they both heard shuffling, uncertain footsteps, saw Braddon coming painfully down the stairs, step by slow step, anxiety contorting his features. For a moment Serroi didn't recognize him, then she scowled at him. The round ebullient man with his warm joy in good food and good neighbors, the exuberant friend of all who came through the door, this man no longer existed. His skin hung in folds over his bones, his hands shook, his bramble-bush hair was thinned and flattened and streaked with white. He stopped on the last step, glanced about the room. He winced at the shadows, swallowed as the door stayed shut. His tongue flicked across dry lips then he cleared his throat. "Cetaj?"

Serroi's fingers tightened on Hern's arm. Without speaking she raised her other hand and brushed back the hood, turned her face to the light.

Braddon gasped. He stumbled off the bottom step and stretched out his hand to touch her cheek. "Meie?" His eyes flew past her, came back to her. "Did he see you?"

"He was there. I don't think he knew me—the hood was up, the cloak pulled around me. Seems to me the old buzzard's eyes aren't too sharp anymore."

"Sharp enough." Braddon straightened his shoulders. "Doesn't matter. Orders are no one's to be out after sundown without a pass."

Hern started to speak but Serroi closed her fingers tighter, digging her nails into his flesh. "Whose orders?"

"Agli's. Backed by a Decsel from Oras." The words trailed into a hiss of fury. For a moment a shadow of his old self returned.

She touched his wrinkled cheek. "So much change in such a little time?"

"Yah, meie." The flash was gone. He caught hold of her hand, his own trembling, held her fingers against his face. "Change, Yah. They had me in their House of Repentance a full month and when they let me out they set him watching me." He nodded at the door. "Soäreh's worm, he is."

"Then we'd better be off."

"He already saw you." Each soft word fell heavily into the silence. "They said if I sinned, they'd burn me out. Sin!" He dropped her hand, stumbled to the bar and edged behind it. Fishing beneath it, he brought up a clean damp cloth and pushed it gently, lovingly across the ancient polished planks. "I don't know why I keep on, meie; this isn't living. It's not that I have anyone now, Matti dying last spring, my grandson gone off. Never thought I'd say this, but I'm glad she's not here no more and don't have to see this." His eyes slid around to Hern. "Think I know you, friend. Shouldna be here, it's a bad place for you. Listen to an old man, both of you. Get from the mijloc and stay out. Nothing you can do alone. And folks here are too shook up to help." He polished absently at the planks in front of him. "Call you perverts, meie, the Followers, they do. I've seen 'em chasing meien." He stared somberly at the cloth. "Getting so a man can't spit without looking first at them damn rules they got hung up all over the place." He flicked a finger at the door where she saw a pale square of white stuck to the middle panel. "Put me in that jail of theirs," he went on. "Young Beyl he come to slip me out, all set for the mountains he was, wanted me to go with him. Good lad, dammit I do miss him. Be dead most like before Winterdeep. Froze or ate or skewered. Meie, you shouldna be wearing the leathers. Not here. Not anywhere. The Worm, he got to dig Agli out of bed and that fat bastard likes his sleep. You got a little time. At the head of the stairs, fourth floor, south side. Beyl's room it was. Most of his clothes left, take what you need and shuck those leathers. Go quiet, we got a Norit sleeping up there, been here more'n a passage now, hanging around snooping into things." He folded the cloth with neat small movements of his hands, stowed it away, straightened. "You, cetaj." He jabbed a finger at Hern then tapped it against his head. "Give me a clout here. Mark me. Worm knows when you got here. I been wasting too much time talking." He sighed. "Han't been able to talk really seems like a year now. If they find me on floor with bloody head, maybe they won't ask when that head got bloody." He moved quickly away, stopped by the foot of the

stairs. "They find me here, they think maybe you got me before I had a chance to yell." He rounded his shoulders and
bent his head.

Hern's eyes widened, but he nodded and drew his dagger;
his movements slow at first then very quick, he crossed the
three-stride space between him and Braddon, the hard tap behind the ear done before Serroi let out the breath she was
holding. Braddon folded slowly down. Serroi ran to him to
break his fall, but Hern caught her arm and held her back.
When Braddon was sprawled on the floor, he thrust her aside
and knelt, his fingers searching out the pulse in the old man's
throat; with a quick, relieved smile he used the blade's point
to draw a long scratch across the rising bump, then jumped
to his feet as blood began trickling through the coarse grey
fleece on the old man's head.

"You are sometimes clever, Dom," Serroi murmured.

He bowed, mockery in the elaborate dip. "Nice of you to
notice." The bitterness in his voice startled her, but before
she could respond, he caught her wrist and started for the
door. "Let's get out of here."

She wrenched her arm free. "Not yet," she said. "Not
now."

"What?"

"You go see about the macain. Bring them around to the
south side, I should be coming out a window there and down
the wall."

"Forget it, you won't be out of the hills long enough to
need those things."

Serroi strode back to the stairs, pulling the hood up as she
went, tugging it so far forward it dangled in her eyes. Standing behind the crumpled body, she stared at him, angry
words flooding her mind, choking in her throat. In the end,
all she said was, "See we have mounts."

She wheeled and ran up the stairs, up and around, anger
driving her like fire under her feet, her toes whispering tsp-sp
on the worn grass matting, pattering on the landings, around
and around, up the squared spiral, first floor, second, doors
all shut, whoever slept behind them ignorant of or ignoring
the meie interdicta flitting up through flickering shadow, third
floor—fourth. . . .

She stopped running, stood panting, bent over hands
clasped tight about the worn sphere of the banister finial,
gulping in the hot still air redolent of lamp oil and hot metal,

blinking at shadows wavering like grandfather ghosts along the narrow hall ahead of her.

A door opened near the hall's end and a man stepped out—a tall, thin man with black hair braided into a fantasy of coils. *He dressed to meet me,* she thought. *He knew I was coming.* The lamp by his door touched russet gleams in his molasses-on-coal skin, pricked azure flecks from his indigo eyes. As Serroi straightened, heart thudding with the violent fear of norim she'd never been able to eradicate, he brought up his hand, long thin fingers like reptile paws spread out behind a pinwheel of white fire. He flung it at her, plucked another out of nowhere, flung it, plucked and flung a third.

Fast as thought they swept toward her. Faster than thought. She had no time to duck or defend herself, no defense if there was time.

The heat touched her face, the glare blinded her.

The tajicho hummed and burned in her boot.

The firestars, one, two, three, swung around and sped back at the Norit. He worked his long fingers frantically to cancel the calling before he burned in his own fire.

Without waiting to see what happened, Serroi flung herself around the newel post and lunged for the door. At first her fingers fumbled uselessly with the latchstring, then she managed to fight down the terror enough to see what she was doing. Behind her she heard a howl of pain and rage. She jerked the door open, heard other doors down the hall open, heard sleepy voices—sounds cut off when she slammed the door behind her. She slapped the bar home and jerked in the latchstring. With the bar like a comforting arm pressing against her shoulders, she leaned on the door, scraping the sweat off her face, struggling to control the panic that the Norit stirred in her.

"Open." The demand was a roar muffled by the wood behind her head. She felt a thump against her back as a fist pounded on door. Coldly furious, the Norit screamed again, "Open this door, meie, open and live. Defy me and die." She sniffed with disgust and stepped away from the door. *Absurd, absurd,* she thought. *No one talks like that, defy me and die. Words of a wooden tyrant in a puppet play. He couldn't mean them, absurd even to say them.* She pressed the heels of her hands against her eyes and struggled to put behind her the paralyzing fear her Noris had etched in her bones those days of pain, endless unrelieved pain, when he couldn't believe she wasn't defying and resisting him. She was tempted to yell back at the Norit, taunt him with his stupidity, but in the end reason prevailed; anything she said he could seize on and use against her. She listened to mutters that might have been curses and smiled.

She ignored the demanding voice and growing noise outside, ignored the cessation of sound that followed a snapped order from the Norit, ignored the droning chant that broke the silence. She dug through the boy's chest, determined to give Braddon good measure for his generosity. Item by item, she pulled out what she thought she could use and rolled these things into a compact bundle, strapping it together with a wide black belt. The chant grew louder, more insistent. When she stood again, she saw the bar shuddering in its iron loops. As if impatient but inept hands tugged at it, the heavy hardwood bar moved a little, rattled in place, moved again.

The single window in the room was a small square by the head of the bed. She thrust the shutters open and tossed the bundle out, hoping Hern had sense enough to collect it and tie it to her saddle, hoping too that he hadn't rebelled against being ordered about by a child-sized female and left her to get herself out of this mess. She glanced at the bar, frowned. It was moving more smoothly now. Grim-faced, she ran across the room, flattened her palms against the bar. "Tajicho," she whispered, "if you ever twisted magic awry . . ." laughed when the chant broke off with a roar of pain. She shoved the bar home again and ran for the window.

She found the bundle in a forked branch of a desiccated bush, one of those she'd helped to plant in that season she spent as stableboy for Braddon, the last step on her trek to the Biserica. She found time to be sad as she tucked the bundle under her arm and reeled in her rope, laying it in coils as she pulled it down, found time to scold herself for slashing at Hern, to berate Hern for his blind refusal to listen to her. The rope whipped to her hands with a soft whisper of leather and a harsh rattle of the bushes, the rattle reminding her that this had once been a cheerful pleasure garden. She'd last seen it with the fountain playing in the middle, with small tables scattered about, a glass and copper lamp burning on each, brightly dyed paper lanterns strung overhead. The tables and the lanterns were gone, the flowers in the squat round tubs were gone, only weeds grew in the dry soil and even the weeds were dying. The stone flags were littered with bits of paper, dead leaves, passar droppings. As she clipped the rope back on her weaponbelt, she looked up. The small window above was still dark and empty. She smiled with satisfaction. "Bit on something that bit back," she murmured. "Serves you right."

No Hern yet. She shook her head and moved toward the front of the Inn, listening intently. The thick walls defeated her ears but through the outreach of her eyespot she sensed a growing turmoil inside.

Hern came around the corner, riding one macai and leading a second. Serroi felt rather ashamed of herself for suspecting him of desertion, especially when she saw that he'd taken the time to switch gear to fresh beasts. She shook her head, her rueful smile widening to a grin as she took note of the fineness of the beasts and realized that they probably belonged to the Norit. She swept him a deep bow, tucked the bundle more securely under her arm and swung up into the saddle. "There's a gate in the back wall."

He lifted a brow. "Looks quiet out front."

"Won't be." She rode past him and was pleased when he followed without a word. The gate was barred, the hinges rusty and stubborn, but Hern dealt easily enough with it. When he was mounted again and riding beside her, she said, "The Norit was waiting for me. He's blocked now, but he won't stay that way long." She turned her macai into the shadow of a small grove on the edge of the commonlands. "You hear? Waiting for me."

Hern snorted. "Fighting shadows, meie. No one followed us. No one saw us."

She shook her head. "No one had to. The Norit's been here a full passage. You heard what Braddon said." She held her mount to a rapid walk as she threaded through the trees, skirting the garden patches (mostly empty now of all but weeds, the produce pickled in crocks or stored deep in root cellars against the rigors of winter). "He knew I'd have to leave the Valley. He stirred up the Kry so there'd be only one way for me to go."

"He. Always He. Who is this 'he'?"

She glanced at his scowling face, looked away. "The last of the Great Nor, Dom," she said somberly. "The others are dead now, most from challenging him. The domnor of the Nearga-nor. The driving force behind all this—or so I think. No, I'm sure of that." She felt his silence, looked at him, shook her head. "You couldn't touch him, Hern. I don't know who could."

Where the commonland ended she saw the tatty hedge she'd expected, the boundary hedge of Hallam's Tar. Sweet Hal the feckless, everyman's friend.

"Puts us back on the road," Hern's voice was mild but she couldn't miss the understated sarcasm.

"No." Biting at her lip, she frowned along the hedge. "Which way . . . which way. . . . When Tayyan and I were coming north to take ward at the Plaz, we stopped off to see Braddon and Matti. The tarom of this holding is the laziest creature on the Plain. He let a small hole in his hedge wear big. A herd of hauhaus got out and started making a mess of the commons." She flipped a hand at the open lands behind them. "We rounded up the beasts and fixed the break with some poles and wire. Ah, I remember now. This way." She started east along the hedge.

Hern gave an impatient exclamation and started after her. When he caught up with her, he said, "After three years?"

She chuckled. "You don't know Sweet Hal. Long as the patch held he wouldn't see any reason to fuss about it." She pointed. "See?"

There was a narrow gap in the hedge, bridged by neatly woven poles and wire. "Tch! Look at that. Hallam's still Sweet Hal." The bushes about the gap were tattered and dying, the wire wound precariously about brittle dead limbs. "Looks like a breath would blow it over. Hallam's luck that it lasted through the Gather storms." She edged the macai closer, reached down and tugged the patch loose with a series of small poppings from the thorn hedge. "Sweet Hal, bless him, even the Followers can't change him."

Hern followed her through the gap, slid off his macai and wired the patch upright again, cursing under his breath as the dry thorns stung him. Sucking at his knuckle he came walking back toward her. Standing by her stirrup, his lips pursed prissily, he said, "One doesn't leave gates open in pastures. It isn't nice." When she laughed, he swung into the saddle. "Dammit, woman, we're supposed to be fleeing for our lives."

"No one's chasing us just yet." She began angling across the field through the silent black shapes of sleeping hauhaus, heading for the distant tarhouse, pleased with the power and grace of the mount she rode. "Trust a Norit to save the best for himself."

"Trust me."

She laughed. "All right, I will." Bending forward she scratched through the spongy growths along the macai's neck, drawing from him small snorts of pleasure after his first startled duck away from her fingers. "No, Norim don't know much about us beasts, do they, my beautiful friend. They don't know how we like to be stroked and praised when we do good." She straightened, glanced over her shoulder at the Inn. She could just make out a small bright square high up near the roof. "Well, well. On your feet again are you?" She pulled the macai to a stop and slid from the saddle, calling Hern to come back. "The Norit's with us again." She pointed.

Around them the dark bulky forms of the hauhaus were rocking onto their feet. A few browsed with the herbivore's constant hunger, restless under the rise of the great moon grown near full and pouring its light down on the Plain. Others dipped their heads but only nosed at the grass.

In the distant window a black form swayed from side to side as if the Norit sniffed the wind for their traces. It stiffened. "Ma-al-chi-i-in." The word was a wild howl rushing by overhead; again Serroi thought she saw the Norit move, stretch more of himself outside the window, his head swinging rhythmically. "Ma-a-al-chiin!" he shrieked. Serroi shuddered.

Hern stirred beside her, touched her arm. "Malchiin?"

"A chini called from Zhagdeep. A demon to track and kill." She kept her voice low and steady but she couldn't control the trembling of her body. Against her will the Noris had used her to make those malchiinin. Demons aping flesh, shaped by the chini essence of the pups she'd raised then betrayed, pups she'd seen driven to their death by her Noris. If anything part or wholly magic could break through the tajicho's distortion, a malchiin could. They knew her, blood and bone they knew her, her scent, her shape, her voice, her touch.

"Can it?"

"What?"

"Track us."

"I don't know. Probably. Take my hand." In the moonlight she saw his pale eyes glint with amusement and his mouth stretch into a mocking grin. "Don't say it, Dom." She thrust her hand at him. "I'm protected from the Norit's far-seeing but you're not. There's a chance he'll think I'm alone but why depend on that?"

"Touching. Your solicitude, I mean." His hand closed over hers, warm and rather comforting. "Difficult to ride like this."

"We won't be riding for a while." She stiffened as she heard the third call; for just a moment she felt a lifting of her spirits, a brief hope that the Noris wouldn't send the beast-demon. Then a streak of utter blackness swept across the sky, dropping chill ferocity like rain onto the earth below. She closed her fingers hard on Hern's hand, fighting down the urge to mount and kick her macai into frantic flight away, away anywhere even though she knew that flight was futile.

Hern raised his brows. "Malchiin?"

"Yes."

Shouts drifted broken on the wind, coming from the Inn, squeals from unhappy macain and other less identifiable noises. The night turned red over there with the glow of torchlight.

"Nice little mob." Hern tried to pull free but she kept her grip on his hand.

"The Norit won't wait for them."

The malchiin began belling, the huge sound bounding and rebounding from earth to sky. The sound swelled and cut off, the subsequent silence as stunning and ominous as the beast's first call had been. Hern jerked loose and drew his sword. "We can't outrun that."

"No." She looked at the sword, shook her head wearily. "You can't think that's any use?"

Around them the hauhaus stopped grazing. As one they faced the gap. As one they groaned in shuddering, terror-filled hoots. As one they turned and galloped frantically away.

The malchiin trampled down the patch and stalked through the gap, a great black form shoulder high to a macai. A silver chain looped about its neck and lifted in a graceful curve to the black-gloved hand of the Norit who followed the demon through the gap, riding a macai mare who stepped with near daintiness into the interstices of the pole and wire mesh. The demon bounded forward, tugging at the chain, its red eyes fixed on Serroi, burning with eagerness to get at her. Foil to that eagerness, unhurried, savoring what he seemed to see as repayment for past humiliations, the Norit rode slowly toward them, stopped his mount a short distance from them, jerking the malchiin back onto its haunches, holding it there with a growled command. The malchiin sat with predator's patience beside the macai, black ears pricking, red tongue lolling from its chini mouth, its chini tearing teeth gleaming in the moonlight like bits of polished jet.

The Norit smiled. "Meie," he said.

"Cetaj-nor."

"He waits."

"Let him wait."

The Norit reached into his sleeve, took from it a chased silver collar with a delicate chain attached, its loops filling his palm and dripping in graceful cascades from each side, the silver very bright against his coal black skin. "Take it, meie."

"No." She looked past him, frowned as she listened to the noise of the mob. It was moving out from the court, coming toward them, getting louder, the torchlight brighter. She shifted her gaze back to his calm face. "You want me," she snapped, hoping to goad him within reach, "you come fetch me."

The Norit eyed her somberly, shook his head. With a quick jerk of the chain and a harsh word, he brought the great demon beast back onto four feet. "He has no use for the fat man. Come, or I loose the malchiin on him."

Hern swore, took a step toward the demon, his sword lifting, balanced lightly in his hand. "Loose that thing and lose it," he said briskly. The past hour had provided a nasty series of shocks to his amour-propre. Accustomed to deference however hypocritical, accustomed to having his own way with little struggle, he'd found himself reduced to a despised appendage, forced to follow passively where another led. To him, despite Serroi's babbling of demons from Zhagdeep, the beast was only an overgrown chini. He knew his own skills and was confident in them.

"Hern!"

"Stay clear, meie."

"Don't be a fool. Steel won't touch him."

"We'll see." He eyed the panting malchiin with anticipation. "Try me, Nor."

The Norit ignored him. "Come here, little misborn." The Norit's voice was a whisper of silver sound in silver moonlight, spider silk whipping about its chosen victim.

"Never." She leaped in front of Hern as the Norit dropped the chain and hissed the beast at him. Two swift strides and it was leaping at her. Hern's hand closed on her arm, he meant to sweep her aside, there was no time for that, no time, she reached out small hands dusky grey in moonlight that leached the color from everything but the glare of the malchiin's eyes, she leaned into the leap of the malchiin, feeling heat surge up through her body and into her hand, a heat so intense she couldn't bear the pain of it but she did bear the pain and, bearing it, she thrust out her hands and touched the malchiin, touched the stone-hard flesh, the horrible cold flesh, she felt a numbing blow against her hands, a blow that sent her stumbling back against Hern, the heat gone from her, gone suddenly, wholly out of her. The malchiin hung in place an instant longer, a hollow chini shape, mouth gaping on nothing.

Then the shape was gone, the eerie silence was gone, what was left of the malchiin fell to earth in a dusting of black ash.

Serroi thought she heard a whimper as the chini shape collapsed, as if the fragment of chini soul trapped inside at last won free of its torment and returned to the Maiden.

She felt herself shoved aside, fell as legs too weak to hold her collapsed under her, lay shaking on the grass as Hern lunged at a Norit numbed by shock, as startled as she by his attack. Before he could calm himself enough to call on his magic, Hern sprang from the ground, caught his arm, fell back, toppling him from the saddle. Hern came down light and sure on his feet but the Norit crashed on one leg which folded under him, bone cracking under the sudden weight put on it, the sudden pain disorienting him yet more. He shrieked and fell silent, eyes rolling back in his head, mouth falling open. Hern sliced his head neatly from his shoulders.

Panting a little, he strolled back to Serroi, caught her hand and pulled her to her feet, grinning broadly. "Maybe not the malchiin, but steel worked well enough on that."

Leaning against him, feeling her strength slowly creeping back into her, she matched his grin. "One of these days we just might make a good team."

CHAPTER V:

THE MIJLOC

For three days the Agli's fist tightened about Cymbank until it was squeezed out of all semblance to its former shape. Peten Jerricks, the Townmaster, sat in one of his own cells, a look of astonishment permanently in his round eyes. The Scribe—tax gatherer, magistrate, Oras legate to the Taromate of RiverCym—hastily examined his soul then put on Follower black and the silvergilt badge of Soäreh.

The women in black chanted at Tuli as she stood with her wrists bound with soft leather straps to iron rings high off the floor:

> There is a pattern for all things
> Blessed be Soäreh the Light-giver
> Every creature has a place, blessed be the place
> Blessed be Soäreh the Pattern-giver

The broad soft strips of the five-tailed lash came down on her naked back. It stung a little but she lifted her head and laughed at them.

The guards quartered in the Center rode out in patrols, fetching the accused back to the Center, shoving them in cells with no pretense of trial. All that was required was an accusation from a Follower in good standing—an accusation of lewdness, blasphemy, secret Maiden worship, disloyalty to Floarin, cursing, a thousand other minor infractions of Soäreh's law. The guards had open warrants from Oras to preserve the outward look of legality, but there was no more law on Cimpia Plain, only the will of Floarin, and that, whether she knew it or not, was the will of the Aglim, the will of the Nearga-nor, the will—ultimately—of the Great Nor, Ser Noris, the unbeliever in anything but his manifest power.

The women chanted:
To man is given stewardship of field and beast
The beasts whose meat is red, the wildfowl and the wild
  beast
Is given to him
Blessed be Soäreh who makes man herder and hunter
  and tie

The lash fell again. Tuli locked her teeth together. Her
back was a ladder of pain. She no longer felt like laughing.

The maiden Shrine was closed, the fountain dry, the vines
uprooted. The columns with their carven maiden faces were
still standing but smeared with thick black paint. Follower
hands had used the same black paint to scrawl Soäreh's sigils
across the delicate patterns of the tiled court. The Shrine
Keeper had vanished into the Center—renamed the House of
Repentance—and no one had heard her or seen her since.

The women chanted:
To woman is apointed house and household
Woman is given to man for his comfort and his use
She bears his children and ministers unto him
She is cherished and protected by his strength
She is guided by his wisdom
Blessed be Soäreh who makes woman teacher and tender
  and tie.

For a third time the lash fell. Her back was on fire. She
gasped this time when the thongs came onto her flesh, then
bit down hard on her lip, ashamed she'd let them draw even
that small sound from her.

Center. Under its new name it was still the center of the
town. It was the place where the "mistaken" were gently
corrected and taught to see things right (right being whatever
the Agli said). The taroms, the ties, the craftsmen and
shopkeepers—they seethed and dithered and struck out clum-
sily and ineffectively. After so long a peace and so mild a
rule, they were accustomed to obeying directions from Oras
(not blindly, and not completely—they were independent
hardheads all. They obeyed as far as they felt like. In the old
days that was enough. Hern was too indolent to drive them
hard and his fathers had been the same. Still—the habit was

there. It was hard for them to think of rebelling; they turned
at last to the old ways of dealing with intransigent Scribes:
they dug in to wait it out, confident Floarin's aberration
would go away eventually and things would return to the way
they were when everyone was comfortable).

    The women chanted:
    Cursed be he who forsakes the pattern
    Cursed be the man who puts on woman's ways
    Cursed be the woman who usurps the role of man
    Withered will they be
    Root and branch they are cursed
    Put the knife to the rotten roots
    Tear the rotten places from the body
    Tear the rotten places from the land
    Blessed be Soäreh the Pattern-giver

The chant continued, led, after the first hour, by the sil-
ver-voiced acolyte. The long slow flogging continued with it.
The words drove Tuli wild until the pain swamped her and
she no longer heard anything over the pounding in her head.
The tenth blow was the last, landing a good two hours after
the first. Her mouth was bloody when it fell, her teeth cutting
into her lip as she held back the foulest curses she knew, as
she held back the cries of pain.

In three days the Maiden was thrown down and Soäreh
elevated in her place. The Taromate was disbanded. The customs and institutions of centuries were overturned and replaced. Those three days Annic Gradin and her younger
daughters spent in a small dirty cell with a rickety cot and
thin straw pallets and a stinking slop bucket in one corner, in
hard and meaningless labor, in a constant din of instruction
until they were angry, disturbed, and most of all afraid. Teras
Gradinson spent the days in the same way, packed in with a
dozen boys his age. Nilis Gradindaughter kept Dris (the
baby) at the Tar, since he was presumably young and uncor-
rupt enough to be reeducated to the service of Soäreh.

After the tenth stroke they cut her down. She tried to stand
but anger and pride were no substitute for strength. Her
knees folded under her and she found herself crouching at
the acolyte's feet. One of the chanters brought her the dingy
black blouse she was forced to wear in this place. She

fumbled her arms into the sleeves and managed somehow to
button up the front. Her warders waited with enraging patience for her to finish, then the two women took her arms
and lifted her to her feet. She refused to cry out though the
pain in her shoulders was greater than that in her back. Because they were under Alma Yastria's angry gaze she expected them to handle her roughly, but they were gentle and
considerate, walking slowly and carefully so she could
stumble along and not be dragged, speaking to her in soft
tender voices, telling her . . . telling her . . . she missed the
first sentences, protected from what would be an intolerable
irritation by the pain that ran like fire through her body, by
her need to concentrate on moving legs and feet that seemed
to belong to someone else, but as her strength came back, she
heard them murmuring lessons of obedience and submission,
telling her over and over of the true womanliness of yielding,
going on and on, meek and mild, until she wanted to scream.
And yet—that would be a victory for them, an acknowledg-
ment that she heard them, so she fought with her fury; she
said nothing, tried to pretend she didn't notice them, but she
couldn't prevent the stiffening of her body, the silent but
fierce denial of everything they wanted from her. She knew
they had to feel this, but they changed nothing, not the firm
but gentle hold on her arms, not their soft-voiced exhorta-
tions.

The way back to her cell seemed endless, but all things end
at last. One of her warders unbarred the door and pulled it
open, the second guided her inside, silent at last. Tuli
gathered herself, stood very erect, swaying a little as the
woman took her hands away and left her. She didn't move
when she heard the door close behind her with a tidy click.
Her eyes flew to her mother's. Annic sat unmoving on the
cot, smiling a little. Sanani stood beside her, hands opening
and closing, full lips pressed together, dark eyes shining. The
three of them waited together.

Several minutes passed. Tuli's hands closed into fists when
she heard the scrape of a sandal outside the door. After another minute she heard soft footsteps as the two women
walked away.

Tuli staggered toward her mother, fell on her knees,
pressing her face against her mother's thighs, muffling the
scream of rage that tore from her. Annic smoothed her short
brown hair as she shuddered and raved and sobbed. Sanani
eased off the blouse. With a small clicking of her tongue she

used a bit of rag and water from the drinking bucket to bathe the weals crisscrossing Tuli's slim back, trying to draw away the heat in them and with it some of the pain before Tuli dissipated her fury enough to notice the pain once more.

After a few minutes Tuli's shuddering eased and her sobs quieted. When she lifted her head, Annic took the rag from Sanani and wiped away the tear stains. Pride gleamed in her eyes as she smiled down at Tuli. "You were splendid, little firehead," she murmured. "Oh I did laugh at that dirty water streaming down Yastria's ugly face and oh my child, you must learn to stay your hands because they won't stay theirs."

Tuli shook her head. "I can't, Mama."

Sanani began bathing Tuli's back once more. "House of Repentance! Lock-up for rowdy drunks, that's where we are." Tuli winced as the rag moved across the weals with a bit too much force. "Sorry. It's just . . . just everything. The Scribe's the Agli's thing, you saw what they did to the Maiden Shrine. They showed us, Maiden curse them, like they were proud of what they did." She dipped the rag in the bucket and wrung it dry, the water making its own music, the only music in the small grim room. "Everything gone, taken apart, thrown away like five hundred years was worth nothing. The world has turned a page and everything is changed but us, we're left over from the old page." Her usually gentle voice held a colder anger than anything Tuli knew. She glanced over her shoulder, surprised. "Repentance." Sanoni looked down at the rag in her hand, threw it across the cell. "For what!"

"For being alive." Tuli's voice was husky. "For being everything they're afraid of, those small-life bloodsuckers who call themselves Followers." She sighed, surprised at her own words. She seemed to see things (though she couldn't have put in words what she meant by things) with an extraordinary clarity. She felt drained of strength and oddly peaceful. Yawning, she sat back on her heels, her eyelids heavy.

"Well." Annic chuckled. "This is a change." She rumpled Tuli's hair. "Mayhap your father and me, we should have beat you before."

Tuli giggled, then the giggling turned shrill, then she was sobbing again, rocking back and forth on her buttocks drowning in an anguish that seemed to have no source and no bottom to it.

Annic slapped her sharply, shocking her still, then rested

her hand lightly on Tuli's head. "Hysteria I won't have. Control yourself, Tuli."

Tuli swallowed hard. She felt like a bird on a storm-tossed branch, thrown helplessly about by the up and down of the forces struggling in her. She screwed her eyes shut, tightened her hands into white-knuckled fists. Her heart thundered in her ears, her throat swelled, shutting off her breath (or so it seemed to her) but when she opened her eyes again, the stone was solid and cold beneath her, the world stood steady around her and for the moment at least she felt steady enough inside.

Annic stroked a finger down her cheek. "That's my brave girl."

Tuli yawned, smiled tiredly at her mother and got to her feet, thinking a little wistfully of her own comfortable bed, so unreachable right now. She glanced at the window. *It's dark out*, she thought and was startled to see it so. *Lots later than I knew.* When she'd doused Alma Yastria it couldn't have been later than midmorning. Taunting she'd taken with silence; cuffs and pinches she endured; the interminable preaching that filled all the interstices of her day she tried to ignore, though that was the worst thing until Yastria started in on her mother. Without a word she'd scrubbed and rescrubbed the same length of corridor, knowing she'd done a good enough job, if not the first time then the second, knowing they were simply trying to break her spirit.

Three full days of this she endured without a word, only a few defiant glowers she couldn't help. But when Alma Yastria, the hard-faced head warder in this antechamber to the deeps of Zhag, Aglu Urith's chief bootlicker, when this woman turned her nasty tongue on Annic, when she grabbed her arm and jerked her around and began pointing out to her what a miserable wife and mother she was, how she'd failed in every sense to be a proper woman, when she started calling Annic whore and mother of whores, Tuli couldn't contain the fury rising in her. On sore knees, holding the pumice block in hands rubbed raw, she stared at the square, lined face, watched the writhing of the thin lips. Quietly she got to her feet. Quietly she bent and wrapped sore fingers about the wooden bucket's bail. She took the two steps needed, swung the bucket with all her strength, flinging the filthy, soapy water full in Alma Yastria's face. And felt a vast satisfaction as she saw her suddenly wordless, saw the brown-grey runnels of water coursing down her face.

They put her in the Silence—a smal black box of a room, four feet on a side, windowless and utterly empty. They left her there in the velvet blackness until they came to fetch her for her flogging, thinking, she knew, that they were punishing her. She settled herself comfortably, legs crossed, back against one wall, and relaxed into the silence, understanding in those first few moments the real horror of never being let alone, never being able to get off by herself. She closed her eyes, smiling because she wasn't closing them on anything, and thought about the nights she'd run under the scatter of Moons, Teras by her side, rejoicing in the cool silver calm, stalking lappets or scutters with sling and stone, laying their catch on the kitchen stoop and giggling together at the pretended wonder of Auntee Cook. As the minutes or hours (she couldn't tell and didn't much care) slid past, she drifted into sleep, a better sleep than she'd had stretched out on that straw pallet with the chill of the stone striking up through it and into her bones.

Restless, unable to relax, hands twisting behind her, Tuli prowled about the cell. Her bare feet squeaked on the grit scattered over the stone floor. She wrinkled her nose at the slop bucket. *The evil old hags, they didn't let Mama or Sanani empty it.* Her stomach growled and she realized that half the shake in her legs was due to hunger. Nothing to eat since a bowl of watery porridge for breakfast. Gingerly she eased her back flat against the wall letting the cold stone soothe the welts. "Did they let you eat, Mama?"

Annic looked up. "Eat? Yes."

"Bread and water," Sanani said. "You?"

"No." Tuli snorted. "Starve me meek, starve me mild, if beating won't do it, hunger will. Hah, lots of luck." The window beside her was shoulder high. She swung around and closed her hands about the bars. Standing on her toes she could see a bit of barren yard, but also a swatch of sky and the face of Nijilic TheDom with the smaller Dancers close beside him. The breeze, warmer than it should be, drifted in, carrying with it the dark pungent smells of night. At that moment she wanted to be out there so badly she nearly started clawing at the stone. She closed her eyes, tightened her grip on the bars, swallowed hard. When the need subsided a little, she pushed away from the window and started prowling about again. "I don't think I can stand this much longer, Mama."

Neither Annic nor Sanani answered. The only sound in the cell remained the pat-squeak of Tuli's feet as she turned and turned in growing desperation. "If Alma Yastria says a word—" she slapped at her side—"one word, one chinjy little word, I'll bite her nose off."

Annic sighed. "Sit before you wear us all out."

"I. . . ." She wheeled, excitement blazing up in her as as a warbling whistle sounded close outside the window, the cry of a kanka passar as it drifted on its gas sacs, wing membranes extended in a hunting glide. She ran to the window, gripped the bars again and waited. The whistle came twice more.

Annic rose, reached her hand to Sanani. "What is it, Tuli?"

Without answering, Tuli moistened her lips, curled her tongue and produced the warbling exhalation.

"Tuli?" The word was a ghost of a sound carried in on the breeze.

"Here." She stretched higher on her toes, thrust her arm through the bars as far as she could and wiggled her fingers. "Teras?"

"Got you. Hold tight, I'll be there quick-quick."

"Be careful." She pressed the side of her head against the bars and closed her eyes, straining to read the air, but she heard nothing except common night sounds.

"Tuli?"

She sank back onto her heels, turned slowly to face her mother and sister. After one look at Annic's worried face, she rubbed hard at her eyes, then grinned at her mother, grinned like a fool and she knew it and wasn't able to help it; she wanted to clap her hands and dance around and around the cell, wanted to let out her tension in shrieks louder than any fayar's hunting call. With some difficulty she pressed down her jubilation and said, fairly calmly, "That was Teras. He's going to get us out of here."

Annic stepped closer to Sanani, laid her arm on her daughter's shoulders, frowning a little, a thoughtful glint in her eyes. But she said nothing.

Sanani leaned against her mother, reached up and pressed her hand over Annic's. "Coming for us, Tuli?" When Tuli nodded, she sighed. "To take us where?"

"Away from here, does it matter?" Tuli lifted a hand, swept it around in an impatient gesture as if she brushed at spider webs in front of her. "Anywhere would be better than this."

"For you." Sanani spoke slowly, choosing her words with

care, her eyes on Tuli's face, measuring and considering what she saw there. "It's different for Mama and me, Tuli." She patted her mother's hand. "I'm not like you, younger sister. I'm good at managing a house and I'm good with people, I can guide them and keep them happy with me." She smiled, a warm glowing look that crept inside Tuli and teased away some of the tension growing in her, that invited her to share Sanani's amusement. "Things you can't say, sister." Sanani lifted one small hand into the shaft of moonlight coming through the window. "Look at my hand, Tuli. What have I done with it? I never had the wish to run wild over the night fields like you and Teras. Of course we knew, we always knew, but what hurt was there in it? I can't ride, Tuli. Macain frighten me. I can walk well enough, but that won't do, not with guards chasing after us. I don't know about Mama. . . ." She hesitated.

"My last ride was a long, long time ago," Annic murmured. "I don't think I can remember how."

Sanani nodded. "You see?" She sighed. "Think, sister, what can they do to me here? Sometimes I get impatient, but I don't really mind the scut work they make us do. I do . . . do mind about Joras, not seeing him, not wedding him next passage like we planned. I mind about Cymbank and the ties being thrown off the land. I worry about Father and about my oadats, especially the ones just hatched. I hate what's happened to the Maiden Shrine. But, Tuli. . . ." She sighed. "I'm not like you. I don't get angry at the same things or in the same way. When Yastria and the other warders preach at me or scold me or dig at me, I just don't let myself hear them. I think about Joras or my hatchlings. I remember them pattering about like balls of grey down, scratching awkwardly in the dust with all four legs or tumbling over when they get their legs crossed, their little beady eyes bulging, their limp beaks opening and closing as if they were saying the worst words they knew with no sound at all coming out. I almost laughed in Yastria's face this morning. She looks twice as foolish as any oadat chicklet if you watch her lips wiggle and ignore the words. I don't care what they make me do, Tuli, they'll never touch anything that's really me."

Annic chuckled. "So that's what happened with my scolds."

Sanani leaned her head against her mother's shoulder. "It was such good training."

Tuli stared, winced at a sudden stab of jealousy. Then she

remembered Nilis's words and opened her eyes wide, seeing with a sickening shift of viewpoint a little of what Nilis had known all her life. With a shudder of revulsion she rejected the insight. *No, never, no excuse for that betrayal.* She pressed her hands flat against the stone, the cold hardness against her palms a reassuring solidity in a world turned strange. "Then you won't come?"

"No. Mama?"

Annic shook her head. "Better not. For now, at least. Tuli, I want you and Teras to go after your father. Tell him what has happened to us all. That's more important right now than getting us away."

Tuli, happier now that she had something definite ahead of her, ran to the door, laid her ear against the planks. When she heard a soft rubbing outside, she took three quick steps backward, her breath coming rapidly.

The door swung open. Teral stepped inside. "Come on," he whispered. "Hars bust the lock on a back door when he come for me." There was urgency and excitement in his whisper. "The others shoved in with me, they already left. Any time now some snoop will see the cell's empty and yell for the Agli." His eyes flickered rapidly from one face to the other.

"They're not coming, Teras." Tuli took a step toward him, then threw herself at Annic. Her mother's arms closed tight around her, her mother's lips touched her forehead, then Annic turned her about and urged her toward the door. "Maiden bless you both," she murmured.

Tuli put her hand on her brother's shoulder, twisted her head around. "We'll find him, Mama."

"I know. Hurry now." She nodded at Sanani. "We'll be waiting. Be careful."

"We will."

Teras swung the heavy door shut, shutting away the image of Annic and Sanani standing with their shoulders touching, their hands clasped. Tuli helped him shove the heavy bar quietly back through the loops then she ran down the corridor beside him, her weariness and pain lost in rising excitement.

Teras pushed at the small door. It wouldn't stay closed. "Hars did too good a job on this."

"Hold on a minute. I got an idea." Tuli darted away toward the river.

While he waited he ran his fingers over the broken lock and the bruised and splintered wood above the lock where

Hars had jammed in the prybar, glanced up along the solid back of Center wondering if there was anyone behind the shuttered windows. Then Tuli was back, a stalk of bastocane in her hand. He frowned at the cane then rubbed his thumb across the crack between door and jamb. "That's not thick enough."

"Fold it till it fits," she said with sharp impatience and gave him the cane.

While Tuli held the door shut by leaning the end of her shoulder against it, he folded and refolded the cane. It wasn't wholly dried out so it was flexible enough to bend without shattering, though the hollow stem broke open in the folding, exposing knife edges he carefully avoided. When he was satisfied with the bulk of it he shoved the roughly wedge-shaped mass between door and jamb, wiggled it about until he forced it in as far as it would go. Cautiously he took his hands away. When it stayed in place he started walking to the river, Tuli beside him.

"Where's Hars?" She followed him onto the river path. "You said he was waiting."

"Other side the river. By the bridge." Teras extended his stride until he was loping along the path through flickering leaf shadow and the undisturbed music of night life, sounds unchanged when everything else in his life had changed. He was suddenly and unexpectedly and deeply contented, as if he'd snatched back a moment from the blighting touch of the Followers.

Tuli sucked in a breath of the warm damp air, the horrid cramped feeling of the past three days melting out of her. She felt like laughing and she trembled with exhaustion. Despite the urgency in her head, her body had about reached its limit. She slowed to a walk so suddenly Teras ran on several strides before he noticed. He turned and came back to her.

"We've got to get on, Tuli," he said. He passed a hand across his eyes, leaned closer so he could see her more clearly. "You look awful. What's wrong?"

She grimaced. "No food all day and a ten-stroke flogging."

Teras jerked back. He stared at Center's watchtower looming over the tree tops, his face hard, a glassy look to his eyes that scared Tuli a little.

"No big thing," she said quickly. "It's just I'm tired and hungry." She giggled. "Teras, you should've seen. I pitched mop water all over Alma Yastria. What they did was a nothing against the look on her face."

Teras relaxed. A short while later, he grinned. "Might've known."

Tuli started walking, pulling away irritably when Teras tried to take her arm. "I'm sick of people hanging onto me," she said. "Even you, twin." She walked in silence beside a silent Teras until she saw the old granary lit by red torchlight. "Another tilun?"

"Yah. That's why Hars went cross the river. Too many folks about, he said. Made him itchy." Teras shook his head. "It was a lot different last time we came along here. Three days—no, four now. Can you believe how much has happened?"

Tuli moved her shoulders, grimaced. "I got reason to believe."

Hars sat with his back against the thick, gullied bark of an ancient brellim watching the water swirl past his feet. Six macai stood ground-hitched in the shadow of the brellim grove, edgy and unhappy but not fighting the training that held them where he left them. Five were saddled and the sixth carried a high rounded pack whose contents were discreetly tucked beneath a folded tarp. Lost in thick shadow and behind a lacy fall of leaves, he could see unseen whoever passed across the bridge. He called the twins to him with the kanka whistle and didn't seem much surprised that only Tuli came with Teras.

Tuli hung back as Teras brushed past the macain and hurried to Hars. "Mama and Sani aren't coming."

"Smarter'n most, your ma." He got quickly and neatly to his feet, surprising Tuli who'd thought him a creaky old man. His hair was white, had been white as long as she could remember. He was bent and gnarled, tough as a centuries-old olive tree, sometimes looked to be older than the earth. In the moonlight this night he seemed different. More alive, maybe? Younger? Tuli didn't know what exactly, but it rather pleased her. She had a sense that like her he belonged to the night. He smiled at her suddenly, a wide, knowing smile that told her he knew what she was thinking and feeling. Another time, another place, another person, her anger would have flared at this, now (and she didn't know why) it was a blessing, a Maiden smile riding oddly on his worn face. The look was gone in a blink and he was tugging at his ear, his narrowed eyes on the spare macai. "Best come for your Mum and sis later when there's a place ready for them." He clipped lead ropes to the halters of the two extra mounts and tied their reins up so they wouldn't trip on them. "Ras-lad, tell your Da to think on the vale where we sat out a rain once."

"Huh?"

"Your Da 'ull know."

"You're not coming with us?"

"Would've if the Tarma'd come." He tied the lead ropes to a ring on his saddle. "Different now." His short, strong fingers made quick work of the buckles on his left-side saddle-bag. He flipped the top back and pulled out a knobby black bundle. "Your sis, she cleared out the house for the tilun. This for you, night runner." He smiled at Tuli again, that quick, flashing smile that erased half a century from his face. "No way you can ride in that mess." A thumb jerked at the skimpy long skirt blowing against her legs. "Be sores on your butt before you make a mile."

Tuli caught the bundle, laughed with delight as she recognized the pair of trousers wrapped round the outside. "Thanks."

"Be careful how you unroll that. Your sling's in there and a hunting knife besides. Now, get yourself round behind that bush 'nd change while I finish with this 'un here." He nodded at Teras.

Tuli clutched the bundle against her breasts and went hastily behind the indicated bush. Though she couldn't see them any longer, she listened intently to what Hars was telling her brother while she began unbuttoning her blouse.

"Here's for you, Ras. Sling and knife. Your own. Got it from your room. Your things're still there, though, since you run off, I expect they'll outlaw you like they did your Da and call young Dris Gradin-heir. Calm down, lad. Most things get worse before they get better. You rather be back in that cell? Thought not. Listen. Your Da, he's a careful man. He shook me awake the night he left and give me this."

"Gold."

"Yah. Here." Tuli heard a series of dull clinks. She stepped out of the skirt and started pulling on the trousers.

"I'll be keeping half, being a careful man myself. You share that out with your sister and keep it hid. Lot of folk been shoved off the land and looking starvation in the ribs. Good enough people, but not so strong against temptation as

they might be. Here, you keep this where you can get at it."
More clinking noises. She fumbled at the laces on the
trousers then called herself to order, pulled the cords tight
and knotted them. "You need something, you pay with that
silver there. But don't go flashing that about neither, you
hear?" Tuli clamped her teeth together against the pain of
lifting her arms over her head and pulling the tunic down
over her aching back. The cloth was soft and supple and she
blessed Hars fervently as she realized he'd found her a larger
tunic somewhere. The shoulders were too wide and the
sleeves hung six inches over her fingertips but the fullness in
the front hid the shallow swell of her breasts and the fullness
in the back fell comfortably across her welts. She rolled up
the sleeves until her hands showed, buckled the sheath belt
about her waist. It slid low on her hips though she'd used the
last hole. She fingered the leather thoughtfully, glanced up at
the moons. TheDom's broad white face floated overhead, the
three smaller Dancers close to passing him. *Late,* she thought.
She gathered up the discarded skirt and blouse and came
rather hesitantly around the bush.

Hars was in the saddle. He looked her over, nodded. "You
make a good enough boy. In the dark anyway. There's a couple jackets tied on the saddles. Better wear one come day.
Don't care how hot it get, you got a kinda slimpsy look might
make some types start crowding you. Bread and cheese and
some dried fruit in the saddlebags. Keep to yourselves. Don't
chat with everyone comes along." He chuckled at Tuli's indignant glare. "Tain't a game, moth."

"I know that."

He looked suddenly bleak. "You think so but you won't
know that till you have to kill a man." He straightened,
raised a hand. "Be seeing you, twins. One of these days."

Tuli dropped everything and ran to him, feeling suddenly
bereft. She put her hand on his knee. "Maiden bless you,
Hars friend."

He touched her head, smiled down at her. With no more
words, not even a wave, he rode into the shadows under the
trees, the three reined macain following in unprotesting
silence.

"What are you going to do with these?" Teras held up the
skirt and blouse.

Tuli turned slowly, frowned at them, then grinned. "Dump
them in the river. Let the Yastria make what she wants of
that."

Teras walked to the edge of the water, wadded the clothing into a tight ball and tossed it out as far as he could. The ball unfolded as it flew, fluttering like dark wings over the river. It landed with a very small splat and went sweeping off, riding the water like discarded leaves from a shedding tree. He stood gazing at the black bulk of the watchtower for some minutes then came back to her. "No alarm yet."

"Still, we better get going."

"Yah. You need help?"

Tuli nodded. "A boost. My arms don't work so good right now."

By dawn Tuli was clinging to the saddle ledge, staying in the saddle by will alone. She followed Teras along the Highroad, drifting in a painworld, the skin inside her thighs rubbed raw in spite of the protection of the trousers. She'd never ridden so long before. In most of their night rambles, she and Teras had kept inside Gradintar hedges. She'd gone with the other Gradins to Oras when they made the pilgrimage to the Temple to celebrate the Moongather, but they'd all walked and taken the miles slow and easy.

A hand closed about her arm, supporting her. Gradually she understood that her mount was standing still. She forced her eyes open. Teras was leaning anxiously toward her. *He doesn't look tired at all,* she thought resentfully. "Tuli?" she watched his mouth open and close. The word seemed to come from a great distance through waves and waves of water. She blinked. "Tuli, you all right?"

She thought over the words, then nodded carefully. The world swayed around her. The hand closed around her arm was all that kept her from sinking in slow circles to the ground somewhere beneath her. "Tired," she croaked. " 'S all."

"We're gonna stop awhile. Hang on." Teras eased the reins from under her stiff fingers and led her down a slope. *Slope?* she thought. The Highroad was flat, no up no down. Flat. Flat. Flat. The shift of her weight broke open some of the scabs on her sores. The pain shocked her out of her haze of exhaustion. She shifted her hands on the ledge and straightened her back. A dark line of trees loomed ahead of her, blocking all but the tip of the dawning sun. *We rode all night,* she thought and felt a vague wonder.

When Teras slid off his mount she looked down at the dew-beaded grass and knew she couldn't dismount, not without

help. She eased her grip on the ledge and shifted about in the
saddle, every muscle protesting. The macai dropped his head
and began tearing avidly at clumps of grass by his feet. She
watched Teras. He was bending his knees, kicking his feet
out, stretching and twisting his upper body. *He's stronger
than me now*, she thought. *A lot*. She turned away, not
wanting to admit to herself that she could no longer keep up
with him, let alone dominate him as she had when they were
younger. He came briskly over to her. "Stiff?"

"Help me down." The edge of annoyance in her voice
brought a flush of shame to her face after the words were
said. She wanted to apologize to him, was angry at him, was
angry at herself for being such a weakly creature; she refused
to be weak and helpless and submissive, and it wasn't Teras's
fault she was so torn up—why was she blaming him. "Please,
Teras?"

If he took any notice of her snappishness, he laid it to her
weariness and ignored it. He took her hands and helped her
ease off the macai. When her feet touched the ground, her
knees buckled and she fell against him. He lowered her
gently to the grass.

She shivered as cold struck up through the cloth of her
trousers and pierced the sores on buttocks and thighs.
He knelt beside her and began massaging her calves, working
ankle and knee until the feeling came back into her legs. She
opened and closed her hands, rubbed at her arms once he
stopped working on her legs. He settled back on his heels.
"Better?"

"Some."

"Hungry?"

"Too tired. I couldn't swallow."

He nodded, got to his feet and went to his mount. A moment later he was back with a waterskin. "Here," he said.
He knelt again and handed the skin to her, then sat on his
heels, waiting with a finger-tapping patience for her to finish
with it. As she drank and drank, his eyes moved restlessly
about the clearing, squinting against the strengthening light
that gave a reddish glow to the shadows under the trees.

Tuli sighed, lowered the skin and shoved the carved
wooden plug home in the protruding mouthpiece. "Much better."

"Think you could get some sleep?"

"Here?"

"Why not? Folks on the Highroad can't see us. I'm going to look around a bit, then catch some sleep myself."

"Teras, what about Da? And the guards—won't they be looking for us?"

"Tutu, the macain have to rest and eat. We got no grain for keeping them going without grazing and if we ride them off their feet, Da 'ud skin us and Hars 'ud think I was dumber than Dris if I couldn't take care of my beasts. So you might as well sleep. The guards. . . ." He shrugged. "If they come, then they come."

She watched him walk off, disappearing behind a clump of brush, then tried to stand. She was shaky all over and cold to the bone. After falling back twice, she managed to get onto numb feet and hobbled painfully into the middle of the small clearing where the sun was touching the grass. She settled in a patch of warmth, curled up and closed her eyes. For a time her sores itched and burned, plaguing her too continually to let her relax. When the sun warmed some of the soreness away, she slept.

Teras shook her awake. She groaned as she tried to move. Her sores were like knives biting into her flesh. He helped her sit up, inadvertently putting pressure on the healing welts from her flogging. When she gasped with pain, he jerked his hands away, then had to catch her arm to keep her from falling over. "Maiden's toes, Tuli. I'm sorry." He held her up while she croaked a laugh, wiggled her feet up and down, straightened and clenched her toes. She tried to swallow and found that her throat was painfully dry. "Water?" she whispered.

While he brought her the waterskin she massaged the back of her neck and eyed the sun, trying to estimate how much time had passed while she was asleep. The sun was past zenith, the tree shadows moving toward her from the west now, not quite long enough to reach the center of the small clearing. *About mid-afternoon*, she thought. She drank. The water was warm and a little stale but it was nectar to her scratchy throat and swollen tongue. "Did you sleep any?"

"Some." As if her words reminded him, he yawned and his eyelids drooped. He jerked his head up, jumped to his feet, reached his hand down to help her up. "We better get going."

They rode at an easy lope along the thick, black, rubbery surface of the Highroad, the road straight as a knife slash and empty of all traffic to the southern horizon, equally empty ahead as far as Tuli could see. She felt horribly conspicuous on the high embankment that raised them near to treetop level, yet it was rather comforting to know there was no one about to challenge her disguise or ask difficult questions about two young people traveling without adults.

When the shadows of sundown were swallowing them and the western sky layered with red and gold, Teras gave a muttered exclamation and pulled his mount to a stop. Tuli looked at him, a question in her eyes. "I thought you wanted to keep going." She frowned. "What's wrong?"

"Boom," he murmured as he searched the sky and the road ahead.

"Gong?"

"Loud and loud. Look!" He pointed at the sky close to the northern horizon.

She followed his finger and saw two dark specks drifting in lazy circles above the treetops some distance ahead. "So?"

"So Hars. Those, they aren't passare, Tuli. Demons, that's what they are. Traxim. Look how big they are, all that way alay and we can still see 'em." His hands closed tight on the ledge in front of him, he leaned forward and peered intently at the black specks. "They look to be watching something."

"For us maybe?"

Teras dropped back in the saddle and kneed his mount to a fast walk. Tuli kept her macai to a trot until she was beside him again, though her tired beast complained with low hoots and a whine or two. "Hars?"

"When we got to talking, remember I told you, after Nilis met the Agli, anyway we got to talking about this 'nd that 'nd he told me about the tilun, you know, 'nd after that he sat fiddling with a bit of leather, you know how he does, 'nd after a while he started talking about when he was a kid 'bout big as me."

Tuli glared at him. "And you didn't tell me!"

"Maiden's toes, Tuli, what happened at the tilun scared all that right outta my head."

"So how come it's back now?"

"Them. Demons. Eyes and spies for the Nearga-Nor. Hars said he smelled Nearga-Nor mixing in where they shouldn't. Said he knew them better'n anyone should have to. Said when he was a kid in Sankoy, he got snatched away from his family by one of the High Nor because he had some kinda talent or other, didn't say much about that. Well, he didn't say nothing about that. Anyway, that Nor started teaching him things 'nd that wasn't so bad though he missed his family a lot and the Nor was meaner than a limping fayar. And he kinda like the idea of being a Nor and doing the things his master could, kinda liked the idea that he'd come back and do some awful things to the Nor to pay him back for the way he treated him. But there was this initiation thing he'd have to go through and he wasn't trusting the Nor much so he sorta snooped around. No one would talk to him but there was this other boy who was a couple years older who'd been initiated already and was getting along good with the Nor and he happened to see him naked one day and so he found out one thing they were going to do to him." He flushed a dark red and scratched uneasily at his upper lip, then along the line of his jaw, then tugged at the collar of his tunic.

"Teras!" Tuli felt like reaching out and shaking him but she didn't. "Don't be like Nilis," she said sharply.

"Well, you're a girl."

"Well, I'm going to snatch you bald in another half-second if you don't get on with it."

"If you must know, they were going to geld him. You know what that means?" He wouldn't look at her.

"I watched Da and Hars when they did that to the rogue macai last year. Mama explained." She stared at him. "You mean the Agli and all them are. . . ?"

"Uh-huh. Anyway, while he was with the Nor he found out all about the traxim. Told me what they look like. Big black devils with leathery wings. Wingspread wider than I am tall. Stink worse than downwind of an oadat coop. Sometimes the Nor put poison on their talons, when they're not just being spy-eyes."

"Teras, is Hars. . . ?"

"No!" Teras exploded. "Course not, Tuli. He ran off before they could. And if you ever tell him I told you. . . ."

"As if I would." She frowned at the specks which were beginning to merge with the increasing darkness of the sky. "You think they could be watching Da?"

"Uh-uh, not unless he started back to the Tar for some reason. He's been on the road near five days now, should be over halfway to Oras, even riding slow."

"They're watching something. And if we get too close, they'll see us sure and if the Agli's the one using their eyes, he'll know where we are and where to send his guards, and if they've got poison on their claws like you said maybe he'll make them attack us. He'd be rid of us with no one knowing." She touched dry lips with the tip of her tongue. "Can they see in the dark? If they can't we could sneak past once it's full dark."

"Don't know. Hars didn't say." Teras glanced at the sky where the last bit of sun had eased behind the Earth's Teeth and the colors were slowly fading. "Let's keep going a while and see if we can think up something real nasty for them."

"Maybe they'll go away or find a perch for the night."

"You really think they would?"

"No." She sighed. "Teras?"

"Huh?"

"Why don't we get a little closer and go off the Highroad? We can hobble the macain and sneak through the trees until we can see what they're watching."

He thought for a moment then nodded. "Better than that, we can take the macain with us and sneak them around whatever it is, then hobble them and come back for a look. That way we'll have a good start on the traxim when we go on in the morning." He thrust his hand into a jacket pocket. "We got our slings. Fill our pockets with good stones and I'd back us against a decset of those city-bred guards, 'specially you with your night sight."

Tuli giggled. "I'd like to get them into those trees in the dark, tripping over their own feet and skewering each other instead of us. We could run them crazy."

As soon as it was full dark, they led their grumbling mounts down the steep embankment and into the trees until they were moving along beside a rambling, badly maintained Tarhedge. Tuli rubbed her stomach, hunger overriding her excitement. A fistful of dried fruit, a torn bit of bread and cheese snatched on the run just wasn't enough. She heard her twin's stomach growl and giggled. Teras glared at her, then moved on as carefully and quietly as he could. She adjusted quickly to the confused blurring of shadow thrown by the Scatter; there were nine of the eleven moons in the sky with Nijilic TheDom now past full and beginning to lag behind the smaller but faster moons, the Dancers and the Drover, the Jewels of Anesh and the smallest of them all, the Dasher. For Teras, adjustment was more difficult; the shadows were a shifting confusion, tricking him into misjudging heights and stumbling over roots and other small obstructions that caught at his feet before he could make them out. He settled down after a few minutes and went more slowly, taking his time instead of plunging ahead, and his progress became almost as silent as Tuli's.

The leaves overhead murmured in the night wind. Somewhere not too close a stink-shell had been disturbed and wisps of its pungent defense came drifting to them. The macain grumbled and whoofed, wanting to stop and graze, which they considered their due after a hard day's work. Their claws dug into the thick layers of fallen leaves, sending fragments of leaf and gravel in an irregular rain behind them. Tuli chewed on her lip as she glided through the dark. The beasts were making too much noise to sneak them past anything more alert than a hibernating doubur. *Sneak*, she thought. *Hah. More like stomp up to their front door and bang on it and announce here we are.*

A different sound came floating to her through the night noises and the tromping of their disgruntled mounts—a few stray notes broken by shifting wind gusts. Tuli caught hold of her twin's arm. "Hear that?"

"Sounds like a flute."

"Yah. What I thought. Gong?"

"Uh-uh."

"Well, we better leave them here." Tuli nodded at the macain. "They just won't be quiet. There's a bit of grass." She pointed. "That should keep them happy."

They left the hobbled beasts cropping eagerly at the grass and slid into the shadow under the trees. Teras kept close behind Tuli, stepping where she stepped, the two of them gliding like moondrift toward the music. It was soon more than scattered notes, blending into a haunting melody that wove into and around songmoth twitters, the whistles of hunting kanka passare, the rising and falling whisper of wind through the trees.

Those trees thinned abruptly, opened out into a roughly circular clearing. Tuli dropped onto her knees behind the high roots of a spikul tree. As soon as Teras was settled beside her, they eased apart a few of the tall thin suckers growing in a thicket on the clearing-side roots and stared wide-eyed at the scene spread before them.

A number of blocky wagons like boxes on wheels were scattered about the clearing, small cook fires burning by all but one. Women bent over pots dangling above the fires (the rich meaty smell drifting to her on the wind made Tuli's mouth water and her stomach cramp), children played in the

dust near their feet. Men sat in groups on wagon tongues or
squatted beside their wagons talking in low tones. The few
words that reached Tuli's ears were strangely accented and
unintelligible; they were speaking some language she'd never
heard before, not the mijlocker that she'd grown up with.
One wagon was drawn apart from the others, closer to the
tree where the twins crouched. Its fire was larger than the
others and had no pots or spitted meat roasting.

The flute player was a long thin shadow beside that fire.
Red light played restlessly on a lined face and a thatch of
pale hair, on thin fingers flickering along the pipe. Beside this
figure a blockier shape with a bland round face held a fat-
bellied lute, fingers and finger shadows dancing vigorously
over the strings coaxing from them mellow flowing sounds
like the leap of water in a mountain brook. Other shadowy
forms squatting by the fire tapped at small drums. A big
woman sat on a chair at the back of that wagon, clapping
with the beat of the drums. After a short while she dropped
her hands. "Vala, Seichi, gelem-hai brad," she called, her
deep voice music as rich as any the lute produced. "Tans pyr
zal."

Laughing, patting at long black hair flowing loose, tugging
at tight bodices, smoothing the gathers of flaring skirts over
slim hips, the two girls left their fires and came running to
the big woman. Men and children, women not still cooking
supper started drifting from the other fires, settled in a circle
behind the musicians. The music stopped a moment. The
flute player stretched, shook saliva from her instrument.
"Kim olim'k?" Her voice was low and husky; she spoke the
strange tongue with a slight mountain lilt. Looking around at
the others, she ran her free hand through her untidy hair,
cocked her head and waited for the answer to her question.

The big woman cleared her throat and the confused babble
among the musicians died away. "Sorriss," she said firmly.

The flute player laughed, glanced at the others, blew a few
experimental notes, then settled into a lively tune. The lute
came in, then the drums picked it up. The girls began dancing around each other, flirting dark eyes, swinging their long
dark hair, arms rising and falling, hands clapping over their
heads, dropping to clap before their breasts. The spectators
picked up the rhythm and were clapping soon in their turn,
laughing and calling out cries of appreciation and encouragement.

The girls swayed and whirled, their feet pattering swiftly on the earth, turning and twisting in their intricate dance. A man rose to his feet. Several of the sitters called his name, then fell silent. He gave a wild cry that brought a gasp from Tuli and a glare from Teras. The man began to sing in a sliding minor tremolo that climbed over and under and around the bouncing melody from the instruments, weaving a thread of sadness through their cheer.

Teras and Tuli watched entranced, so absorbed in the strange spectacle that they failed to hear the two men coming up behind them, were not aware of these until hands closed on them and jerked them to their feet. Teras struggled then went still when he found his first effort useless. Tuli tried to wrench herself free. When she failed she blazed up, flailed out with her feet, threw herself about, tried to bite her captor. Since he was stronger than her and skilled in the control of struggling animals, she got nowhere.

"Tuli!" Her twin's voice was like a slap in the face, bringing her out of her blind rage. She quieted and hung panting in the hands of her captor.

He lowered her until her feet touched the ground. "T'at way, yoonglin'." With a shove he sent her stumbling toward the fire and the dancers. Her hands shaking, she straightened her jacket and tried to swallow the lump of fear in her throat. She moved closer to Teras, wanting to take his hand, unwilling to show that much weakness.

"Vat ye got, cachime?" A small man walked from the fire and stopped in front of her. He spoke the mijlocker with a strong accent that made him hard to understand. Tuli lifted her head defiantly and stared at him. His face was a congeries of wrinkles, his nose a blade of bone jutting from that sea of folds. Eyes lost far inside somewhere flicked over her, turned to measure Teras, then fixed on the face of the biggest man. An eyebrow rose. "Mijlocker."

Her captor smelled of musk and sweat. He shrugged. "Thom 'nd me, 've check d' snares." He held up a cord with six lappets dangling from it, their forepaws limp, their necks broken, their powerful hind feet soiled with dirt and oil from their fear glands. "Ve find d'two sneakin' 'nd watchin'."

"Spies?" The little man's lips stretched in a thin smile, spreading out the wrinkles in his cheeks, his eyes narrowed yet further—shooting out little gleams of amusement. "These? Some young for it."

Behind them the music died away, the dancing stopped.

Tuli shivered under the threat of all those eyes. They looked hostile, certainly unwelcoming.

"What were you doing there, boys?" Perhaps by conscious effort his accent smoothed out a little.

Tuli looked at Teras, thinking he'd better do the talking. At least they'd taken her for a boy, but she didn't trust her tongue or temper.

Teras rubbed his arm. "We were just watching the dancing. My brother and me."

Tuli nodded, watching the wrinkled face, relaxing at the little man's calm acceptance of what Teras said. She began to think they'd come out of this without more problems, swallowed a smile at the ease with which they they were fooling these people.

"Yoonglins like you ought to be in bed this late."

Teras licked his lips, scuffed his toes in the dirt. He was enjoying himself, Tuli felt that. Men were sometimes so dumb, they just didn't think anyone younger than them had any brains. His eyes on his boot toes, Teras muttered, "We sneaked out. Climbed down a tree. My brother and me, we do that all the time." He started to put his hand in his pocket, but the man Thom grabbed his arm. "I'm not gonna do anything." Teras jerked his arm loose. "I just wanna show you. . . ." He pulled the sling from his pocket. "See?"

"Any good with that, yoonglin?" The little man looked mild and disarmingly simple; his wrinkles trembling, he was almost beaming at Teras.

"I usually hit what I aim at."

The little man moved to one side, the firelight catching the folds of skin, deepening the lines until he looked grotesque, as if he wore a mask painted with red and black lines. He waved his hand at a wagon a short distance from the fire. "See that basin on the side of the drogh?"

"Drogh?" Teras was running the sling through his fingers. He was shaking a little, blinking and a bit worried. Tuli looked where the little man was pointing. The basin was a dim round that flickered as its shiny bottom reflected the cookfire close by. It seemed big enough to be a fair target. Tuli crossed her fingers, hoping the fire was bright enough to ease Teras's problems with moonlight.

"The wagon there. Make that basin sing, boy."

Teras nodded. He reached in his pocket and brought out a pebble. He whirled the sling about his head until it sang, then with a quick expert flick of his wrist sent the small worn stone flying. The basin rang like a gong.

"Good enough, boy." The little man shoved his hands into the pockets of his short black jacket. "Take back a lappet or two these nights, do you?"

The tension went out of the watchers. They began to wander off, back to their fires or their groups to talk over what had happened.

"Can we go now?" Teras shoved the sling into his pocket and moved a step closer to Tuli. "We didn't mean to bother you."

"Bring the boys here, Gorem." Tuli jumped. The big woman's voice startled her. She began to feel apprehensive again when she realized that the woman spoke without any accent. Why this bothered her she wasn't sure, but she dragged her feet as she followed Teras and the little man Gorem around the fire. He stopped them in front of the woman, walked on another step to drop on his heels beside her, his head just a little higher than the line of her massive thighs. Her face was broad across the cheekbones, narrowing to a squarish chin. Her mouth was large and mobile, set now in an intimidating downcurve. "Rane," she said, "you and Lembas stay, the rest of you scat." She thrust out her hands, fluttered them as if she shoed away a clutch of oadats.

Rane was the flute player, a tall thin woman in a man's tunic, trousers and boots. She had a mountain-bred's lanky build and pale hair. Her eyes were unexpectedly dark. In the fire and moonlight their color was indeterminate, but they certainly weren't the pale blue usual in her kin. They tilted down at the corners above high narrow cheekbones. She smiled at Teras and Tuli, amused and tolerant but maybe not so easy to fool.

Lembas was shorter, stockier, with arms that looked too long for his broad body. His hair shone like silver in the moonlight; his face was round like a baby's and rather too pretty. He stood tossing a stone idly from hand to hand, his delicately curved mouth set in a slight smile that failed to reach dark eyes.

"Your names, boys." The big woman leaned forward, the chair creaking under her. "I am called Fariyn."

"Teras, cetaj, and this is my brother Tuli."

"Not cetaj, Teras. Fariyn." She settled back in the chair; it creaked alarmingly with each shift of her massive body but that didn't seem to bother her. "Now then, what are we going to do with you?"

Teras lifted his chin, stared defiantly at her. "Do? Why do anything? Just let us go. We can get back home easy enough." Tuli nodded vigorously. "Let us go," she said. "We didn't do nothing."

Fariyn glanced up, her eyes searching out the circling forms of the traxim, her face grim. She looked from Teras to Tuli. "This is not the time to be fooling about after dark, boys. I think you need a lessoning. Who's your pa?"

Teras pressed his lips together and shook his head. Tuli prodded at her own brain, frightened in earnest now, trying to find a way out of this closing trap. "No!" she burst out, then wished she hadn't when she felt Teras stiffen beside her. "No," he said firmly. "Da 'ud tear hide off if he found out we were night running. Just let us go, we won't do it again."

Fariyn rubbed at her nose. "We got trouble enough these days being what they are. Who's your pa?"

Teras shook his head.

Fariyn turned to Rane. "There's a town a few miles east of here, isn't there? You know this part of the Plain better'n me."

Rane nodded. "About a half hour's ride."

"Good." Fariyn scowled at Teras. "You won't talk to us, boy, then we take you and turn you over to the Agli there."

"No!" Tuli cried out, her shout blending with her brother's. They whipped around and darted away, ducking and dodging as Rane and Lembas chased after them. Tuli stumbled, scrambled to her feet, but Rane's long fingers closed on the neck on her jacket; she twisted hard, a sudden skilled jerk of her hand that brought Tuli whirling around.

"Be still," Rane said. Her cool fingers slid up onto Tuli's neck, nipped hard suddenly. A roaring filled Tuli's ears and blackness slid across her eyes. Then the pressure was gone and she could hear and see again. "Be good," the long thin woman said, her voice quiet, a little amused. "We won't hurt you."

Tuli heard a scuffle, then Lembas came past her, pushing Teras ahead of him. Rane urged her after them, her strong slim fingers a warning pressure on Tuli's neck. The twins were marched back to Fariyn and left standing dejectedly in front of her.

She was smiling, an amused twinkle in her dark eyes. "Boren," she said, "these two don't seem to relish talking to

an Agli." The little man's wrinkles spread again as his lips
stretched in his version of a smile. "So." Fariyn looked from
Teras to Tuli. Her smile faded. "Rane, bring me that one
closer." She pointed to Tuli.

Urged by a hand in the small of her back, Tuli stumbled
forward. She knelt at Fariyn's command. The big woman
bent over her, looked intently into her face. She slipped long
strong fingers under Tuli's chin, forced her head around,
drew a firm forefinger along her jawline. "So." A soft,
drawn-out hiss, filled with satisfaction. Fariyn took her hand
away and settled back in her chair. "I don't think you're a
boy at all."

Tuli kept her head stubbornly down. She said nothing.

"Go back to your brother, child. I have to think a minute."

Tuli scrambled to her feet and stood beside Teras, rubbing
at her neck where Rane's fingers had bitten hard into the
muscle.

Fariyn rubbed her broad thumb against her forefinger,
slowly, repeatedly, her dark eyes focused on the fire, a con-
templative look on her face. After a moment she scratched at
the drooping tip of her long nose, tilted her head back, her
eyes following the black shadows circling high above the
camp. Finally she nodded as if she'd made up her mind
about something. With a vast fluttering of petticoats, she got
onto her feet. "Rane, Lembas, bring those two inside. Come,
Gorem, there's more here than we want to spread about."
She looked past him at the dark figures around the cook fires.
"Yes, well." She started up the back steps of the drogh, the
box swaying back and forth under her weight. The little man
followed behind like an oadat chicklet at its mother's tail.

The inside of the drogh was something of a surprise to
Tuli. It was lit by several delicate oil lamps with bowls of
etched glass. The oil in the reservoirs was scented and filled
the small neat room with a smell something like that of
fresh-mown hay. The wooden floor was covered by a Sankoy
rug that glowed with jewel colors. Along one wall a chest
with a padded top served as a seat. It had carved panels with
floral designs and pillows piled thick over the embroidered
pallet. Fariyn sat in an armchair placed against the wall opposite the door, an elaborately carved seat almost like a
throne. She nodded at Gorem who threw two pillows on the
floor by her feet. "Sit yoonglins," she said briskly. "Be welcome in my house."

Lembas stopped in the doorway, one shoulder pressed to

the jamb, his free hand tossing and catching the stone he'd been fooling with before, his eyes turned outside, a sentry watching to see that no one came close enough to overhear what was said inside.

Rane and Gorem sat on the wall seat, Rane at the far end, her face lost in shadows, Gorem nearer to Fariyn.

Feeling helpless and afraid, Tuli did what she was told and sank onto one of the pillows; she crossed her legs and spread shaking fingers on her thighs. Teras stood beside her. His hands were fisted against his side as he struggled with his own inner turmoil. He hated giving away to emotion, needed the feeling that he was in control of his body if not of his life. He faced Fariyn determined to give nothing more than he absolutely had to.

Fariyn sighed. She rested her arms along the carved wood, her fingers closing on the worn finials. "Sit down, boy. We're not going to eat you."

He flushed, his ears turning pink. Moving stiffly, he folded down, perching on the pillow like a scutter about to run.

"I thank you." Fariyn smiled, her eyes amused again. She turned to Gorem. "We have a mystery here, friend. Two local lads sneaking out to hunt small game, he tells us, innocent as a new-hatched foal. But one of the lads isn't a lad at all, though a sibling certainly, given the strong likeness between them. Brother and sister, I think. And he won't name his pa, a simple enough thing one would think. And the two of them panic when I talk about giving them over to an Agli." She chuckled. "Though I don't fault their taste in that."

"Nor I." Gorem leaned back against the wall, relaxed, the lamp over his head lighting gleams in his sunken eyes. "It does give us a strong bargaining point."

Teras glanced at Tuli. She reached out and took his hand. "I don't know," she said softly, slowly. "Gong?"

"No." His fingers tightened around hers. "No warnings."

"What do we do?"

"What we have to."

Fariyn nodded. "Sharp, aren't they. We don't have to spell out their choices."

Rane spoke, her voice calm and remote, cool as falling water. "Don't tease them, Fariyn."

Tuli stared down at her knees. "Nilis wouldn't like that dance."

Teras grinned. "No way." He looked up at the painted ceiling, not seeing it, his thoughts written on his face. "The traxim, Tuli. They wouldn't be watching their own." He turned to gaze at Rane. "Or her, a woman wearing man's clothes. We could ask."

"Do it."

Teras faced Fariyn. Beside him Tuli fixed her eyes on the big woman, striving to read behind the smiling surface. "Are you for Soäreh?" he asked.

"No more than we have to be." The answer came from behind them. Rane earned a sharp look from Fariyn for her interference. As the twins slued around to stare at her, she said, "Sometimes we have to trust. Isn't that what we're asking them to do?" She rubbed her thumb thoughtfully over a section of her jawline. "Besides, Fariyn, I think I know these two." She smiled as at a pleasing memory. "I stopped at your father's Tar six years ago at spring planting. I was a meie then. My shieldmate and I helped set out the pot-grown diram and strew the maccla seed. You two were a pair of zhag-born brats wilder than panga in rut. Twins. No, Teras, I won't say the name, better not even here, but that's a long way south of here. What happened?" She leaned into the light. "Look close, young Tuli. Remember the night of the Primavar? You were chasing Teras across the green and slammed into me, knocking me sprawling. My face bounced off a crock of cider someone had left sitting beside one of the fest boards. It broke and I got this." She tapped a short curving scar, a gouge out of her jawline. "I was bleeding like a throat-stuck hauhau, but I grabbed at you." She chuckled, spread out her left hand, wiggling her thumb to call attention to a ragged scar that circled it near the base. "You nearly bit it off."

Teras and Tuli scrambled around and scooted closer to her, stared up into jewel-bright green eyes, a dark, shining green like brellim leaves with a faint hint of blue behind the green. Tuli reached up, touched the scar on Rane's face. "I remember." She grimaced. "Da whaled us some good. And made us stay in our rooms till the whole fest was over."

Rane chuckled. "Zhag-born brats." She shook her head, sighed. "You're in trouble, twins. Tell us. Mayhap we can help."

"If this reunion is over?" Fariyn's voice trembled with laughter, but it brought Teras and Tuli back to the pillows.

"Foarin's tithe. It started with that . . ." Teras began.

"No. With Nilis," Tuli broke in.

He frowned. "I don't think so. I think it started for Cymbank when the Agli came. And the weather was so bad we had a hard time getting the winter plantings done. Spring was almost worse. Storms. And come harvest everyone was out in the fields trying to save as much of the crops as we could, even the Cymbankers shut down their shops and come out to help and a lot was lost. We know we're facing a hard winter. Used to be when Hern was still in Oras, a harvest like this, he let most of the tithe go and then this Decsel comes down from Oras from Floarin Doamna-regent saying she wanted the full tithe, same as she'd get from a regular harvest, and the taromate they decided to protest and Da was going to go to Oras. . . ." He looked down at his hands and in a dull, weary voice told them the rest of it.

"So you're going after your father." Fariyn tapped the finials of the chair arms.

"Yah. 'Nd if the guard already has him, we're going to bust him loose." When Fariyn raised an eyebrow, he scowled. "We can."

"I don't doubt that, yoonglin, no, I don't. How d'you know about those stinkin beasts?" She jerked a thumb at the ceiling. "Not many here on the Plain would."

"A tie, he worked in the stables of our Tar. What was our Tar. He's the one bust us out of the House of Repentance." He rubbed his hand along his thigh. "We wondered why they were watching so we sneaked up to see."

"Mmm, they been following us since Oras." She closed her eyes, seemed to drop into a light doze. Tuli glanced at Teras's face. The lines of strain in it were softening. He was blinking slowly, having trouble keeping his eyes open. His head trembled a little on his neck. She looked away, saw Fariyn wide awake and watching her.

"Tired?"

Tuli started to shake her head, then glanced at Teras and nodded.

"You had macain?"

Teras stirred. "Yah, we left them by the hedge. They made too much noise." He dropped his hand heavily on Tuli's shoulder and lurched up onto his feet. "We can go?"

Tuli got up slowly. She slipped her hand into her twin's and straightened her shoulders.

Fariyn leaned forward. "Why not stay here and catch some sleep? Mmmm, and some food. You hungry?" She didn't wait for an answer. "We'll wake you before dawn and you can get on your way. We'll fetch your mounts, grain 'em for you."

At the mention of grain, Teras's eyes started to glow. He really cared about the affectionate ugly beasts. Tuli smiled to herself, delighting in Fariyn's tact. His fingers were hot and tight around hers. He was beat and he knew it but he wanted to go on, he wasn't sure he trusted these people that much, he'd rather depend on just himself and Tuli. Finally, he nodded. "Thanks."

"Good. Rane, take care of them, see they get something to eat." She leaned back, sighing, her face relaxing into a smile. "Yoonglings, Maiden grant you find your pa; my blessing with you if we don't meet before you leave."

"And blessed be you, cetaj," Teras said gravely, bowed with a grace and courtesy that surprised Tuli and made her feel like pinching him.

Chuckling, Rane shepherded them from the drogh. Tuli danced ahead of Teras, stretching and yawning, glad to be outside and on her feet again. She swung around and danced backward, giggling and patting her stomach. "Food. Food. I'm hol-ul-ul-llooow."

CHAPTER VI:

THE QUEST

Serroi pushed away from Hern and walked to the Norit. Behind her she heard his impatient exclamation and before her she heard the muted clamor of the mob as it left the road and started along the hedge for the gap the men of Sadnaji knew quite as well as she did. She grimaced, annoyed at herself, but she didn't go back to her macai. When she looked over her shoulder, Hern was wiping his sword blade with a bit of soft cloth, his hands moving with quick impatient darts along the shining steel. And when she looked ahead, the red glow of the torches was coming toward the gap more swiftly than she liked. She rubbed her thumb across her fingers as she gazed down at the body, at the silently screaming head rolled several feet away, remembering the feel of the sprite rupturing at her touch, remembering the heat tearing through her when she dissolved the malchiin, remembering the shivering with fear. Distantly, she heard leather creak as Hern swung into the saddle. "Torches getting close," he called to her, his voice sharp. She couldn't blame him for it, what she was doing was foolishness, but she couldn't bring herself to mount and ride away, not just yet. She knelt and flattened her hands on the headless torso. At first, nothing happened, then she felt a rush of heat tearing up through her body. The flesh beneath her hands burst in blue flame. She leaped back, shook her tingling fingers, watching the Norit's body burn, watching the eerie blue fire leap across and consume the staring head. She opened her hands, inspected the palms, surprised when she saw the skin smooth, unmarked.

"Serroi, dammit . . ." Hern came plunging at her; he leaned over, caught her up and bore her off just as a guard rode through the gap, his torch flaring into rags as he tore across the grass after them. With Hern's arm clamping her against his body, jarred by the jolting gait of his macai, it was hard for her to concentrate, but she fixed her eyes on the

106

guard's mount, her eyespot throbbing as she reached into the beast.

The macai reared, threw itself into a frenzy of bucking and curvetting that tangled it with the riders following, driving them back, using claws and teeth and the lurch of its heavy body to drive the others back and back to the hedge. Serroi stabbed deeper. The macai screamed, threw itself up so violently it fell over, rolling on its rider. The torch flew from his hand and landed in the hedge; the flames caught in the dead dry twigs, whooshed high and wide, drawing yells of alarm from the men still outside the hedge.

Hern dumped Serroi into her saddle. She spent a moment quieting the beast, nervously aware that the three guards were pulling their mounts back under control. She glanced at Hern, nodded, then pricked her macai into a plunging run that got her halfway across the pasture before she heard the shouts of the pursuing guards. She glanced back. The fire was leaping twice man-height, threatening the trees behind it and the houses beyond them. *Poor Hallam*, she thought. *They'll be on him like a plague of bloodsuckers.*

"Serroi!"

"Huh?"

"How do we get out of here?"

"Gate." She jabbed a forefinger about two degrees east of Hallam's dark watchtower. "There."

The gate came too quickly out of the darkness at her. She risked a glance over her shoulder. The guards were still having some trouble with their macai but coming stubbornly after them, leaving them no time to dismount and open the crude three-pole gate. *Damn leeches.* She stroked her hand over the smooth thick skin on her macai's shoulder. Some macain refused to jump. The one she rode was a highbred mountain beast, more of a racer than a stayer. She bent over his neck, patting him, crooning to him, urging him on, straight toward the poles. He gathered himself, shoved off with powerful hind legs, cleared the gate with room to spare. She laughed aloud as they flew over the poles, sheer joy in the flight drowning fear and anger. Hern's beast soared over behind her, clearing the poles as her mount landed on stride, swung gracefully around and took off down the twisting lane outside the hedge. She slowed him to a smooth canter until Hern caught up with her. Still laughing, she tossed her reins to him. He caught them, dipping and straightening, laughing too, his mind making leaps as easily as his mount. He asked nothing, simply kept her macai moving smoothly beside his while she held onto the saddle ledge, closed her eyes and sought for the three macain following them.

She prodded them, heard shrill cries of crazy rage as the beasts went berserk, heard a wordless shout from Hern as the guards thrown from their saddles yelled, cursed their beasts, cursed the blasted witch they chased. Serroi shivered at the screams of the tormented macain. Hern glanced at her, saw her eyes open, handed back the reins. "Useful talent," he said, jerked a thumb over his shoulder. "Got all three of them?"

Serroi felt her excitement dwindle into self-disgust. "I hate that," she mumbled, not caring if he heard or not.

As the macain ran on, stride matching stride as if they were used to running in double harness, he reached over, balancing with some care, caught her hand and held it briefly, a gesture of understanding and attempted comfort. For the time he held her, she felt that comfort then the hand was gone and she was colder than before.

They rode along a winding lane barely wide enough to let them move in pair. She knew this road, if such a track deserved the name of road. It ran like a drunken snake along the edge of the Plain, going from Tar to Tar until it cut down from the foothills of the Vachhorns and drove toward Sel-ma-Carth. For several minutes they rode with the flutter of leaves, the call of distant birds, the innocuous night noises, then she heard a macai scream in pain and rage, felt the pain of its beating in her body, flinched at the short whip cuts that drove it along, cuts and blows multiplied three fold until she shuddered under them, gasping and anguished with her guilt and their suffering. She felt the sprite's husk rolling beneath her fingers. *I had to do it*, she thought. *Had to stop them.* But she knew she couldn't do it again, nor right now, not to these beasts. She reached back after a moment and soothed them, knowing she was acting against her own interests, yet happier with herself when she felt the pain diminish and the beasts settle more contentedly into the run after her.

Hern was watching her, frowning. "You know the ground," he said. "What now?"

Know the ground, she thought. *I wonder. How many years since. . . ?* She lifted her head. Over the heavy breathing and thudding pads of the hard-pressed macain, she heard a faint boiling sound—rushing water. *CreekSajin. And there's a ford somewhere along here. Not far, I think. I hope not far.* She looked back. The tracks of their macain were like wounds on the pale earth, easy to follow with TheDom high and only a shade past full, the Dancers and the Drover up with him, easy to follow even for those city-bred guards. She could no longer hear sounds of pursuit but she could feel them back there, coming eagerly on; they must know who they followed; the chance to get their hands on Hern would drive them far beyond prudence. She felt a momentary lift of her spirit when she thought of the Sadnaji men busy with the fire. It was too close to their own houses for them to let fanaticism take over for sense; the available trackers were occupied. She blessed the idiot guard who'd charged at them with a lighted torch in his hand. If anything saved them from his fellows, that would, he would, she smiled to think how chagrinned he would be if he knew how much he'd helped them.

Her macai stumbled, righted itself and ran on. She chewed on her lip. *Racers not stayers. All but run out.* After listening a moment longer to the ragged breathing of her mount, she pulled him down into an easier canter, nodding with satisfaction as Hern matched her without comment. She began scanning the thick growth of trees on her right, willing them to thin and open on the ford.

After an eternity of anxiety she caught a glimpse of moonlight sparkling on water. "Hern. Ahead right." She slowed her macai, swung him around and sent him into the water, kicking up crystal glimmers, stirring up the glistening white sand of the bottom. He surged up the far bank, throwing the white sand wide as his claws dug into the slope. At the edge of the brush she pulled him to a stop and waited for Hern. "Uphill." She pointed. With a last worried look at the stream, she rode into the brush, Hern quiet beside her, both of them holding their weary mounts to a walk, slanting across the rising rolling hills, weaving in and out of broom and brush. As she topped the third hill, she glanced at the ground behind her, smiled with satisfaction. On this hard rocky soil with its cushioning of tough, sun-cured bunchgrass, the macain left few traces of their passage. Over and down, right around a puff-ridden clump of brittle, dying broom, left around a pungent circle of vachachai brush, deep-ribbed leaves like vach antlers, flat, palmate, tougher than vachhide. Up again. On the slope of fourth hill, too close still to the stream for her comfort, she heard shouts from the guards, the distant splash of water as they plunged across the ford. She listened, tense, but relaxed when they began cursing furiously as the tracks

Jo Clayton

they followed disappeared on them. However dangerous they might be on city streets, here in the wild they were out of their element and easier to fool than an infant lappet. Down again, threading with some caution between ripe puff-balls perching on dead broom branches, winding up along a dry streambed, the small clatter of rock against rock, macai claws clicking against rock, back to the quieter pad-pad on dry grass. She heard the guards casting about futilely for the trail, heard the hooting and honking of their macain as they came too close to puff-balls and touched them off. She swallowed a chuckle, knowing the fiery itch that followed a touch of the red dust inside the puffs. They were very vocal over their discomfort, cursing and snarling at each other, vocal too about the hopelessness of their pursuit, yet greed drove them on. Miserable, itching, close to being thoroughly lost, they blundered about the low hills as if they expected to fall over their quarry somehow. A moment later, Serroi did chuckle, very softly, a gentle agitation of the air. Hern heard, lifted a brow, grinned in his turn. She stretched and shifted about in the saddle, more than willing to put an end to this day. They were reasonably safe now unless the guards regained some sense and rode to the nearest Tar to commandeer a tracker or a chini-handler to sniff out their trail. She wrinkled her nose at the thought, shook her head, and began edging around toward the creek.

When he caught sight of the waterflow, Hern scowled. "Riding in circles?"

"Half-circle." She patted the neck of the macai, then turned him toward the creek's bank. Over her shoulder she said, "For the benefit of inquisitive noses."

On the bank she slid from the saddle and dropped down on a convenient rock. "Get your boots off, Hern." She suited action to words and began tugging at her own. "We're going to be walking in water for a while." She slipped the second boot from her foot. "We can't count on them staying stupid."

After she tucked the boots into a saddlebag, she led her macai into the creek and started wading along, the water pushing strongly against her, rising halfway up her thighs. It was cold as the ice it ran from, the ice caves high in the Vachhorns ahead. She kept glancing up the hills, feeling too exposed on her right with only scattered clumps of broom to conceal her and Hern from a lucky blunder of the searchers on the slopes. When she reached a section where trees grew on both banks, she breathed a sigh of relief though this was no unmixed blessing since the increased darkness made footing doubly treacherous. She smiled a little when she heard Hern floundering behind her, cursing under his breath as stones on the bottom turned under his feet or barked his toes.

The trees thinned again as the stream began to curve back to the south. Serroi and Hern had to climb as well as force their weary legs against the strengthened current pouring down an increasingly difficult slope. Moonlight silvered the bow waves curling round Serroi's legs and turned the trees and broom along the bank into stark patterns of dark and light. When she looked back she could see the clouds of soil the macai's claws stirred up slipping rapidly away, carried farther than she could make out before it settled back to the bottom. Now and then she heard a distant shout from the guards still stubbornly combing the brush. She was glad they hadn't thought to go back yet because anyone with half an eye could see there was something troubling the water upstream, even they couldn't miss that. And now and then she had a momentary vision of wading around a bend to come face to face with a scratched, dirty, irritable guard. When the voices finally dropped behind, she began to relax—and become more aware of her multiple discomforts. She looked over her shoulder at Hern, chewed on her lip. He was putting his feet down with great care, his face frozen into an absent-minded mask. She wasn't feeling too brisk herself, her legs had nearly lost all sensation and her back ached. She let the macai walk past until she could hang onto the stirrups, glad of the support though her fingers started cramping.

For the next half mile she progressed one step at a time— forcing a leg against the current, feeling out a fairly stable foothold, bringing up the other leg, repeating that over and over. Serroi began searching the creek banks, sighed with relief when the tumbled stone and thick brush on the banks drew back and a gentle grassy slope slid down to a flatter stretch of water. She sent the macai up the bank letting it carry most of her weight until she was standing in the cool thick grass. As the beast began cropping eagerly at the grass, she dropped to her knees, stretched, rubbed at her eyes, yawned, swung her legs out in front of her and rubbed cautiously at her feet.

Hern settled beside her, sat wiggling his toes, scowling dubiously at them. With a soft disgusted sound he lay back, and looked over at Serroi. "Lost?"

"No."

"What about them?"

"Lost? I doubt it."

"Did we lose them?"

"Maiden knows. I think so. Unless they set trackers on us."

"Think they will?"

"They were your guards. You're a better judge than me." She got wearily to her feet and walked toward the macai, crooning at them so they'd let her approach. She took her boots from her saddlebag, hesitated, then untied the bundle of Beyl's clothes; the leather of her skirt was clammy and miserable against her skin, she could feel the shake of cold as well as weariness in her legs. Silently she blessed old Braddon for his gift. She swept the cloak along with the bundle and after another moment's thought, she circled round to Hern's mount and took down his boots.

She dropped the boots by his side and settled to the grass again. With a sigh of pleasure she began drying her feet and legs with the cloak. His eyes were closed. He looked half asleep. *Yesterday,* she thought, *yesterday I'd have told him the track I wanted to take is just a little way upslope. I'd have said, but for your folly we could have been miles closer to the Greybones Gate. I'd have thrown that in his face with pleasure and spite.* Smiling, she shook her head. She tilted onto hands and knees. Dragging the cloak with her, she crawled to Hern's feet, began patting them dry, going gently over the stone bruises and abrasions.

Startled, he sat up. "What?" When he saw what she was doing, he flushed and reached for the cloak, embarrassed at having her perform a service for him he'd thought nothing about a thousand times before when it was one of his wives or concubines attending him. She smiled, appreciating the subtle change in his perceptions, let him have the cloak and started undoing the bundle.

Some minutes later she said, "There's a track a few hundred yards upstream. Cuts through a small meadow. Be a good place to camp, plenty of fodder for them." She nodded at the macain as she unrolled a shirt and trousers and snapped out the wrinkles. "I could use some rest. So could they."

"A track." His voice was dry. He didn't say anything else but he didn't have to. She was glad she hadn't let her bitterness show, blinked when she realized that she wasn't really angry with him any more or even with herself. As he was pulling on his boots, she got to her feet. Taking shirt, trousers and her own boots with her, she retreated behind a bush and stripped off the wet leathers, the sleeveless tunic and divided skirt. The homespun wool of the boy's clothing felt soft and warm against her skin and once again she blessed her friend and spent a moment hoping he'd escaped the threatened burning. *He'll survive,* she thought, knowing as she did so that it was more wish than real possibility. *There's a core of toughness in him, in all of them, those mijlockers. Ser Noris will find them harder to swallow than he thinks.* She laughed aloud at this, knowing her own foolishness—still, there was a thread of hope she couldn't deny no matter how absurd it seemed. She slung her weaponbelt about her waist again and marched into the small clearing. "Hern, the macain are beat. We'll have to walk."

"Walk." Hern stretched, groaned, looked down at his small feet in their finely crafted riding boots. "Walk."

She chuckled, called the macain to her with eyespot outreach and soft clucks of tongue against palate. Knotting the reins into a ring on the ledge, she stroked the macain with her outreach and implanted a command to follow. Over her shoulder she said, "Next time forget vanity and settle for comfort."

He snorted and came after her, walking with great care, bending his feet as little as possible, shortening his already short stride. He raised his brows as he watched the macain pacing placidly along behind Serroi, then stretched his stride as movement eased some of the soreness in his muscles. He caught up with Serroi and together they walked along the bank of the creek in a silence more comfortable than any words they'd shared as yet.

"Floarin must be mad," she said suddenly.

"Power mad."

"She's a fool if she thinks she'll keep any power once the Nor close their fists on the mijloc."

The wind was beginning to rise, stirring the leaves over their heads. Night prowlers rustled through the grass and brush growing around the scattered trees. Serroi nodded, tucked her thumbs behind her belt. "You're right about that. The Nor don't work well with women, that's why they tried first for you, Dom." She glanced at him. "Floarin says she's pregnant."

"None of mine if she is." He grunted. "I haven't gone near her for years." Dappled moonlight played over his form, leaf shadows flickered over his face. He was scowling, his lips

compressed into a thin line, the anger that'd been simmering
in him the past year boiling up close to the surface. Glancing
at him now and then, she moved along beside him prudently
silent until he started walking more painfully, then began to
limp.

"Blisters?" Serroi touched his arm. "You'd be better with
bare feet."

Dislike glinting in pale eyes, he pulled away. "Don't try
mothering me, meie. You aren't equipped."

"Cripple yourself then." She walked on, frowning at the
ground in front of her. *Sorehead,* she thought. She grinned.
Sorefoot. Still grinning she swung around, walked backward,
unable to resist the wordless crow even though she knew she
was exacerbating his irritation.

He smiled. His pale eyes glittered. Ignoring the pain in his
feet, he limped faster. He reached out. His fingers stroked
along the curve of her neck where it rose from the opening in
her tunic. He drew fingertips over the smooth flesh, slipped
his hand around her neck to rest warm and disturbing under
the blowing ends of her curly mop. She felt a moment's
panic, started to pull away but he was too strong, he pulled
her closer until her slight body was hard against him. Slowly,
sensuously, he moved his lips along the curve of her cheek,
brushed them lightly across her mouth, kissed her very thoroughly, his hands moving over her, until she was limp, holding onto his arms to keep herself from falling on her knees.
With a triumphant smile he stepped away from her.

She stared at him, trembling, rubbing shaking hands along
thin arms. *He couldn't beat me,* she thought. *I'm too small, it
wouldn't do any good. For his pride's sake. So he uses
his. . . .* She swung around and walked away from him. After a few strides, she looked back. "Dom, don't be a fool.
Take the boots off before your feet start bleeding." She managed a small smile. "If you bleed all over them, you'll just
ruin the leather."

With a bark of laughter Hern dropped onto a root and
started tugging at a boot heel. "Make a habit of being right
and you'll turn into a worse irritant than puff-ball dust."

A habit of being right. She winced.

He rose, his bare feet pale and absurdly small against the
dark grass. A look of pleasure on his face, he stood wiggling
his toes, shifting his weight from one foot to the other.

Serroi shook her head, started on. He came up beside her,
swinging the boots with a jauntiness that sent laughter bub-

bling through her though this time she was careful not to show it. Amazing how sore feet could ruin a man's disposition; that wasn't all, she knew it well enough, she was beginning to realize how galling he'd found her all-too-obvious contempt and how ill-founded that contempt actually was.

"Beyl can't be the only boy running for the hills," Hern said. "The mijloc will fight." He made an impatient brushing gesture. "Eventually."

"Except for a few bands of half-starved outlaws that they let your guards run down, they haven't had to fight for a long time now." She spoke absently, her eyes tracking the course of the creek, trying to see how far they had to walk.

"Not since Heslin united the Plains."

United. Serroi smiled at the roots she was climbing over. *Conquered is more like.* "The mijloc's isolation helps," she said mildly. "No close neighbors to covet what you have."

"And we rode them with light reins, we sons of Heslin. They like us well enough."

At least that's true, she thought. *Most of the time. Not so much at tithing.* She glanced at the rotund figure strolling beside her. *You Heslins have been too damn lazy to worry about taking more power.* "They'll like you a lot better when they've tasted a few years of Floarin's rule."

"Years." Hern spat, kicked at a root forgetting that he wasn't wearing his boots, swore fervently, limped on, a grim look on his face.

The trees opened out into a small round meadow. The stream danced through its middle and a muddy line of stones marked the track that cut the halves of the grassy circle into quarters. Along the track moonflowers glowed like white lace, shoulder high off the ground, swaying gently on their thick hairy stems, gifting the wind with their cool, hardly sweet perfume. The meadow soil was thick, black and soggy under the matting of grass roots. Serroi kept to the stream bank until she reached the track then stepped from stone to stone till she came to the trees on the eastern side of the clearing. Hern took a bit longer to follow, the stones hard on his bruised feet. He was careless once or twice and sank ankle-deep in the muck—which didn't improve his temper. Cursing under his breath, he followed Serroi to a level stretch of drier earth under the trees, sank onto the springy air roots of a solitary spikul and began scraping at the mud on his feet with a handful of the meadow's coarse grass.

Serroi ignored him, thinking that was the best way to

maintain their somewhat precarious accord. She stripped the
gear off the macain, wiped them down with wisps of grass
and sent them ambling out into the meadow to graze on the
succulent pasturage.

"You aren't going to hobble them?"

"No need." She didn't look at him, busied herself with
draping saddles over a low limb on a gnarled brellim and
spreading the pads to dry. "They won't go far. Too tired."
She squatted by her blanket roll, undid the straps and began
loosening the ground sheet wrapped around her blankets
"Not going to rain, I think."

"Hot for this time of year."

She set the groundsheet aside and began clearing small
rocks and twigs off of a section of earth. "I noticed." She
rose stiffly, tossed a small rock aside. "You want to hunt for
firewood or fix supper?"

"Kind of you."

"What?"

"To offer a choice."

"Don't be tiresome, Dom. Which?"

"Firewood." He padded over to the pile of gear and bent
down, grunting with the effort, to catch up the small ax.
"How much you want?"

"Enough to last till morning." She frowned at the sky.
"Not long now."

He nodded and moved with stiff painful strides into the
darkness under the trees.

Serroi stretched, yawned. She was sleepier than she was
hungry, but she knew she should eat since she'd need all the
strength she could find on this quest. She caught up the
waterskin and the kettle, taking them to the stream, thinking
pleasant thoughts of a steaming hot cup of cha.

When Hern came back with an armload of wood, she was
kneeling beside a small circle of stone, fitting the last stone in
place, at her elbow a pile of fresh herbs and knobby tubers,
dried meat and everything else she needed for supper, all of
it waiting for the fire. He dumped the wood beside her, tossed
the ax down without watching where he threw it. It banged
off a stray stone and bumped out into the meadow's tangled
grasses while Hern rubbed at his hands and scowled at broken skin on his palms.

Serroi sighed with exaggerated patience. "Dom."

"What now?"

"We've got one ax between us. You want to gnaw the next

batch of firewood down to size with your teeth?" She lifted one of the smaller limbs, broke it over her thigh, inspected the pieces, broke one of them again, then began fitting them into the space between the stones.

He made a face at her back, stepped reluctantly into the mud and began weaving through the grass hunting for the ax.

Hern poked through the shell fragments in his palm, searching vainly for any more nutmeats. He brushed the shell away and eyed the pot. "Any stew left?"

Serroi glanced into the pot, shook her head. "Trail rations, Dom." She lifted the kettle from the dying fire and poured the last of the hot water over the already soggy leaves in the bottom of her mug. "You're too fat anyway, short rations will be good for you." She took a sip of the weak cha, sighed and held out the mug. "Want this?"

"Better than nothing." Sipping at the hot pale liquid, he watched her rinse out the stew pot and scrub the interior clean, dumping the used water onto the grass. She broke a few dry twigs from one of the branches, blew on them until she had a small but briskly crackling fire, then added more twigs and some larger branches. She sat back on her heels, yawned, her eyelids drooping, her shoulders sagging.

Hern spat out a cha leaf, picked another off his lip, drank again from the mug, watching with weary amusement as she rose, brushed herself off and moved to the groundsheet. She pulled her boots off, wiggled her toes, sighed with relief, met his eyes and smiled at him. Unbuckling the heavy weapon-belt, she laid it out flat on the blankets beside her. "Come here, Dom, and let me work on your feet." She laughed at the expression on his face. "Don't be a baby, I'm not going to hurt you."

He got to his feet. "I don't see why you weren't strangled at birth."

Her face went still. "I nearly was, Dom. Not strangled, but given to the fire when my grandfather saw this." She touched the eyespot on her brow, spread out her hands to remind him of the odd color of her skin.

"Damn." He eased himself stiffly down beside her. "I didn't mean it."

"I know. Never mind." She worked one of the belt pockets open, brought out a small pot of salve. Holding it, she looked around, wrinkled her nose. "Hang on a minute, I need water." She fetched the waterskin and knelt at his feet. With

gentle hands that still managed to hurt when she touched the
broken blisters, she washed his feet clean of heavy dark dust
and the stains from the meadow muck, then spread the salve
on the abrasions and the blisters, worked it patiently into the
stone bruises on his soles. He flinched and fisted his hands at
first, then sighed with pleasure as the soothing balm eased the
pain from his sores and the heat of it penetrated his bruises.
He lay back and closed his eyes, was almost asleep when she
finished. She sat on her heels gazing at him with something
close to affection. After a moment she rubbed at her eyes
with the back of her hands, crawled up on the groundsheet
and shook him awake. "You want to take first watch or second, Dom?"

They rode undisturbed along the track for the next three
days, the quietness and solitude of the mountain slopes easing
the tension from both of them so that by the time they
reached the Greybones Gate late on the third day, the bad
beginning was almost forgotten.
A hot leaching wind with a dry musty smell like the dust
of dead fungus blew against them from the Gate, a tall narrow crack between fluted cliffs of dead stone, wind-carved
into elaborate convolutions, singing an eerie, ear-piercing
melody. As they sat on sidling nervous macain, blinking away
dust-generated tears, somewhere in the Gate before them there
was a sharp crack, the clatter of stone against stone, an over-
stressed section of cliff breaking away. Cupping a hand over
nose and chin though that wasn't much help, she blinked furiously, felt herself beginning to float. She lost touch with arms
and legs, swayed in the saddle, had to grab the ledge with
both hands. She turned to Hern, started to speak but her
words were lost in the singing of the wind. She caught his
eyes (glazed and wandering like her own, slitted in a slack
face) jerked her head toward the track, back along the way
they'd come. He nodded and followed her away from the
Gate.
There was a shallow hollow in the barren stone, protected
from the wandering dream-winds, death-winds, behind a
screen of scraggly stunted brush with tiny leaves whose unas-
sertive green was dusted to a dead gray. Serroi hitched her
mount to the brush, shook it clean of dust in case he wanted
to browse and settled herself in the hollow to wait the cessation
of the song in the Gate which would mean the dropping of
the wind. Shadows raced into long distorted shapes that were

swallowed by the dropping night. She gazed out over the Plain and saw the gathering of thick dry clouds, dust clouds not water bearers, yellow-tinged even in the pale, bleaching light of the rising TheDom. The edge of the Plain marked the edge of the clouds. They were there, she knew, to keep heat pressing down on the land, a blanket spread by her Noris. Serroi wiped at her sweating face, the sun-heated rock behind her still holding the day's warmth. The sky over the Vach-horns was clear, it'd be cool soon enough, cooler than she liked. She thought about the cloak still tied behind her saddle, made no move to fetch it, lassitude heavy on her arms and legs and sitting like sleep in her head. She couldn't keep still; itches ran along her legs and played on the inside of her knees, worse when she scratched at them. They ran along the sides of her back and in between her shoulderblades where she couldn't reach. A tic jerked by the corner of one eye and the inside of her nose tickled. She thought of trying to sleep, but was afraid to sleep, afraid of the dreams that would haunt her in this place.

What Hern was thinking she couldn't tell. He sat toward the front of the hollow, turned away from her—all she could see of his face was the convex curve of his cheek, the jut of his brow. He sat very still, his square rather beautiful hands resting lightly on his thighs (she saw one and assumed the other from the shape of his back). There was a quality of repose in him that she'd hadn't expected, another jolt to her image of him. Briefly she envied that repose (scratching with industry at an itch on the inside of her thigh) then she wondered what he was looking at, shifted onto her knees and crawled over to him, followed the direction of his eyes.

Beyond the Gate the mountains curved north, wave on wave of wind-carved stone, naked and barren and eerily beautiful, their patterns of dark and light slowly oh so slowly changing, evolving as the great moon rose higher pulling the smaller moons after him, like a dance in slowtime requiring infinite patience to know all its cycles.

Still the wind sang, sometimes so loud it raised echoes from the slopes around the Gate. The rock leaked its heat away into a clear and cloudless sky while the yellow clouds boiled and tumbled above the Plain. Serroi and Hern waited without talking for the tedious vigil to end. About two hours after midnight the windsong died to a whisper. They gave the macain all the water they would drink, then rode warily into the Gate.

The rutted, wrinkled floor of the pass was littered with rock fragments and more rock fell before and behind them, small bits clattering loudly from bulge to bulge to shatter into smaller bits on the rocky floor. It was very dark inside the Gate. TheDom was on the far side of the sky, his light touching only the upper few feet of the eastern cliff. The Jewels of Anesh floated overhead, three small glows the size and tint of copper uncsets, their feeble light only adding to the confusion among the shadows at the base of the rotten cliffs. Hern and Serroi rode straining to hear the crack and clatter that would announce a major fall, their uneasiness transmitted to the macain, already unhappy and moaning with distress at the sharp bits of stone pressing against their tough fibery pads.

The Gate wound on and on, undulating up and down, never straight anywhere for more than a dozen macai strides, up and down and around, until Serroi was dizzy with the switches, suffocated by the dust kicked up by macai paws, near screaming with frustration at the slow pace—and still the ride went on.

After two more hours—or a small eternity; both perceptions being true—she saw a pale deep vee ahead, and heard a tentative moan from the walls as wind began to tease at her curls, wide-spaced tentative tugs. Then it blew a cloud of grey dust around them and she no longer saw the exit ahead. The faint starlight reaching them, the only light they had now, was eaten by the dust and they rode blind, dependent on macai senses, battered by moans and whistles and howls from the fluted stone around them.

All things end at last and they came out of the Gate into the faint red light of the earliest hint of morning. Hern pulled his mount to a stop on the flat space atop a cliff, wiped at his face, scraping away a layer of grey dust, leaving streaks behind. He fished in his pocket for the cloth he used to clean his sword and scrubbed it hard across his face, searching by feel for the burning streaks, growling with distaste each time he inspected the rag and refolded it for a bit of clean surface.

Serroi cleaned herself with less fuss and gazed around. They were on a kind of lookout, a flat area edged with boulders whose orderly array hinted that intelligence rather than chance had set them in their places. She looked at the boulders and remembered that this was the Sleykyn road, the way that most of those assassins and torturers took to reach the mijloc, Oras and across the Sutireh Sea since Skup was closed

to them, their own southern coast was impenetrable marsh
and their northern reaches swept by hostile nomads. The
eastern sky was rapidly brightening into conflagration, the
sun's tip a molten ruby resting between two peaks. The
mountain dropped steeply from the lookout, its dead stone
and long dead vegetation layered over with large grey-green
crystals that caught the red light from the east and turned it
into a purple-brown murk. On the floor of the basin the lake
was a shimmering bloodstone, muted green water with trails
of bloody decay winding through it. And on the basin floor
shimmering short-lived dust devils walked the desolation, continually dying, continually reborn. If she looked at them too
long she saw eyes in the dust that gazed back at her.

With Hern ahead (she was in no mood to dispute leader-
ship) they wove back and forth down the slope in the exasperating tedium of a dozen switchbacks. The trail was
crumbling, neglected and starting to melt back into the
mountainside, a result of the Gather storms when passage
through the deadlands became impossible, the mijloc protected from more Sleykynin by Air and Earth herself, matron
face of the airy Maiden, Mother Earth who brought forth her
fruits for the delight of man. Delight not Duty. Dance in the
moonlight for the joy of it, the joy, dance the two-backed
dance for the Maiden's delight the Matron's joy, drink down
the wine and warm the spirit, warm the body with cider hot
and spicy, foaming headily in earthenware crocks, in earthenware mugs, splashed to celebrate the earth, sloshing in hu-
man bellies, leaping in the dance, laughing the water music,
watch the moth sprites dance, spin the light-lace on the water
. . . Hern stop . . . Hern dance with me, the two-backed
dance . . . make joy with me. . . . Serroi blinked and
tugged her hazed mind free, blushing, hoping rather desperately that she hadn't said those things aloud, that Hern hadn't
heard her. She swallowed. Her mouth felt dry already but she
knew better than to drink here.

They reached the basin floor without incident though twice
more Serroi had to discipline her wandering mind and body
and stiffen herself against the insidious influence of the ever-
present dust. The road across the basin was marked at intervals by large cairns and scraped flatter than the seamed
surface on each side, the crude finishing of the surface over-
laid by a deep, muffling layer of grey dust. Dust devils
danced thick on the road and blew to nothingness against
them. Serroi began to hear whispers in the wind despite her

efforts to deny them, voices whose sibilant syllables were almost clear enough to gel into intelligible words, whispers that teased at her to listen harder, just a little bit harder, there were secrets to be heard. She scolded herself out of listening again and again but always the temptation returned. Beginning to feel a little frightened, she kneed her mount to a faster gait until she came up with Hern. She let the macai slow to a walk, the two beasts matching strides again, content to move side by side. Hern was staring intently at the dust devils whirling through their brief lives ahead of him. She wanted very much to talk with him, using the commonplaces of ordinary conversation to hold her raveling mind to ordinary paths. "Hern," she called, then coughed and spat as dust flew in her mouth. He didn't seem to hear and she didn't try again.

The macain paced steadily on, perhaps seeing their own visions, hearing their own spectral sounds. As the hours passed the whispers came closer, grew louder and more insistent though she still could not understand them. Sometimes she thought she heard her name, though she couldn't be sure. She blinked now and then at Hern, wondering if he heard the same. There was a dazed dull look on his face, a touch of pain in it and self disgust. She turned quickly away, feeling like an intruder on his privacy.

The dust thickened and lumped into half-formed creatures that loped or undulated or slithered beside her. She tried to ignore them. At first they were little more than blurred lumps with indeterminate outlines, but gradually the outlines sharpened as if she herself, by looking at them, acted on them. She looked away, but always looked back again, drawn to look by a force within herself that beat down her feeble attempts to assert her will.

Tayyan rides beside her, a sketch in grey and black, a blur at first but even so Serroi knows her by the tilt of her head, and angular grace of her body. The wind whispers now in Tayyan's voice: *Serroi. Serroi. Serroi.* Serroi weeps, tears cutting runnels through the dust mask on her face.

A tall form comes drifting in the dust between Serroi and the dust Tayyan, an elegant black form with pale face and pale hands and a shining black ruby drop hanging from one nostril (the black ruby bothers Serroi for a moment but she forgets it when the scene evolves). His mouth moves and the wind's whisper takes on the dark music of his voice: *Serroi. Serroi.*

Tayyan reaches a long-fingered hand to the Noris. Pale hand closes on pale hand. Riding the dust macai with her knees, Tayyan pulls the Noris astride facing her, his long narrow robe riding high on thin muscular legs. He leans to her, they kiss, a long slow terrible kiss where they seem to melt together. He is suddenly naked, enormously rampant. Serroi stares, knowing this is impossible, forgetting why she knows this is impossible. Tayyan is naked too now. It is absurd. Serroi would laugh but she cries instead, sobs her hurt and pain as Tayyan and the Noris couple, though frantic, somehow manage to maintain their balance on that walking dust macai. Eyes burning until tears blur away the scene, sick yet unable to look away until she sees nothing but the sliding dust, until she rides blind and sobbing, fighting a terrible sense of loss, a chill anguish of betrayal, a hurting beyond healing.

When at last she fought back to reality and wiped her eyes of muddy tears, the hurtful images had faded into the dust. She glanced at Hern. There was a scowl on his face and as she watched he seemed to wince away with a look of horror in his eyes. She wondered what he was seeing, then decided that she didn't want to know.

Beads of light begin gathering about Serroi, sharpening into moth sprites, their tiny glowing bodies weaving a lace before her of mind-dazzling beauty. She gasps with pleasure, gasps with horror as one by one the lights begin to die, the small forms breaking like puff balls, the broken husks raining against her face, dead and gone with the world worse off for lack of them.

Chini pups play beside her, jumping in exuberant delight at the wonder of being alive; chini pups run beside her, silent, eyes calling her betrayer and murderer. "I couldn't help it," she cries. "He was too strong for me. I fought him, yes I did. You know I did." The pups run together, melt together into a great black beast that lopes beside her, grinning at her until it too melts into the dust.

Dead men, her dead, dead at her hands float around her, grinning at her, cursing her, each curse simply her name: *Serroi. Serroi. Serroi. Serroi.*

The land began to rise. Slowly, painfully they left behind the level of the dust devils and climbed into a cleaner wind. Serroi had wept herself empty; she rode with her hands clamped on the saddle ledge before her, sunk in a dull stupor that stayed with her until the wind carried the clean spicy odor of vachbrush and snowline conifers strongly to her, the smells of vigorous life rekindling her own life. She sat straighter, scrubbed at her face, drew in several cleansing breaths that flushed the last of the poison dust from her lungs. When she tilted her head back, following the steepening slope to the peaks, she saw not far ahead two great horns of stone. The Viper's Fangs. The Gullet ran between them. An hour or two more, that was all. An hour or two and she'd be pouring cold clean water over her. She closed her eyes, swallowed with difficulty. Cold clean water, outside and in. She let her shoulders sag, her back curve into a weary arc.

The macai went steadily onward shifting from its sluggish walk to a jolting trot that broke her rapidly from her daze of exhaustion. She glanced at Hern. He wore his court mask, his bland rather stupid smile, a face he could put on without effort while his mind worked busily behind it. For a moment only she wondered what he was thinking, then shrugged her curiosity away, and settled herself as comfortably as she could in the saddle while her macai turned into the first of the switchbacks.

CHAPTER VII:

THE MIJLOC

The hour before dawn was silent and cool, as cool as the blanket of clouds would let it be, and the Traxim were gone from over the Players' camp when Rane woke Tuli and Teras. She gave them food, hot cha, more grain for the macain and sent them on their way with a thoughtful scowl on her long face.

Teras and Tuli kept to the trees though the riding there was not especially easy or quick; they had to work their way around tangles of dying, thorny underbrush, through root mazes and past thickets of saplings where a viper would have had trouble wriggling between the trunks. When the color had faded from the east and the sun came clear of the horizon, bloating as it rose, Teras worked cautiously to the outer trees. On the edge of shadow he watched the sky above the road for a long time and still saw nothing. "They've really gone off," he said. "Come on." He kneed his mount to a quick walk and started up the embankment to the Highroad, Tuli coming quiet and thoughtful after him, glancing repeatedly at the empty sky. The clouds were gone now, burnt away by a sun that had already grown half again as big as it should be.

They had the Highroad to themselves until about an hour before noon when a brownish dot popped up from the northern horizon, resolving itself eventually into a Pedlar coming south, ambling unhurriedly beside his esek, a small brownish-orange beast padding steadily along on three toed feet, the pack on its back almost as big as it was and far noisier. Metal pans dangled from the side of the pack, along with clutches of spoons and forks, long-handled ladles and digging tools, all of them clattering musically with each of the esek's swinging strides. The Pedlar—a small dark man with long thin arms and legs—waved as the macain trotted past him, called a greeting. Teras grinned back, waved. Tuli heard the clank-clunk-clang for a long time before it finally faded into the distance. When the cheerful noise was gone, she sighed. "I wonder how much longer the Aglim will let folk like him and the Players be?"

"Don't know." Teras uneasily rubbed at the back of his neck.

"What is it?" Tuli rode closer, anxiously scanned her twin's face. "Gong?"

"Not exactly." Teras pulled his hand down. "Sorta like someone's staring at me, you know, you get that itchy feel on the back of your neck."

She twisted around, "There's no one back there now."

"I know that." He kicked his macai into a trot and pulled away from her and her questions. Tuli sighed and rode after him.

About midafternoon when the heat was so bad they were beginning to think about leaving the Highroad and moving back under the trees, a stenda lordling and three stenda herdsmen brought six macai yearlings out of the foothills and drove them up onto the Highroad in front of the twins. Arrogant as always, the young stenda ignored them as beneath his notice, didn't offer them the customary traveler's greeting but the herdsman on their side grinned at them and waved as the twins took to the steep grassy slope alongside and edged their way past the boisterous young macain. Teras and Tuli returned both grin and wave, Tuli's spirits rising as she was taken for the boy she pretended to be.

The heat grew oppressive. The wind fell and the air twisted and distorted ahead of them as the black paving turned to an oven floor. They left the the Highroad to ride along at the edge of the trees, letting the macain drop to a shuffling walk, stopping frequently to water the beasts and splash a little water on their own reddened, burning faces.

Near evening when the road became passable again, they began meeting other riders. Two Sleykyn assassins were moving south. *I wonder who they're after*, Tuli thought. She shivered, hoping it was no one she knew. She only relaxed where they were small figures far behind. They passed guards, traveling craftsmen, passed tithe wagons going south after grain flanked by more guards, footloose laborers hunting work from Tar to Tar, scattered young men much like the twins appeared to be, rootless and ragged with a feral lost look to them even when they laughed and joked together. Most of them were walking. Teras and Tuli got a number of speculative looks, the macain they rode drew more. Teras grew edgier. He began keeping the width of the Highroad between them and the larger groups they met. And he began looking back more often. "Tuli," he said finally. "The itch is a lot worse."

"Someone following us?" She twisted around, stared along the Highroad behind her. There were several riders wavering in mirage riding north just as they were, but no one close. "I can't see anything to worry about."

"Let's stop a while."

"What about Da?"

He moved his shoulders irritably, leaned over the saddle ledge and scratched at the spongy fringe on the macai's neck. "They need rest. Look ahead there." He pointed. "The Blasted Narlim." A high pale pole of a tree (dead for a hundred years or more but still standing as a landmark because the oils in the wood repelled insects and retarded decay) the narlim was like an ivory needle rising above the blue-green leaves of the broader, squatter brellim. "We stopped there when we went to Oras, remember? It's got a well." He shook the limp waterskin by his knee. "We're about out of water."

"We can't camp there." Tuli scratched at her chin. "You saw how those landless looked at our macain."

"You always argue," he burst out. "No matter what I say." He kicked his mount into a heavy run, leaving Tuli gaping at this unexpected and quite unfair attack. She followed without trying to catch him, a cold hollow spreading under her ribs. Not that she and Teras never had arguments, but there was a different sound to this, an angry resentment that troubled her. He slid from the saddle and began working the pump handle with a vigor that seemed to ease some of the tension in him. Uncertain how to act with her brother now, Tuli rode her macai down the embankment, silent and hurting. She slid from the saddle and led her macai to the water trough, stood patting his neck as he gulped down the cool water.

When the trough was full, Teras untied the grainsack given by Rane, pushing past Tuli to do so. He felt dark to her, dark and closed away from her. Then she saw him glancing at her, not meeting her eyes, glancing repeatedly and shyly like a chini pup who'd misbehaved and she saw that he was ashamed but didn't know how to speak to her again. The coldness under her ribs went away. She grinned at him and led her protesting mount to the pile of grain he poured for

her. He smiled back tentatively then left the macain whuffling
at the grain and moved under the trees. He settled on a thick
air-root, his back to the spikul's scratchy trunk, his eyes on
the Highroad.

Tuli straddled a root on a neighboring spikul, leaned forward, arms braced, hands circling the shaggy wood. "Will
you know who it is?"

Teras leaned his head against the trunk and closed his eyes.
He scratched slowly at his thigh, his fingernails pulling
wrinkles into the heavy material of his trousers. "I think so."

"How long we going to wait?"

"An hour, mayhap." He opened his eyes and smiled
dreamily at her. "If he's not by us before then, he's not coming. The macain will be rested enough by then so we can go
along for a while more."

Tuli bounced a little on her root, then jumped off. She
stretched a while, bent and twisted, until she remembered she
was hungry. She edged toward her macai. The beast was licking up the last grains, the ones sunk in between the stiff
springy blades of grass. He shied as she set a hand on his
flank but kept his head down, wrapping his tongue about the
grass, tearing it up and swallowing it. She dug into a saddlebag and pulled out a packet of cold meat, bread and cheese.

After sharing with her twin, she settled herself back on her
root, chewing vigorously and watching the thin trickle of pas-
sersby. Floarin's moves in the past few days obviously hadn't
touched everyone in the mijloc, not like Cymbank anyway.

As the sun moved slowly toward the peaks of Earth's
Teeth, losing a portion of its swollen coppery strangeness, the
twins spoke at intervals, exchanging only a word or two.
More seemed unnecessary now, the rents in their accord
healed (at least on the surface) as if they'd never occurred.
When she finished eating, Tuli was up again, too restless to
relax as Teras was doing. She began prowling through the
quiet sun-dappled grove, watching tiny talkalots running
about the limbs, watching the abasterim swooping after near-
invisible bugs, listening to wild oadats rustling through brush,
airroot tangles and fallen leaves. Eased by these comforting
reminders that some things weren't changing out of all recognition, she strolled back to Teras. "We going to wait much
longer?"

He was staring intently at the Highroad. His head jerked a
little when Tuli spoke behind him, but he didn't turn. "No."

She looked from him to the empty road, then started past

him to see more of it. He stopped her, his hand hard and nervous on her arm. "Wait."

She stepped back reluctantly and stood at his shoulder in the shadow under the drooping limbs. A single figure rode slowly toward them. He looked thin and short though he was still too far away to judge the actual length of arms and legs. He wore a cowled jacket, the hood pulled up over his head in spite of the lingering heat of late afternoon. His mount looked lean and rangy with powerful legs longer than the average—mountainbred, a racer by the look of him.

When the rider came even with them, he pulled the fractious macai to a stop. While it jerked its head about, clawed at the blacktopping, sidled and backed, the rider stared intently into the trees, his face a circle of darkness under the cowl. Teras slipped his hand into the pocket of his jacket and brought out the sling, draped it over his knee, slid his hand back and closed it about one of the stones. He sat tense, waiting.

"Gong?" Tuli whispered.

"No." He didn't relax. "It doesn't always," he whispered back.

The macai continued sidling about, whoomping softly until the rider urged him off the Highroad and down the embankment. The man's long-limbed body moved easily and gracefully with the dip and sway of the racer. He rode straight toward them, stopped the macai at the edge of the shadow, lifted a hand to the cowl with a familiar angular grace. Even before the gesture was completed, the cowl pushed back, Tuli knew. "Rane," she breathed.

Teras stuffed the sling back into his pocket. "Why?" he demanded.

"Why?" Rane shrugged. "Say curiosity. I was leaving anyway this morning." Her eyes moved from him to search the shadow behind him. She smiled at Tuli. "How go the sores?"

"Well enough." Tuli glanced at Teras. He nodded. It was Rane who was following, no one else. "Why didn't you just come with us? How come you waited?"

"You look like you were waiting for me."

"Someone." Tuli spoke before she thought. Teras's fingers closed tight about her arm, but his warning came too late.

"One of you is a sensitive. You?" She nodded at Teras.

He drew back until his spine was pressing against the trunk of the spikul. Tuli chewed on her lip. *Did it again, Maiden bless, ran my mouth before I thought.* She moved closer to

Teras, closed her hand around his. She felt him stiffen, then relax and knew he'd forgiven her. With a brief reluctant nod, he said, "Me."

Rane crossed her arms on the saddle ledge, smiled down at them. "Owleyes and Longtouch. You make a good team."

Teras grinned. "Well," he said. "Sometimes." He slid off the root. "You didn't answer Tuli's question."

"I had things to do before I left." Rane's voice went cool and distant. She waited until the twins were mounted again, then the three of them rode back up the embankment and set their macain to an easy lope. The mounts of the twins were rested and well-fed, full of frisk though not as high-strung as Rane's racer.

Tulu studied the lanky ex-meie, wondering just why she'd come after them, why she'd really come, not what she said, wondered if they'd ever get any answer to that, one they could believe, not that laconic non-explanation she'd given them. She shifted in the saddle, suddenly aware of her sores as if Rane's question had stirred them into life.

The ex-meie rode closer. "Bothering you?"

"A little."

"Ummm." She inspected Tuli's mount. "A good flatland beast with a steadyish gait." She paused. "How's your balance?"

"Huh?"

"Ever walk corral poles?"

"Course. Lots of times."

"Good at it?"

"Some. Why?"

"Never mind. Try taking your feet from the stirrups and letting your legs hang. Don't grip with your thighs—hold yourself on by balancing your upper body. Hang onto the ledge if you start slipping, that should be enough. Teras." Her call was quietly spoken but insistent. Teras twisted around, saw them slowing and dropping behind, pulled his mount to a stop and waited for them. When they came up with him, Rane said, "We're going to have to move slower. Your sister is having some trouble again."

Teras nodded, rode beside Tuli ready to give her a supporting hand if she needed it. After wriggling about in the saddle until she felt comfortable, she kicked her feet out of the stirrups, then tried to deal with the consequent feeling of instability. With a startled gasp she clutched at the ledge as she found herself tilting inexorably to her right. Eventually she slumped like a sack of grain in the saddle, legs dangling loose, her body moving bonelessly with the swing and sway of the macai's stride. It was a rather exhilarating feeling. She was rooted in the macai and through him into earth herself, wholly relaxed, almost giddy with the unexpected pleasure in this sort of riding, the ease of pain only a minor though welcome, bonus.

After watching her closely for a while, the quiet ex-meie nodded and her smile stretched to a broad grin. Her worn face relaxed. The warmth usually hid behind her controlled bearing shone from her blue-green eyes like sunlight on rain-wet brellim leaves. "You should have seen me trying to ride when I ran away to the Biserica." Her voice had a tender, musing quality. She might have been talking to distract Tuli from the questions seething in her head, or might simply have been in a remembering mood with Tuli just by chance riding beside her. Or she might have other reasons, helpful or threatening. Tuli wondered as she listened, but she listened avidly.

Rane made a clown face, ran long, rather bony fingers through her thatch of straw-colored hair. "Stenda women, ah stenda women, what a life they lead."

Tuli added, "A while back we passed a stenda boy with a herd of macain."

Rane chuckled. "And he wouldn't even give you greeting."

"Yah. A snot."

"A Stenda, moth. A lord of creation. Born knowing he's infinitely above the rest of us."

"You couldn't ride?"

"Oh no, Tuli. A stenda lady—never. It wouldn't be at all proper. We sew and we smile, we learn our genealogies until we can recite them in our sleep. We gossip and protect our complexions and wait to be married. If we're lucky and a little talented we may even learn some music." She patted her flute case. "And it's so damn dull one wants to scream aloud but that wouldn't be permitted. A stenda lady has a low and pleasant voice at all times no matter what the provocation."

"So you ran away."

"So I ran away." She sighed. "Not before I was beaten bloody more than once. I used to slip out at night like you and Teras when I couldn't stand it any longer, usually when TheDom was full, I couldn't bear to stay inside when he painted the world silver. I used to play with the macai foals or just wander about feeling free. I was very bad at escaping then, they caught me nearly every time and every time they caught me my father examined me to make sure I was still virgin. Examined me publicly. Called all the family together. The times I wanted to kill him, chop him into bloody shreds. . . ." She sighed again. "Ah well, that was a long time ago."

"Sounds like the Followers are first cousins to stenda men," Tuli said. "They kept yammering stuff like that at me." She slanted a look at Rane, then gazed down at hands resting lightly on the ledge in front of her. "Do many stenda girls reach the Biserica?"

Rane's lips twitched, but she answered seriously. "Not many. Just the stubbornest." She shrugged. "Most stenda women seem to like the way they live. My youngest sister is quite happy, no pretense about it."

"Sort of like Nilis."

"Sort of, I suppose." Rane's eyes twinkled at her.

Tuli fell silent. Her ankles and feet started to swell, hurt when she moved them. She lifted one foot and rested her toe in the stirrup. It threw her off balance, but felt better, so she slipped in the other toe. When she was settled again, she glanced at Rane, started to speak, clamped her lips tight.

"Why did I leave the meien?" Rane's voice was gently teasing. "You want to ask that, don't you."

"It's none of my business." Tuli was embarrassed. Her face felt hot and tight.

"No, it isn't." Rane looked away. Her profile was all Tuli could see in the slanting light from the setting sun. "Still, it's certainly no secret. You met my shieldmate but I don't know if you remember her, it was a long time ago, nearly half your lifetime, moth." She rode silent for several minutes, her profile altering as her lips moved into a brief tender smile. "Meien always ride in pairs. Sometimes for companionship and protection, sometimes because they are lovers. We were lovers, my shieldmate and I. You probably can't understand that, moth, but it was so. Passion and affection, an affinity of souls. Together we made a whole, apart we were uneasy and imcomplete. I was fourteen, your age, moth, when I stumbled through the Northwall gate. Fourteen when I met her. I was thirty-nine when she died. . . . she died—do you know, there were months when I couldn't say those two words together. She died for two years, a wasting disease that even our healers couldn't cure. I left the Biserica because there were too many memories there. Out here. . . ." She moved her hand in one of those innately graceful gestures Tuli now knew were a lingering result of stenda drilling. "Out here I can let go of her. And remember the good times if I'm in a mood for memories." Tuli saw with surprise that she was smiling. "I'm just a wanderer now, moth, playing flute for those who want to hear it. The Players make me welcome for the sake of this." She patted the flute case with laughing affection. "And I'm useful if they run into trouble with drunks or men who pester the Player women under the delusion that they're little more than whores. It saves a lot of bad feeling if I'm the one to tunk the louts on their thick heads and leave them for the Townmaster's men to cart off to the lock-up." She tapped the saddle ledge. "A caveat here, Tuli. You and Teras did right to trust Fariyn and her friends. The other Players are something else. They're fiercely loyal to their own but outsiders are fair game. If you run into them again, trust them only as much as you have to. And keep an eye on exits."

Tuli frowned, suspecting that there was a lot about Rane and her activities the ex-meie wasn't telling. She swallowed her curiosity, knowing she'd get no satisfactory answers. "Tchah," she whispered.

"Hurting again?"

"No. Just thinking."

"Oh." Rane's lips twitched. "That can be painful."

Thick yellow clouds were piling up above the Earth's Teeth, pushing at the sharp peaks like hauhaus shoving against a corral fence. The sunset stained them rose madder and rust, garnet and gamboge, amethyst and indigo, great rolling puffs of barren dust given momentary glory. Rane watched the clouds, silent and still, her hands relaxed on her thighs. Tuli saw the colorplay that enthralled the ex-meie and paid it perfunctory tribute, but she was filled with fear for her father and she had little mind left for anything else. When she looked at Teras, riding stiff and unyielding beside her, she knew he was feeling the same fear.

His head started moving, turning slightly side to side. He was scanning the road ahead, scanning the sky. Tuli waited for him to speak but when he said nothing she grew impatient. "Anything?"

"No." He lifted a hand, let it fall. His gong occasionally deserted him when it would be most useful. They'd learned long ago never to depend on it when they were trying to sneak back into the house after one of their night runs. Tuli stared at the sky ahead, not knowing what to expect, then she leaned tensely forward, ignoring the pain as she pressed sores hard against the saddle flaps.

A black shape barely distinguishable from the sky flew across the road, flew back. She strained to see. *Not a trick of the twilight,* she thought. *One? Yah, only one.* "Teras, Rane." She pointed. "A trax. There. Just one."

Teras tried to follow the line of her pointing finger. "You sure?"

"Tcha! Would I say it if I wasn't?"

"You think it might be watching Da?"

"Maiden knows."

Rane wiped sweat from her forehead, her eyes on that black shape still far ahead. The sun's murky glow picked out the planes of her high cheekbones and the long slide of her nose, sank her eyes into smears of shadow. She pulled her cowl up over her head with a crisp movement of one hand as if she were issuing a challenge to that unnatural thing that waited for them. Her macai caught her mood, tossed his head, sidled about, his claws pricking delicately at the blacktop. "That thing's already seen us, don't you doubt that." She tugged at her cowl. "We'll ride slow and steady till we're a quarter mile, maybe a little more, past the snoop."

"Past?" Tuli blinked. "Oh."

Teras grinned. "And come back through the trees."

"Didn't think I'd need to explain."

Tuli eased a hand down along her thigh and rubbed gently at the sores. After a minute she said, "If Da is there, what are we going to do about that trax?"

Rane dipped and tapped on a flat leather case behind her right leg. "Crossbow," she said. "Its range is longer than those lethal slings of yours." When she straightened and saw Tuli's face, she shook her head. "I'm not making fun of you, child. Are you as good as your brother?"

"She's better, 'specially at night." Teras touched Tuli's arm.

Tuli closed her hand about his, happy with this renewal of their closeness. "Maybe I can see better'n him, but he can sling harder and farther."

Rane nodded slowly. "I see." Her head tipped forward, she brooded in silence as they slowly drew closer to the circling trax. It was bigger, like a child with great leathery wings. The air near the surface of the Highroad was still, the only sound the clack-pad of the clawed feet on the resilient paving, but high overhead the clouds were spilling, wind-driven, from be-

hind the peaks and spreading out across the Plain, veiling the
pale light from TheDom while he was still low in the east.
"Maiden curse them!" Rane slammed a hand down hard on
the saddle ledge, then soothed her startled mount. She jerked
the cowl off her head again, her short hair standing out from
her head like tumbled straw. "Look here, Tuli, Teras." She
pressed the hair back from her face, tapped at her temple. "I
hate this, it shouldn't be necessary." She straightened her
shoulders. "This is a good place to hit if you want to lay a
man out with your slings. You'll either kill him or put him out
of action for a good long while. If his back is to you . . ."
she bent her head forward, felt at it with long strong fingers.
"Here. Try to hit about here. If his hair isn't too thick." She
straightened. "If it is or he's wearing something on his head,
one of you sting him, the other be ready for the temple when
he swings around. If you're lucky. He could dive for cover
and make a nuisance of himself instead." She went on talking
as their macai walked briskly over the blacktop, giving cap-
sulized advice in a hard, steady voice.

Time passed—and distance—faster than they knew. Tuli
looked up, gasped. The trax was directly overhead, drifting
ominously on the wind. It was huge. She gaped at it. Far
huger than she'd thought even when Teras relayed what Hars
had told him. Vast and shadowy in the starless sky. Vast and
terrifying. She couldn't look away. She tried to swallow but
there was a huge lump shutting her throat.

"Tuli." Rane shook her loose from her paralysis. "Don't
look at it, just keep riding." She smiled tightly. "Not that I
blame you. That one's twenty times the size of most traxim."

Tuli nodded. Though she still couldn't speak, Teras asked
the question plaguing her. "How much longer?" he whispered.

"We'll see. Watch the roadside, twins. The trax came back
to look at us, but it's been doing most of its circling about a
quarter of a mile ahead." She loosened the reins a bit and her
macai scratched into a slow canter, pulling ahead of them.
Tuli rode closer to Teras, shivering and unhappy.

They cantered past an oval clearing, another campsite.
Near the trees was a small herd of grazing macain, hobbled
and enclosed within a wide circle of rope tied from tree to
tree, from spear to spear, the short stabbing spears of the
guards, by them a guard sitting cross-legged on the grass. In
the center of the clearing there were more guards moving
about a fire. Tuli held back her excitement until the guards

were out of sight behind the fringe of trees, then she leaned
over and dropped her hand on her brother's arm. "Did you
see? Wasn't that Patch?"

"I saw him," Teras muttered. A muscle was jumping beside
his mouth. Under Tuli's hand his arm was rock-hard with
tension.

She took her hand away, struggling to control a growing
fear and the surge of rage that threatened to burn away all
reason from her brain. Her father's favorite mount, the one
he'd ridden when he left three—no—four nights ago, she was
sure of it, that big splash of ocher on his flank like a distorted
handprint. *He's there,* she thought, *he has to be. Just because
I didn't see him . . . they wouldn't have. . . .* "No!" She
kicked her heels into her mount's sides, sending him into a
scrambling trot until she was riding beside Rane again. "He's
there," she said in an urgent whisper. "We saw his macai."

Rane said nothing but after a few more strides of her
mount she pointed to the trees and edged the macai down the
embankment, Teras and Tuli following close behind. Still
silent, the three of them rode into the thick shadows under
the trees. When the road was out of sight, Rane stopped
beside a large spikul and slid from the saddle. Holding the
reins loosely in her left hand she settled herself on one of the
larger airroots and waited for the twins to dismount and drop
their reins, ground-hitching their more placid beasts. "You're
sure?"

Teras nodded. Tuli beat her fist against her thigh. "Patch,"
she said, her voice cracking.

"You didn't see your father?" When they shook their
heads, she sighed, stood and knotted the macai's reins to the
airroot. "Then we better take a look at that camp. Those
guards, hunh! Town-bred and easy meat for experienced
night creepers like the two of you." She tousled Tuli's short
mop with a quick pass of her hand. "Thing to remember,
though, twins, is they could get lucky. So you're going to be
very, very careful. For your father's sake. And you, Tuli, you
keep that temper hitched. You hear me?"

Tuli stiffened. "I'm not stupid."

"Easy to say. I'll see." She reached out and caught Tuli's
arm as she started off. "Listen, both of you. Think before you
do. Saves a lot of doing over. Now, I counted five macain in
that herd. You say one was your father's. Which means that's
a guard tercet. We'll wait till they bed down, cut down
the odds that way. Two on, two off, that's the usual watch

pattern. One will stay with the macain, the other should rove, but probably won't, lazy bastard." Her hands lowered onto her thighs, fingers trembling. She stared at the ground, kicked back against the springing arching airroots. "It's wrong, dammit." She lifted her head. "When we hit, go for the kill if you can."

Tuli nodded, feeling fierce. "We can do what we have to."

Rane's mouth twitched into a quick half-smile. "You might find that a bit harder than you think." She stopped Tuli's protest with an upraised hand. "Argue later if you want to." Her eyes flicked from Tuli to Teras and back. "If you get shaky, think of what they're going to do to your father. Come on, we'll go take a look—and I mean just a look, you hear?" Without waiting for an answer, she slipped into the shadow, moving like a shadow herself, fading through the tangled underbrush as if she had no feet.

Three guards sat by their fire, sipping at mugs of cha, their faces fire-red and shadow black. The clouds were thick over the moons now, very little light trickling through their boiling dust. Tuli crouched behind a thin screen of brush, her eyes sweeping the shadows. At first she couldn't see any sign of her father. She strained forward. Teras's hand was hard and hot on her shoulder.

Near the back of the clearing beyond the edge of the firelight there was a moonglow sapling. A man was tied to the slim trunk. A broad, sturdy man. The slowly rising wind stirred through the fire and momentarily brightened it, the light lifting to the man's face. Tuli sucked in a breath. Teras dropped his head, his mouth against her ear. "Da?" he breathed. She nodded. Tesc's hands were pulled around behind the trunk. Dark rope lines crossed and recrossed his torso. Several windings around his throat held his head tight against the tree. His eyes were open and there was a grim hard look on his round face.

Tuli touched her brother's hand. When Teras took it away, she stood and faded back into the shadow under the trees until she was far enough from the clearing to speak without the men hearing her whispered words. Rane drifted up to join them.

"He's there," Tuli whispered. "Tied to a tree."

"I saw," Rane murmured.

"You found the fourth guard?" Teras asked.

"Watching the macain. Half-asleep." Rane looked down at

her hands. "I was tempted to take him out. Would've been easy."

"What do we do now? Just wait?" Tuli moved impatiently.

"Right. Just wait." Rane tapped Tuli's cheek with a long forefinger. "Can you?"

Tuli sniffed. "As easy as either of you."

In the clearing two of the guards were rolled up in their blankets, one of them snoring like a whistle. The guard on duty moved restlessly about, stamping around the sleepers. Now and then he tossed a chunk of wood on the fire, now and then he kicked wood chips into the darkness under the trees. He ignored the prisoner, glanced repeatedly and with a sullen resentment at the blanket-wrapped form of his Tercel. Now and then he stared up at the black shape still drifting overhead, riding the rising wind with no effort, stared up and muttered about stinking demons, then went on slumping about the clearing, blind to everything he was supposed to be watching, sunk in a thorough bad temper.

Tuli dipped her hand into her jacket pocket, smoothed her fingertips over the stones that made it bulge. Now that the time to act was on her, she felt cold inside at the thought of killing a man, even such a loser as that guard. It had seemed easy when she wasn't looking at him. She worked her mouth, remembering what Hars said, that she'd know it wasn't a game when she had to kill someone. Her fingers slipped over the stones, feeling their cool roundness, hearing the tiny clinks as they knocked together. She fixed her eyes on the dark skin under the sweep of the thin stringy hair, sought to convince herself that it was the same thing as the lappets and scutters she'd used as targets to hone her skill. She shut out the moving man, the sullen animal face, focused on that curve of the temple.

Rane came drifting back, warned them of her presence with a brief breathy hiss. She dropped onto her knees beside Teras. "Time to go. I've taken out the fourth guard."

Tuli drew her sling through her fingers, trying to keep them from shaking. "Say when," she growled, almost forgetting to keep her voice low.

Rane bent back, bracing herself on one arm. She hooked to her crossbow she'd left leaning against an airroot, rested it on her knees while she straightened, wobbled, caught her balance. Patting the stock, she said, "When I skewer the trax." She got to her feet with a quick smooth unfolding.

"Start around to your father now, Teras. Wait till Tuli drops the walking guard before you begin cutting him loose."

Teras nodded, jumped to his feet and disappeared into the thick, steamy darkness. Tuli fumbled through the stones in her pocket, shaking with a cold that had nothing to do with the air around her. For a minute she had no feeling in her fingers. She went still, breathed deeply. And a stone was cool against her fingers, fit like an egg against the curve of her palm. She brought it out and set it against the pocket of the sling, held it there pinched between thumb and forefinger, got slowly to her feet.

Rane laid the back of her hand gently against Tuli's cheek. "If you can't, don't fret about it." Then she was gone, heading for the road side of the clearing where she'd have open space for her bow.

The trax was a triangular shape against the cloud blanket, growing in size when it dipped lower, shrinking again as it climbed. Tuli didn't see the bolt fly, only saw the trax flounder suddenly, the great wings losing their grip on the wind, starting to beat irregularly. With a harsh cry that reverberated like high-pitched thunder across the treetops, the demon fell, tumbling over and over, sweeping toward the east as the wind caught at the lifeless, now clumsy wings.

At the first flutter Tuli swung the sling over her head, her eyes fixed on the hollow curve of the guard's temple. He was gaping up at the falling dead thing, making a perfect target of himself. With the trees whispering loudly around her, she forced everything else from her mind and swung the sling faster and faster until it sang over her head.

She released the stone, waited, bent forward tautly, her eyes on the guard.

His eyes rolled back, the stone bounced away in eerie silence, the sound when it crunched into flesh and bone swallowed by the wind. His knees bent. With a slow awkward grace his body folded, melted in on itself and hit the ground without a sound, the sounds of his abrupt dying lost in louder noises, the ordinary noises of the windy night.

Tuli straightened, numb again. It seemed rather terrible to her that she felt nothing. She looked away and saw the sleepers thrashing about, tangled in their blankets, startled from sleep by the dying cry of the demon, the crash of its body through the trees. With stiff fingers she fumbled for another stone.

Rane came flying across the clearing. One guard was dead

before he was fully awake, his throat cut with an almost careless flick of her knife. The other managed to kick away the
encumbering blanket, scoop up his sword and leap back. Before he was set, Rane had the dead man's sword and was attacking.

Tuli came slowly into the clearing, the sling dangling from
her fingers. All her life she'd heard tales of fighting meien,
but hadn't believed that much of what she heard because
she'd met dozens of meien pairs stopping the night at her father's Tar or spending a fest in Cymbank and couldn't imagine any of them hurting anyone. What she saw happening in
front of her was therefore unreal, she saw it but couldn't
really take it in.

Tesc came from under the trees, rubbing at his wrists
where the ropes had left deep red marks, Teras grinning at
his side, eyes shining. Tesc stopped beside Tuli, touched her
on the shoulder but said nothing. She glanced at him, moved
closer until she was leaning against him, then went back to
watching the contest in front of her.

Rane's cowl was pushed back. Her face was serene. She
seemed to look past and through the guard. Their swords
floated before them, flickering into shimmering dances without contact, dance, dance, contact, a soft slither of steel
against steel over almost before it started, recoil, return. She
was long and lean and fast enough to blur sight when she
needed to be, apparently tireless, shifted out of ordinary time
into a state that let her see and react without need for
thought. The guard was a big dark man with long arms and a
rangy, well-muscled body. He fought grimly, knowing he was
the stronger, trying to overbear the blade that seemed like
smoke when he came against it. A cut opened on his arm, another high on his thigh. He began breathing harder. Sweat
glistened on his face. Rane was unmarked, unhurried, her
breathing as even as if she were out for a stroll under the
scatter of moons.

"Zhagbitch!" the guard spat at her; he attacked furiously,
filling the clearing with the tink-hiss of sword clashing with
sword, driving Rane back and back, expending his strength
recklessly, gambling that he could batter her into brush or
against a tree where her greater speed and skill would be ne-
gated. She slipped from one trap to another, turning and
twisting like an eel in a net, baiting him with possibility, running him off his feet, watching, always watching, no ex-

pression in her face, her eyes calm, remote, infuriating beyond sense.

His blade faltered. There was fear in his eyes, a realization that his gamble was lost. He backed away as her point, adder swift, flicked at face and body, backed again, stumbled as his feet tangled in one of the abandoned blankets. As if her arm were somehow connected with his feet, her blade darted past his faltering guard and slipped effortlessly between his ribs, out his back. She dropped the hilt and leaped away, stood watching as he folded quietly down, his dark eyes bulging, his mouth stretched wide in a silent scream. The point of the sword caught on the grass and tipped him onto his side so he curled up like a sleeper on the blanket that had betrayed him. When he was still, she knelt beside him, closed his staring eyes. "Maiden give you rest," she murmured. Then she stood, crossed the clearing and stopped in front of Tesc. "Good to see you again, tarom."

"Rane." Tesc studied her face. "How goes it with you?"

"Well enough."

Tuli stared at Rane. The serenity was gone from her face. She looked old and tired and deeply melancholic as if the sadness and pain of the world sat on her shoulders. She glanced up at the breathing clouds, sighed, looked down, smiled at Tuli, her face warming briefly, then she turned more briskly to Tesc. "Ready to ride, tarom? I think we'd best be far from here when more traxim come to investigate the death of that one."

CHAPTER VIII:

THE QUEST

The valley stretched out below them, long and sinuous like a sleeping dragon tamed by a patchwork coat of field and farm. Clean and rested, her stomach comfortably full, Serroi followed Hern along the flint trace and onto a stingy path that wound past the edges of the higher terraces, a hard stony track barely wide enough to accommodate macai pads. Fifty terraces and a scatter of farms below, riverMinar swung lazily between a double line of trees, dots of chrysophrase and peridot, olivine and emerald, and clumps of giant reeds, strokes of saffron and jade against the water's azure, under the narrow wooden bridges lovely even from this height, and—far in dusty blue distance, it slipped without fuss into a terraced city packed behind shimmering sapphire walls. She gazed a while at the palaces of Skup wavering like mirages against the sky, at a few stray glitters beyond them from the Sinadeen.

The sun rose higher, a normal sun this side of the Vachhorns. There were minarka working already on the lower terraces, loosening soil about the plants, pulling weeds, some few emptying bulbous waterbags into the small areas within the earthen dams raised about each plant, hoarding the water with such care not a drop was wasted. The minarka looked up as Hern and Serroi passed, blinked dark eyes at them without much interest and even less welcome, then went back to their work. They were small and slender, even the men, with long limbs and short torsos, all shades of brown from deep amber to burnt honey, with darker brown hair and umber eyes. Both men and women wore short wrap-around skirts and sleeveless shirts tucked behind broad sashes wound round and round before they were knotted at the side. Some of the older men and women wore sandals of braided straw, many of the younger went barefoot.

Serroi began to envy them their cool clothing as she followed Hern lower and lower down the mountains, dropping

142

into the dry heat of the Vale. The long narrow valley lay between two mountain ranges, getting little rain but enjoying a
vastly extended growing season, its fertility a gift of riverMinar. The minarka on the terraces were most likely tending the
third planting of the year.

As the track flattened, its nature changed. It broadened until it was cart-wide and the surface was no longer hard mud
or stone but sun-baked brick painted with soft pastels like
colored dust and set in patterns of delicate symmetry. Listening to macai claws clicking on the brick, Serroi rubbed her
nose and contemplated Hern's back. The black tunic was
hanging straighter. The fat was melting off his sturdy frame
though he never stopped grumbling about the meagerness of
trail rations. The pavement flowing past was neat as a house
floor as if someone weeded around it and swept it every day.
The verges bloomed with fall flowers or had miniature trees
and mosses arranged in exquisite landscapes. Serroi stroked
her lips, swallowing a chuckle (Hern was in no mood for
laughter of any kind, especially that directed at him), wondering which he'd head for first once they reached Skup-
port—a brothel or a cookshop? The fields beyond the verges
were enclosed in low stone walls, fieldstone carefully fitted together without the aid of mortar. She thought of riding beside
him and coaxing him out of his sullens, then shook her head.
Not yet. Within the walls the minarka farmed on three levels,
fruit trees in neat rows, between them taller plants of various
sorts strapped to strung wire supports, between these,
ground-hugging plants—berries, tubers, bulbvines, root vege-
tables. *I wonder what he saw in the deadland's dust?* she
thought for the hundredth time and for the hundredth time
recoiled from the thought, exceedingly reluctant to remember
her own visions, and wondered again, unable to leave the
image alone. Whole families were working in their plots,
from the tiniest who could barely toddle but who could carry
away the debris of other minarks' work to ancients who
moved with inching deliberation but handled the plants with
great love and greater skill. When Hern came through the Viper's Gullet he looked subdued, withdrawn. Even when he
splashed vigorously, noisily in the cold, clean water in the
Cisterns, he kept some of that brooding melancholy. He came
to her, clean and sleek and fed, seeking another kind of comfort—and was turned down hard (perhaps harder than she'd
really intended; she was fighting her own ghosts and had
nothing left for him but anger). All of the minarka, even the

youngest, straightened as Serroi and Hern rode past and
stared at them from dark, hating, hostile eyes. Once when she
looked back, she saw young children industriously sweeping
the bricks as if to brush away any sign or taint of the
strangers' passage. Her anger fired Hern's. Their hard-won
accord shattered about them and they flung unforgivable
words at each other, yet they couldn't leave each other, there
was no place to go, the land bound them to each other. The
heat, natural here even this late in the year, was unbearable.
She wiped at the sweat on her forehead and eased out of the
blue wool jacket. She pulled loose the neckties of Beyl's shirt,
sighing with pleasure as the gentlest of breezes caressed her
sweaty skin. *Just as well I'm not wearing the leathers,* she
thought. *They'd rot right off me.*

The road dipped slightly, went round a clump of olivine
weepers and turned onto a wooden bridge, a single humped
curve with a lovely arch and side rails of bent and molded
watercane. Serroi exclaimed with pleasure. Hern looked back
for the first time since they'd started down the mountain,
raised his brows, then urged his macai onto the bridge.

Serroi stopped at the top of the arch. A comparatively cool
breeze was drifting along with the water. She drew her sleeve
across her face, looked at the brown stain on the fine white
cloth with distaste, looked at the blue-green water and sighed,
started on after Hern.

He was waiting for her in the shade of a clump of watercane. With a flip of a hand at the sun, he said, "Time to eat."

Again suppressing a smile, Serroi nodded, slid out of the
saddle and stood bending her knees and kicking briskly to
work some of the stiffness out of her legs, gazing thoughtfully
at the bridge and the river. "Be better to get out of sight;
those minarka back there weren't exactly friendly." Without
waiting for an answer she led her macai around the reeds and
along the riverbank.

A tree grew out of the water, some of its roots clinging to
the gently sloping bank, the dirt washed away from the others, a weeper with dark yellow-grey-green leaves like flat
teardrops on fawn and saffron withes that hung to the water,
ticking at the surface, dancing and swaying with the wind.
Serroi led her macai to the water beside this tree. As the
beast drank, she pulled off her boots, rolled up her trousers
(dark blue wool, Braddon's gift), dug into her saddlebags for
the nourishing but monotonous trail bars (nuts, dried fruits,
honey) and the tough strips of jerky. Dropping Hern's share

into a shallow pannikin, she set it down on the grass and took her own food to the tree, where she straddled a root and dangled her feet in the eddies teasing at the other roots. She ate slowly, relaxed except for a niggling little itch that continued to plague her, a warning of some danger to come or simply her own reaction to the near stifling hostility that filled the Vale.

Once his mount was drinking Hern stripped off his tunic, tossed it down beside the pannikin. He dumped the bars and jerky on the tunic and used the pannikin to dip water from the river which he dumped over his head and torso. With a sigh of relief he settled on a patch of grass, pulled off his boots and inspected his feet. The abraded places were still faintly pink but had healed without sign of infection. The blisters were redder but they too were healing. He wiggled his toes and looked at the water, then at Serroi. Grunting with the effort it took to bend that far, he rolled his trousers above his knees, scooped up his food and came over to the tree. He found a stouter root, settled with his back against the trunk, his feet in the water. His eyelids came down sleepily over his pale eyes as he contemplated her a moment, then he looked down at what he held in his hand and grimaced. He began eating, chewing slowly as if he wanted to make the meager meal last as long as possible. Except for several considering glances, he didn't acknowledge her presence.

Serroi brushed her hands off, bent precariously and dipped first one hand then the other into the water, swishing them about, straightened, slanting a glance at Hern, daring him to match her acrobatics. Smiling, she wiped her hands dry on her trousers, kicked her feet gently in the water. "Sulky little baby boy," she murmured, her voice a whisper just loud enough for him to hear.

He chewed steadily, his eyes on the swaying withes. In his face or body there was no sign he heard her.

"The meie's always right. You said it."

He brushed the sticky crumbs from his hands, but he made no attempt to reach the water. Lacing his fingers behind his head, he stared dreamily at the river and the withe tips, at the ever changing shadows breaking and reforming on the water.

"Hern, I don't know what you saw in the dust." He stiffened as if she'd flicked him with a whip. "I can only hope your ghosts weren't as . . . as troubling as mine." It was an indirect apology for the things she'd said to him at the Cisterns. If she had to, she'd say the words; for her own pride's sake, she'd rather not. If he made her say them, it would be deliberate; she had (she hoped) stopped underestimating his intelligence and sensitivity.

He folded his hands over his shrinking paunch. "You've got a nasty tongue when you turn it loose."

"You're no gentle soul yourself, Dom."

"It'll probably happen again, cutting at each other like that."

"Probably." She kicked her foot up, watched the crystal drops fall back. "I've always felt that grudges were a profitless waste of time and energy."

Hern smiled. "I'm a lazy man, meie."

Feeling absurdly buoyant, she balanced on her root and grinned at him. "As long as we know."

"Uh-huh." He glanced up at the fragments of sun visible through the leaves. "Hate to say it, but we better get moving if we want to reach Skup by sundown."

They rode through a silent land, the laughter and high-pitched gabbling of the minarka dying away as soon as the strangers were spotted. Hern's face grew slowly grimmer as he took in what she'd sensed so strongly before. "They'd make a fine mob," he said finally. "Better than that bunch in Sadnaji."

"They've had more experience with Assurtilas as a neighbor. We should be safe enough as long as we stay on the road and don't bother them."

"I would like to depend on that."

"They're used to Sleykynin riding through the Vale, going from Assurtilas to the Mijloc; they've learned to leave them alone if they stick to the road."

"Good for them. But we're not Sleykyn."

"The habit should hold."

"Habit." He snorted, then looked about. "I haven't seen any houses."

"They live in walled villages." Serroi wiped at her face. "Maiden bless, it's hot. Villages built on the least fertile ground, of course."

"Walled?"

"Sleykyn raids. When they don't keep to the road."

They crossed the river twice more as its wide bends swept it away and back, then away again. Not long after the second bridge, when the sun was perching on the points of the Vachhorns, the road widened and the plantings ceased. Herds of hauhaus and rambuts—cream-colored hooved beasts with crimson strips running vertically along their barrel bodies—grazed on the grassy pasturage that lay before the high blue walls of Skup. Straight ahead of them, on the far side of a broad moat, two high square towers flanked the gates of Skup. The outer gate was higher than two houses and made of ironwood planks, a wood so dense it weighed as much as the metal it was named for. Behind the ironwood gates, black iron gates stood open. Only closed in wartime, they were oiled daily and moved a little on their hinges. The minarka took no chances. Skup had never fallen, not even when the Mad Prime of Assurtilas two centuries before had assembled a Sleykyn army and burned the rest of the Vale to dust and ashes. Serroi saw with relief that the outer gates were still open. She glanced at Hern. He was scanning the walls, his eyes narrowed, a measuring intentness in his face. "Dom."

"Mmmmh. You know who built those walls? When this is over. . . ."

Serroi pulled her mount to a slow shuffle and waited for him to match his speed to hers. "Do you speak the sulMinar?"

"No. Why should I? There was. . . ."

"No need before." She tilted her head, ran her eyes over him, grinned when she finished. "Probably just as well you don't."

"And what's that supposed to mean?"

"That you're less likely to get us skinned."

Hern looked pained. "Viper."

"O mighty one."

"Crawl for them?"

"Want to spend the night with the hauhaus?"

"Not especially."

"Thing to remember is that most of the minarks in the High Palaces . . ." She nodded at the villas on the higher terraces partly visible above the walls, catching the colors of the sunset in their glittering sides. "They're getting madder by the moment, apt to act on whatever thought flits through their crazy heads. Which can be very dangerous to the hapless passerby. We'll have to hope we can avoid being noticed, that's the safest way through Skup."

"Why not go around?"

"Can't. The walls go into the sea, faced with tiles like those." She flicked a hand at the blue walls (turning purple now as they sucked in red light from the sunset). "Too slippery to climb and too high to jump." She rubbed at her eyes, patted a yawn. "Maiden bless, I'm tired. That's the only gate. Let me do the talking."

His brows lifted, then he said amiably, "Viper."

Serroi patted her macai's neck. "Poor man, his brain's rotting. That's all he can say now."

"If I answer that, we will be here till morning." He looked around at the herd of blocky hauhaus grazing close by. "I can think of pleasanter bedmates." He kneed his beast into a faster walk, his brows rising again as he took in the guard strolling to the center of the gate.

The minark wore elaborately chased and gilded plating. Three tall white plumes swayed above a gilded helmet whose outer surface was molded into spikes that glistened in the light from the setting sun. His long thin legs were uncovered from mid-thigh to ankle, his feet thrust into gilded sandals. He stood waiting for them to come across the drawbridge, leaning on the pole of a halberd whose head shimmered like silver above the sway of the plumes. Hern's eyes narrowed.

"Watch it, Dom," Serroi whispered.

"Stop nagging at me, meie, you're worse than Floarin in a bitchy mood." Reason prevailed over irritation so he kept his voice low, though he scowled at her.

"I like my skin, Dom, even if it is green. I want to keep it right where it is, wrapped around my bones." She sniffed, then lifted her head, her eyes twinkling, the corners of her mouth twitching. "Relax, man, and remember you're no longer Domnor of Oras and the Plains. Here, now, you're a beggar. No, less than a beggar. If it helps, so am I."

He shook his head, tilted it and contemplated her. "You look like a scruffy boy. Why should you have such a boundless capacity for annoying me?" His rueful grin dissolved into a scowl. "I'm not a half-witted infant."

They stopped before the guard, waiting with an assumed patience while he inspected them. Hern slumped in the saddle, looking sleepily moronic. *He's not the half-witted one,* she thought, *I am.* When the guard spoke, she blinked, then forced her tired brain to take in his words, her mind having to shift from the mijlocker she'd just been speaking to the sulMinar she was hearing.

". . . want?" the guard finished.

Serroi blinked again, bowed as low as she could. Picking

careful between phrases, she addressed him in the seeker's mode, low to high. "If the magnificent one before me in whose shadow this one is unworthy to stand, the incomparable and compassionate guardian of this most glorious of cities, this worm beneath his feet would contrive to find the words in his ignoble head to reply." It was hard to keep her face straight as she mouthed this nonsense, but minark culture demanded this formalized hypocrisy.

Mollified by the string of compliments and the mode of address, the guard preened himself and repeated the question. "Where you going, slave-dung, and what do you want here?" His blunt speech was the worst of insults but Serroi was glad enough to get to the point that quickly. The sun was almost gone and the guard was quite capable of shutting the gate in their faces.

She bowed again, slipping her fingers quickly into the pouch hanging at her side, drawing out two of Yael-mri's grudged gold coins. With them concealed in her hand, she spoke again. "Oh most honorable and warlike of guardians before whom these worms tremble, this useless and disgusting uncle of this person who is less than the dust on your divine feet and he who speaks these stumbling words have ridden across the Mountains of the Dead at the bidding of They-Who-Heal. It is required that we take ship at Skup and proceed on their business. This one who is blinded by the glory of your person. . . ." She let one of the coins fall as she raised her hand and placed it before her face, fingers spread, thumb holding the second coin against her palm. ". . . must ask passage through this domain of mind-dazzling glory. Noble sir, may this unworthy one note that in the liberality of your wealth you have dropped a trifle of gold. Doubtless you have so many coins that it has escaped your notice."

The guard's eyes searched the paving stone. The breath hissed between his teeth when he spotted the golden round. He scooped it up, tucked it into a pouch, then began looking round again.

Greedy bastard, Serroi thought. She dropped the second coin.

The minark straightened, sneered at them, then waved them past. "Keep to the low way, dung."

As they rode through the ironwood gate, he stood watching them, making no move as yet to close the gate behind them. They rode past the towers that looked down on the open way between ironwood and ironmetal gates, their shiny blue surfaces pierced at various levels by bow slits. When Hern and Serroi emerged from between the black iron gates glistening with oil, they passed into a narrow ugly street more like a posser-run than anything men should be expected to traverse. On both sides of the inner gate, ornate grills shut off wider streets that climbed steeply up and around the dark foliage of stiff, spear-like conifers. Hern glanced at these, then ahead. The corner of his mouth twitched up, but he made no comment.

The low way was a narrow cobbled passage between two high, dirty walls. On each side of the roadway were deep stinking gutters filled with sewage and scraps of garbage. The farther they got into the city, the more noxious the air became. Hern wrinkled his nose. "They make it obvious what they think of us."

Serroi yawned and immediately regretted it. "What I told you." The street curved sharply some distance ahead. She straightened, stretched out a hand to stop Hern as she heard a blare of horns, several instruments played loudly with no attempt at anything but noisemaking. "Maiden grant. . . ." She heard a clatter of hooves, high giggling laughter in between the blasts of noise, cursed softly, looked up to meet Hern's startled gaze. She urged her macai to the edge of the gutter and motioned Hern to ride close behind her. "A Brissai," she said quickly. "Young minarks from the High Terraces out on a tear, juiced to the ears on dream dust or worse and up to any mischief that appeals to them. Chasing some unfortunate, sounds like." She chewed on her lip, anxious eyes on Hern's face. "If they only push us into the gutter and sweep on past, we'll be lucky."

"Into that?"

"A little stink is better than a skinning, and that's the nicest thing that will happen to us if we so much as touch one of them." The sounds were coming rapidly nearer, more raucous than ever. "They're after blood. Don't move, don't say anything no matter what, don't even breathe."

She heard the pattering of bare feet on the cobbles then a ragged furtive little man bleeding from hundreds of small wounds came stumbling around the curve. He was so blind with his terror he blundered past them without seeing them, struggling to reach the great gates before they were shut.

The Brissai came round the bend a moment later, five young men in loose robes that whipped open about naked

golden bodies. Long loose tresses of russet hair fluttered in
the stinking air, golden eyes were fire-hot, golden skin wore a
film of sweat, not from exertion but from emotional extrava-
gance. They rode sleek rambuts with silken ribbons braided
into their crimson manes, strips of azure and silver, red and
gold and green, fluttering in the wind of their tempestuous
passage. Each youth carried a long slender rod with a
needle-spiked knob at the end of it. The leader saw Serroi
and Hern, pulled his mount to a sliding halt, sitting the
plunging beast with the easy grace of a superb rider. He
looked lovingly at them, delight shining in his metallic eyes, a
tender smile on his delicately curved lips. With an unregarded
grace, he pointed at the stumbling fugitive. "Ban Abbal, get
that."

One of the five rode after the little man and smashed the
spiked ball into the back of his head. The minark went on a
few strides then jerked his mount around and forced it to
trample on the small body before he left it lying, flung out on
the cobbles like a bit of rubbish and came back to the Brissai.

The leader danced his mount closer to Serroi. "Green," he
said, then laughed, the sound like music above the clatter of
the nervous rambut's hooves. "The boy has green skin." The
snickers of the other four sounding behind him, he twitched
the rambut two steps sideways. "And a fat man. A little fat
man full of juice." He giggled and prodded at Hern's shoulder with the ball of needles, their points sliding easily through
the black cloth to pierce the flesh beneath. Hern sat without
moving, without even a wince, his eyes fixed on the cobbles.

The minark looked at the blood on the spikes, smiled
sweetly. "Little fat man's so stupid he can't feel." The look in
his eyes heated to a glare, his playfulness changing to rage as
if he sensed the pride and strength behind Hern's unim-
pressive exterior. He rode his rage with a light hand, taunting
Hern, jeering at him, punctuating the jeers with passes of the
needle ball. Small cuts opened on Hern's hands and face,
trickles of blood crept through his tunic and trousers, though
he sat stolidly until the highborn started swiping at his eyes.
Even when the ball danced in front of his face, though he
was pale with fury and frustration, Hern kept himself under
control, moving just enough to save his eyes.

The other four were beginning to get bored. They milled
back and forth past the intent pair, hooting and yipping.
They sniped verbally at Serroi, teased at her hair with their
needle balls, but otherwise left her alone. She belonged to

their leader, his prey after Hern. *He must be Falam's kin at least, a son maybe,* she thought. *Highest of the high. Maddest of the mad. He's going to kill Hern. No way we can make it to the Port. Have to get out of here.* She closed her eyes and fumbled for the rambuts; the beasts were strange to her and slippery, a little mad like their riders. She couldn't read them well enough, was taking a long time to control them, too long.

The minark raked the needle ball down the side of Hern's face, laying it open to the bone. With a roar, Hern snatched the rod away, his strength waking a spark of fear in the minark's golden eyes, flipped it over and used the butt of the rod to punch the youth in the stomach, driving him backwards off the rambut, spilling him into a particularly evil-smelling section of gutter.

As he splashed down with a shirek of mindless rage, Serroi finally got the hold she wanted and sent the rambuts stampeding toward the gate. "Hern, this way," she yelled and kicked her macai into a plunging run after the beasts and their struggling riders. Hern bent low over the neck of his mount and followed after, laughing with satisfaction and derision at the minark youth, stained and filthy, cursing, slipping, clawing his way out of the gutter.

The guards were beginning to close the ironwood gates for the night, but fell back before the wild panic of the rambuts and their near helpless riders, recognizing their status even if they didn't know their faces. Serroi and Hern bowled through the gap before the guards could react. As soon as they were across the bridge, Serroi swerved to one side so Hern wouldn't plow into her and pulled up. She closed her eyes again and stabbed deeper into the rambuts. They began bucking and sunfishing, rearing and flinging themselves into reckless leaps, went to their knees, rolled with abandon until they were free of their riders. Leaving the minark youths groaning on the grass, they ran wildly across the pasture land plunging through several herds, scattering the hauhaus and rambuts there into terrified flight. Drained by her outreach, swaying in the saddle, Serroi let her control fade.

Hern edged his macai closer, caught her as she almost fell. "Very nice. What now?"

Serroi scratched delicately along the periphery of her eyespot, trying to get her weary mind to think. "Back," she said finally. "The Sleykyn road. East."

"You all right?"

"Will be. I can stick in the saddle."

"They chase after us?" He twisted around, clicked his tongue against his palate as he saw one of the guards running toward a draggled screaming figure limping over the cobbles and pointing a shaking finger at the pair sitting their macai beyond the bridge. "That answers that." He kicked his macai into an easy lope. Serroi settled herself more comfortably in the saddle and sent her macai loping after him, frowning as she wondered how much the beasts had left in them after a full day's riding.

They were some distance down the side road when she heard the alarum gong ringing out over the valley. "What else?" she muttered. Nijilic TheDom was a handspan above the eastern mountains, flooding the plantings on the left and the pastures on the right with shimmering white light though he was several days past his prime, a light she could have easily done without because it silhouetted them far too clearly against the pale earth of the rutted road.

"What's that for?"

"The gong? That's to warn the pass guards to watch for us and stop us."

He looked across the fields to the towers. "They've got a good view." Still looking back, he grunted with disgust. "Armored troop riding out." He swung around. "They want us bad. Me."

She made a face. "The one you ducked in that muck most likely is the favorite son of the Falam, or close to that. Not your fault," she added hastily. "Nothing else you or I could've done. Bad luck, that's all." She shifted position, stretched carefully. "I could sleep for a week. How's your face?"

"Sore." After a minute he said softly, "I'd like to have that little bastard for just five minutes."

"He's probably warped enough to enjoy a bit of beating."

With a bark of laughter he ran a hand through his hair, "Right again, meie."

"Right, hunh!"

The land began to rise. The mountains ahead were worn, their contours rounded as if their substance had been eaten by time. Sounds floated along the road, carried on the east wind that rustled in the grass and tugged at their hair, sounds of hooves on paving bricks, the clatter of armor. The turnoff was hidden by a gentle swell of the ground but she knew the minarka were close behind and getting closer by the minute—and they couldn't push the macai harder without running them into the ground.

Hern bent forward and patted his laboring mount on the shoulder, murmured encouragement to the tired beast. When he straightened, he said, "We going somewhere or just running?"

"Both. First we've got to get out of the Vale." She paused. "Next, we've still got to get across the Sinadeen. That means Shinka-on-the-Neck, since Skup is now thoroughly closed to us."

"Shinka." He said it like a curse. "An extra passage at least."

"Looks like."

"Pass guards. How many? How good are they?"

"Four. Sweepings. Punishment detail. Not really guards, more like sentries, watching for Sleykyn raiding parties. They've got a gong too."

"Sleykyn. Maiden's tits, Serroi."

"Yah. I know." She yawned, swayed in the saddle again, the ground ahead blurring, swinging, blurring again.

Hern caught hold of her halter and pulled her macai to a stop. Ignoring her protest, he untied his water skin and filled a cup, then threw the water in her face. She gasped. He filled the cup again and handed it to her. "Drink this." He watched her gulp the water down. "You got anything in that magic belt that will wake you up? You're about out on your feet." He grinned. "Or seat in this case."

Serroi rested the cup on the saddle ledge, her fingers searching along the belt for the pocket with the waxy green buttons that gave her energy but exacted a high price in return. She chewed a button, swallowed, washed away the bitter taste with the rest of the water and handed him the cup. "Thanks."

"Self defense. I want you bright and awake when those bastards come over a hill at us."

She wrinkled her nose. "And I was beginning to think you liked me."

The land began to roll more steeply upward toward the ancient mountains; her head began to roll with it. The plantings on the left stopped and there were no more farms, only the hills and knee-length moon-silvered grass with scattered herds of hauhaus, rambuts, woolly linats. They pulsed, growing and shrinking, flicking in and out, visible at the corner of her eyes, gone when she looked directly at them, there when she looked at them, rippling into nothing when she looked away, until she couldn't be certain the herds were really there. It was the drug, she knew, it didn't sit well on an empty stomach. She looked back as she topped one of the hills and saw the band of armored men topping a hill a lot farther behind than she'd expected. She brought her macai to a stop and sat gazing back at them, watching them waver and shift, ballooning into transparent giants, shrinking again.

Hern's voice sounded suddenly at her ear. "The fools, they've overridden those beasts. Look at them wobble." He stroked his macai's neck, chuckling at the beast's groan of pleasure. "Give me a macai any day. Rambuts are all flash and no stay."

The moonlight caught a breastplate and flashed fire at her. She winced, gave a sharp, frightened gasp. White fire from halberds and helmets stabbed at her. She squeezed her eyes shut, opened them, saw nothing at all on the hill and gasped again.

"What's wrong?"

"Nothing there. All gone." Forgetting about the mirage on the hill—maybe a mirage, Hern saw them too—she stared at his face, at the savagely torn cheek, dried blood black in the moons' light. "Let me fix that."

He touched his cheek and winced. "Must be a sight to frighten children." He turned his mount and started down the slight slope toward the next and steeper ascent.

Serroi caught up with him. "No," she said. The word was a black bubble. She blinked at it. "No," she said experimentally, giggled at the drifting black bubble. "No. No. No." The bubbles danced in front of her, went pop! pop! pop! She blinked again and tried to concentrate, having momentarily forgotten what she'd been talking about. "No, you won't scar if I can just tend to your face. I'm good at tending. The Silent Ones, they wanted me to learn healing. My gift, don't deny your gift, only brings trouble, besides you're too little to be a meie. Little. Skinny. Green. Be a nice little healer. Magic. Too much magic in it. Too much like the Noris. No. I'm going to be a meie. Sword and bow and fist. Real things. No magic. Not ever. No and no and no." She giggled again. "I'm stubborn."

"You're also flying high. Can you hear me, Serroi?"

"Uh-huh."

"No time for tending now, we have to get through the pass."

"Uh-huh."

"How long you going to be like this?"

Serroi blinked slowly, spoke even more slowly. "Because no food, I mean Tarr on empty stomach, works too hard. Too fast." She pressed her hand against her eyes. "Don't know."

"Hold up." Hand still on her eyes she heard him breathing hard close to her, felt a tugging on her gear. She would have protested but it didn't seem worth the effort. A moment later a strong hand pulled hers down from her eyes, put a trail bar in it. "Eat that."

She was still nibbling on the bar when they rode into the trees and began the climb to the pass.

High on a mountain slope, stopping a moment to rest her mount, Serroi looked back. "Hern!"

"What is it?"

"Look. They must have switched mounts." The minarka were coming fast out of the band of trees, riding up the steep grade almost at a gallop. "I wasn't dreaming the herds on the hills."

"You can stop the rambuts, turn them around."

She grimaced. "To be honest, I'd rather stop the riders." She unclipped her bow, urged her macai forward at a steady walk, slipped the reins under her knee and rode by balance and thigh-grip alone. Setting the stave on her instep, she strung the bow, tested the pull, drew two arrows from the case by her knee. She frowned at the road ahead, pleased to see several bends as it hugged the side of one mountain and curved against the next. "When they get close enough, if they do, I'll pick off two of them and damp their enthusiasm a bit."

"Thought you didn't like killing."

"I don't." She shrugged. "Mad minarks, no loss to anyone." She sounded flippant, looked miserable. "Maiden bless, Hern, I've killed men before when I had to. And to be honest, I don't know if I could control the rambuts right now." She looked down at the arrows in her hand, sighed, dropped them back in their case. "Maybe they won't catch up."

The pursuing minarks drew inexorably closer. The steep grades of the road were hard on the already weary macain. They started shuffling, stumbling, gulping in air, wheezing it out, letting their heads hang low. Serroi slid off her mount and was quietly pleased when Hern did the same. They started walking, leading their macain, hearing behind them shouts of triumph from the minarka. They went around one bend then another, then started laboriously up a triply looping switchback. On the third and shortest loop Serroi stopped. She took two arrows from the case by her shoulder then handed the reins to Hern. "Go on ahead, Hern."

He touched the side of her face. "You sure?"

"Very." She pointed. "When they come around that bend I'll have a good clear shot at the leaders. And I can be around there before they can shoot back—if they even have bows. I didn't see any." She nodded at the curve behind her.

Hern closed one hand on her shoulder, squeezed it in a wordless expression of fellowship, then began walking away, the macain plodding after him. He was taking short cramped steps, his own strength drained by the long, long day.

Serroi got set, arrow nocked, then eased off stance. She walked back and forth along the short level stretch, afraid her muscles would grow stiff if she stood still too long.

She heard the hooves of the beasts before she saw the riders. Nocking one arrow, holding the other between the last two fingers of her drawing hand, she waited, breathing slowly, steadily, sinking herself into the mindless receptive state she'd labored long to achieve.

Two men came round the bend riding side by side. She pulled, loosed, flipped the second arrow into place, pulled, loosed, then lowered her bow and smiled. The minarks were collapsing off their mounts, arrows lodged in the narrow space between the two sections of chest armor, having sliced neatly through its leather backing. She watched a man crawl hurriedly, nervously, to the bodies and start hauling them back around the bend, then she turned and began walking after Hern.

He was waiting for her around that first turn in the road, sitting on a rock. He got to his feet slowly and stiffly. "Do you ever miss?"

"Not often." She took the reins of her macai and walked on in silence, unwilling right then to say anything more.

The minarka hung back for over an hour though she knew they were coming still, feeling them like a black fog behind her, stubborn in their malice. Again she chose a place of vantage and waited. This time she dropped only one of them because they were riding in single file and more cautious about coming around bends. Hern and Serroi plodded on, winding up and up through the mountains, reaching the saddle of the pass at the end of another hour.

Hern wiped at his neck with a sodden rag. "Still behind?"

"They expect to catch us at the wall."

"Wall?"

"There is a wall of sorts up ahead." She looked back along the trail. The minarka weren't visible yet but they were creeping up again; she picked up a rising expectation and a touch of anticipation. "I didn't tell you about the wall?" She frowned, tried to remember but found recent events too hazy to sort out. "About a mile past the saddle. Road goes through a long narrow canyon. Guardhouse with a well. Gate's usually not barred, they don't try stopping the Sleykynin, just beat the gong once they're through." She started down the long straight incline, stepping carefully over and around the ruts, slanting a glance at Hern. The elegant boots were scuffed, stretched, and beginning to sag at the ankles—far less elegant and far more comfortable than before. But the soles were still thin and slippery; his feet had to be sore and burning. She sighed. Once again she looked back.

A minark stopped at the top of the slope, stared down at them. Another man came up behind him, yelled and beckoned. Serroi dropped the reins and lifted her bow. The minarka scrambled hastily out of sight.

Hern chuckled. "You've got them pretty well trained." He was standing on one foot, leaning against a drooping macai.

She scooped up the dangling reins and slapped her macai on the rump, grimaced at the sorenes of her calves and started down again. "Just as well," she said. "TheDom's getting low and the Jewels don't give much light." She yawned. "Another hour at least."

"Walking." Hern grunted. He looked at the macai pacing beside him. "Walking."

When they reached the canyon floor the night was very dark, very quiet. The guardhouse was a blotch of darker shadow in the shadow of the wall. Serroi patted her macai's shoulder. "Hern," she whispered.

"Mmmh?" The sound came out of the darkness edged with pain and a growing irritation.

"I think they're sleeping up there."

"Good for them."

"I'm not sure, though." She patted the macai again, remounted. "At least they're a little rested. They should be able to carry us long enough." She waited. Hern was a quick-rising blackness. He whooshed as he landed in the saddle, groaned at the pure pleasure of being off his feet.

They reached the gate without a challenge. When Hern bent down to lift the bar, they both heard a long-drawn, whistling snore. "Definitely asleep," he murmured and swung the gate open with the flat of one hand. The snore turned to a juicy sputtering. As Serroi followed Hern through the gap she heard a confused muttering; it grew louder as the negligent guard thrust his head out an embrasure and looked blearily around. "Who there?" He withdrew his head a moment then thrust his shoulders out, a short throwing spear in one hand. "Get back here, you, or I skewer you."

Serroi laughed. "You couldn't hit a mountain with the head you got. Better think about saving your neck," she yelled at him. "Bar the gate again and tell those following us we must've snuck around you somehow." She kept looking back as the guard lowered the spear and considered her words. When he pulled his head back inside, she chuckled again.

"What was all that about?"

"Giving that drunk some good advice. Hush, I want to hear . . . ah!" Behind them the gates swung shut. "Good man. You look after you and let the rest go hang." She raised her arms over her head, twisted her body about, then slumped in the saddle. "Ay-mi, the tarr is beginning to wear off. Hern."

"Hummmh?"

"I'm going to crash any minute."

He rode closer, looked back at the black bulk of the wall. "The minarka?"

She rubbed at her eyes, yawned again. "Wall's it. We're in Sleykyn land now." Sleep was clubbing at her; it was hard to talk, harder to think. She clutched at the saddle ledge feeling horribly insecure as if she were trying to walk underwater and making sorry work of it.

Hern caught hold of her shoulder. "Dammit, Serroi, where do we go from here? Where!"

The pain from his grip, the shouted word penetrated her haze. "East," she thought she said, repeated it when he shook her and demanded an answer. "East," she mumbled.

Hern shook her awake about midmorning. She was roped to the saddle, stretched out along the macai's neck, her arms dangling, every muscle in her body stiff and sore, her head throbbing as if borers were gnawing their way through her skull. He began working the knots loose and in a few minutes she was able to push herself up. She ran her tongue over dry and cracking lips. He was shrouded in dust. His grey-streaked black hair was pasted close to his head and powdered near white with the dust from the track. Weariness was an aura about him nearly as visible as the floating dust. When he put his hand on her knee, she felt it tremble. "Serroi." His voice was harsh, cracking. "Can you find water?"

Water. She touched her tongue to her lips again and tasted the bitter alkalinity of the dust. *Water.* His hand was warm on her knee. She sucked in a breath, winced as her throat hurt, squinted her eyes against the hammering of the light reflected from the white, white, terribly white soil and rock around her. *Water.* His hand was warm and alive, the fingers trembling with weariness. *Water.* Her eyespot throbbed, sought, tasted the air, reached out and out. She twisted her torso about until she faced the direction of the pull; she could almost smell the cool green liveliness of the water. *Good water. Close.* She lifted her arm, faltered as its weight seemed beyond her strength, lifted her arm and pointed. "There." Like him, she croaked through the coating of dust that dried her mouth and thickened her tongue.

His hand touched her arm. She looked down. He was giving her the reins. "Can you. . . ." He moistened his lips, worked his mouth. "Can you manage?"

She flexed her fingers, closed them stiffly about the reins. After a moment, she nodded, touched the reins to the side of her mount's neck, eased the macai off the track and down the rocky bank and started across the parched and cracking land toward the water that pulled at her.

They came into a wide ravine, a great jagged wash slashing acrost the barrens. A dry streambed ran down the center of the wash, bits of desiccated brush and sun-bleached bones strewn about among its boulders. To the south the wash ran against a line of weathered stone as if a giant cleaver had sliced the land away and beaten the sliced-off part into rubble that lay in grey and white heaps along the base of the scarp. Directly ahead of them the rubble was swept away. Serroi could see sunlight glinting on small pools of water in the stream bed and beyond these an arching blackness that was the mouth of a cave.

They dismounted and led the macain inside, released them to drink at a deep oval pool of ice-cold water. When Hern judged they'd had enough, he drove them out of the cave. Moaning and whoomping with displeasure, they ambled down the slippery streambed and started grazing on scattered clumps of coarse dry grass.

Serroi sat where she'd dumped herself, all her small pains dissolved in the larger agony in her head. She pressed the heels of her hands hard against her eyes, trying to throw a line about her exploding head and tie the pieces together. After a minute she drew her legs up, rested her arms on them and let her hands dangle.

Hern brought her a cup of water. He knelt beside her, took one of her hands and closed her fingers about the cup, then wrapped his fingers about hers. With his help she lifted the cup to her lips. When she was finished, he stood. "Better?"

"A little. Thanks."

He turned away, pulling up his tunic as he turned, still holding the cup. Black cloth bunched over his ribs; he looked at it, laughed and tossed it to Serroi, then jerked the tunic over his head and dropped it to the damp stone. He sat down heavily beside the water, pulled off his boots, sat, still laughing, wiggling his toes, bending his knees and working his ankles. Serroi chuckled as she watched him though it hurt her head. He grinned at her over his shoulder, jumped to his feet, stripped off his trousers and launched himself into the water. With a great deal of splashing and swearing at the icy liquid, he managed to scoop up a handful of sand from the bottom and begin scrubbing away the crust of his long walk.

Serroi watched drowsily, thinking it would feel good to be clean and cool; she ought to join him, but she was too tired to move. Her head dropped lower, her eyes wouldn't stay open. Murmuring incoherently, she eased onto her side, curled up on the rock. The sounds in the cave took on eerie distant echoes, then she was asleep.

When the dream began she was aware that time had passed and she knew that she was dreaming——

She rose and looked around, naked now, with a tingling sense of freedom from the dragging weariness and fear of last night and the morning. Joy filled her. She spread out her arms like wings and soared on the wind, flying across the moons over a landscape of black embroidery on a textured white ground. She lay out on two winds, one cold, one warm, drifting idly on one or the other for a long time, rising on the warm wind, sinking on the cold, until she was suddenly aware that a line was curled about her ankle. She looked down. A string like a kite's tether joined her to something on the ground. Curious, she spiralled down, swinging in slow circles about the fragile black thread. She saw herself curled on her side, Hern lying asleep beside her, holding her against him; his breath was warm across the matted hair of her distant body. She felt it and trembled, looked down wistfully, wishing that the tenderness she saw there was real. She saw her boots standing beside her discarded clothing. This bothered her but she couldn't think why. With shocking unexpectedness the kitestring shortened and thickened, jerked powerfully at her leg. She faltered, thrashed about; the air wouldn't hold her. Screaming in silent terror, she tumbled down and down.

A hand caught hers and she was a feather wafting upward again. She looked for her rescuer but saw no one. She felt the fingers warm and reassuring about her wrist, she saw nothing, no one. The hand pulled her away from the sleeping figures, faster and faster. She began to be afraid, tried to free her wrist, turning and twisting it. The unseen fingers were strong but gentle; they held her loosely but she couldn't pull away from them. The tie between her and her body stretched and stretched until it was an agony of fire about her ankle. She began to panic when she thought of the tie breaking. Something terrible would happen if the tie broke.

The hand pulled harder, fighting the pull of the tie. At last it brought her lightly down on the top of a mountain, a barren black and white mountain, the stones and vegetation disciplined into abstract geometric forms. Her toes touched down in the center of a five-sided figure that looked familiar enough to chill her though once again she didn't know why. She was alone on the mountain top, there seemed to be no point to bringing her there, but the hand held her when she tried to leave.

There was a shimmer in the air. She watched with a feeling of inevitability as the shimmer solidified into the dark elegant form of Ser Noris.

There were more lines in the beautiful arrogant face. He smiled at her and his ruby glimmered as it moved and caught the unnatural light. His hair was black smoke floating about his face. That and the ruby she remembered. The sadness and pain in his black eyes was more than she remembered except perhaps in the last dreams, the ones that drove her from the Valley. He came closer to her, reached out to touch her. She tried to back away but the hands held her still; his servants, she remembered that now, the hands that had washed her and tended her as a child. "Serroi," he murmured, his voice dark music as it always was; she would have wept but there were no tears left in her. "Why fight me so?" He slid long elegant hands through her tumbled hair, each touch like fire against her skin, pulled one of her curls between thumb and forefinger. She gasped. Too many memories. She couldn't bear it, any more than she could weep. She trembled and burned. "Come home, little one. I've missed you." He touched her face tenderly. "More than I thought I could miss anyone or anything."

Again she tried to weep, again she could not. She looked down, saw that her hands were transparent. She looked at the Noris and he was transparent also, a wavering image that firmed, turned smoky, firmed again. "Serroi," he called, his voice pleading, caressing, tearing at her. She looked down at herself. Her legs were rags, translucent blood ran down the insubstantial flesh. "Ser Noris," she whimpered. She drifted closer to him, caught at his hand, held it against her face. "Why do you torment me so? Why do you want to destroy what I love?"

"Serroi." He sat, pulling her down with him, settling her head onto his thigh. He brushed the hair back from her face, smiling a little, a flush of life in the glassy pallor of his face. "You don't understand, child. There's so much waste in that life you love, things rot and die, they hurt you and betray you. I only want to bring order out of disorder." He touched her nose with a fingertip, pointed at the moons. "Look. Like the circuits of our eleven moons. They make a thousand patterns, more, but move always in a neatly regulated manner; if you study them long enough you'll always know what they're going to do. More than a thousand patterns, my Serroi, all of them different. No sacrifice of variety, but a great gain in peace."

As he continued to stroke his fingers along her face, she felt that peace. She felt safe, enclosed in the surprising warmth of his love. There was no more loneliness, no more yearning for someone to receive and return the pent-up flood of affection that threatened to drown her some days. She looked up into the face of her beloved, saw that he was smiling, his black eyes filled with triumph. That jarred her

out of her drift into contentment and acceptance. She tore
herself loose from his hands. "No!" she cried. She flung herself into the air. "No," she wailed as the ebon tie snapped her
swiftly back to her body.

She was thrashing about, legs caught in a blanket, back
bruised by the stone. Strong square hands were hard on her
shoulders, pinning her down. Warm hands, solid and alive.
Still whimpering and whispering the *no* she'd screamed in her
dream, she pried her eyes open and stared up into Hern's
anxious face. It was very dark in the cave but enough moonlight came in to show her the taut hardness in his face, the
worry in his narrowed eyes. She sighed and stopped struggling. Cold bit into legs and arms where she had kicked free
of the blankets. His thigh was warm against her. He was bent
over her, his hands pressing down on her shoulders until she
finally went quiet, then he moved them to the blanket on either side of her head. He continued to lean over her, shifted
his weight onto one hand, touched her face with the other,
tracing the wetness of tears, stroking very gently over her
pulsing eyespot. "It's only a dream," he murmured. "Nothing
so bad, only a dream."

She couldn't explain. Tears flooded her eyes. She began
crying desperately, her body shuddering, her head twisting
back and forth as she tried to turn away from his probing
gaze.

With a soft curse, he pushed onto his knees. He picked
Serroi up, pulled her onto his lap, then struggled with the
blankets, wrapping them awkwardly around himself and the
sobbing shivering woman. He held her against him, pressed
her head into his shoulder, stroked a hand gently over her
clotted hair and down her narrow back. Over and over he repeated the soothing sweep of his hand, saying nothing much,
not knowing what to say, reduced in the end to simple crooning sounds. Slowly her sobbing grew easier, the shuddering
body quieted, then she lay relaxed against his body. The layers of fat were soft and yielding though she could feel the
hardness of the muscles underneath. He was warm, warming
her aching chilled body, warming away her aching desolation
until she was drowsily surprised to find herself happy, content, murmuring with pleasure as Hern shifted her around
and drew his fingertips in a slow spiral about her nipple. He
continued to caress her until she was responding eagerly.

They made love on the hard cold stone floor and fell

asleep curled up one against the other, the blankets tucked around them, Serroi exhausted and content, the terror of the dream wiped from mind and body.

Serroi woke filled with energy and well-being. Outside the cave Hern was moving about, whistling. She rubbed at her eyes, stretched and yawned.

Abruptly the two parts of the night came together for her. She shivered then smiled. Nothing could bother her this morning. She yawned again and sat up. The sun was streaming into the mouth of the cave. She jumped to her feet, stretched again and looked around. Her clothes were tossed carelessly aside, covered with dust, stiff with sweat. Hern wasn't much good as a maidservant. She swallowed, grimaced. There was a monster of a foul taste in her mouth. Rising onto her toes, thrusting her hands toward the cave roof, she strained upward, twisted her spine, flopped down, straightened, danced across to the dark deep pool and plunged in.

Laughing, sputtering, teeth chattering she bounced from the rim of the pool, stepped suddenly off a ledge and went under. With a strong kick she drove herself up again, broke surface with a whooping cry, paddled about the pool, her body growing accustomed to the icy cold. The whistling outside retreated, growing fainter and fainter. She started humming the tune, feeling as cheerful as Hern, feeling like laughing. She splashed carelessly about, diving under, kicking up again. Finally she scooped up some sand from the bottom and began scrubbing her body and her hair. Soap would have been better, but her weaponbelt with its bit of soap was in a crack somewhere and she didn't feel like searching for it. When she was as clean as she could make herself, she ducked under a last time, then waded out of the waterhole and used one of the blankets to rub herself dry.

She shoved at the borrowed clothing with her bare toes, kicked it into the water, wrapped a blanket about her body and went outside, lifting her feet hastily when she touched the hot stone. She found a bit of shade, pushed the wet hair off her face and looked around. The sun was about an hour from zenith, the macain were standing nearby, munching at the tips of the branches of a scraggly bush. Her brows rose when she saw that they were saddled already. Her saddlebags were tied in place, her weapon belt slung across the saddle. Hern was nowhere in sight. She felt for him, her eyespot throbbing, groping beyond the range of her eyes with the immaterial fingers of her outreach. When she touched him, he was some distance to the east; he seemed cheerful and busy about something. Shrugging off her curiosity, she picked her way across the stone and sand, wincing at the heat and the pricks of the sharp rock flakes. Scratching absently at her macai's neck, she gazed up at the sun. *Going to be hot.* She closed her eyes. *Hours. I'll fry in my leathers.* She shrugged. *Not much choice.* She started digging in her saddlebags.

When she heard the whistling again, she was spreading Beyl's borrowed clothing to dry on the rocks outside the cave. Minutes later Hern came half-running half-sliding down the north slope of the wash. He sauntered toward her, a grin on his face, a hint of swagger in the swing of his shoulders, three lappets dangling from his left hand, in his right hand a sling waggling with a jaunty beat. He held up the lappets. "Dinner."

Serroi straightened, eyed them, her hands on her hips, her head tilted (feeling a tickle of amusement and a maternal affection she refused to show—he looked in that moment so much like a small boy, the son she'd never have, she wanted to hug, pat and praise him, and she couldn't do that either because he wasn't a small boy). "So I see," she said. "Very interesting. Just how do you plan to cook them?" She looked deliberately around at the rock and withered grass, the tough and scanty brush.

He chuckled, "Here. Start skinning." He tossed her the string of lappets and strode off, leaving her torn between amusement and annoyance.

She was down at the streambed burying the offal and bloody hides with the neatly trimmed bodies laid out above on the flat top of a rock when he came back carrying an armful of grey-white wood, wood so dry the surface powdered when she touched it. "The heart's sound enough," he said. "Tested it."

Serroi stamped sand down over the entrails and dusted off her hands. She lifted her head suddenly, closed her eyes and felt about for other lives, anything that might threaten them, but touched nothing except a few rodents and fliers, widely scattered, far more concerned with surviving in a harsh land than with any possible intruders. She touched the wood again, rubbed her thumb across her fingers. "Too dry to smoke. Still—we better build the fire in the cave."

He swung around, pale grey eyes suddenly alert. "You picked up something?"

"No." She shivered. "Just a chill. It's gone now."

His eyes searched her face. She smiled. His face lightened; he smiled at her, reached out and took her hand. Shifting his load so he could balance it comfortably under one arm, he pulled her close and set his arm around her shoulders. As they moved up the streambed, he spoke casually about his hunting walk, pride in his success strong in his voice. She glanced at him. He was relaxed, contented, his face appreciably thinner. She let him hold her, even though it made walking more difficult for both of them, happy for the moment in his happiness, suppressing her own reservations.

Hern sat back and sighed, his hands folded around the cha cup that rested on the diminished bulge of his belly. "That was good."

Serroi smiled. "Thank you, master," she said demurely, her eyes lowered, her head bowed meekly.

"Viper." He sipped at the cha. After a moment's comfortable silence, he said, "Let's stay here this night. You need the rest and I can use it."

Serroi smoothed her hands along her leather skirt. She looked up. He was smiling sleepily at her. She caught her breath, didn't breathe for a dozen beats of her heart, then she jumped to her feet and walked to the front of the cave. Over her shoulder she said, "My clothes should be dry now. You'd better fill the waterskins. I can't guarantee we'll find water again before sundown."

He put the cup down with exaggerated care. "Serroi." The word was a command.

"No." She set her shoulder against the stone, narrowed her eyes against the white glare of the desert.

"Why?" He came up behind her, curled a hand over her shoulder.

She moved restlessly under the touch. Very briefly she let herself lean against him, her head against his chest, his fingers playing gently in her hair, but when he began fondling one of the curls, she pulled away and went to fold up the trousers and long-sleeved shirt.

He watched her, frowning. "Because of your shieldmate?"

"No." She lifted the white shirt, scowled at it. A short dunking in icy water and a bit of banging on the rocks cleaned the sweat smell but did nothing for dirt and sweat stains. She folded it, held it against her, smoothed the sleeves down, then rolled it into a tight cylinder.

"Why then? Last night you didn't object."

She set the shirt roll down, scooped up the trousers, snapped them vigorously, then started to roll them up also. "Last night." She looked down at the dark blue cylinder. "I need . . . I need affection, Hern. Given and gotten. Water for a killing thirst. Bread against starvation." She tapped the cylinder of blue wool against her thigh, shrugged. "Passion." She smiled at him. "Pleasant as an extra, but not necessary, not for me."

He ran his fingers impatiently through his hair. "Serroi, that doesn't explain a damn thing. You don't have to sleep with me if we stay here another day. What in zhag does it matter? You need the rest. I need the rest."

"And I have bad dreams. He knows I'm here."

"Serroi . . ." He took a step toward her.

"And don't take my boots off again, no matter what. He can get to me then." Her hands were trembling; she saw him smiling at her, the ruby riding his lip, a fire in its heart. He smiled at her and beckoned. She shuddered.

Hern caught her by the shoulders, pulled her to him, his strength overcoming her instinctive resistance. He held her without words until the stiffness went out of her body.

They rode in a companionable silence down the chalky track toward the alkali plain glittering between the worn hills. Hern was lost in thought, riding with automatic skill, holding his rested and restive mount to an easy walk. Serroi frowned at the bobbing head of her macai, her mind plodding in relentless circles about Hern and Ser Noris and the weary ride to Shinka that lay ahead of them.

Intent on their concerns, neither of them heard the padding of half a dozen macain or the low, irregular rasping of velater hide against metal. They rode around a bend and found themselves in the middle of six armored and alert Sleykynin.

CHAPTER IX:

THE MIJLOC

Burin Blanin stumped into the circle of moonlight, tugging at the sleeves of his tunic, scowling. "When a man has to sneak out of his own house like a thief . . ." he muttered.

"You're not the only one." Vrom Santinin stopped beside one of the violated Maiden columns. He touched the thick black paint splashed inexpertly in a long swipe up and over the carved face, scanned the court, his eyes moving over the painted pavement (more black paint, in thick almost unreadable letters) to the fountain now dry, the dancing figure that used to stand clothed in water and now had a thickening coat of dust over more disfiguring black paint. His lips tightened and his long narrow face pulled together in a worried frown. "What I'm bothered about most is spring. How we going to plant if Floarin takes all our seed?" He moved past Burin, his long legs scissoring rapidly across the court, his moonshadow jerking across the black paint and the delicate floral design beneath it. "How you, Tesc."

"Well enough, better than the Plain."

"That's for sure." Burin glanced with some sadness at the silent fountain. "I used to like the sound of that." He crossed to Tesc holding out a massive hairy paw. "You looking good."

Havor Kalestin and Kimor Gradsigornin came into the court together. Havor looked around, pursed his mouth to spit, then changed his mind and swallowed. "The rot's in all our houses," he grumbled. "You look around and all you see is black. More'n half your folk are wearing it. Getting so even the food taste like hauhau shit. They won't let us Maiden-bless it, we have to listen to some git preaching at us, enough to make a posser puke."

Kimor chuckled. He stopped in front of Tesc. "Salah sends greetings and good wishes, says you're to know you're welcome in our home." He wrinkled his long humped nose.

"Says you're her brother and zhag can swallow any damn
traitor in her household."

"Thanks, cousin. How you put up with that tongue. . . ."
He grinned, shaking his head.

"And if Annic needs anything, clothes, you know. . . ."
He chuckled softly. "What a hoo-haw. First the terrible twins,
then you bust Annic and Sanani loose a couple weeks later.
The Decsel he went roaring about with the Agli, digging into
every stinking corner. How're the twins, by the way?"

"Enjoying themselves."

"I bet."

Vonnyr Mallin was the last of the five taroms to show up.
He came striding into the court, his impatience blowing before him like a summer storm. "Hah! Tesc. You looking
good. What'n zhag we going to do about this stupidity?" He
flung out a long thin arm, forefinger jabbing at the silent
fountain, swooped his whole hand to encompass the mutilated
pavement, the disfigured columns. "Look at this mess.
Maiden's sweet breath, I'm ready to hang the bunch of them
from the nearest brellim. Those Soäreh-posser who watch and
watch and wrinkle up their silly faces when a man does a
natural thing. Cousin, when that idiot norid comes snooping
around pretending to be so holy, hah! Agli, hah! Posser dung,
that's what." He distorted his face, thrusting out his chin,
pulling on his nose, his hand fisted, rounding his eyes, moving
his head in the lazy arcs of an ambling posser, squealing eagerly, sinking the squeals into staccato grunts.

Eyes watering, face red with suppressed laughter, Tesc
caught hold of him and pulled him toward the small schoolroom behind the sanctuary. "Shut up, you fool, or you'll have
the town on us."

The schoolroom was empty, all the furnishings burnt in a
bane fire the day the paint was smeared on. Tesc settled himself facing the door which he had Burin leave open. For
several minutes the men said nothing, simply stared at the
gritty floor, the spray of leaves blown inside and left to decay. Havor coughed against the back of his hand, wiped it on
his trousers. "Tallig come home t'other day in Soäreh black.
M'own brother. Now when I look at him, which I don't if I
can help, churns my belly worse'n a three-day binge, I see
him eating me with his eyes. Wishing me to step out of line,
make a mistake, do anything he can get a handle on."

Tesc frowned. "Then you keep out of this, Hevi-chal. No
need to let them get their hooks in you."

"Hanh! How long before he starts inventing things? You think the Agli-dung'll want truth? All he give one damn about is the look of things and that to keep honest folk quiet. Lot of them in Soäreh black they're honest enough, just stupid's all. They won't stand for naked grabs, I know my folk, but it don't take much to fool 'em." When the others nodded in solemn agreement, he rubbed at his nose, grinned more like a mischievous boy than a man well into his middle years. "Know what I did? Climbed out the window. Went up a tree and over the wall. Felt damn silly, I tell you. But he don't know I'm out and Lelice will keep a closed mouth. She can't stand him, never could. And she for sure don't like this Soäreh business. Says her maids have stopped laughing, go around looking pious and superior. Makes her want to slap them, then check the stores to see how much they're stealing." He shook his head. "Don't know how much more of this she can take. With her temper. . . ." He spread his hands in a quick helpless gesture then folded them on his knees.

After another interval of heavy silence, Tesc said, "I'm the example that's supposed to keep you all in line. You don't make any bad breaks, the Soärehmen should let you be." He cleared his throat, stared out the open door at the cloud shadowed moonlight. "Why I wanted to see you—wanted to warn you, things might be getting tougher. Tithe wagons'll be starting back to Oras any day now. I got Annic and the others tucked away up in the Earth's Teeth. We're collecting quite a bunch of mijlockers up there—from all over, more coming in as time passes, most of 'em with about what they got on their backs, men and women and kids. Now, the weather's not been right for more'n a passage, but winter's coming like it or not and we need food, clothes, arms and shelter." He held up a hand, shook his head. "Not from you, friends. From the bastards that sent us up there. We going to start taking the tithe wagons, one thing. Another, we start making the days hard for Followers. We are going to hassle Soäreh black till they feel like they're sitting bare-assed on a hill of bloodsuckers." He passed a hand across his round face. "Wanted you ready. Keep your noses clean. They get on you too hard or on your kids, come on up, just ride into the hills, someone will see you and collect you. Could be dangerous, they're not going to let us sit up there and hit them when we want; we're trying to set things up to deal with that."

The six men sat once more in a heavy silence. Outside the open door Teras and Tuli sat with their backs against the wall, their legs drawn up, listening to what was being said inside, watching the clouds gather and break up as if whatever was herding them in place was distracted by something. Tuli wiggled her thumbs slowly, glanced now and then at Teras. His head back, his eyes half-closed, he might have been dozing but his body was taut with a nervous intensity that was beginning to worry her. She brushed a hand over her short hair, chewed on her lip and thought about talking to him. Eyes drooping wholly shut, Teras began tapping the tips of his fingers on the paving bricks.

Inside, Vrom burst out, "Dammit, Tesc, they're impossible to live with. A couple of the laziest ties I ever seen, you know 'em, that slattern Tink and her blockhead brother Doddle, since they took the black, they even started bathing. Hah! Clean, neat, do their work. Never thought I'd say it, liked 'em better before. Now they make my skin crawl." He wrinkled his bony nose. "Times I want to kick ass so bad I just gotta walk away."

"Me, I'm mad and scared and don't know what'n zhag to do about it," Kimor said suddenly. "Listen, yesterday afternoon, I come home from arranging the cull. A couple my tie kids had been going at it hot and heavy in the strawbarn and got themselves caught." He grinned. "What'n zhag, they're ties, no problem, even if the girl gets pregnant. She just gets married a bit sooner than she might otherwise or takes off to the Biserica for a while. No one the worse for a little fun." He growled low in his throat. "The Followers on my place they were going to take a whip to the pair, said they were immoral and damned unless they repented and changed their ways. Well, I rode up and wanted to know what all the fuss was about. The kids wriggled loose and got to me. Dammit, Tesc, I thought those fools, the Followers I mean, were going to take their whips to me! I hauled the kids inside and chewed them out, told them they were brainless gits being that careless when they knew how things were. Told them to get off home to their parents and next time they had an urge they should make damn sure they were well hid." He snorted. "Getting so a man feels eyes on him even when he's in bed with his wife. Salah's complaining a lot about that. Says it's worse than trying to cook a big dinner stark naked. Bug eyes and grease popping out of the pan on you. She's some tetchy these days."

Burin laughed, cleared his throat. "Tesc, got a feeling one of those you might be getting up there is ol' Zeb. He started coming round to the tars like he always done before and some fool got word into Cymbank and the Decsel came for him; Maiden be blessed, the old fayar he smelled trouble and got away, but you tell me how we're going to get our pots mended if the guards chase all the tinkers off like that. And the cobbler here in town, he put on the black. Now he won't do work for anyone but Followers." He slapped at his boot. "Look at that hole. Tried to get it fixed yesterday. Not a chance. Bastard looked pious and said his hands were given for the service of Soäreh. Talk about wanting to kick ass. Phah!"

"You want to talk about bad. . . ." Vonnyr's flexible voice dropped to its lowest register. "First couple weeks they were all sweet as honey. Rest of you know this, but I don't know if you heard, Tesc. Hihnir and Innal?"

"What happened?"

"We got public whippings now, ain't it wonderful. Made Hihnir forge the irons and set the post himself. In the middle of the green. I tell you!" He spat. "Decsel come around to all the shops. Joras and me, we were in town for some chain, needed to fix up another hoist for the butchering. Made us go too, and us just riding in no idea what we were getting into. Got no chains, just got to see the blacksmith and his helper hung up on that stinking post and whipped bloody. Every soul in town there. Had to listen to the Agli rant about natural and unnatural till I was ready to rot. Then they marched the two of them to the House of Repentance, said they were going to teach 'em to live normal Soäreh's way. No one's seen 'em since and no one, me either, has got the nerve to ask about 'em. I don't hold with the way they lived, but sweet holy tits, they've lived here near on forty years not bothering no one." His feet scraped on the floor and he coughed again. "I don't see where this is going to end."

"Thing I'd like to know is what happened to Hern. He might be fat and lazy like all the Heslins but he wouldn't stand for this."

There was silence inside for a few breaths then Tesc said, "You remember Rane the meie?" There were a few rasping sounds as the men shifted about, a grunt or two. "She said the Biserica took him in after Floarin turned the guards on him, let him live in the gatehouse."

More silence.

"Pretty good with a sword, Hern, or so they say." Vrom chuckled dryly. "Me, I'd cut my foot off."

Burin slapped his hand against the wall. "What do we know about battles and such? That's what we got Domnors for. Maybe we should send someone to talk to Hern, see what he thinks we should do."

"Could do that." Tesc sounded tired. "Me, I can't afford to wait for him to get busy. Got mouths to fill and shelters to put up. Things should settle down, though, when the first snow falls."

"If it does." Vonnyr's gloom spread to the others. Again there was silence in the gutted schoolroom.

Teras sat up suddenly, his face wrinkled with concentration. Tuli stopped trying to juggle her two stones and clutched them tight in one sweaty hand. "What is it?" she whispered. "Gong?"

"Uh-huh." He rubbed furiously at his eyes, scowled at her. "There's someone snooping about, at least I think so," he whispered, his esses spraying in her ear. "If they heard . . . take a look, will you?" He got quickly to his feet. When she was up beside him, he finished, "I'll tell Da and the others."

She nodded and started off, circling the fountain and fading into the deep shadow under the vine trellis linking the carved columns, filled with a restless energy that made her glad to be moving, whatever the purpose. She trotted through the columns, her feet dancing between and around the heaps of dead dry leaves, floating, it seemed to her, without effort or sound, feeling the Maiden peace settle over her in spite of the desolation. She felt like singing, like laughing, then she came out of the columns and slowed as she moved along the front wall to the main gate of the shrine, most of her senses tuned to the road outside. She tripped suddenly over something soft and crashed to the paving, knocking the wind out of herself, scraping her palms bloody. The noise of her fall seemed to echo louder than a gong. She jerked around, switching ends like a spooked macai, and found herself nose to nose with a familiar face. "Joras," she whispered. She pressed her hand to his neck under the angle of his jaw, breathed more easily as she felt the strong, slow beat. She sat back on her heels. *Must've been standing watch and the sneak got to him.*

The dying vines whispered in quick papery rustles, the wind blew bits of grit over the paving. In the distance the flute song of a kanka ended on a sharp high note as it loosed its gas and swooped on a prowling rodent. She reached toward Joras's shoulder intending to shake him out of his stupor.

Leather scraped against stone. Someone out in the darkness took an incautious step, arrested the movement, but not before she heard. She sprang to her feet, looked wildly about, plunged into the columns as a dark figure came leaping at her.

She yelped, but didn't bother screaming. Her father and the others knew about the prowler, no use alerting the town. She twisted and turned through the pillars, trying to get around him and back to her father, gasped with horror as a dark shape came round a column and fingers caught her arm. She jerked loose, panting, sweat breaking out all over her, her heart thudding in her throat, plunged again into the darkness under the columns. She was intensely angry, but it wasn't like one of her rages, more like Sanani's bitter anger that was cold and mind-clearing. She was afraid but in her body and her mind was the memory of the guard in the clearing folding slowly to the ground, killed by a stone from her sling. She slipped a hand into her pocket, felt the stones and the long strips of leather. She made one last desperate turn, ran flat out for the middle of the court of columns, hearing his feet slapping on the bricks, his breathing hoarse as he labored behind her. Sling in one hand, stones in the other, she skidded into the processional aisle, flew along it and out into the street, skidded about again and ran round the outside of the wall toward the grove behind the shrine. Halfway there, she stopped, whirled, stood shaking and unsteady, eyes burning and blurred, gulping in great bites of dusty air. Still shaking a little, she thumbed a stone into the pocket of the sling and started whirling it about her head, her eyes on the corner.

The acolyte came plunging around the corner, stumbled to a stop, then started for her, triumph stretching his mouth and glittering in his eyes. His exertions had knocked the hood back from his head. She saw with a clarity that startled her the polished gleam of his shaved pate, his ears standing out like handles on a jug.

The sling whirred over her head. He was a half-dozen steps from her when she loosed the stone. His last step aborted, a look of surprise in his one remaining eye, one hand starting to lift toward his face, he crumpled to the pavement and lay in a heap, the wind playing with the folds of his robe.

Tuli waited. He didn't move. She lifted a hand grown

leaden and pushed the sling into her jacket pocket. The wind sang eerily along the wall, tugging at the flattened folds of his robe, pressing the cloth against his bony length. She longed to run to her father and feel safe in his arms. Her stomach churned. She rubbed her sleeve across her eyes, realizing with some surprise that she was crying. She looked up. Nijilic The Dom was riding heavily across a crack in the yellow clouds, his light touching a Maiden face visible above the top of the wall, lovely, serene, compassionate, seeming to smile at her. She walked past the fallen boy (he couldn't be more than three or four years older than her), walked past the black heap, her eyes fixed on the gentle face, the forgiveness she read into it helping her to forgive herself.

She flattened her hand on the wall, walked along it, turned the corner, her hand slipping over the rough stones, the tension flowing out of her back and shoulders as soon as the body was out of sight. She went through the gate, her feet scuffing on the bricks.

Joras was sitting up, breathing hard and poking at his head, cursing softly but with great feeling. Vonnyr was propping him up, his mobile face squeezed into a scowl of rage and concern. The other taroms, Tesc with them, clustered around him, throwing muttered questions at him that he'd given up trying to answer.

Teras was the first to see Tuli. He started toward her, calling her name. Tuli tried to smile at him, couldn't, brushed past him and threw herself at her father, shaking all over as reaction hit her a second time.

"Tuli?" He smoothed his broad hand over her hair, patted her shoulder. "What's wrong?"

"The acolyte. He was listening. He came after me, chased me. I killed him. Out there." Her face pressed against her father's well-covered ribs, she waved a hand awkwardly at the street. Her words muffled and indistinct, she said, "Around the corner."

With a muttered exclamation Burin shifted his heavy body into a light-footed run and disappeared out the gate. He was back a minute later. "Dead all right. Little one here, she whanged him good with her sling. Wonder how much he heard?"

"Enough to get us all proscribed." Kimor dropped his hand on Teras's shoulder, smiled at Tuli. "Terrible Twins just saved our necks."

Vonnyr helped Joras onto his feet. "You all right to ride?"

Joras smiled at his father, a small twitch of his lips, his face sweaty and pale. "I can stick in a saddle."

"With the sneak dead, we got time and room to move." Vonnyr looked anxiously at Joras. "Take it easy. We can haul the body off with us, bury it somewhere."

"No," Tesc said sharply. Tuli stared up at her father, startled to see him so grim. He shifted her around until she was standing beside him, his arm curled protectively around her shoulders. "No," he repeated. "You want the Agli to call him from the grave to tell the tale of what he heard?"

Vrom gaped. "Huh?" Vonnyr looked uneasily around, his eyes drawn to the silent street visible through the gate's elegant arch. The others shifted with the same lack of ease.

Exhausted by what she'd done and the tumult of her emotions, Tuli leaned against her father's side, watching them, hardly taking in the import of her father's words.

"You heard of Necromancers," Tesc said.

Kimor scowled. "Norits maybe. Aglim ain't norits, just norids. Can't light a match without sweating."

"Rane said Nearga-nor's behind this, feeding the norids more power. I don't want to take no chances." He patted Tuli's shoulder. "No one's going to raise that body if it's ash. The twins and me, we'll dump it in the Agli's own fire."

Burin strangled on a snort of laughter. Vonnyr beat on his back grinning. "Be damned to you for a grand fool, cousin."

Tesc smiled, sobered. "You all take care, keep in your heads what happened tonight. We been careless, nearly paid for it." He shook his head. "Going to be a tough winter."

Once the taroms were safely away, Tesc walked back from the grove and stood looking thoughtfully down at the boy's body. When Tuli and Teras joined him, he shifted his gaze to the old granary across the street. The flame in the outer basin was burning low and the place looked deserted. He dropped his hand on Teras's shoulder, tapped Tuli's cheek. "Think the two of you can carry him?"

"Yah," Teras said. Tuli felt her skin crawl at the thought of touching the dead boy, but she nodded.

"Good." Tesc frowned. "Let me look the place over first." He moved quickly across the weedy ground, stopped at the corner of the shrine to look up and down the street, moved rapidly across it, a bulky man walking with the silence and grace of a hunting fayar. He melted into the shadow at the base of the granary, hesitated in the doorway, disappeared inside. Tuli looked down at the dead acolyte and shuddered. She moved closer to Teras. The minutes passed slowly; it hurt to breathe.

Tesc reappeared in the entranceway. He beckoned, stood waiting for them.

Teras knelt and turned the body on its side. He looked up at Tuli, his eyes shining liquidly in the dim light from the cloud-obscured moons. The wind whipped his short hair about his face. "Grab his legs, Tuli." He straightened, hugging the boy's torso against his side. The skinny legs trailed limply on the ground by Tuli's feet. She suppressed another shudder and forced herself to lift them. Her twin looked over his shoulder. "Ready?"

She nodded. As they moved swiftly across the empty street, she was all too aware of the cold flaccidity of the dead flesh she carried; she stared down, saw coarse black hair curling over the pale flesh, saw long thin toes, saw every crack in the horn on the heels, the stained and crooked toenails, the dusting of dirt between the straps of the worn, sweat-stained sandals.

Tesc vanished inside the granary. Tuli shivered at the change that the last weeks had made in her father. His usually amiable face was harder, leaner, angry in a way that sometimes frightened her. She shifted her grip on the acolyte's legs and looked sadly at her brother's back. Some of the same anger was churning in him. He'd always been the one to keep her steady, the sane one, bubbling with an infectious sense of fun, a quieter appreciation of the ridiculous. Like the change in her father, the change in her twin frightened her, even more, it chilled her. He moved without looking back at her. She pinched her lips together, the sense of loss deepening in her.

Teras circled the exterior fire. Tuli followed awkwardly, her fingers cramping about the thin legs of the dead boy. These new things she was being forced to learn, the killing and the capacity of people to hurt others, the things she was learning about her father and her brother, these things reached back into her memories and corrupted them. Nothing was the same. Nothing was safe. She blinked back tears and forced herself to concentrate on the present, to be alert and ready to act if she needed to.

They trudged along the curving hall that followed the turn of the outer wall, new-panelled and new-painted, stinking of the fresh paint, glistening white paint that caught shadows

and images of the small lamps bolted high on the walls,
caught them in its wet film like a sun-dew catches insects for
its supper. The sweet sickly smell of incense came drifting
back to them, mixing with the stink of the paint. When they
turned into the meeting room, Tuli was fighting down nausea,
concentrating so hard on her rebelling stomach that she didn't
at first see what was waiting for them. Teras dropped the
shoulders of the acolyte with a hiss of disgust. Tuli let the
feet fall away and stood rubbing her hands on the sides of
her jacket.

The Agli was stretched out on a mat, his head close beside
a brazier that sent up a heavy oily smoke. The smoke moved
slowly out and over the gaunt man, wreathing his still form
with ragged black claws. The smell was powerful enough to
make her dizzy; she pinched her nostrils together, trying to
shut out the stench and the choking smoke.

The Agli's eyes were open, but he seemed to see nothing.
Tesc loomed over him, looking down at him with disgust—
disgust and a brooding satisfaction.

"What's that?" Tuli pointed at the brazier.

Tesc snorted. "Tidra." He moved until he was standing by
the Agli's head. "They put a pinch of it in the fire at the tiluns to help them work up the folk and make them pliable."
He snorted again, and as she gasped in surprise, he carefully,
precisely, kicked the Agli in the head. The drugged body
jerked, the Agli's head slammed over against the mat then
rolled back. This time the glazed eyes were closed.

"Is he dead?" Tuli leaned against the door jamb, frightened
by the barely controlled violence in her father.

"Not him." Tesc glanced at the brazier, scowled, kicked it
hard away from him. It skimmed over the floor for several
feet, bounced onto its side and began to roll noisily along the
floor, spilling coals and the gummy resin that was the source
of the smoke. He nodded with grim satisfaction then walked
to the acolyte's body. With a grunt he scooped it up, carted it
to the altar, the broad flat basin where the fire was dancing
high into the heavy air, hot and crackling. Turning his face
away, he dumped the boy's body into the flames and leaped
back, nearly tripping over the Agli's outflung arm. He
steadied and stood watching a moment as the flames shortened and blackened then started building up again as the
black robe kindled.

Tuli shivered as the sweet smell of roasting flesh joined the
mix of odors, remembering suddenly and unwillingly Nilis

thrusting her arms into that very fire. She moved over to the
door. The paint stink was welcome now, something cleaner
than the odors fighting in the meeting room. She leaned her
head against the jamb, breathing shallowly, waiting for the
others to come past her. Their job was done; it was time to
get out of here. She wanted terribly to get out of here. When
she didn't hear footsteps, only the soft murmur of voices, she
gathered herself and turned around.

Tesc and Teras were standing on opposite sides of the
Agli's unconscious form, looking thoughtfully down at him.
A cold smile curled her father's lips; he rubbed a hand along
his chin. "Think you could find some of that paint?" He
jerked a thumb at the doorway.

Mischief danced in her twin's eyes. "Yah," he said. A grin
on his face, he ran past Tuli without seeming to see her. Tuli
watched him disappearing back toward the front of the structure. Her uncertain temper flaring, she flung herself back into
the meeting room, glared at her father, scuffed about the
room, glancing repeatedly at him, snapping her fingers, hissing to herself trying to work out her anger. She kept well
away from the fire that was beginning to send up oily black
smoke to coat the clean whiteness of the new-painted ceiling.
She stared at the film of grease, took a deep breath for the
first time since she'd entered the room, realizing for the first
time too that she'd been almost not breathing as she wandered about. She looked up again, her hand over her nose and
a mouth. *What's left of a man.* She shivered and went to
stand beside her father, seeking comfort from his strength
and vitality.

He was kneeling beside the Agli, using his knife to cut
away the dark robe from the man's arms and shoulders.

"What're you going to do with him?" Tuli shoved her foot
into the Agli's side, nudging him so that his arms moved a
little.

Tesc lifted his head, frowned at her. "I forgot," he muttered. He sat back on his heels. "Rope. Tuli, go find me some
rope. Keep your eyes and ears open. I don't think there's anyone in the building, not with all this wet paint." He rubbed at
his nose. "Enough to strangle a bull hauhau."

Happier to be included even though she still didn't know
what was happening, Tuli ran out. She was only a few steps
down the hall when she met Teras coming back. He was carrying a large paint pot. A coil of rope was looped over one
shoulder; when she saw it she quivered with disappointment

and annoyance. She bit at her lip, then turned to walk beside
him, glancing at the paintpot and brushes. "What's all that
for?"

He grinned. "You'll see."

"Tchah! Teras. . . ." She took hold of the rope and began
working it off his shoulder. "Sometimes I could hit you."

He stopped walking to let her slide the rope over his arm.
"Use your head, Tutu. What do you think we could do with
paint, rope and that clown?"

The rope dangling from her hand, she snorted softly, repeatedly, at the use of her baby name and followed him into
the room. She dropped the rope beside her father and stepped
back, pressing her lips together to contain her laughter.

Tesc was slicing off the Agli's thick black hair, having
some trouble since his knife wasn't a particularly good razor.
The Agli's head had a number of slow bloodworms crawling
over the pale skin. When he heard the whispery splat of the
rope, he rose to his feet, frowning at Tuli. He took hold of
Tuli's shoulders, turned her about and pushed her toward the
door. "Go outside and keep watch."

Tuli wiggled away from his hands, swung around. "I want
to watch here."

"Do what I told you. Get."

Her eyes fell and she shuffled backward to the door, her
gaze sullenly on the naked body of the Agli. When her shoulder touched the jamb, she lifted her head.

"Get," her father repeated. The look on his face showed
her the futility of argument, so she stumped off down the hall
grumbling at her exclusion from the fun.

"Just because Da stripped him." She blew a gust of air
through her nose. "Just because I'm a girl. Girl! Who took
care of the spy? Me. And now they sent me away to protect
my young eyes. Tchah! Girl!" She kicked at the dirt of the
street, went to stand leaning on the edge of the smaller basin,
glaring at the pile of pale ash and scattered coals with a
flicker of red left in them. Overhead the clouds had closed in
again until only TheDom's broad glow shone through, a
vague circle of dull yellow light. The wind blew stronger and
too hot; the night was stifling; in spite of the air's pressure
against her, she felt smothered as if someone had dropped a
blanket over her. She rubbed at her eyes. They were sore, felt
swollen. Waiting was hard, a lot harder than the running and
fighting she'd done not so long ago. She was suddenly tired,
very tired. Her arms ached. Her legs ached. She wanted to

cry, she curled her fingers into claws, wanting to tear at someone, anyone, her father and her brother for pushing her out here to wait alone while they played their games with the Agli's naked body.

She heard a whispery scraping sound. Tesc and Teras came through the entrance, dragging the Agli behind them. They'd fitted a sort of rope harness about his body, looping rope between his legs and under his arms, the second length of rope, the tow rope, knotted to the harness between his shoulder-blades, they were pulling him along on face and belly. A smear of paint trailed off behind him along the tiles of the hallway. He was still unconscious, his head lolling about as they let him fall and strolled over to stand by Tuli and inspect the twin timbers projecting from the wall over the entranceway, left over from the days when the structure was used as a granary. Tesc looked at Teras. "Ready?"

"In a minute." Teras cocked a thumb at the hall. "Lost his drawers he did." He stooped beside the Agli, rolled him over and began slapping more paint on his groin and genitals. Tesc watched a moment, then tossed the end of the tow rope over one of the timbers. "Don't forget the Maiden's Sigil," he called over his shoulder.

"Got it."

"Start working on the wall, I'll pull him up."

As the Agli rose in the air, hanging limply in the harness, the ropes cutting in his soft but meager flesh, Teras hauled the paintpot a little way down the wall and started scrawling characters on the mud bricks. Wrapping the rope about his arm, Tesc began walking back along the wall until he reached a hitching post. He glanced around, narrowed his eyes as he saw Tuli watching with a face-splitting grin. "Get over here, little bit; tie this off for me." He held the rope taut while Tuli knotted it to one of the rings bolted to the post. The rope stretched a little as he let it go. The Algi's body jerked up and down. Out in the street again, Tuli bounced from foot to foot, a hand clamped over her mouth to stifle the giggles that threatened to explode out of her.

The once-formidable priest was a comic figure, dripping slow drops of thick white paint. From knees to navel he was slathered with paint. On his hairless chest Teras had drawn the Maiden's Sigil. While paint coated most of his head, Teras had left circles of unpainted flesh about his eyes and mouth and ears. He looked like a toy clown dangling from a string.

Teras tossed the paintpot into the street. The clatter drew Tuli's eyes to what he'd been doing. "Soareh's pimp?"

Tesc caught hold of her shoulder and swung her around. "Never mind that."

Tuli stumbled ahead of him as he kept tapping her lightly on the back urging her along. "Don't see why you didn't put that rope around his dirty neck."

Tesc moved up beside her, took her hand. "Folks don't laugh at corpses." He glanced over his shoulder, smiled with satisfaction, led her briskly across the street toward the grove where their macain waited. He swung Tuli into the saddle, watched to be sure Teras was up, then mounted quickly and led them out of the grove. "Seems to me a good belly laugh can cure a lot of foolishness."

CHAPTER X:

THE QUEST

The well was a hole in the ground, a burrow gnawed from the chalk and sandstone. The water was twenty feet down, off center, a well within a well, hidden from the light by the overhang, protected from the blowing dust though not completely. A sweethorn tree grew some distance from the well itself, yet each year a squad of vassals had to cut away the web of hair-fine white roots that crept into the hole to steal the water. A few grey-green needles about an inch long clung to the first spans of the shiny black branches as they slanted precipitously upward. The rest of the needles lay scattered about the hard pale earth while the outer portions of the branches bore only hard black thorns longer than needles with upcurving points finer than the points of needles. Smaller doerwidds with foliage like scabby green-grey lichen clustered in a west-facing arc about the sweethorn.

Their Sleykyn captors had spread one of Serroi's blankets in the shade of that arc beneath the sweethorn tree. They were kneeling in a ragged circle on the brown wool; now and then one or more of them looked at her, eyes animal-blank, inhuman because to them she was inhuman, more than that, less than beast. The interaction between meien and Sleykynin had a long, unhappy history. The Sleykyn order was implacably hostile to the Biserica as if the meien threatened them on such a deep level they had no need to think, only to react, were driven to humiliate, debase and destroy any meie so unfortunate as to fall unprotected into their hands.

A burst of raucous laughter came from the kneeling men as they tossed oblong ivory dice and watched them wobble and slide about on the dark brown wool. She knew only too well what that was about, she looked at them and forced herself to show none of her fear. A Sleykyn groaned and cursed, fell back off his knees until he was sitting with his feet stretched out before him, removed from the circle on the

blanket. *Bad luck*, she thought. *First out, last in*. She almost
laughed at that bitter joke, but turned instead to Hern.

The Sleykynin had dumped him on a dusty flat some yards
from her, left him unprotected in the sun after kicking and
beating him with casual brutality, something he owed to her,
owed to the fact that he dared ride with her in Sleykyn lands.
He was sitting hunched over, short sturdy legs stretched out
before him, tied at the ankles with the quick but effective
hitch herders used when they threw bull hauhaus. Sweat
rolled down his grim, intent face. He wouldn't meet her eyes
even when she tried smiling at him. His broad thick shoulders
moved slowly, the deliberation of power kept under stern
control. She remembered suddenly how she'd seen him the
night of the Moongather, tied naked to a chair, waiting to be
demon-swallowed, working with iron patience to win at least
one hand free. Serroi tugged at the ropes around her wrists
but the Sleykynin knew how to bind without pity. The turns
cut into her flesh, cut off her circulation. Already her hands
were swollen and numb. Her weaponbelt was gone, thrown
casually across the saddle on her macai, her bow was clipped
to the saddle. They'd pawed her cautiously (snake-handlers
holding a viper) to make sure they had all her weapons—but
they'd missed the knife in her boot, paper-thin and balanced
to a hair. The tajicho was busy at what it did best, protecting
itself, protecting the knife as it did so.

A yell from the kneelers. A Sleykyn stood, the second man
out. He stood watching the others, shucking himself out of
his armor as he watched. He made a comment, most of
which was lost in a sudden burst of laughter, something
about leaving some meat on the bone. He threw corselet and
bracers into a careless heap, stooped to unbuckle his greaves.

Velater hide. Deep-sea predators, the velaterim. They spent
most of their lives out in the middle of the Ocean of Storms,
spawning every five years in shallow coves a little north of
Shinka. Hunted in their spawning by magic and desperate
greed. Velater hide. Inner side soft, supple, breathing like live
skin. Outer side covered with tiny triangular scales with razor
edges. One swipe of a velater glove would rip skin and flesh
away to the bone.

A third man out, one who kept sending her sour looks as if
his lack of luck was somehow her fault.

She was left waiting deliberately; she knew that. How does
one get ready for rape? Sit and watch and know it's coming,
fear seeded and growing in the mind. She was supposed to

participate in her own degradation. That was important to them—that she validate what they did to her by helping them do it. *Let me get my hands free,* she thought, sighed, *and give me time to get the feeling back in them.*

The macain were groundhitched between Hern and the half-circle of doerwidds: the beasts shifted restlessly about the dangling reins, scratched crossly at the hard white soil, suffered more and more from standing without water in the hot afternoon sun. She could feel temper rising in them all and most of all in the macain that served the Sleykynin. Her mount and Hern's had eased away from the Sleykyn beasts, turned edgy by the malignity in them, the fermenting turbulence in them, sidling step by step, heads jerking, the reins rippling against the ground, until they were several feet away from the others. Serroi saw this with considerable satisfaction since she wasn't quite sure what would happen when she prodded the Sleykyn macain across the line into madness and into an unnatural attack on the masters they served with dull sullen hate. She looked at them and they looked back, all of them swinging about to fix their soft, brown-gold eyes on her, as if they somehow knew what she was going to do, as if they waited and watched for the violence to begin, a violence that would relieve a tension in them growing near unbearable. She pressed her leg against the side of her boot, felt the long slim presence of the knife.

Wait. Watch the game. Know the order in which you will be forced. Look at the faces, see them all alike, all animal faces, all dark, dark eyes, dark skin, all of them young, faces unformed, smooth as masks. Watch them unbuckle their armor and throw it in careless piles. Know they want her to last through the rape and linger for the other torments they plan for her. A man in velater moving on her would rip the flesh from her bones. Red rags, gristle and wet white bone. Make her last. Do the first thing. Take their time doing it, driving into her bones, into her soul how helpless she is before them, not a warrior, nothing at all. Make her beg, if they can, or whimper, yes a whimper would be enough to satisfy them in the beginning.

The dice go round and round. A fourth Sleykyn is gone from the circle, sullenly stripping himself to the soft leather undertunic, moving aside to squat and fondle himself as he looks at her. Raising lust with rage, laying hate on hate until he builds a tower of hate.

She looks at Hern. His shoulders still move in that slow,

controlled way, but she has little hope he can win free, even a hand. He is looking at her now, shame and anger, frustration and fear, these are in his face, not fear for himself—she knows that—fear for her. She smiles at him, tries to tell him to be ready for what she is planning. His tongue moves along his upper lip, wipes away the beads of sweat clinging there. He follows her eyes to the macain, to the gamblers. He smiles.

She looks at the sun, twisting her head over her shoulder, squinting against the white glare. It is halfway through its declining arc. She looks away, blinking to rid herself of the black-tailed spots that swim in liquid arcs before her eyes. *Soon,* she thinks, and even as she thinks this she hears a shout of triumph from the blanket. A Sleykyn is backing away scowling, another is kneeling, unbuckling his greaves. The kneeling Sleykyn stands slowly, very slowly, his eyes fixed on her. His leather tunic hangs to mid-thigh. He lifts the bottom and she thinks he is about to strip but he does not, only grabs hold of himself and starts walking toward her, his eyes wide and staring like a half-tame macai with a saddle on his back for the first time. He hangs limp at first though the gentle friction of his hands begins to stiffen him as he walks toward her. Surprised and not surprised, she sees that he is afraid of her, he doesn't want to touch her. He struts toward her, leering at her, but he feels nothing of that, that is for the others behind him. He would have given almost anything to be one of the first out, to have to wait for the others, to move insulated from her peril in their slippery spendings.

He stops in front of her, lets his tunic drop. The pale pink tip of his tongue darts about his mouth, there is sweat collecting on his brow, his eyes glaring past her. With quick jerky movements he stoops, thrusts two fingers into the neck of her tunic, drags her onto her feet. He reaches behind his neck, pulls out the short dagger he keeps there, spins her around, slashes her wrists free, shoves her onto her face and leaps back as if she is suddenly doubly dangerous, a viper cocked to strike. "Get up," he snarls; in spite of his efforts, his voice shakes.

She gets up without saying anything. She has said nothing the whole time, not since the Sleykynin surrounded them and took them prisoner. She knows they will not hear her, that her voice will act on them like nettles. She turns slowly once she is on her feet, wiping her abraded palms on her tunic. He is grinning at her, there is no humor, not even any enjoyment in that stretching of his lips or in his staring eyes. "Strip," he growls. She pulls the neck thongs loose, jerks the neck opening wider then turns the sleeveless leather tunic quickly over her head. Behind her she hears Hern's quick intake of breath, feels his shame, feels his suffering as his too-active imagination paints images for him he can't endure. Suddenly, like a burst of light in her head, she knows how deeply she cares for him, a caring of many complexities, even now she couldn't call it love or passion or anything so simple. She drops the tunic and fumbles with the lacings of her divided skirt. For Hern's sake as much as her own, she has to stop this. The Sleykyn is watching avidly, not trying to hurry her, as she begins easing the skirt down over her hips. He is fondling himself again, having trouble gaining and maintaining an erection. She lets the leather skirt fall and steps out of it, reaching as she does so in to the Sleykyn macain. He is a rather beautiful boy with long-lashed dark eyes and a touch of rose on his cheeks and delicately chiseled lips. He can't be more than eighteen or nineteen at most. She drops back on her boulder though the hot stone is uncomfortable against her bare buttocks. She can almost hear the meat sizzle. She bends over and puts her hand on her boot.

The next happenings are faster than thought; her plans made, she doesn't have to think. She twists her mindblade deep into the macain, driving them into a squealing screaming frenzy, setting them at the Sleykynin sitting in their undertunics, unprotected, unaware, eyes focused on the tableau in front of them. Claws and teeth tearing unarmored flesh, feet stomping soft, unshelled bodies, the attack is too sudden and the five are dead almost before they know they are hurt.

As she drives the mindblade into the macain, she flicks the hideout from its bootsheath, flips it over, catches the point and sends it wheeling at the Sleykyn boy.

He drops flat, fast enough to dive below the knife. Her throw misses.

He scrambles to his feet, his face suffused with crimson, the madness in his eyes matching that in the eyes of the beasts still doing damage to the flesh and bone under their stamping claws. She turns and flies over the ground toward the carnage, getting ahead of him only because even in his madness he is appalled by the unnatural fury of the macain. He slows, his long stride hobbled by that fear. She reaches the piles of Sleykyn armor several body lengths ahead of him, plucks a knife, a sword, a velater whip from the weapons thrown carelessly about.

Moving on her toes among the bits of flesh and splashes of blood, she edges around the sullen macain, milling about, no longer tearing at the dead Sleykynin though two of them still paw at a leg, a torso, rolling them aimlessly about as if they half-remember what that meat once was. When she is past them, she runs back to Hern. She drops the sword behind him, tucks the whip coils under one arm and cuts his hands free. Leaving him to work at them, she wheels and hisses the Sleykyn boy back, flicking the whip against his calves and retrieving it too fast for his stabbing grabs. With the boy hovering just beyond the reach of the whip, she cuts Hern's ankles loose. The boy looks from Hern (rubbing at his wrists, stamping his feet now that he was on them again, his face white with pain as circulation returns), to the macain (snapping viciously at each other, not quite at the point of mutual self-destruction), finally to Serroi. He begins edging toward the armor, his eyes moving skittishly between the three points, easing nearer, a step or two at a time, gaining confidence little by little as Serroi stands without moving and the macain-milling shifts them slowly away from the field of death. The boy seems cooler now, moving with the easy grace of an athlete. He takes another step toward the armor. The whites of his eyes glisten as his gaze shifts restlessly about. Any minute now he will have his sword. She can stop him but for Hern's sake she will not. There is a waterskin by the sweethorn tree, a Sleykyn waterskin plump and full.

"Sleykyn," she calls.

He shies like a nervous macai. He says nothing. He won't look at her.

"Throw that waterskin here."

His face goes stubborn, his chin juts. He won't do it, she knows that, not without threats.

"Throw it here," she repeats, putting a snap in her voice. She starts to say *boy* but changes her mind. "In exchange for the sword you want."

He looks at her now, his eyes wide and staring. He considers what she said. He can get the sword with one quick leap—he knows his body's capacity that well—but he makes the mistake of looking beyond the sword at the sprawled bodies, at the sullen frothing macain. He turns greenish pale. His throat works. His resolution slides away with the sweat suddenly slicking his body. He bends with an aged stiffness,

lifts the bulging skin and flings it at her. It bounces twice and
lands at Hern's feet. Hern laughs. The boy stares wide-eyed,
shies again, dives for the sword. He comes up quickly to his
feet, crouched and ready to fend off any attack. He goes
crimson to the ears with mortification. There is no attack, no
treachery. Hern has the waterskin upended over his head. He
has been drinking, now he is letting the water splash down
over him. He is not even looking at the boy.

Serroi, watching the boy, thinks: Odd that this is what he
won, not first rights at a rape but a choice of deaths. Probably he prefers this death to the one that struck down his com-
rades. She knows he is going to die. Hern will kill him. The
boy doesn't believe this. She watches the glow come back into
his dark eyes. He sees Hern only as a little fat man a head
shorter than him, twice his age, grey in his hair, laughter not
ferocity in his pale eyes. Sword balanced lightly in his right
hand, he walks toward Hern.

Serroi watches him coming, his bare feet light on the
chalk, his eyes flicking from her to Hern. Always back to her.
He still expects treachery. She looks down at the whip in her
hand, flings it away. The boy is Hern's problem now, she has
other things to worry about. She walks toward the two macain huddling close in their nervous fear of the others. She
croons to them, eases toward them, strokes them with her
outreach so they will let her come up to them. She puts her
hand on her mount's nose, hears a soft moan, smiles. She
scratches vigorously among the folds of skin at the macai's
throat, laughs as Hern's mount butts his nose against her, demanding his share of attention. She unties her waterskin, it is
only half full but better than nothing right now. She finds a
hollow in the hard earth and empties the skin into it. All this
time she hears behind her the kiss and slither of steel, the dull
sound of feet quick on the ground. She pats the macain as
they drink.

Hern and the boy prowl warily about each other, alert for
the slightest opening. When she looks over the necks of the
drinking macain she sees that they've tested each other already. There is a small cut on Hern's forearm, a slightly
larger one, still bleeding, across the boy's thigh just below the
edge of the tunic. She watches, thinking that the match looks
ludicrously unequal. The boy is strong, fit, quick, confident,
and he is young, near the peak of coordination and reaction
time. Hern is not actually fat now, thanks to the strenuous
riding of the past few days and the limited meals, but still

sweetly rounded. He is battered, the weariness in his face a
cruel contrast to the boy's freshness. Serroi sees the contrast
and knows it is true and not true. Hern has depths in him,
strengths the boy would never have, a core of stubbornness
that would keep him fighting even when everything seemed
hopeless, a quickness of mind to match the quickness of his
body, the general amorphous attribute called character. She
watches with appreciation as Hern's point slips past the boy's
guard and tears a jagged gash in his arm. He is away before
the boy's riposte can reach him, escaping without a touch.

She scratches her mount's shoulder, watching with guilt
and anxiety as one of the Sleykyn macain curls his head
around and sniffs suspiciously at his own flank. Before she
can move, he sinks his teeth into his flesh, tears out a chunk
of muscle and screams with pain. Then the five others are on
him, ripping at him with already bloody teeth, clawing at him
in a return of their mindless rage. Though it dies quickly,
Serroi feels every wound in her own flesh. She has a moment
to know she'll never again be able to drive any beast to such
frenzy, even to save her life. She tries reaching into them to
ease the rage, but they are slippery, hard and slippery, and
she can't penetrate the wall of madness. They are locked in
the world she has made for them and there is nothing she can
do about it. *Except kill them,* she thinks. She unclips her
bow, strings it, plucks five arrows from the quiver and starts
for them.

Hern is breathing hard, but he hasn't lost his speed. The
boy is bleeding from another cut. He is much warier. Twice a
feint has fooled him so thoroughly only his agility has saved
him, the unthinking quickness that dropped him under Serroi's knife. Another time he'd recognized the feint and
reacted to what he expected only to have his sword nearly
twisted from his hand by a move he'd never even heard of
with all his schooling in swordplay. The move fails by a small
margin, not because of anything the boy does, but because
Hern's wrists do not have their full strength, his hands are
just a hair clumsier than they should have been. As the careful, controlled bout goes on, the boy slowly sees that he is the
one expending most energy, attacking three times to Hern's
one, moving along a consistently wider arc. Confident in his
skill and his youth, contemptuous of Hern, he has spent himself more recklessly than is wise. He isn't stupid, he has
fought well, perhaps—if he lives—he will never again fight so
well. But Hern is better. That is it—the whole thing—a better

swordsman, a quicker thinker, a better tactician. When the
boy finally knows this, the fire goes out of him. He fights
grimly on, seeks to inflict what damage he can, but he is
beaten. The edge is gone off his speed, the grace has fled his
body. He is a dead man walking.

Serroi nocks an arrow, carries four others in her drawing
hand, moves away from the sane beasts, circles behind their
stubby tails, their plump haunches, so they won't see what she
is going to do. Drawing and loosing, running in a shallow arc
as they drop, she slays the five macain, kills them quickly,
cleanly. And when the fifth one falls, she stands with her
arms hanging, her bowstring scraping against her knee, staring silently at her dead.

The end of the contest comes quickly after the boy knows
himself outmatched. A parry falters, his arm is thrust aside
and the swordpoint slides with an easy and a welcome
neatness into his heart.

Hern pulls the sword free, stabs it into the ground and
stands leaning on it, the excitement of the bout gone out of
him, fatigue like lead on legs, arms, shoulders. He has felt
nothing during the fight, not even the cuts and bruises. Now
these burn. His face burns too, about the half-healed wound
from the minark's needle ball. He stands bent over the hilt of
the sword, too spent to move, too weary to keep standing, too
weary to sit down, watching with dull eyes as the boy finally
dies, his mouth open, his eyes rolled back in his head, his
body flattening as if some plumping pneuma had leaked away
with his heart's blood.

Serroi brings him a cup of water, touches his arm, wakes
him from his haze of weariness.

He straightens with some difficulty, takes the cup.
"Thanks."

"Let's get out of the sun." She tugs at his arm.

Hern empties the cup, looks over her shoulder at the
ripped and savaged bodies, the tumbled armor, the bloody
shredded blanket occupying the only bit of shade for miles
around. He drops his eyes to meet Serroi's anxious gaze,
shrugs and walks away from her to lower himself into the
patchy shade near the trunk of the sweethorn.

Serroi pinches her lips together, her mind closing in on itself like fingers into a fist. She has gone beyond horror, re-
fuses to think any more about what has happened or about
anything else. She locks herself in the present moment, does
what must be done, does it without overt emotion.

With Hern unsmiling, thoughtful, his cup refilled, sipping at the water, watching her, not steadily but now and then as if he is checking to make sure she is still there, she collects their scattered gear, dumps it at Hern's feet, starts rifling through the Sleykyn belongings. Waterskins, weapons, trail food, these she adds to the pile. When she is finished she stands by Hern's feet, wiping at her face. Her mind aches from the tightness of her grip on it; there is a burn of tears behind dry eyes. She tries a smile but her face is too stiff.

Black bloodsuckers are swarming over the corpses, some of them transferring their attention to the living. Serroi slaps at a sucker on her leg. "You'd think they'd be satisfied with all that." She moves a hand in an irritated gesture that takes in the field of death.

Hern glances at the corpses and at the dead boy. She can't read the expression on his face. "Should I thank you for the crumb you threw me?" His voice was hard with irony. "To make me feel more like a man, I suppose."

"Don't be stupid. I missed my throw, that's all." She shrugs. "You want honesty, I was a lot more concerned about the macain than I was with the boy." She looks around, lifts a hand, drops it. "I forgot my knife." She walks back to the scuffed flat, kicks around in the cream-colored dust until she finds it. She looks down at herself, clucks her tongue; she picks up her leathers, shakes them as free of the dust as she can, dresses herself. Wiping the dust off hilt and blade, she strolls back to Hern. "My turn. Thanks." She bends and slides the knife into its sheath.

He yawns, looks lazily at the sun then back at her. "Why?"

"For what you haven't said. If we'd stayed at the cave like you wanted we'd have missed all this." She starts for the nervous, snorting macain.

He stands, stretches. "No point. Bad luck, that's all."

She glances over her shoulder, surprised into a short laugh as he echoes her words, the ones she'd chosen to ease him after the fiasco in Skup. She leads the macain across to the pile of gear, watching him as he moves his shoulders. He turns slightly and the light streams through the branches of the sweethorn onto his face, lighting up the partly healed scar from the needle ball. A trickle of dried blood runs down his cheek and dips under his chin. A Sleykyn fist had caught him there an age ago—though she remembers now noting the blow and his involuntary outcry. She pulls the weaponbelt from the saddle.

He opens his hand, closes it into a fist, raises his forearm, winces, lowers it, closes his fingers about the cut in his arm over the sash in the black sleeve, its edges stiffened with dried blood. He runs his eyes over her. "Hadn't you better get rid of those leathers?"

"In a bit. Sit down a minute, will you?" She slides the weaponbelt through her fingers until she finds the proper pocket and takes out the salve jar. Slapping the belt over her shoulder, she opens the jar, wrinkles her nose at the slather of salve left. She looks around, firms her mouth and closes her mind. Slipping the knife from her boot, she kneels beside one of the corpses and cuts off a piece of his leather tunic, one relatively free of bloodstains. She stands, rubs at her nose. "Sit down," she says again, more sharply than she intends. She swallows, presses the back of the hand holding the piece of leather against first one eye then the other. More quietly, she says, "Let me fix your face."

Without speaking, he settles back to the blanket. She hefts one of the waterskins from the pile close by her knees and soaks the piece of soft leather, uses it to wash around the tear on his face, working as carefully as she can but hurting him in spite of her care. He winces now and then but makes no other sign of the pain. When she is finished she takes salve on her fingertips and spreads it carefully over the lacerated flesh. She sits back on her heels. His eyes open and his tightly compressed lips spread in a relieved smile. "Feels a lot better."

"Good." She leans toward him and catches hold of his right hand. There is a short but ugly scratch on the back. As she cleans it, she says, "We can't camp here."

"Who'd want to. What're you getting at?"

"Floarin must be buying Sleykynin."

"An army?" He closed his fingers, opened them, closed them again. "Why? She's got the mijloc nailed."

"Not the Biserica." Serroi unbuttons his cuff and rolls the sleeve up so she can get at the cut on his forearm. "Sits there like a thorn poisoning her." She tugs at his arm until she has it firm along her thigh. He is bending forward now, his head close to hers. She bends over the cut, spreading the lips apart, cleaning carefully inside. When she has the black threads and dirt cleaned out, she scrapes up the last of the salve and spreads it over the raw flesh. Hern has his teeth sunk into his lip, his face is pale, sweating. "And Ser Noris wants the Valley," she says.

"An army," he repeats softly. He lifts his arm absently so she can roll the sleeve down and button the cuff again. She sees that the thought disturbs him. He looks at the sun, moves impatiently, frowns at her. "You keep talking about him, that Nor."

She wipes her hands on the bit of leather. "I lived with him from my fourth to my twelfth year. He tried to use me. . . ." She drew the tip of her forefinger around her eye-spot. "To open the Valley for him."

"You escaped?"

"No." She gets to her feet, starts stowing the extra supplies in the saddlebags. "He threw me away like a broken pot."

"Left you to die?"

Her fingers are very busy packing Sleykyn food in with their own. "I don't think so," she says finally. "I don't understand it. I've thought about it the seventeen years since. I don't know."

He finds his swordbelt and sheath in the pile of gear. "Twenty-nine. You don't look it."

She shrugs. "Who knows how a misborn ages. I'm probably the first to escape the fire." With gloomy satisfaction, she slaps the saddlebag shut and ties the thongs.

"Time we were out of here." He steps around a body, over another and makes his way to the dead macain. "It's turning you spooky." He kneels beside a macai and starts cutting her arrow from the cooling flesh. "He wants you back?"

"So he says." She moves around to the other side of the macai and continues with her stowage.

"And you want to go back."

"I can't."

"That's not what I said."

"I know." She begins rolling up a Sleykyn blanket to replace hers. The sun is setting and the air is already much colder, with the suddenness of temperature drop characteristic of high desert. A few stars are already blooming in the darkening sky. Further discussion avoided by mutual consent, they finish what they are doing and start away from the well, riding on the lamentable track the Sleykynin call a road, riding this time with their attention on the land before them, not on whatever speculations disturb their minds.

They rode at night and holed up by day, depending on Serroi's outreach to warn them of danger ahead or behind. The day camps were wretched—little shade, much wind and dust.

Hern, Serroi, the two macain were white with the om-
nipresent alkali dust that leached away what little moisture
the sun left in their skin. On the first day, lying in the meager
shade of a clump of doerwidds atop a low rise not far from
the road, they watched three bands of Sleykynin ride past,
heading for the Vale of Minar and probably for the mijloc
beyond, all of them young, just-fledged sword fodder like the
six at the well. Hern withdrew further and further into himself, brooding over a helplessness that was for him too strong
an echo of the helplessness of the mijloc. He grew grimmer,
more irritable; having to depend on Serroi to such an extent
made him feel his helplessness all the more keenly. The brief
interval of tenderness at the cave might never have happened.

On the third night they needed water and crept down to a
well about an hour before dawn when the band of young
Sleykynin camping there were deep asleep—being still in
their own land, they mounted no guard. While Serroi kept
watch with arrow nocked and ready, Hern filled the skins.
They left the well behind them without incident and rode on
through land illumined by a shrinking TheDom, the radiant
Dancers and the irregular sparks of the Jewels. Now and
then, when they topped a higher rise in the South road, they
caught glimpses of tilled land, an occasional heap of stones
that might be a walled city or a Sleykyn Chapter House.
Most of the time they saw only the anhydrous, lifeless earth
glowing with the moonlight it sucked in.

On the ninth night there was an armed guard at the well
when they came down for water, not Sleykynin, but Assurtiles of the Prime's elite guard. News of the slaughter at the
first well had apparently reached into the North. The two
guards were jumpy, twitching at every noise. They huddled
close to a small fire, blankets wrapped around their shoulders,
the chill of the night making noses drip, eyes fill with rheum.
Four others lay wrapped in blankets on the flat around the
hole that was the well.

Serroi and Hern withdrew carefully until they were back
with their macain. Serroi drew her hand along the flat waterskin, scratched gently at the warty neck of her mount. "We
need water. Even if we could do without, they can't." The
macain, used to a temperate climate with constantly available
water for drinking and rolling in, were beginning to suffer
from the desert heat and the stinted gulps of water.

Hern drew a powder-laden sleeve across his face, spat.
"Assurtiles," he said. "Not Sleykynin."

"You said it yourself once. Sleykynin make chinjy guards. Besides, Sleykynin are probably too busy hunting us."

He frowned. "You know that?" His voice sharp, he laid a heavy stress on *know*.

She shrugged. "Obvious, isn't it. Why guard that well unless they know we're coming? Count the days. Two for the first band of Sleykyn to race for Assur after finding the dead. Three more back to the well with the best pack of chini trackers they can locate, *they* being full assassins this time, not those hatchlings we saw on the road. Two more to send news back that we're headed east more or less along the road. Two more to get Assurtile guards scattered out along the line of wells. I haven't felt them yet but I'd say the Sleykynin aren't that far behind us. They're limited by the speed of the pack but they probably aren't stopping much, just long enough for food and water."

Hern grimaced. "Almost as stupid as running into the middle of those boys, forgetting about chini trackers."

"I won't argue with that." She looked past him, narrowing her eyes and staring intently at the eastern horizon. "If we can reach the scarp there." She pointed. "You can just about see it, a heavier darkness along the horizon. If we can reach that before they come up with us, we won't have to worry."

"Why?"

"Tell you later. Let's get that water and get out of here."

By the end of the tenth night the hunt behind them was audible, the chini pack close enough for the belling of the beasts to reach them. The land was arid, desolate, even emptier than before, crossed unpredictably by deep gullies that were often just too wide to leap. Twice they attempted to leave a road starting to curve toward the north and cut straight across the land toward the great scarp that lay before them as a ragged black line like a heavy brush stroke across rough paper, but each time they were forced back after losing a worrying amount of time searching for places narrow enough to jump the gullies. Behind them Serroi felt the fury of their pursuers like the effluvium from a stink shell, choking her, sickening her. Then the road swung almost straight north. She pointed at the Scarp. Hern nodded. For the third time they left the road and tried cutting across the broken lands.

Dawn found them riding at a fast walk along the rim of a broad wash, moving almost directly south, hunting for a

place where they could jump their weary mounts across. The
scarp lay less than a quarter mile away on the far side. Hern
was sullen, tired, angry, impatient. He wanted to stop and
ambush the Sleykynin. Serroi refused. Her arrows, she told
him, wouldn't pierce velater hide unless she was almost nose
to nose with the wearer and the Sleykynin wouldn't let either
of them get that close. He wouldn't do much better with the
spears he'd picked up at the well. Hern wanted her to prod
the macain into attack again. She couldn't force herself to do
that, not again, never again. She tried to tell him that but he
couldn't or wouldn't understand. This was life or death and
as far as he was concerned you fought with what weapons
you had. Through persistence and shouting, she convinced
him it was a weapon she no longer had.

The band of assassins kicked up dust behind them, the men
visible as black dots like seed in a cottony white fruit. They
were leaving the chini behind, pushing their mounts now that
Serroi and Hern were in sight, closing the gap faster than was
comfortable in Serroi's eyes. And the wash stubbornly refused
to narrow, though it did begin to curve toward the east just a
little.

"Serroi," Hern called suddenly, bringing her head back
around. His words spaced by short silences as he spat out the
churning dust, he continued, "Look ahead. Am I dreaming or
is that a neck a couple lengths ahead?"

Serroi rubbed at her eyes, squinted ahead. "I think so.
Doesn't look much better than the last two we passed, could
be it's enough. Want to take the chance?"

"We got a choice?"

"No."

They angled out from the wash to give their macain running room. Behind them they heard shouts from their pursuers, screams from the Sleykyn macain as their riders tried
to whip speed they didn't have from the tired beasts. Bent
low over macain necks, whispering encouragement to them,
Serroi and Hern sent them racing at the wash. Powerful hind
legs kicked against the earth; the macain flew in shallow arcs
across the chasm. Serroi's mount landed a safe distance from
the lip, claws out, digging into the hard soil; he pranced a
few strides farther, halted as she tugged him to a stop and
turned to watch Hern's struggles. His mount had landed on
the very rim of the wash, brought down early by Hern's
weight. He flung himself up over the neck of the macai as the
beast scrabbled frantically at the crumbling rim, the shift of

his weight finally enough to turn the balance. The macai scrambled to safety and minced delicately up to Serroi, Hern settling himself back in the saddle. Across the wash they heard a roar of frustration. There was no way the Sleykynin could emulate their feat, their mounts were exhausted and their full armor made them heavier even than Hern.

A short spear hummed past Serroi, plunking into the crusty earth. Hern patted his trembling mount on the shoulder and set him into an easy lope, frowning at the ragged breathing of the beast. Serroi, startled, looked over her shoulder at the Sleykynin. Two of them were on the ground, throwing sticks in hand. As she looked, the second whipped his arm down. The spear hissed through the air at Hern, faster, it seemed to her, than any arrow. She kicked her macai to the side, heard the spear slice past her, heard a grunt from Hern. When she looked, he was crumpling from his mount, a spear shaft protruding from his back. She only had time for a glimpse of this before there was a terrible burning pain in her back and she was falling too.

Mordant bite of dust in her nose and mouth. A yielding hard bulk under her body. She blinks, sits up, pushing against a resistance that is sticky like thick syrup. With almost a pop! she breaks through it and stands.

At first she can see nothing, it is very dark. No moons— Are the clouds back?—then it seems to her she can see a form in the darkness, a long slim form looming high over her. She blinks, wishing she could see more clearly though she isn't frightened, something that surprises her since she can vaguely remember a moment of extreme fear and pain. With the wish comes clearer sight as if all she needs is to will something and it is so. She sees a slim woman with a stern lovely face, it is like one of the Maiden carvings in the great Temple in Oras, but this vision lasts only an instant, the image fades—or changes—or was never there at all. A dark bulk is in front of her, closer to the ground. She blinks. Reiki janja sits cross-legged on the cold gritty earth. The janja beckons. Serroi glides to her at first delighted to see her, then puzzled because she is somehow not walking. She looks down at herself. She is naked. She puts her hands to her face, ashamed to be naked before her friend. She is confused. She can't remember stripping. She holds out her hands and looks at them. She can see the ground through them. She is dreaming. As before. She is suddenly afraid. Before her is Reiki

janja, her friend, she is certain of this, then not certain, she
gazes painfully at Reiki, trying to see into her but she cannot.
The memory of pain grows suddenly stronger, she looks back
at what she left behind her.

In the cold austere moonlight, softly rounded in the stark
black and white angles of the landscape, she sees her body
draped over Hern's, the stubby shafts of spears growing from
both their backs. She gasps and is back hovering over herself.
She sees the trampled dust around the two bodies, the prints
of many macain circling them. Her weaponbelt is gone. Their
mounts are gone. Hern's sword is gone. The Sleykynin have
left them for dead, she knows suddenly. She looks back at
Reiki. "Am I dead?"

"Not yet. Not quite." The janja's voice is quiet, reassuring.

Serroi kneels. The janja is right. There is life burning in
both the bodies, in her abandoned body and Hern's, though
the fire is flickering low. She takes hold of the spear shaft, intending to pull it from her body, but there is no strength in
her hands. Reiki is beside her as she takes her hands away.
"Reach deep," the janja says.

"How?" Serroi looks helplessly at the shaft. "I don't understand."

Reiki kneels beside her, getting down with difficulty and
many muttered complaints, presses her hands on Serroi's
green glass feet. "Reach into earth for the strength you
need."

Her body knowing what to do though her mind is clouded
with confusion, Serroi reaches deep and quivers as a surge of
warmth comes from earth into her.

Reiki takes her hands away and grunts herself leg by leg
back on her feet. "You know what to do," she says. "The
knowledge was born in you."

Serroi sets her hands on the spear shaft again. Before she
can gather herself to try pulling it out, it moves of itself and
begins working out of her body's back. As it comes loose,
blood surges from her back. She lets the spear fall and drops
to her knees, flattening her hands on the wound. At first the
blood flows through her hands, then the warmth flows out of
them. Her hands sink into the lacerated muscle. She doesn't
know what is happening, but the warmth knows, her body
knows—how to heal itself is what it knows. She realizes this
almost immediately and relaxes, letting what is happening
happen of itself. Her body uses the warmth to make new
flesh, new blood, pushing her hands up as it repairs itself,

layer by layer. When her hands emerge from her body, she stares at them. Her dream-flesh is translucent green glass and there is no blood on it.

"You want to hurry a little or Hern will die on you." Reiki's grave voice breaks into her wonder.

Dream-Serroi nods. She tugs at her body but can't budge it even when the warmth surges back into her. Reiki pushes her aside and lifts Serroi and lays her flat, face up, on the ground. Dream-Serroi flits to Hern. She roots herself in the earth again, the feeling is like extruding tendrils from her dream body, she sees them growing down deep deep into earth's heart. She grasps the spear shaft, feels it come alive and begin working up through the thicker meatier muscle of Hern's back. When it is out, she lets it topple and presses her hands into Hern's flesh. Again the body knows its business. She doesn't have to fuss, just provide the energy and let it work. She is much more confident this time, feels a great serenity, a happiness that is partly joy that Hern will not die and partly the joy she finds in the healing itself. Again the flesh knits under her palms, little by little pushing her out. When the wound is closed and healed except for a faint pinkness of the skin, she sinks back on her heels and looks thoughtfully at the delicate green glass of her hands. She turns and smiles at Reiki janja, weary but happy with it.

The janja smiles a bit distractedly, waves her big hand at Serroi. "Back home, little one. You've been out long enough."

Serroi drifts across to her body. She stands looking down at it for a moment. Her body's eyes are closed. There is a half-smile on her face. She looks quietly happy and at rest at long last as if all her agonizing has been washed away. Dream-Serroi hesitates. But—in spite of the pain she knows is waiting for her—she isn't quite ready to die yet. Rest is seductive, but there is too much left for her to do to succumb to that seduction. She steps onto her body and merges with it.

She sat up. Hern was still out, his body recovering from its strenuous business. She felt some of the same weariness, a dragging tiredness as if she'd been heaving forkloads of wet hay all day long. She pulled her legs up, wrapped her arms around them. Her herbs and drugs and other small supplies were gone with her weaponbelt, the macain were gone and all the food and water with them. The gold was gone. She sighed as she thought of Yael-mri's annoyance when she heard this. Gone to Sleykynin, that was the worst of it. She propped her elbows on her knees, dropped her chin into her hands and contemplated Hern. He was sleeping, no longer unconscious, she realized that when she heard a faint snore. *Left for dead,* she thought. *They'll regret that, probably are already with the Prime of the local Chapter House chewing their ears off about not bringing the bodies back. Wonder what time it is.* She dropped her hands and looked up. Most of the moons had already set, though the three Dancers were still up, their light touching the face of the scarp and illuminating the rotten ragged stone. *They'll be coming back.* She spared a moment's thankfulness for the wash she'd cursed so fervently before. Without that, without the Sleykyn fear they'd escape, she'd be back in the trap she'd been in before at the well, facing a course of rape and torture, this time with less—far less—chance of escaping it. She touched the side of her boot, felt the long slim hardness of the hideout, blessed the tajicho. She watched Hern snore for a few minutes then turned to search for Reiki expecting to see nothing, thinking that the old woman had vanished with the ending of the dream, but the janja sat quietly, waiting with wordless patience for Serroi to finish her musings, passing a soft leather bag from hand to hand, the long drawstring draped over her thick wrist.

"Take off your boots, little one," Reiki said softly. "For a while now you must keep touch with the Mother."

Serroi touched her boots, outlined the small round of the tajicho. "I can't. I dare not."

Reiki tossed her the small pouch. "Put it in this. Wear it around your neck."

Serroi fished out the tajicho, looked up to meet Reiki's smiling eyes. "You shouldn't be able . . . how . . .?"

"I couldn't if I wished you harm."

"The sprite . . . Hern. . . ."

"I know. Don't worry about it."

"Oh." The tajicho was warm in Serroi's hand but not burning. She slipped it into the pouch and hung the pouch around her neck.

She pulled off her boots and sat rubbing her feet. She looked at the boots, pulled the hideout from its sheath. She set the knife on the ground beside her and dug into the other boot for the silver box and the lockpicks stowed there. She set the picks and the box beside the knife, looked at them a long moment, sighed, restored them to their pockets and set the boots on the ground. She got to her feet, feeling bones and muscles creak. She stretched, working her sore muscles until they protested, then strolled over to smile down at Hern.

Still deeply asleep, he looked uncomfortable but there was nothing much she could do about that. Even back in her body she wasn't strong enough to lift him. Stepping back, her foot touched something. She looked down. The spear. She bent and picked it up, rubbed her thumb along the dried blood on the point, pounded the shaft against the ground. It was long enough to serve as a walking staff. She dug the bloody point repeatedly into the hard earth to scrub the blood away. *Good for digging too*, she thought. She stopped and stared at the spear. *Digging?* She shrugged, cleaned the second spear and laid them both out beside Hern. She scratched at her nose, twisted her mouth, went back to her boots. Holding them in her hands, she gazed at Reiki. "Digging?"

"You know already."

"I know nothing. I understand nothing. What's happening to me?"

"You're changing. Shifting from his hand to mine."

"Who are you?"

"You know me."

"I thought I did. I'm not sure now."

"I'm Reiki, janja of the pehiir. What did you think?"

"That only?"

Reiki shrugged, spread out her hands palms up. "Sometimes I think so, sometimes not."

"Now?"

"Does it matter?"

"Yes. What is he to you?"

"He has made himself my enemy."

"Does he know what we're after? Do you?"

"I know. He doesn't yet. He thinks you're running from him, trying to pull his attention from the Valley. And he's worried about you."

Serroi looked down at the boots in her hand; she lifted them and smoothed the tops over her arm. "Why is he doing this?"

Broad hands palm down on her thighs, Reiki janja sighed. "An end to uncertainty. He's tired of seeing things and people he cares about darting out of control, out of his control. He's not an evil man."

Serroi echoed Reiki's sigh. "I know. He doesn't understand anything."

Silence. The whisper of dust on dust, the acrid taste of dust in her mouth. The soft regular puffs of Hern's breath. Serroi

flattened her feet on the earth, feeling the currents passing
between earth and her, understanding now a little why she
must walk barefoot for a while. She wiped her face with the
sleeve of Beyl's shirt. "What else do I need to know?"

"Eat no meat up on the plateau."

"Hern won't like that."

"That's not laid on him, just you."

Serroi grimaced. "For always?"

"No. Only on the plateau."

"So. What can I eat?"

"Learn to listen."

"That's a big help. Will you be coming with us?"

"No, little one. I'm not here."

"Am I still dreaming?"

"No. Yes. Does it matter?"

Serroi rubbed her feet back and forth in the slippery dust.
"We've got no water, no food, nothing."

"Learn to be still. Empty yourself and listen to the voice of
the Mother."

"Words. Can't eat words. You won't help us."

"You're survived before and in worse case. The plateau's
no desert. You don't need help." Reiki got heavily to her feet,
grinned at Serroi and was suddenly not there.

Serroi blinked. Somehow what she knew as reality and
what she thought of as dream blended so completely that she
had no idea where one began and the other left off. She
closed fingers about the soft leather bag hanging between her
breasts. That was real, it was here, she could touch and see
and smell it, even taste it if she wished. She slid her feet back
and forth in the cold dust, feeling morning in the air, something about the darkness and heaviness in the wind pressing
against her back, the extra chill in the dust beneath her feet.
She went back to Hern, knelt beside him.

She reached out to shake him awake, instead drew her fingers very softly across his broad low brow, brushing the
sweaty strands of hair off it, drew her fingers down along
the side of his face, smiling as she touched short stiff whiskers.
His razors were gone with his gear. He wouldn't like that. He
was fussy about his person. Fastidious. The quest had already
been hard on him that way, it would be worse now. She
smiled tenderly as she traced the outline of his lips, leaned
down, kissed him lightly, straightened to find his eyes open
watching her, a twinkle of amusement shining in them. She
sat back on her heels. "Sneak."

"Viper." He sat up stiffly, rubbed his hands together, moved his shoulders. "Thought I was dead."

"Not quite."

He moved his shoulders again, caught sight of the two spears lying beside him. "Another little talent?"

"So it seems. Newly acquired."

"Good timing." He lifted the spears, examined the points, raised his brows when he saw traces of blood on both points and on the shafts near the points. He got to his feet, gave her a hand, swung her around so he could examine her back. "Got you too."

"Uh-huh." She pulled free, stooped, picked up one of the spears, straightened, scanned the sky just above the top of the scarp. It seemed to her she could see a faint lightening just above the dark ragged top of the cliff looming over them, though it could have been imagination only.

Hern's hand dropped on her shoulder. "You thinking what I think you're thinking?"

"Yah, Dom."

"Why?"

She leaned back against him. His arms closed around her, holding her quietly, without fuss. She sighed. "I have to. Don't ask why because I damn well don't know." She rested against him, reluctant to go on. "Wild magic up there. The Sleykynin are afraid of it," she said. "You don't have to come with me. There's a river not too far north of here. You could steal a boat and ride in comfort down to Shinka."

He said nothing for several minutes, only stood holding her, his chin resting warm on her head. Then, laughing, he turned her around and gazed down at her, his hands on her shoulders. "You won't take orders even when you know I'm right, you won't answer questions until you're ready, you're bad-tempered, intolerant, self-centered, annoying." Still laughing he left her, collected her boots and the other spear. "Let's go."

The ascent of the scarp face was more exasperating than difficult, a crawl from crack to crack with rock that seemed solid splitting away from under hand or foot, every hold tested and not excessively trusted. By the time they reached the top Serroi's hands and feet were bleeding, Hern's hands. The sun was just coming up, a red dot on the flat line of the horizon. The morning was cool and fresh, an erratic breeze stirring the grit and the clumps of limp dry grass, the low scraggly brush. Serroi dug her spear point into the hard earth, left the spear standing as she turned to Hern and took his hands.

"What . . .?"

"Be still." Healing is not so easy in the body. She feels his startled resistance, his subsequent relaxation, as she roots herself into the earth and lets the warmth of the Mother surge up through her and into him. He feels it and shies but she is holding him tight and he can't pull away without hurting her. He grows quiet as the healing drains his strength a little, not much this time; the wounds are minor, but she has an urge to do something about that small weakness. She fills him with the strength of earth herself then takes her hands away. He stares down at his hands as she is noting that she has, without intending it, healed herself. She meets his eyes, sees his brows raise, sees also that scar on his face is gone, though the break in his whiskers remains to show where it was. She backs away to the spear, takes hold of the shaft, feeling a brief euphoria, a high that slowly leaks away as she faces the sun and starts walking.

She took a few steps, turned. Hern was watching her with an odd expression on his face. He brushed his hands across his shirt front, shook his head, came up with her, asking no questions.

They walked in that companionable silence for some time. The plateau near the edge of the scarp was mostly rock with scatters of thin soil, a few patches of wispy sun-dried grass, small crawlers disturbed by the passing feet. As they got farther from the edge the soil got deeper, the grass thicker, the brush taller, a new kind of brush with a dusty, pleasantly pungent odor. Short crooked limbs with a smooth leathery bark so darkly red it was nearly black, teardrop-shaped leaves of a dusty grey green. She stepped over a dried-out vine with a few touches of green left in the ropy stems and leaves, dried out fruits, wrinkled, dark purple, clinging to desiccated yellow stalks. She felt a sudden bite in the soles of her feet, lifted first one foot then the other, brushed hastily at her soles, trotted after Hern.

A second vine. The prickle again. She stopped. *Listen,* she thought. *Reiki said listen.* She slipped one boot from under her belt, knelt beside the vine, stripped the dried fruits into the boot. Hern watched a moment, walked on, impatient, growling in his stomach, thirsty already and getting thirstier.

She knew what he was feeling but at the moment she didn't know quite what to do about it except keep gathering roots and anything else she found edible. She rose and walked after him, listening at last, listening through the soles of her feet.

A lappet scurried across in front of them. With an explosive exclamation, Hern was after it, the spear reversed, poised for the throw. He disappeared between clumps of brush, running with a speed and energy that surprised her, though she wasn't surprised to see that he could use that spear, he seemed to know something about any weapon she could think of. She forgot about him and began "listening" to the earth again, digging up crooked yellow tubers, dropping them into her boot with the fruits. She found a patch of tulpa, broke off the thick crisp stalks and added them to her collection. She was prodding thoughtfully at the soil with the point of her spear when he came back, three lappets not one dangling from his left hand, a wide grin marking his delight with himself. He mopped at his face with his sleeve. "Think you could find us some water?"

She leaned heavily on the spear, wondering what she could do. Not needing his prodding, she'd already sent her outreach searching for water. As far as she could tell, there was none on the surface of the plateau. *Water,* she thought, and as she thought of water now, she had an itching on the soles of her feet, a writhing wriggling feel as if immaterial roots were struggling to break through the skin. Alarmed, she lifted one foot, felt a pressure on her back and neck. "Wait here," she said, "let me see." The push driving her, she struggled to keep some kind of control over her body, to avoid the snatching thorns on the brush; she felt confused, ignorant, helpless in her ignorance.

When the push lets up she kicks her feet through the matted grass until she is standing with her feet partly buried in the gritty dirt. The roots break through, drive into earth's cool heart. She touches a cold so intense it is a terrible pain. The cold gushes up through her body. She cannot pull away, not without tearing loose from those roots and she is afraid of doing that. The cold bursts forth and flows over her feet. She looks down. Crystalline liquid is gushing from beneath her feet, the flow increasing until it is bubbling up past her ankles.

She stepped out of the water, wiped her feet on a patch of grass, wrinkled her nose at the clammy feel of the sodden last inches of her trouser legs. She looked at the water, laughed, an uncertain rather frightened sound, stopped when she heard that fear. "Hern," she called. "Here's water."

Hern wiped his greasy hands on a patch of limp, dry grass, broke the improvised spit into bits and dropped them into the small hot fire. Serroi sighed, peeled another tulpa stalk and bit off a piece of the crisp white flesh, the smell of the roasted meat making head and stomach ache.

Hern dug his boot heel into the dirt, inspected the groove. "You think this so-called quest is worth all the trouble it's giving us?" He turned his head, his grey eyes considered her gravely. "Or something Yael-mri cooked up to get us out of her hair."

Serroi shook her head. "If it was anyone but Yael-mri—no." She yawned, surprising herself, covering the gape with a sluggish hand. The warmth of the sun and her exertions were making her sleepy. "It's a real chance." She yawned again, blinked. "Chance. Win or lose, what else is there?"

CHAPTER XI:

THE MIJLOC
(IN THE EARTH'S TEETH)

Stretched out on her stomach on a narrow flat high up the mountain, Tuli dragged the twig through the stony earth, gouging out a line beside others scratched at random in front of her, using the control she imposed on her hand and wrist to help her tighten what little hold she had on the turmoil in her head. She slanted a glance at Rane. The lanky ex-meie was sitting cross-legged beside her, perched on a hummock of grass, fingers stroking continually along and along the smooth old wood of her flute, her face controlled, serene. "You think I'm crazy?"

Rane turned her head slowly, smiled slowly. "No," she said.

"They do." Tuli stared down the slope dropping away close by her left shoulder at the turmoil below, the miniature black figures of busy mijlockers, some scurrying about without apparent destinations, others trotting in double lines from the quarry below to the semi-circle of stone backed against the near vertical cliff on the far side of the long narrow valley, or in double lines carrying blocks of roughly dressed stone to the quickly rising wall that was beginning to block off the valley between two crumbling cliffs near the point where it opened out onto gently rolling hills. Below her, stone cutters worried granite from the hillside using what makeshift tools they had with them, worked the quarried stone into blocks, the steady ring of iron hammer against iron chisel, chisel against stone making bright singing sounds that rebounded from the face of the mountain across the way. A creek wriggled along the valley floor, making a demanding unresonant music. Shouts and laughter bounded up to her ears. The air so high was thin and cold and carried sound with the clarity of cracking ice.

"Teras went scouting with Hars," Tuli said. "Five days ago. Without me."

Tuli dumped the water from the canvas bucket into the big pot backed up against the fire and stretched hands blue with cold to the blaze. The heat reddened her face, made her skin itch, but she didn't draw back, the warmth felt especially good after the splashing of the icy stream. She closed her eyes, sniffed with pleasure at the fish frying in the pan, abandoned for the moment while her mother beat at batter in a thick-sided crockery bowl. Tuli sat back on her heels, yawned idly, watching her father as he came up the streambank toward them, stopping a few minutes at each of the nearer camps to talk a bit with the other outlaw taroms that had settled in the valley. Sanoni was a little farther up the mountain, fussing with her oadats, a half dozen of the grey-furred ground-runners kept for the moment in rough wicker cages. They weren't adapting too well to the higher altitude though they still produced an egg or two, Annic's batter testified to that. They tended to droop and forget to eat except when Sanoni teased and caressed them into a happier state. Teras didn't seem to be anywhere about. *Da must've sent him to get something,* she thought, then tried to dismiss him from her mind. He'd been restless and irritable, snapping at her with no excuse at all, hanging around with the boys when he wasn't working. As her father came up the slope to their camp, red-faced and vigorous, oddly content for a man who'd lost everything, Tuli got to her feet, stood rubbing her hands down along her sides. "Where's Teras? He better hurry back, breakfast's almost ready."

Tesc lost his smile. He bent over the fish in the frying pan, picked up Annic's spatula, prodded at them, flipped them over neatly with a quick twist of his wrist, surprising Tuli who'd never before seen him try anything connected with work of a house, though, of course, this rough camp was far from being a house.

Tuli started to repeat the question. "Where . . .?"

"He left early," Tesc said reluctantly. He frowned down at the fish, tapped them with the spatula. "With Hars," he said. "We need to know when the next tithe wagons are loaded and ready to roll."

"Left? No. He wouldn't go without me." Tuli tightened her hands into fists, knives in her head and belly, a surge of heat up her body. She wrestled with the newborn rage, tried to shove it down. "He wouldn't, Da. He knows I want to go."

Tesc came around the fire and took hold of her shoulders with gentle strength, stood looking gravely down into her face. "Try to understand, Tuli. I don't want you riding with them. It's too dangerous."

Mouth working without making words, Tuli stared up into her father's round blue eyes, saw anxiety in them and something else she didn't understand—unless it might be pity and she shied away from that because she couldn't endure the idea that her father might pity her. "No." She folded her arms tight across her tender breasts to damp the waves of anger surging in her. "No. I don't believe you." Her voice was not quite shrill and broke on the words. The pity she refused was stronger in her father's face. "It was him, wasn't it? He doesn't want me." With a hoarse scream as her fury burst on her, she flung herself onto her father's chest, fists beating on him, a voice hers and not hers shouting things she couldn't bear to remember later. Annic came around behind her, pulled her away from Tesc, turned her, slapped her hard first right cheek then left, shocking her from her fit, holding her close after, patting her shoulders, murmuring soothing, meaningless sounds until her shuddering passed away and she was limp and exhausted in her mother's arms.

"It's time you let him go," Rane said.

Tuli gouged repeatedly at the soil with her bit of twig, brushed the broken earth away. "I don't see why."

"You aren't children any more."

"He wasn't just my brother, he was my friend."

"Was, Tuli?"

"Is."

"You don't have many friends, do you?"

"That's not my fault. Can I help it if they're too stupid to care about real things, not just gossip and giggling? There's no one I can talk to, not really, not like Teras. No one understands." She looked at the twig. "They're boring. Besides, they don't want me around, they laugh at me." She broke the twig in half with a quick vicious twist of her hands and flung the pieces away from her. "Fayd came up from the mijloc a couple days after Teras left."

"Fayd?"

"A friend, at least I thought he was; he used to run around with Teras and me, we had a lot of fun then. . . ."

"Eh-Tutu."

Tuli dropped the stone block she was carrying and wheeled at the sound of the familiar voice, a grin threatening to split her face in half. "Eh-Fada," she cried and held out her hands.

Fayd slid from his weary macai and caught hold of her hands. His brows rose—very bushy and so blond they looked like small straw stacks sitting over his dark blue eyes. "What've you been doing to yourself?" He drew his thumbs over rough, abraded palms grey-white with stone dust.

"Working, you nit." She pulled her hands free and stooped for the stone, straightened, cradling the awkward mass in the curve of her arm. "You just wait, you'll be hauling too once the council knows you're here." She began to stroll not too quickly toward the wall. "What happened? And how'd you find us?"

He walked beside her, leading the macai. "Saw Teras— well, he saw me, told me where to come."

Tuli glanced at him, saw he was waiting for her to ask about Teras. She looked away from him and walked stiffly along without saying anything.

"What happened? Eh-Tutu, you know my father, what he's like. He caught me. . . ." He stopped. His brilliant blue eyes narrowed a little, slid slyly toward her. He wore the too culti-vated look of rueful deviltry that gave him the air of a naughty sprite, a look that had too often helped him to slide unscathed out of trouble. Tuli didn't like it much. "Anyway," he said, "he disowned me, foaming at the mouth with righteous rage over my iniquities as he called them, was going to have me hauled off to the House of Repentance. I didn't wait around for that. Adin's heir now."

"I'm sorry, Fayd. I knew you and your Da didn't get along too good but I didn't think he'd do something like that."

"Eh-Tutu, it's not so bad, just Soäreh junk, folks getting tired of their ranting already, it can't last that much longer. I admit it sent Father off his head but he never was any too. . . ." He broke off when he saw the distaste in Tuli's face. "What's Teras doing below?"

"Looking around." She started to explain but found herself oddly reluctant to say anything more about it to Fayd. "Look, Fayd, you'd better go check in with Da. He's up along there somewhere." She waved her hand toward the creek. "He don't like folks wandering about without him or the council knowing."

"Council? That's the second time. . . ."

"Da 'ull tell you." She grinned at him. "I know you, lazy, you want to lie around in the sun all day. Hah! You'll be groaning louder than the creek tomorrow. We got lots and lots of work to do to get ready for winter."

"Work," he moaned. Though he still smiled, there was strong dislike in the glance he gave the stone she hugged to her side. With a laugh and a wave he swung into the saddle and rode off.

Tuli looked thoughtfully at her hands, then at the stone; with a discontented sigh she straightened her back and started for the wall.

Rane lifted her flute, looked at it briefly, raised it to her lips and blew a few experimental notes. She lowered it again, a question in her eyes. "There's more, isn't there."

Tuli nodded. Her lips were pressed so hard together they disappeared; a hectic flush reddened her cheeks.

"You don't have to tell me." Rane started playing very softly, coaxing a breathy, near inaudible tune from the lowest notes of the flute, a strange soothing rise and fall that blended with the brisk rustle of the stiff grey-green leaves of the vachbrush. Tuli relaxed gradually. She pressed her thighs together, moved her hips restlessly back and forth across the crusted earth. She was embarrassed, ashamed, afraid, most of all afraid and unsure. She listened to the flute music, glanced at Rane's long gaunt face, envied the tranquility she saw in both face and body. She rocked her pelvis against the ground, scrubbed her thumb hard against the grooves she'd scratched in front of her. She closed her hands into fists, rubbed the back of her fist across her mouth. "I . . . I missed Teras a lot," she said suddenly. Panic rushed her into speech again when Rane stopped playing and turned to look at her. "Don't look at me or I can't."

Rane nodded, shook saliva from the flute, began playing again, the same slow drifting melody, the same low singing notes.

Tuli slipped from her blankets late on the second night after Fayd showed up. She wriggled under the heavy canvas, dragging boots, jacket, tunic and trousers with her. Gibbous TheDom was hanging low in the west almost sitting on the points of the Teeth and the night air was dry ice against her skin. She ran shivering to a clump of brush, pulled off her sleeping smock and dressed as quickly and quietly as she could, suppressing the chattering of her teeth, hampered by the cold-induced clumsiness of her hands. She pulled on her old jacket, thrust a hand into her pocket, felt the leather straps of her sling coiled in the bottom and began to relax for the first time in days, all those people around, people she didn't know, people who didn't want to know her, she couldn't get away from them. She stamped her feet down in her boots and prowled off along the creek crossing to the far side on the stepping stones, taking care not to wake any of the sleepers in the camps, flitting like a shadow along the valley toward the wall, shedding as she moved more of her tensions and constraints until she was having a hard time keeping her laughter inside. It was like old times, all she lacked was Teras at her side but she wouldn't think about that, at least there was Fayd. She grinned at the moon. Good ol' Fayd. She swung her arms vigorously, hopped a few steps every few strides, her soul expanding with the night her eyes soothed by the familiar black and white and multiple greys. There were no kankas up here to fill the night with their flutings and their wavering kill-cries, but another sort of passar occupied the same niche, a slimmer flier with long pointed wings, smaller gasbags and a piping song almost too high to hear. Small furry predators, long and lithe with a humping, bounding run, flitted from shadow to shadow, pounced on smaller rodents and fled with their prey as Tuli ran past them. There was no guard on the half-finished wall, not yet, no point to it; she circled around through the gap where the gate would be and came back to the creek bank, trotted along it until she came to the lone brellim growing among the scattered conifers, an aged gnarled tree whose lower limbs were so heavy with years that their outer ends rested on the ground creating a cavern of darkness even in the daylight. Fayd had promised to meet her there.

She put her hand on one of the low limbs, felt it creak under her palm. There was a knot in her stomach suddenly, a vague foreboding that rather spoiled her pleasure in the icy beautiful night. Angrily she flung out a hand as if she pushed the feeling away from her. "Fayd," she called. "You here?"

"Eh-Tuli." The answering whisper came from the shadow under the brellim.

"Come on, I brought my sling, let's go." She was impatient, refusing to share the nonsense of whispers out here where there was no one to hear them.

"Come in here first, got something to show you."

"Fayd?" Still impatient, still refusing to acknowledge the coldness inside her that had nothing to do with the bite in the night air, she pushed into darkness that even her nightsight was unable to penetrate. "Where in zhag are you?"

He laughed, a nervous kind of sound almost like a giggle but too excited and too something else she had no name for to be a giggle. He bumped against her. His arms went around her. She began to feel trapped. His breathing was hoarse and ragged as he rubbed his body hard against hers. She was horribly uncomfortable, but she didn't move, sensing that if she pushed him away as she wanted, she'd lose him too and she couldn't bear that. She stood stiff and unresponsive, waiting for him to finish whatever it was he thought he was doing. "Relax, relax," he whispered, "you want to do it, you know you do, you came, didn't you." He moved a little away so he could slide a hand between them and knead at her breasts. It hurt. She tried easing herself back from him, but he wouldn't let her go. "Don't be like that, Tutu, you want it, I saw you looking at me, you want it, relax, I'm not going to hurt you." He hooked his foot behind hers and pulled them out from under her, catching her as she toppled and lowering her to the ground, doing it gently enough that she wasn't shocked into a panic. There was a blanket on the ground. *He planned this*, she thought, *he knew all the time what he was going to do, Ay Maiden help me*.

"Fayd," she said, her voice breaking over the lump in her throat. "I don't want to do this."

In the darkness she could hear the slide of cloth then he was down beside her. He laughed, that same strained breathy laugh that had disturbed her before. "You haven't done it before, that's all, Tutu, you'll like it." He kept talking in that husky coaxing whisper as he eased her tunic up until it was rucked up under her arms, leaving her breasts exposed.

"Fada," she said, pleading with him, using his pet name to try to remind him of old times not now. "Fada, don't."

"You're being silly, Tutu," he whispered, he bent over her and took her nipple in his mouth. She gasped and wriggled on the blanket as heat very unlike her anger heat shot through her body. "See, see, you like it." His breath was hot against her skin. He kept on and on until all she felt was a growing pain and a feeling of nausea at his touch and the knowledge that he wasn't going to stop, he was going to do what he wanted no matter what she wanted.

"Fayd, stop," she said sharply. "I won't. . . ."

He didn't answer, didn't even seem to hear her, was too busy with the lacings on her trousers to pay attention to anything she said. He got up on his knees to ease her trousers down over her hips then he was on top of her. *It hurts, oh Maiden help me, it hurts, I don't want this, I'm not ready for this, oh let it end, let it end, please let it end.* She bucked and writhed under him trying to throw him off her, but he was too heavy, too much bigger, she was helpless, she screamed and cursed and clawed at him, it meant nothing to him, made no difference to what he was doing. He groaned and shuddered on her, then rolled off, got to his feet and laughed, he laughed at her.

Tuli lay back, colder inside than she'd ever been in her life. For the first time, she wanted to be angry, wanted to have that fire in her head that blanked out everything but the need to hurt. She lay on the blanket, cold and nauseated, empty.

"Little sicamar." There was an awful kind of triumph in his voice as he pulled up his trousers and tied the laces. "You drew blood, you know that? Whee-oh, what a ride you give, Tutu. Told you you'd like it, didn't know how much, did I?" He didn't understand anything, he thought—oh, Maiden bless—he thought she was pleased, he didn't have the faintest idea she wanted most of all to tear him into bloody shreds, how stupid he was, how stupid I was to think I wanted him for a friend, to let him even get started in this. "You better get back before someone misses you." She could hear his feet kicking through the dead leaves on the ground as he walked toward the outer circle of hanging limbs. "Eh-Tutu, don't forget to roll up the blanket, tuck it in the hollow on the backside of the trunk, we'll need it next time." The leaves rustled as he pushed through to the outside. She could hear him whistling as he strolled off.

Tuli sat up, slowly, painfully. She still hurt but more than that she felt soiled inside. "Next time," she said. She pulled her tunic down with trembling hands, grateful for the slight increase in warmth. "Stupid," she said. She got painfully to her feet and started to pull her trousers up, changed her mind, pushed them down over her boots and kicked out of them. "Stupid." Standing first on one foot, then on the other, she tugged her boots off and threw them on the blanket. "Never." She bent and felt about for her trousers, then her boots, carried them out into the moonlight. "Not with him."

She dropped her clothing on the greasy creek bank and plunged into the water, shouting involuntarily as the liquid ice closed around her reaching to her waist. She waded to shallower water, scooped up a handful of sand and scrubbed vigorously at herself, ignoring the pain, scrubbing away the feel of him, wishing she could scrub the memory of him from her mind, until she felt cleaner though she didn't know if she'd ever feel clean again, not really. She ran from the water when she was finished, rolled on the grass to dry herself a little, then scrambled back into her clothes, her skin tingling, the blood racing in her veins. "I won't let him spoil this," she said. "I won't let him steal the night from me," she shouted to the moons, shouted futilely, she knew that. Her sureness was gone, she couldn't get it back, that sense of invulnerability when she ran the night. Nothing would ever be the same again, the change that she'd rebelled against before was almost complete now. Nothing would ever be the same.

Rane kept playing the flute even though Tuli stopped talking. Tuli gathered courage and lay watching her, taking pleasure after a while in the neatly chiselled features of her stenda face, in the unconsidered grace of her lanky body, in the sense of control she got whenever she looked at the exmeie. Rane's calm helped her reduce the thing with Fayd from the monstrous horror it had grown to in her mind to a mere unpleasant and uncomfortable episode. Tuli dropped her chin onto her fists and listened, smiling inside, to the slow, sighing music from the flute. Far down the slope the noises of the work continued unabated, but that all seemed terribly remote from this patch of grassy brush-free mountainside, sheltered from the wind, warmed by the late afternoon sun. Tuli yawned lazily, her eyelids dropping. Rane finished her song, shook out the flute, set it on her thighs, reached out and brushed a straying lock of hair off Tuli's face. "He wasted no time boasting about the two of you?"

"None." Tuli folded her arms on the ground in front of her, dropped her forehead on them, hiding her face. She felt Rane's hand touch her head once, then withdraw. She spoke to the dust. "I was carrying stone. About halfway through the morning he walked past hanging on to Delpha, you don't know her, she's a tie-girl from down south, she's. . . ." Tuli sighed, then sneezed as the dust came into her nose and mouth.

"You don't get on so good with the tie-girls."

"No." Tuli turned her head so her cheek rested on her arms, her face turned away from Rane. "No, they don't like me much. He ignored me, the lout. Fayd ignored me. Not that I wanted him to fuss or anything, but he went past me more'n once like he didn't even see me. And Delpha was giggling, she'd look at me and look away, sneak a look and look away, and a couple tie boys kept hanging around and grinning at me. And touching me. You know. Ayii, Rane, I hated it, but I didn't do nothing. When things got too bad I went off, up here sometimes, it helped a bit, but they wouldn't leave me alone. And . . . and then Fayd and Delpha came by. They should have been working, both of them, they'd got no business lazing around like that. And Delpha stopped and stopped him when she came up to me. And she looked me up and down. And she pushed out her chest and flopped that red hair around and flapped her eyes at Fayd and told him, I didn't know you went with boys and she laughed and . . . and . . . things kind of exploded and I jumped her and I don't know much what happened after that till you pulled me off her except Delpha kept screaming I was crazy and Fayd sort of hung back and flopped about with his stupid mouth hanging open. Am I crazy, Rane? I don't know anymore, I can't . . . can't hold onto myself even when I know I have to, I do things I hate after, things I know are wrong when I'm doing them but I can't stop. Everything's wrong. Everything."

Rane laughed, shocking Tuli. "Don't exaggerate," the ex-meie said, her words like Annic's slaps serving to unseat the fit of whatever threatened to overtake her. "Tuli, I'm setting out on a swing around the mijloc to Oras and back. Tomorrow, early. You want to come with me?"

Tuli felt a sudden flush of relief, a lightening of her spirit. Then she drooped. "Da won't let me go."

"I think he will. He understands more than you think." Rane laughed and got to her feet. "You stretch out up here and get some sleep."

Tuli flattened her hands on the sleeping pad, forced her eyes determinedly shut and kept herself lying still until she couldn't stand it any longer. Small itches raced across her skin as if thousands of chinjim were infesting the blankets and crawling over her body, their threadlike legs running, running, all over her. With an explosive sigh she kicked the blankets off and sat up, scratching vigorously at arms and legs. The odor of the tent's heavy canvas was sharp in her nostrils, Sanani's steady slow breathing an irritation to her nerves, a reproach almost. Tuli rubbed absently at her arms, shivering more and more as the cold sank to her bones. She snagged one of the blankets and pulled it around her shoulders. The itches started traveling over her again and a dull ache spread across her back. She sighed and got to her feet. *No good. I can't sleep and I can't just sit around and scratch.* Not bothering to dress or pull on her boots, the blanket clutched around her, one corner dragging on the ground, she pushed through the entrance slit and stood awhile in front of the tent, sore in body and spirit from the strain of the past days.

Shaking hair out of her eyes, she gazed around, wondering if she dared go for a walk, tilted her head back to watch the shrunken TheDom drift through wispy clouds because she didn't want to think about that anymore, jumped and gasped when she heard a crash behind the tent, clamped a tardy hand over her mouth though the small sound she made was lost in the night noises, the creak of tent poles, the rustles of leaves, the tiny rattle of grit blowing across the mountainside.

"More than enough wood for morning." Her mother's voice.

"Good. I'm beat." Her father.

Tuli crept along the side of the tent to the point where it joined the canvas windbreak that blocked off three sides of the cookplace.

"Some coals left. Hand me those two short pieces, I don't want to go in just yet, been a long time since I've had you to myself." Laughter, warm and low from both of them, blending. The sound of liquid pouring into mugs just barely audible above the night noises, the subdued crackling from the fire. Tuli spread apart the edge of the tent and the end of the windbreak, saw Annic set the cha pot back on the iron plate at the side of the fire, saw Tesc sitting on the section of treetrunk rolled there to serve as a crude bench. Annic settled herself on the ground by his knees, worked herself around until her head was against his thigh, her back partly against the wood, partly against his leg. He sipped at the mug he held in his left hand, caressed her hair, the side of her face, with the other. Tuli got a queer feeling in the pit of her stomach and pulled back, but put her eye to the slit again after the silence between them had persisted for several minutes, not sure what she was going to see, not sure she wanted to see it, unable to resist the prodding of her curiosity.

They were just sitting there drinking their cha; they looked comfortable with each other, content just to be there. They looked happy and for a very very brief moment, as long as she allowed herself to be, before she drove it away as if it were something white and loathsome that lived in dead meat, she was almost sick with jealousy.

Tesc sighed and set his cup on the trunk beside him. "The ties are getting edgy. They want representation on the Council."

"Mmh, that means Ander Tallin's been acting natural again."

Tesc laughed. "Trust you to see through a wall. He wants to collect all the food and tools and keep them locked up in a shed and doled out every day—by him, I suppose. He says the ties are getting a lot too uppity." Tesc chuckled. "I suspect he tried ordering someone about and was called on it."

Tuli frowned. She'd never paid much attention to anything but the way people acted to her; what they felt about each other and what that might mean to life up here hadn't been important—now it opened out vague but fascinating possibilities that distracted her from what her parents were saying. She rubbed at the wrinkles on her forehead, thinking about the other taroms and their families, startled to find them only cloudy outlines without names and faces.

Annic got up, refilled her cup and brought the pot back with her. "Looks to me like you'd be better off with a couple good ties backing you. Want more cha?"

"I shouldn't, never get to sleep." He grinned suddenly at Annic. "Fill it up, I just thought of a better way of rocking myself to sleep."

Annic chuckled. "The woman tempted him."

"Always." He reached out and took her hand. They stood like that for several minutes, smiling at each other in a way that shut the rest of the world out. With a soft laugh Annic finally pulled away, poured cha into his cup, handed it to him, and settled back leaning against him.

"Problem is," he said, "what we do up here is going to set patterns for a lot of years when this is all over. Hard to see what's going to come of it."

"Tell you this, I don't want to live anywhere Pleora Tallin can order me about. What a chinj. She thinks Anders should be headman."

"So does he." He drained his cup. "Forget them. Let's go in."

Tuli got hastily to her feet and ran along the tent. When Annic and Tesc came in she was curled up in her blankets with a roll of wool tight over her ears.

Tuli looked back. Her father had walked down to the wall with them. Now he stood watching as they rode away, a blocky solid blackness in the gap where the gate would be. She felt a sudden surge of affection laced with grief, a premonition that it would be a long time before she saw her father again, if she ever did. After looking back until she couldn't see the ragged top of the unfinished wall, until her neck and shoulders ached, she swung around and stared at the silent black and grey hills in front of her not sure what she felt now, excited, happy, uncertain, lost; it was good to get away from the valley, that was true, but she was already missing Da and Mama and Sanani and she wouldn't think about Teras. Rane was interesting, but when Tuli thought about it the ex-meie seemed as shadowy and shapeless as the outlaw tarom families had been last night, interesting was a cold word, a distancing word. She glanced around to Rane, saw the woman smiling at her with wordless friendly understanding. Tuli began to feel better. Immersed in that slowly warming silence they rode through the cold pre-dawn morning, following a rambling trail torn by macai claws, compressed by the iron-tired wheels of supply wagons.

"Should be snowing soon." Tuli looked about at the white patches of frozen dew on ground and grass, lingering on the leaves of isolated trees.

"Should be."

"You don't think it will?"

"No."

"Oh." Tuli inspected the broken earth before her, shook her head and laughed.

Rane tilted her head, a question in her dark green eyes.

"I asked Fayd how he found us." Tuli waved a hand at the rumpled earth. "A blind man could."

"Too many people to hide. Anyway, what's the point?"

"I didn't sleep much last night. I got to thinking."

Rane smiled.

Tuli snorted. "I did. Why hasn't Floarin wiped us out? She could pretty easy."

"Why should she?" Rane leaned forward and patted the

shoulder of her macai. "The mijloc is culling itself without much effort on her part. And there's the Biserica, she has to deal with the Biserica first."

"She's going to attack the Biserica?" Tuli was horrified. "She can't do that. It's . . . it's. . . ."

"It's obvious, Tuli." Rane shrugged. "Shrine Keepers are trained there, the core of Maiden service is there. If she wants to force the Maiden out of the mijloc, she has to take it."

"Can she?"

"I don't know, Tuli. That's one of the things this trip is about."

The sun started up, turning the tops of the hills to a shimmering red-gold. As they left the last of the frost behind them, the thick matting of yellow cloud over the mijloc began to break apart. Though they were still a good half day from the bottom slopes, they soon started to feel Plain's heat leaking up into the hills. No more patches of ice-white, no red glitter of dawn-lit dew. The scattered clumps of brush and the now-and-then trees were wilted and drooping, no frost to bring the leaves down or turn them to familiar fall colors. They rode along the winding wagon track, moving at an easy walk, Rane apparently in no hurry to reach the Plain.

"What do ties think about being ties?"

"I've never been a tie. What brought that up?"

"Something I heard Da say."

"Ah. I see." Rane rubbed at her nose, stared ahead between the spiky ears of her mount. "What do you think about ties?"

"I don't know, they're ties, that's all."

"What do you think about being a tarom's daughter?"

Tuli opened her eyes wide. "What?"

"Would you be any different if you were born a tie?"

Tuli brooded over that for the next three hills. The yellowish light and the heat were increasing together. There was some wind stirring the heavy air but it didn't help much. After the sharper, colder, thinner air of the higher reaches, this was oppressive and rapidly growing unbearable. "Most of the ties I knew seemed content enough."

"What if they were unhappy about something?"

"All they had to do was tell Da and he'd fix it if he could."

"But what if your Da was a different sort of man, what if he didn't give one damn about what ties wanted, what could they do?"

"Nothing, I guess, except go off the land and see if some other tarom would take them in."

"Would that be any too likely?"

"No, I s'pose not. But most the taroms I know are pretty much like Da." Tuli scowled at her macai's bobbing head. "They'd starve, most like, if they had to leave the land like that, ties I mean. There's no place for them to go."

"And people don't like change. In fact, if you think of it, Tuli, things haven't changed much on the Plain for several hundred years."

"Up to now," Tuli said.

"Up to now, yes. If you were still back up there, Tuli, what would you want most?"

"To have some say in what happened to me. Not to be told to run and play like a good child and keep my mouth shut and do what I'm told." At first Tuli spoke without really thinking, just responding to Rane's question. When she heard what she was saying, she stopped and stared at Rane. "Oh."

"Answered your own question?"

"Oooh, you're sneaky, you are." Tuli nodded. "I see what Da was saying. Setting patterns." She spoke gravely, rather proud of herself, looked shyly at Rane, blushed at the wide grin on the ex-meie's face. "Well, isn't it so?"

"Very much so." Rane mopped at her forehead with a bit of rag she pulled from a pocket. "Dammit, it's not an hour after sunup and look how hot. We're going to have to lay up for a couple hours come noon." She patted the rag over her face, dragged it into the neck opening of her tunic. "On the whole, Tuli, I'd say the next hundred years will be hard ones for the Plain, even if we win this fight. Might take that long to settle everyone down again."

Tuli licked her lips and thought of the waterskin by her knee, but she wouldn't say anything before Rane did. "You know, I think Da's kind of enjoying himself. Oh sure, he hates it too, but when he's not reminding himself about the tar and the Aglim and all that, he . . . well. . . ." She shook her head.

"He was bored, I think. On the tar. Too easy."

"Oh."

The clouds were gone and the swollen sun was clear of the horizon. They were riding right into it, forced to keep their eyes turned from it, focusing instead on the withered grass and the rattling brush close to the ground. There were more trees along the hills now, big wide-armed brellim whose stiff

leaves were starting to rot, hanging limp and wrinkled from
withered stems, smelling of rot too, a smell at once wet and
musty and sickening. The silence around them was eerie, as if
everything had died or left except grass and brush and trees
and they couldn't leave only die slowly and unbeautifully.

"Do you think I could be pregnant?"

Rane blinked, swung to look at Tuli out of startled shiny
green eyes. "How could I know? It's possible, I suppose."

"Oh." She chewed on her lip, scowling at nothing. "How
could I tell?"

"Wait till your next flow. If it comes, you're all right, if
you miss, not too good."

"Maiden bless, that's two weeks off. Do I have to wait till
then?"

Rane grimaced, not too happy with this conversation. "I'm
no healwoman, Tuli." She grinned suddenly. "I've never had
to face your problem."

They started down the long slope toward the Highroad, a
streak of black slashing south to north, visible sometimes,
sometimes obscured by thick bands of trees, still a little over
an hour's ride away. Tuli gazed thoughtfully at the velvety
black of the paving.

"Not him."

"What's that, Tuli?"

"Not Fayd. I don't want his kid."

Rane ran her fingers through her mop of straw-pale hair.
"You probably got nothing to worry about."

"Probably, huh!" Tuli sneaked a glance at Rane. The ex-
meie had lost some of her usual calm; Tuli regretted disturbing her, partly because she liked Rane, partly because she
depended more than she'd realized on that steady serenity to
help her maintain her own calm. Still, her need was very
pressing. "I've got to make sure," she said.

Rane tapped restlessly on the saddle ledge. "Think hard
what you're saying, Tuli."

Tuli set her mouth in a stubborn line, said nothing.

Once again Rane thrust bony nervous fingers through her
thatch of unruly hair. "Keep thinking, Tuli. You've got the
time."

"Huh?"

The older woman smiled, her green eyes laughing as she
began to lose the tension in her face. "There's a man in Sadnaji I was planning to visit. Might as well detour to the Val-

ley—it won't be much of a jog, it's that close—so the healwomen can look at you."

"But. . . ."

"It doesn't matter, an extra five days, it's nothing."

"I'm sorry."

"Don't fuss."

Tuli heard the sudden irritation in Rane's voice and fell silent.

They rode south during the mornings, starting before dawn, laying up when heat became too oppressive, starting again late in the afternoon to go on past sundown until the moonless, starless darkness made riding too dangerous. As the days passed they sighted occasional traxim circling high above the Road but these spying demons paid no attention to them—just as well for the traxim, Rane had her crossbow cocked and ready. They saw no one, spoke to no one, spoke seldom to each other. At long intervals Tuli asked questions—at long intervals so she wouldn't wake resistance in the ex-meie—as she groped toward an understanding of Rane. The past few days had taught her how very little she knew about other people.

"What was it like, growing up stenda?"

"Like trying to breathe in a flour sack."

"Did your folks chase after you when you ran away?"

"Yes."

"But they didn't catch you."

"No. I was desperate."

"How did you feel when you finally saw the Biserica?"

"Tired."

"What was your shieldmate's name? You don't mind talking about her?"

"Merralis. Not any longer."

"What's it like, living at the Biserica?"

"Different."

"How?"

"I couldn't begin to tell you. You'll see."

"Merralis. How did you know?"

"Know what, Tuli?"

"That you . . . that you loved her?"

"Don't ask me about that, Tuli."

"I'm sorry."

"It's not that I mind talking about it, but I promised your father I wouldn't."

"Are you going to leave me at the Biserica?"

"I don't know. Do you want to stay?"

"I don't know."

"Rane, please, what did you promise Da?"

"Tuli, I really don't want to talk about this."

"I need to know, Rane, I NEED to know."

"It's nothing much, not worth all this fuss. Oh, all right. He was worried about you. I promised not to tamper with you."

"Tamper?"

"Think about it."

"I want to go with you. I couldn't bear being left with strangers and I want to see what's happening on the Plain. If I won't be too much trouble?"

"No trouble, Tuli. I want the company. Camping alone can be a pain."

"Rane, did you ever . . . uh . . . with a man?"

"Tuli!"

"Rane, did you want to . . . to tamper with me?"

"No, Tuli."

"Oh."

"You're much too young, Tuli."

"Oh."

"You're sure you don't mind taking me along?"

"You're getting tiresome, Tuli. I've told you a dozen times I'll be glad to have you with me."

"What are we going to do? After the Biserica, I mean?"

"We." A laugh. "Good girl. We're going to visit some friends here and there on the Plain, swing up to Oras to see what Floarin is up to, report back to Yael-mri and the Biserica. And to your father."

"Do I have to go back?"

"You could stay at the Biserica. I talked to your parents and they told me to leave it up to you."

"Up to me?"

"Uh-huh. Take a look around while we're there and see what you think."

Sadnaji. They rode through the place a little after midnight because Rane wanted to get a sniff of what it was like before she talked to her friend. It was hot and dark and dead. The air was thick and still with a staleness to it as if the bloated sun by day and the clouds by night had pressed it down on Sadnaji until it was drained of virtue. Lifeless—that was it—the whole place was like a preserves crock lost in the cobwebs of an abandoned store-cellar so long its contents were rock hard and near unrecognizable. Lifeless. No lights. No lights anywhere, not even over the Inn door. No sounds, not even hunting kankas or the buzzing night bugs. The macain were twitchy, breathing hoarsely as if they too found that trapped air unusable, wincing at the overloud pad-click, pad-click of their clawed feet. Tuli stared wide-eyed and sorrow-filled, struggling to believe what she saw and sensed. Even Cymbank hadn't seemed so bad as this the last time she was there, but, she reminded herself, she hadn't seen Cymbank for over a passage and "things" were probably worse there now, things being what people were doing to each other. They rode through Sadnaji without stopping; both breathed easier when they passed by the large old Inn that even in the darkness had a plaintive look to it as if it was sinking slowly into the rot of disuse.

Moth sprites danced rigid little patterns on the sadly diminished waters of creekSajin. Rane glanced at them and looked away with a sigh.

The sun was an hour up as they halted on the outlook at the topmost of the switchback turns.

The valley glowed with heat. The fields burned yellow, brown and black, the south lost itself in a merciless shimmer of yellow heat. Dry—dry as ancient bones. Sterile. Dead—that was how it looked to Tuli. The trees dead, charred, in the orchards. Nothing moving anywhere. The structures, half-concealed by blowing dust and the distortions in the air, shivered with heat, the very stones seemed to burn. A limp

and languid wind blew into Tuli's face, hot enough to burn
her lungs when she breathed. Appalled, she turned to Rane.

"It's bad," Rane said, her voice hoarse. "But not as bad as
it looks." It seemed to Tuli that the ex-meie spoke more from
hope than any real belief, but Rane turned away before she
could say so, and started down toward the valley floor.

CHAPTER XII:

THE QUEST

the plateau—the fifth day
Hern stands before her. He holds her hands. His eyes are closed; he is smiling just a little. Serroi probes deep into the mother rock and calls ancient water up to her. The coldness is pain. Hern's fingers tremble about hers. She feels him feeling the pain. For one startling moment, when his eyes suddenly open, she looks through those eyes at herself, sees the appalled and frightened look on her gaunt face, then the image is gone—a heart beat there then gone.

the same day, much later
Serroi leaned against Hern's shoulder. He sat with his legs stretched out before her, his back against the sloping side of the ancient shallow wash, one arm resting heavy on her shoulders. He was relaxed, content, humming a rumbling, near tuneless sort of song that was a pleasant counterpoint to the singing of the water that tumbled past their feet gradually filling the gravelly holes that rainy season spates had dug out. She ignored the hunger beginning to twist inside her, enjoying her laziness too much to haul herself onto her feet and go digging around for a bunch of tough and knobby roots.

There was a flash of grey overhead. Serroi moved her head lazily on Hern's shoulder so she could see the small grey flier more clearly, thinking at first it was some kind of passar attracted by the new water, realizing almost at once that she'd seen no passare up here, not even ground-hugging wild oadats. She blinked.

The odd little creature hovered above her, a tiny man with long thin arms, talons instead of feet, leathery wings covered with fine, grey-brown fur. Longer fur was tufted over his ears and along the outside of his limbs, grey-brown fringes that rippled in the breeze stirred up by the sweep of his wings. Behind him, farther up the wash, she caught glimpses of other fliers, some dipping almost to the water, others zipping from bank to bank. As she watched with wonder and laughter, she could feel a similar mix stirring in Hern—almost as if she were tied into his head in an extension of that brief moment of intrusion when she called the water. Both of them held very still, watching the maneuvers of the tiny flier with relaxed concentration. He flitted back and forth in front of them about an arm length over their heads.

Having gathered his courage, he spilled some air from his wings and swooped closer, bolder still as they made no threatening moves, no moves at all. His round dark eyes were lively, bright with curiosity and intelligence. His small mouth pursed and he uttered a few high humming sounds. Serroi had to force herself to stay motionless at the jolt that the sounds gave her, a powerful sense that they were language, not just animal noises; the jolt was doubled as Hern's equal reaction fed into her system.

Another winged man dropped down beside the first; he was smaller and brighter, creamy fur on his wings, rusty brown tufts and plumes down arms and legs. He glided by them, swung around, fluttered back.

Moving very carefully she pushed off from Hern's shoulder until she was sitting upright. At her first move the flying men worked their wings vigorously, swooped back and up. At a more comfortable distance they hovered and watched her stretch out her hand, palm up. "Friend," she said, singing the word. At the same time she projected as warm a friendliness as she could dredge up out of herself, friendliness and reassurance. "Friend," she repeated, knowing they wouldn't understand the word, hoping they could tell it was a word. "Friend."

They circled out over the burbling water, retreating nearly to the far side of the wash, their wings beating furiously for a few seconds. Then they were gliding again, riding the current of air flowing along the wash. They drifted slowly closer, responding to the reassurance she was pouring out, the hair on arms and legs rippling to that as well as the wind supporting them. "Friend," she said once more.

Bright eyes watched her as they glided back and forth, back and forth, then she heard a modulated squeak from the darker flier. She stopped projecting (after a last burst of delight) and leaned forward listening intently. After a few more repetitions she resolved the squeak into what seemed to be two words. "Kreechnii asiee," he said—or seemed to say.

"Kreechnii asiee," Serroi repeated, taking her voice from

the top of her throat, trying to match the lilt he gave the phrase.

The fliers tumbled into laughter. Wings beating, soaring and curling into great loops, they pantomimed their joy. Then they were back in front of her. The darker male slapped his chest, then worked his wings to get himself out of the tumble the gesture had thrown him into. "Pa'psa," he squeaked. The second male swooped past him, skimming perilously close to Serroi's curls. "Soug'ha," he shrilled, once he was safely away.

Serroi slapped her own chest. "Serroi," she said, again keeping her voice high with a hint of lilt in the word.

The tiny males went into aerial giggles. Their antics woke an answering lightness in Serroi. Hern's hand was warm at the small of her back, his fingers moving in a soft slow caress. His laughter mixed with hers and made a kind of muted music for airborne dance in front of them.

The Pa'psa straightened out and glided closer, pointing past her at Hern. "Qeem heeruu?"

Hern chuckled. "Hern," he said.

Serroi's stomach grumbled. Pa'psa and Soug'ha chattered excitedly. She laughed as Pa'psa rubbed his middle, nodded to show he understood rightly what he heard. "Hungry," she said. Black eyes watched with bright interest for a moment longer, then the two fliers darted away. She leaned back against Hern, laughing.

His hand curled warm and gentle about the back of her neck. He yawned. "Part of that wild magic you were talking about?"

"Don't know. Nobody knows much about what's up here." She leaned into the slide of his hand. "That feels good."

"Mmmm. Not animals."

"No." She sighed with pleasure, frowned suddenly and jerked upright. Grabbing at the pouch, she pulled the leather thong over her head and tugged the pouch open.

"What is it?" As she stared down at the gently glowing crystal, it seemed to her that Hern was responding as much to the spurt of panic that had sparked her actions as he was to those actions.

"Remember what happened to the Norit you killed when I touched him?"

"Uh-huh. So?" He pushed away from the bank, his eyes on her hand.

"I don't want to take chances. I forgot before." She took

her boot from under her belt and slipped the silver box from
the pocket, glancing at him as she did so, surprised to see him
frowning thoughtfully at the crystal glowing in the nest of the
pouch. "Things *are* different up here." She shut the tajicho in
the box, put the box in the pouch and pulled the neck shut.
"You aren't supposed to notice the tajicho."

"Ah." He settled back against the washwall, yawned
sleepily. "Thought it was something serious." He grinned at
her indignant snort. "Where you think the fliers went?"

"No idea." She slipped the thong over her head, sat silent
one hand clutched about the pouch feeling the corners of the
box hard against her palm. Afraid—a little. An oddly distant
fear as if something about the plateau put a barrier between
her and him who she feared. With a hissing intake of air between stiffened lips, she uncurled her fingers and dropped her
hand on her thigh. She felt suddenly naked without the
tajicho touching her, bereft, aching as if she'd been beaten on
every limb. She rubbed her thumb across her lips. *Addiction*,
she thought. She laughed but the laughter trailed off as she
began to wonder just how true that was.

A peremptory call brought her eyes up. Pa'psa hovered
above her, clutching in small three-fingered hands the skinny
neck of a fat tan gourd. Soug'ha was behind him with a second gourd. The darker male descended until he was just out
of reach. Serroi sat very still, wondering what was about to
happen.

Soug'ha giggled suddenly, dived past Pa'psa, skimmed past
Serroi's head, the tip of one wing brushing her nose. As he
scooted over her lap, he dropped the gourd. With more
giggles he climbed at a steep angle, his wings biting deep into
the air. Pa'psa snapped with rage at this presumption. He
dropped his gourd beside the other and went whipping after
Soug'ha. With a hard kick he sent the younger male tumbling, wings working frantically to recover his hold on the
air. Leaving Soug'ha temporarily chastened, he came back to
Serroi, hovered close in front of her, eyes like black beads
moving over her face. He reached out and touched her cheek,
his tiny nails moving across her skin in scratchy lines. not
hurting her though she was aware of their sharpness. For an
instant only he touched down on her knee (and she was very
glad she'd thought to tuck the tajicho away, though perhaps
up here nothing much would have happened), his hard talons
pricking through the fine wool of her borrowed trousers, then
he shot up and away until he was some distance over her

head. He circled up there, a look of intense satisfaction on
his small round face. Soug'ha flitted about behind him, a
small drooping image of chagrin, his daring far outplayed by
his elder.

Serroi rubbed her stomach as it grumbled again.

"Shiapp-shap," Pa'psa cried. "Shiapp." He swooped down,
zipped across Serroi's lap, climbed again and mimed drinking.

Serroi lifted one of the gourds. By the weight of it there
was something inside, probably a liquid of some kind. She
looked up. Pa'psa looped over and over, threw his head back
and once again mimed glugging from a bottle. He
straightened himself, his black eyes shining. "Shiapp," he
said.

"Shiapp," Serroi said. She lifted the gourd, touched the
stopper to her lips.

The little man nodded his head and darted off downstream,
Soug'ha trailing less enthusiastically behind.

Serroi turned the gourd around in her hands. It had a
light-tan ground speckled with orange and ocher. The outside
was smooth with small smooth lumps scattered lavishly over
the swelling belly. The stopper was a chunk of pithy vine.
She worked it loose and laid it on her thigh, tilted the gourd
over her palm. A thick, flower-scented liquid crept out, oozing into an amber pool that caught the light and glowed with
it. She touched her tongue to the liquid. It was sweet-tart, not
so cloying as she feared. She let the viscous liquid roll off her
palm and into her mouth. Her lips and tongue tingled. Her
mouth tingled, went numb, then was flooded with sensation, a
dozen different tingles and tastes at once.

She felt Hern's worry. "Isn't that taking a chance?" he
said.

She shook her head, frowned as she touched her tongue to
her lips, moved it slowly along her lower lip trying to isolate
the tastes, giving that up when they faded too quickly. A slow
explosion warmed her middle. "Good. Have some." She
reached the second gourd around to Hern.

Pa'psa came back, several smaller pale brown females
trailing after him, brushing wingtip against wingtip for reassurance. Shyly they circled over Hern and Serroi, then retreated to cling to the far side of the wash, watching and
whispering rapid syllables to each other.

Serroi laughed, Hern laughed. Serroi lifted the gourd to her
lips and sucked the rest of the liquid out of it, Hern lifted the
gourd to his lips and sucked the fluid out of it. Serroi felt the

double swallowing, the double explosion in two mouths, turned her head slightly and saw she was feeling the movements of Hern's throat and her throat in tandem. She turned back, blinked up at Pa'psa. The hair on the tiny man's body was outlined in light. For an instant, like the fleeting touch of the flier's talons on her knee, she felt tied to him as strongly as to Hern, sharing and passing on his delight—then it was gone, though the link to Hern still lingered. Well-being flowed through her-Hern. She laughed, Hern laughed, Pa'psa went tumbling over and over in soundless aerial laughter.

The glow gradually muted into a calmness that left her tired but happy. Pa'psa continued to circle over them for a while, then grew bored and went soaring off. Leaning comfortably against Hern she watched more of the fliers as they flitted past, carrying webbed loads to the section of cliff where others of their clan were gouging out shallow holes in the crumbly earth. The amber fluid sitting warm in her stomach, in Hern's stomach, they watched a vee of tiny kits fly about, chattering, wheeling away before they got too close, not daring to come really close, squeaking challenges at each other, prodding each other into darting swoops above her head. She laughed, Hern laughed. The kits went climbing frantically up the air, wings clawing for height, a little uncoordinated, lacking the smooth bite of the adults. For a moment she was annoyed at herself, at Hern, for scaring them, then she realized it was simply their flight-reflex, sighed, relaxed, felt Hern relax. The kits climbed high enough to feel safe then they were playing over Hern and Serroi, throwing loops and chasing each other with noisy exuberance.

"Setting up house." Hern's voice was low and amused. He straightened his legs carefully, moving his calves up and down to ease out cramps from sitting so long in one position. Serroi moved her legs to ease cramps she hadn't noticed before. As she continued to watch the antics of the kits, her vision doubled. She saw the kits, saw the adults working away at the wash bank, the second image alternately background and foreground. She pushed slowly away from Hern, lurched up onto her knees and worked herself around until she was facing him. He jammed the heels of his hands onto the sand, pushed himself up to face her.

She looks at him, sees herself staring at him, him staring at her, him seeing himself looking at her, the seeing and the see-ers replicated into infinity as if she and Hern, he and Serroi, crouched between parallel mirrors. Outside that pairing both hear the whiffle of the fliers' wings, both feel their bounding curiosity and their fizzing excitement. Serroi is distracted, Hern is distracted by the high singing chatter flung between them. Hern and Serroi break apart, blink, are dazed and bereft.

Serroi stretched out her hand, Hern took it. "You all right?"

She nodded. "You?"

He laughed, the sound a bit shaky. "Shaky," he said.

"Me too," she said. She pulled her hand loose, got to her feet, looked around for her spear. "Want something else in my stomach." She glanced at the busy fliers. "Better lay off meat for a while."

Hern grunted up, using the two spears to help him push onto his feet. "You're being right again." He handed her the spear. "Watch it, little bit."

the tenth day

They were moving more slowly, inadequate diet putting some strain on their strength, the continual need to hunt for food slowing them more than either liked. Hern ate the tubers she baked, the sweet fruits of the vines, the tulpa stems, the nut-flavored grains they stripped from small patches of grass, shared the meatless diet. Slow progress, meals that for the most part didn't end, a continual eating as they walked, a continual digging and collecting. Still, they kept going. The days were warm and cloudless, the night clear, cool, brilliant.

The fliers traveled with them. After a few days the shy females gathered courage enough to fly close and pat her cheek, pat her hair. They were fascinated by the springy sorrel curls.

The plateau stretched out nearly flat to a distant horizon with wide expanses of grass breaking up the expanses of brush. It was a gently monotonous landscape dominated by pale browns and dusty muted greens. There was an inconspicuous abundance of vegetation, much of it smaller than the palm of her hand. A rather pleasant biting odor clung to everything growing and blew in the air they breathed and was concentrated in the honey drink the fliers kept feeding them.

They slowly grew accustomed to living in two bodies. It made walking difficult and nights interesting. It was sometimes confusing when, for an instant at first, for expanding snatches of time, they couldn't be sure which pair of eyes they were looking through or who was really doing the talking no matter which voice sounded. They touched a lot, walked when they could hand in hand, they came back together often just to touch hands. They slept curled up together, body pressing against body with not the slightest hint of sexual desire.

On the tenth night they first shared dreams:

HERN'S DREAM: "Fat boy. Greedy little fat boy. Why am I cursed with such a lump of lard?" His father's back. His father walking away. His father ignoring him. The room is huge. There are cobwebs of shadow in the distant corners and cobwebs of shadow layer on layer brushed across the ceiling. His father's footsteps boom even after he is no longer in sight, having passed through the door, a gaping hole in one wall.

The boy stands up, the room echoes with every move, the sound buffetting him. He is a round little boy nearly as wide as he is tall but he moves with a quick grace that he knows nothing of. His father is tall and lean, one of the bony Heslins, and continually berates him for greed, his father has been disappointed in him almost since he was born. The boy's footsteps echo as he crosses to the gap in the wall, following his father though he is cold and sad and knows his father doesn't want him around.

The hallway outside the room constricts about the boy. Sweating, gritting his teeth he forces himself into the darkness. The air is lifeless and chill, there is a threatening feel to the passage. The walls come in closer and closer until he is terrified of getting stuck, but he won't stop or go back, his urgency drives him on in spite of his fear. The passage opens with shocking suddenness and he is in his father's office before he can stop and he bumps into a one-legged table with an oil lamp on it. The hot oil splashes over everything, sets the rug and some papers on fire. His father stands over him, his face contorted with rage, purple with fury, his chin beard waggling furiously as he shouts curses at the cowering boy, kicks at him, growing larger and uglier by the minute. The boy shrinks back, literally shrinks, getting smaller and smaller until he is rat-sized and his father's huge foot is poised over him about to step on him.

He is cowering on his bed, trying to strangle his sobs before they can sneak out of his throat. A young woman comes in, one of his nursemaids, charming and neat in her crisp white blouse and pleated black skirt. The skirt whispering about her quick little ankles, she hurries to him, exclaiming with distress. Gathering him in soft herb-scented arms, she murmurs soft affectionate coos. She is warm and soft. She reminds him of when he has just taken a bath and dried off and it is just a little cool and he has on a clean crisp sleep smock and is crawling in between sweet-scented sheets. He leans against her, smelling her, revelling in the feel of her, revelling in the warmth and affection pouring out of her. She pats him a few times more, tucks him into bed, leaves the room.

In a blink she is back. Others are with her. A half dozen nursemaids laughing and teasing him, kissing him and fondling him, feeding him cakes and tartlets and hot, spiced cider. Then they tuck him back into bed and go out with subdued giggling and gossiping.

He is sneaking out with his nursemaid early in the morning. She lets him trail her like a friendly pup. She pats him like a pup, ignores him like a pup. She is sneaking down to the guard barracks to see her "friend," taking the boy with her, knowing he won't tell on her, knowing he'd lie like anything to protect her. She has done this before. He watches her cuddle in the bushes with her guard; he is jealous and unhappy, fidgeting from foot to foot, trying to whistle, producing a few abortive notes. The guard scowls at him over the nursemaid's shoulder—and it is his father's face scowling at him. He screams. The nursemaid ignores him, it always happens when his father is with a woman, even his mother, no matter how close the woman has been to him. They pet and spoil him and forget him when his father is there. He runs off into the bushes, shrunk to rat size again, bumping from trunk to trunk in his blind frightened scurry.

A large man with dark pewter hair is sitting on the barracks steps. He looks ancient to the boy. The boy halts, sucks on his lip, watches the old man draw a piece of soft leather along a shining blade. The old man frowns at him but says nothing. The boy sees that the old man knows him and disapproves of his wandering about by himself. The old man slides the sword into its sheath and sets it down beside him, leaning along the steps. Ignoring the boy, he picks up a piece of wood carved into a knife shape, a twisted hilt and a long hooked blade, blunt along the inner curve. He slices off shaving after shaving with slow patient care, putting the finishing touches on the carving. The boy sits down some distance from the man, watches him, fascinated. The carving goes on and on. The old man works with patient care, the boy watch-

es with the same patience. No one else comes, there is, as far
as the boy is concerned, no one else in the world.

The old man holds the carved knife up, tries its balance,
throws it suddenly at the boy. It turns in the air, end over
end, the boy watches open-mouthed, it comes at him, a little
to one side, going to go over his shoulder. On a sudden impulse, giggling, the boy snatches the tumbling knife from the
air. He runs his hand over it, delighted by the fine detail of
the carving.

"Bring me it," the old man says. His voice is brusque,
abrupt, but not unfriendly.

The boy looks down at the knife. His small, sweaty,
chubby hand is closed tight about the hilt. He doesn't want to
give the knife back. He looks up at the old man, meets stern,
dark pewter eyes. Reluctantly he gets to his feet. Feet dragging over the paving, he takes the knife back to the old man.

The old man takes the knife. "Go back," he says in the
same abrupt, not unfriendly voice. "Sit where you were."

The boy is puzzled, but the voice of the old man has
charmed him. The man is neither shouting at him nor cooing
over him. He turns and rushes back, settles himself with that
incongruous grace that no one ever notices. The old man
sees it with interest.

"Catch it again." The old man flips the knife at him. The
boy snatches it from the air, picks the wheeling knife out of
the air by its hilt with a quick neat snap of his hand. He
starts to get up to bring the knife back to the old man. The
old man smiles, a small tight upcurve of his stern mouth.
"Keep it," he says. The boy settles back, feeling a warm glow
of pleasure as he fondles the carving.

The old man lifts the sword in its sheath and gets to his
feet with a quick smooth flexing of his body as if he is much
younger in the body than in the head. "Come back here tomorrow," he says. He taps the sword and smiles again.
"You're old enough to begin training."

SERROI'S DREAM: She is in the courtyard playing with
half-grown chini pups. The sky is cloudy, the air is heavy,
getting a little too cold for comfort. Beside her the tower of
the Noris rises brown-black and massive. It would be forbid-
ding if it weren't so familiar. It starts to rain, first a few large
drops then an inundation. Laughing, the little girl runs into
the tower, the pups at her heels. In spite of the grimness of
her surroundings, the miserable weather, she is intensely

happy as she is always intense about whatever she is. The chini pups are responding to her mood, bounding up the stairs behind her, around her, before her. Sourceless light travels up the stairs with her, winding round and round the spiraling wormhole. She bursts into her own room, pulls to a stop, startled.

A tall lean man is standing in the center of the pleasant room. He is not smiling. He wears a gold ring through one nostril from which dangles a glittering ruby in the shape of a teardrop. It glitters and shifts with each movement of his lip as he speaks, but for a moment he says nothing, no muscle in his face moves. She laughs with delight and rushes toward him, though the chini hang back silent in the doorway. She doesn't quite hug him. He shows no response for a moment then a small smile curls his delicately chiseled lips. The ruby flashes fire. His austere face softens. Something of the small girl's joy is reflected there. He reaches out, touches her hair, draws one silky sorrel curl through his long pale fingers. Then he fixes his fingers in her hair and flings her onto the bed.

She scrambles onto her knees. "I tried," she whimpers. "I tried."

Shaking with rage, he speaks a WORD and sets pain on her. Without looking at her, he runs from the room.

She moves a hand, brushes it against her thigh and gasps as pain sears through her. The pain gets worse, burning all over her body. She tears off the soft robe that is suddenly a nettle shirt. Her body is bathed in sweat. She pushes off the bed. The soles of her feet burn. She sits on the bed again and feels fire searing her buttocks. She stands. The air presses against her skin and burns. She weeps, knowing that he has done this to her out of the knowledge he has gained through her, weeps, feeling tears roll like drops of acid down her face. Weeps, too, knowing there is no way she can satisfy him, no way she can take him into the Golden Valley. She tried, she really tried, but she couldn't do it. She forces her fingers closed over the latchhook intending to make her way to him and beg him to remove his curse. Her fingers slip off the latch. She tries again. The door is locked.

The torment goes on and on. The night passes. She burns. She can't think. She can't move. After an endless time the door opens and the Noris steps inside. "Please," she moans.

He speaks a WORD. As the fire dies out of her skin, he lifts her, carries her to the bed. She cringes away from him, lost in terror, unable to think, unable to control her body. He

blurs and clears, blurs again as she tries to see his face. There
is sadness in it but she cannot accept this. He puts her on the
bed, sits beside her and tries to untangle her curls until he
sees how stiffly she is lying. He lifts her and holds her until
the stiffness melts in her. She starts shaking, he holds her until
the shaking goes away. He lays her back, touches her cheek,
smiles and leaves.

The Noris is standing at the foot of her bed, his face somber. He waits in silence while she rubs the sleep from her
eyes, then he says, "Get dressed, Serroi."

She scrambles into one of her white silk robes and pulls
the soft slippers onto her feet. Hesitantly, her eyes on his still
face, she takes his hand.

The room blinks out, changes into rolling hills of sand with
scattered clumps of scraggly brush. The Noris speaks. A dark
robe drops onto the sand and rock beside him. He speaks
again, a small WORD, and a banquet is spread out beside the
robe, steaming savory food on delicate porcelain, wine in a
single crystal glass, a crystal pitcher full of water.

Serroi and the Noris are standing on a slight rise in the
middle of the most barren and inhospitable land she'd ever
seen. Her eyespot throbs but she can find no touch of life
anywhere close, only ripples of rock and sand, cut across by
straggling black lines where rainy season run-offs had eaten
into the earth. A little frightened, still aching from the agony
of the past days, she looks up at the Noris.

He lays a hand a moment on her head, then steps back.
"Good-bye, Serroi." And she is alone in the middle of a
desert.

"Why?" she whispers. She stares at the empty space where
the Noris had been. "Why?" She turns helplessly round and
round. "Why? Why? Why? WHY?"

Serroi pushed up, wiped a hand across her eyes, struggling
to hold herself separate for a few minutes at least. Hern sat
up, wiped a hand across his eyes, struggled to hold himself
separate from her for a moment.

"Dream?" he said.

"Yours?" she said.

"More a memory," he said.

"A kind of memory. Squeezed up," she said.

"Why did we dream them?"

"Don't know. Why any of this?"

"Don't know."

"Don't know much, do we."

"Not much."

the fifteenth day—the dragons of glass

Serroi looked at her hands, wrinkled her nose. "I'm turning into a twig," she said with Hern's voice; with her voice she said, "We been doing better than I thought. Should be almost halfway across."

Hern said in his voice, "Our little friends." He smiled, she smiled, at the antics of the fliers air-dancing for their own pleasure over the water she'd just called forth. In her voice, he said, "Putting on a show. They like that water."

A small jewel form flitted past, plunged into the spring, fluttered up again, shedding crystalline drops of water, a very small dragon shape, long and sinuous with small spiky wings, transparent as glass, like a glowing glass statue given magical life. Brilliant rainbow colors rippled across the small snaky form, ruby and topaz, amethyst, emerald and aquamarine. The tiny thing was voiceless, its voice was the pulse of colors along its wavering length, she couldn't read it, Hern couldn't read it, they knew it was speech nonetheless. Hern held out Serroi's finger, laughed with Serroi's voice, his voice also, as long-toed feet tightened about the finger.

More of the tiny dragons arrived and darted into the water, playing joyously with the fliers and dancing with them in tumbling, slithering, shimmering, fluttering exuberance.

the sixteenth day—more dragons

Hern stood in Serroi's spring scrubbing himself with a handful of sand, whistling cheerfully, Serroi could feel the abrasion of the sand against her skin as she lay stretched out on a patch of grass, her hands laced behind her head, smiling lazily up at a cloudless sky. A shimmering form drifted into view, a glass dragon undulating in vast loops, delicately etched against the clear blue of the sky. More of the giants floated past, singing intricate silent chorales of colored light, the faceted bodies pulsing with light, winding about each other in knots of celebration.

The tiny dragons continued to dart about Hern, weaving their small sparks into a spirited capriccio. Slowly Serroi stood. Slowly she walked to join Hern in the water. Without interrupting their jubilant song, the tiny dragons split apart to let her through their shell. Hern dropped his arm on her shoulders, she pressed herself against him; both seeing

through both eye-sets, they watched the play of the giant
dragons through the quicker shimmers of the small ones.

As the days passed Hern and Serroi ceased to search for
food, ate only what the fliers brought them and what the
small dragons gave them (not food exactly, more like bee
stings, not as unpleasant as that, little jolts that gave them
energy with each touch of the cool smooth bodies). Hern and
Serroi walked hand in hand as a beast with four feet and two
heads. The great glass dragons drifted over them singing their
soundless songs in praise of the day, winding in slow dances
one about the other. Each night Serroi-Hern called water and
watched their companions play in it, the tiny dragons bits of
sun and sky, the flier kits noisy and funny, filling them with
another sort of joy, a laughter that celebrated the earth and
the things of the earth, love and friendship and rollicking delight.

When they slept they dreamed, most of those dreams
memories good and bad of childhood and adolescence. They
didn't speak of them, for one thing it was very hard by this
time to separate one from the other enough to be aware that
another spoke. They did speak sometimes, but it was more
like one who takes a leisurely walk to mull over some problem and talks aloud to himself.

The days passed and the miles crept past unnoticed
beneath their feet. They forgot everything but the present
moment, they were children of the present moment, bound to
the now, all anxieties washed away with memory, all agonies
gone except in now-and-then-dreams and those were distant
things like reading a story in a book. They played with the
days like happy children, all sadness exorcised into the night.

Unnoticed, the miles did pass. One morning there were no
more glass dragons in the sky to celebrate the dawn. One
night there were no small dragons to dance in the newborn
spring.

One day Pa'psa circled about them, chattering his distress,
the little brown females flew around them singing a high sad
song—a song of farewell.

One day Hern and Serroi woke and looked at each other
and saw the other as other.

Aches and pains came flooding back, the old tensions and
urgencies came flooding back. Hern rubbed at his jaw, his
hand rasping over the short stiff beard that blackened the
lower half of his face. He started to jump to his feet, grunted

as his knees threatened to give, pushed himself up more cautiously to stand looking west across the plateau. "How long?" he whispered.

Serroi crooked her leg, inspected the leathery dusty soles of her feet, fingered the tattered bottoms of her trousers. "You know what I know."

He swung around, stared at her, gave a short bark of laughter.

Chuckling a little at her unintended double meaning and at his appreciation of it, she got to her feet. "We manage to bring the spears with us?"

He looked around, saw them thrown down beside the new spring. "Seems we did." He bent carefully, picked them up, stumped back to her. "Just as well. I'm hungry."

They were both reduced to rags. All excess flesh was burnt away though they suffered few of the debilities of extended starvation. Serroi nodded when she felt her stomach knot at Hern's words. She took the spear from him and started probing about for tubers and tulpa. A moment later he joined her. "How far to the end of this?" He pushed his hand through his hair. She saw with a touch of sadness that the streaks of gray in the black had broadened into bars and his face looked lined and weary. Involuntarily her hand rose to touch her own hair, wondering if the sorrel was peppered with white. She thought of asking him, glanced at him and changed her mind.

"Don't know," she said. She pointed east. "Where that cloudbank rises, I think."

The next three days were painful. They quarreled a little, not much, it was too dangerous, there were still empathic links between them that were activated by strong emotion. They made love and that was difficult also, the feeling went too deep and their bodies were to feeble still to contain the emotions unleashed. And from the shared dreams they knew far too much about each other's vulnerabilities. If they lost control each could wound the other too deep for healing. It put a constraint on them that only gradually wore away as the soreness scabbed over and they rediscovered the safer uses of tenderness and affection.

About midmorning on the fourth day they stood on the eastern rim of the plateau.

Far to the east there were brilliant flashes of blue, the Ocean of Storms. In the south they saw a dark mass that had to be the walls and towers of Shinka-on-the-Neck. Directly

below them, stretching to that distant coast, the land was a
patchwork of fields and a dotting of dark blotches that were
living compounds scattered along a yellow road that led to a
larger blotch nestled in the loop of a large river winding
down to Shinka. At their feet a path zigzagged down the
steep slope of the scarp.

Serroi moved her shoulders, rubbed at her neck. "Holiday's
over once we're down there."

Hern touched the ragged curls a handspan longer than she
liked to keep them. He was silent a long time, then he moved
away from her and turned to gaze across the plateau. She
looked around. From this edge as from the other it seemed
an arid and uninteresting landscape, some brown and yellow
clumps of limp grass, some patches of short scraggly brush
liberally powdered with a grayish dust, scatters of rock and
gravel. "Eerie," he said. "I don't know what to think of that
time."

"Nor do I," she said. She moved her shoulders again as if
she were trying to free herself from the burden of those
memories, pulled her boots from under her belt, sat down on
the sandy stone. Hern walked past her to stand on the rim of
the scarp looking out at the land below, frowning, a degree
of tension hardening the muscles of neck and shoulder, at
least what she could see of them as his heavy long hair blew
about in the strengthening wind. She upended the boots one
after the other, knocked on the soles to drive out the last
grains of wild seed or any lingering purple berries. He was
thinking about what lay ahead of them, she knew, and what
lay behind. She set the boots beside her and pulled open the
neck pouch. As she pushed out the silver box, she watched
Hern watching the land. *What changes in me?* she thought.
What happens now? She rolled her tattered trousers above her
knees and pulled on her boots. He kicked a pile of broken
rock over the edge and watched the stones bounding down,
striking now and then with a flatter tone on the turnings of
the trail. Serroi drew her thumb across the tarnished silver of
the box, firmed her mouth and opened it. She took out the
tajicho, held it in her hand until it warmed and began to
glow. It had already saved life and sanity, it seemed to her,
half a dozen times, yet she was slowly growing to be afraid
of it, afraid of what it might be shaping her into. She could
feel its radiance creeping into her bones, could feel an odd
flutter in her head. Hern left the edge of the scarp and came
back to her. "It's a long way down. We'd better get started."

"In a minute." She tucked the tajicho into her boot pocket, the spear under her arm, looked at the silver box, extended her hand to Hern so he could pull her up.

When he started down the crumbling path, digging at the stone ahead of him with the point of his spear, she looked again at the silver box, shrugged and flung it away from her to sail with vanishing sheen toward the rolling hills far below.

The descent was more tedious than difficult—hot, straining, and slow; it was late afternoon before they reached the bottom of the scarp. They started east through brush-covered swells that weren't quite large enough to be called hills, the land dipping with some haste toward the intensely cultivated fluvial plain.

They walked in silence separated by a small space, neither touching nor speaking. Hern was struggling to fit himself back into the man he'd known for thirty odd years, the self he was uncomfortable without, trying to tuck in his growing outreach like a woman pushing flyaway curls back under a cap.

By the end of the day they were well into the swells, hungry, thirsty, tired. While Serroi slipped off her boots and kicked about feeling for water, Hern went off with his spear, stalking lappets or wild oadats or whatever small game he could find. She had to reach very deep for the water and expend more energy than she liked to pull it to the surface. Kneeling beside the cold little spurts, she drank until she began to feel bloated, splashed the icy water on her face, pulled her boots back on and went poking desultorily about for edible roots, wondering as she did so if her vegetarian existence was finally over. Her mouth watered at the thought of a hot oozy chunk of roasted lappet.

After unearthing a few withered roots, she found an old oadat's nest, blown out of a clump of brush, no eggs, it was much too late in the year for that. As she touched it with her toe, she heard oadats scratching in the brush and gabbling at each other in their high nervous voices. She straightened, rubbed slowly at the small of her back.

The small flock ambled out of a clump of brush a short distance to her left, a dozen oadats, four smaller than the rest, all of them kicking the covering grass aside with one-two jerks of powerful hind legs, scratching busily with smaller forefeet through the debris of bark, dead leaves and small sticks, hunting for grubs, worms, seeds. She watched them

work their way closer, watched them shy skittishly as they
moved past her, though since she was standing very still, they
didn't scatter in panic-flight. Several tilted onto stubby tails,
skinny forearms tucked close to their sides, taloned feet
pressed against bulging keelbones, heads, wobbly on scrawny
naked necks, turning from side to side to look at her with one
beady black eye then the other, leathery beaks opening and
closing without sound. She stared at them and started
sweating. She moved her leg in her boot until the calf muscle
was pressing against the slim outline of the knife. She stared
at the oadats, swallowed painfully, stood without moving,
watching them scratching past her, her hand sweating,
aching, curled tight about the spear shaft. Her hands
wouldn't move. She couldn't move her arms. She could have
killed one oadat, two, more, easily, but her arms wouldn't
move. She watched the last swagger of the last stumpy, grey-
furred tail as the last half-grown oadat disappeared around a
scraggly grey-green bush. "No sense," she whispered. "This is
stupid." She touched her forehead, drew her fingertips around
her eyespot. Her fingers were shaking. She flattened her hand
under the arch of her ribs, swallowed. "I'm going to eat meat,
whatever Hern kills." She said it tentatively, listening to her
body, listening, as she had expected, to nothing, there was no
reaction to her intent. "So I can't kill, but I can eat what
someone else puts before me. No sense, no sense." Her stomach knotted and unknotted. She sighed, a long shaky miserable sound that made her laugh at herself, then start poking
about for some more roots.

Midmorning on their third day down from the plateau they
reached the rutted road that led toward the river.

Hern stepped on a stone, winced. He crooked his leg,
braced his ankle on his knee, glared at the sole of his boot.
"Thin as paper."

Serroi touched his arm, feeling a nip in her own flesh.
"Want me to. . . ."

He let his foot drop, shrugged. "Stone bruise. It's nothing."

"Don't be a hero, Dom."

"Don't be a heroine, Domna."

She took her hand away, smiling rather wryly. "Point
taken."

He dropped his hand on her shoulder, then stepped away.
"We're a disreputable looking pair."

She looked him over, then gazed down at herself, grimac-

ing as she did so. His black trousers and tunic were not quite
filthy; water cleaned out body smell but didn't do much for
ground-in dirt and assorted stains. The rubbed spots over elbow and knee were almost transparent, as was the seat of his
trousers, more like cheesecloth than the heavy wool they'd
once been. Her own ragged trouser legs were tucked into her
boots, that was one touch of neatness. There was a long tear
beside her right knee, a smaller triangular tear by her left.
The fine white cloth of her shirt was stained with blood and
sweat and a dingy grey now, all over, holes over her elbows,
cuffs frayed to threads. The seat and knees of her trousers
were worn thin, thin enough for her to feel acutely the chill
wind sweeping down against them, a north wind that tried to
push them off the road, that whipped her hair into eyes and
mouth. "Just as well we're getting back to someplace we can
get more clothes."

He nodded. "Though how we're going to pay for
them. . . ."

"Services, Dom. I'll heal and you heave."

He raised his brows. "Heave?"

She laughed. "Use your muscle."

"Hunh."

They walked on, moving slowly and rather painfully along
the road, worn, tired, and more than a little hungry. Walked
side by side, not touching yet still companionable, friendly,
feeling more comfortable with each other than they'd been
for days.

Rounding a bend and a thick stand of cane they saw a man
kneeling beside a rambut, holding its foreleg folded up,
resting on one of his knees, prodding at the hoof with a long
bony finger. He was a short wiry man with a fringe of coarse
grey hair like steel wool running around the back of his head
at ear level, the dome of his skull rising above it like a tight-
grained shell of a wanja nut, shiny and dark brown. The rambut moaned and jerked its leg but couldn't pull free from the
powerful grip of the old man's fingers.

Serroi walked away from Hern and stopped beside the old
man. "Stone?"

He looked up. Grey fuzzy eyebrows flicked up then down
as he held onto the beast's hoof with an absentminded
strength, then scrunched together, his mouth pursing with
them. He stared at Serroi, visibly disconcerted by the dusty
green of her skin. His lively brows straightened with relief as
he looked past her at Hern, reassuringly normal though a

stranger here. His eyes flicked to Serroi again, then away until he was looking past her with the careful politeness of one
not-staring at some blemish inflicted on another person.
"Stone," he said, his brows moving up and apart. He used
them to punctuate his thoughts, his words, the way another
man might use his hands.

She knelt beside him, reached out a hand. "May I?"

After his brows contorted themselves again, he nodded.

She took one of her lockpicks from her boot and with a
quick twist of her wrist had the stone out. She stroked her
fingers across the bruised frog and the rambut moaned. She
closed her eyes, kept her fingers on the bruise, soothed the
nervous beast with a touch of her outreach, called upon the
healing force that flowed up through her knees from the
Mother. It was easy, almost quick now. She had a feeling of
unfolding, something growing in her, a sense of something
huge and perilous just beyond the veils of her mind. She felt
the warmth rising in her, passing from her into the rambut.
She used no mystic passes or esoteric chant as did fenekeln
witchers and felt the old fenekel's puzzlement because of it as
she knelt quietly in the dust of the roadway, her small green
hand resting gently on the rambut's foot, her eyes half-closed,
a half-smile on her too thin face.

The old fenekel's eyebrows changed position a dozen times
to express curiosity, impatience that only politeness kept
silent, more curiosity as his black eyes shifted from Serroi to
Hern who was leaning tiredly on his spear, watching without
surprise or even much interest, darted back to Serroi, then to
the rambut's frog—and finally the mobile brows went high
and round with wonder as Serroi took her hands away,
touched his hand so he would let the beast's leg go. While
Serroi knelt weary and silent on the road, the rambut
stamped his foot vigorously against the road's hard soil,
whistled with pleasure at the absence of pain, then curled his
head down to nuzzle at her tangled oily mop of dusty russet
curls.

The old man turned to Hern, more comfortable dealing
with him. "Tis a wonder," he said gravely, but his black eyes
twinkled and his brows wriggled energetically, telegraphing
amusement and delight.

"My lady is a healer," Hern said then stopped, rather surprised that he could understand and speak a tongue he'd
never studied. He looked at Serroi, smiled at her smile as he
realized where he'd gotten the language.

The old man's brows scrunched together. He whipped his head around to examine Serroi. "Lady?"

Serroi rose wearily, gave him a one-sided grin. "Though appearances be against me, that I am." She moved to Hern's side, looked up at him. "Diplomacy's your forte, my friend."

Hern laughed. "Eh-viper." He turned to the old man. "A good day to you, fenekel-besri."

"A better day than most, thanks be to the lady." His eyes projected worth and self-respect. "There is a debt."

"A very small debt. The lady heals without thought to payment, though. . . ." One hand swooped down to point out his rags, over to indicate Serroi's tattered state. "If your gratitude would run to helping us repair some of our deficiencies, our blessings on you."

Brows butted together, exuding shrewdness, the old man smiled tightly. "We always got a need of this and that in the holds. The lady heals." His voice still laid a slight question on the word *lady*. "And you?"

"I serve my lady. What I know is beast and weapon." He kept his face straight when Serroi pinched him.

"Umphm." The old man gazed past them at the distant line of plateau, his brows shot up, his broad forehead corrugated into deep wrinkles. He took in their tattered grimy appearance, glanced at the frisky rambut whose leadrope kept jerking in his hand. "Were it not wholly discourteous, I would be asking what your road is. There are no holds back along there." He waved toward the west. "Only fields and pastures. Be that so, that it would be a sad reply to the courtesy of your acts, I will not ask." He cocked his head, bright twinkling eyes traveling between them, eyebrows in high inquiring curves. "But 'tis plain to the eye that you've had no easy traveling."

"It's possible we might do a bit of trading, besri, this and that for what we need and perhaps a tale or two to while away the hours after supper?"

The old man's eyes darted once again from one to the other, his brows contorted with lively curiosity. "A tale or two, that is a good thing. The evenings, they're long this piece of year." He nodded at the rambut, short brisk jerks of his head. "Seeing your lady she healed the hurt, it being only right she ride."

Hern bowed with a pared-down grace, the bending of his back a courteous recognition of courtesy He gave his spear to the old man to hold for him, bent with ease to retrieve hers. She watched him go down and up and saw lines of force dance through his body. He reached out his hands to her. She looked at them. They were strong and beautiful. She touched them and they burned her. He lifted her with ease onto the rambut's back, swung her up as if she weighed less than nothing which was not far from truth. His hands spanned her waist and swept her up and deposited her on the rambut's back before she was ready. She had to scramble to crook her leg up, swing it to the far side of the beast. He took his hands away, she was sorry for that, she looked down at him, not smiling, and saw in narrowed gleaming eyes that what had been dead or difficult between them for so long had come powerfully to life. She smiled then, felt a rollicking inside her, remembering as suddenly her telling him so gravely once that passion was only decoration and not necessary and she saw that he was remembering that also and laughing a little at her, a little with her. "Bath and bed," she murmured.

He patted her thigh with a subtly exaggerated possessiveness calculated to stir her fury which she felt a little of but which was mostly drowned by the deep-pooled laughter bubbling in her. They knew each other so well now that tiny muscle twitches spoke volumes of implication and association.

The old man watched them, a little puzzled, but more complacent perhaps because the offer to trade put them on familiar ground. "Bath and bed for sure, young friends. For sure." He tugged on the leadrope and started east along the road with the rambut pacing behind him, head bobbling by his left shoulder, Hern walking by his right. "Harvest is in and the Seed-moons blessing celebrated so things be extra quiet this end of the Seed-passage. And the Raider's moon is not yet. The majilarn they watch their herds too far in the north yet for the raiding, or so the scouts they tell us. Not a vachai alone within a hundred marches. No. Not a one, not a herd. So it's quiet and quiet do be good for raising quarrels in the kin. The tales we know we've heard a thousand times though some be willing to repeat forever like some foolish tinkitink singing evensong over and over till you think you throw a brick at it and knock its silly head off."

The leather on the rambut creaked, the wind blew a ceaseless whine. The butt of Hern's spear thumped rhythmically on the hard earth, syncopated with the thud-squeak of his boots. And the old man talked. Hekatoro he was, he said. Atoro of HoldHek where they were going. They passed fields growing quickly more prosperous even in their nudity. The crops were in, the stubble plowed back into the soil and a winter crop planted. The earth was dark brown and glistening, new-turned in some fields, the plowed furrows hard-edged. Others had a softness of wind, wear and time, the winter cover already seeded and sending up the first new leaves in a mist of green. Neatness, skill, hard work—all visible in these fields stretching away from the road to the horizon. Hekatoro rumbled on about the fine season they'd had, the harvest that had their storerooms groaning, about his fifteen sons and their families and his grandchildren, more numerous he said than the grit blowing south on the Raiders wind.

They turned a grove of squat trees and a clump of dry cane with stems thicker than her arms and long yellow leaves stiff and thin, rustling, whispering, rattling like strips of paper. Hard against the horizon sat a solid structure, long and heavy, hugging the ground, three towers at its center point, one at each of the far points of the tetrahedron. They moved forward along the rutted dirt road, Hern and Hekatoro talking quietly as they walked, gravely, in slow bursts as things occurred to either. She paid no attention to what they were saying, but watched the movement of Hern's shoulders, the side of his face as he turned to look at the old man. She saw the twitch of his wide mouth, the dart upward of a brow, the liquid gleam of dark eyes. The too-draining closeness they'd shared was gone but neither could be quite the same. Though he didn't seem aware of it, right now he was blending her knowledge and her unconscious assumptions with his own skills and experience to achieve just the right note of detached politeness and unobtrusive interest, using the language he'd acquired without effort from her, using the knowledge she'd had tucked away about fenekeln customs. She smiled. So wholly different from the brittle sparring outside Skup. The rambut twitched his ears, pulled gently against the leadrope so he could look around at her. It seemed to her he was smiling at her, inviting her to share in some enigmatic rambut joke. She leaned forward and scratched slowly through the bristling scarlet mane growing along the top curve of his neck, laughing silently, herself aware of the changes in herself, not sure just what they were or how deep they went, but there was time now, even the pseudo-urgency of their quest couldn't change that. Time. Distance. All of that stretching between her and him who pursued and troubled her.

She'd reached a peak of terror and died of it before the plateau, now she felt on a gentle slide into a new calm she wasn't yet prepared to question.

HoldHek drew closer. Walls. Yellow white, spreading back in a shallow vee from a central point between two tower-shadowed gates, a higher tower broad and powerful between the gates behind the obtuse angle of the tetrahedron's front corner. The gates were purplish-brown—rather, one was, the other stood open, too narrow a target for eyes at a distance.

Closer. A tight roll of dark green almost black at the base of both walls. Thornbush. Evergreen, a tangle of black crooked limbs and inch-long needle thorns coated with an irritant dust, a sticky drop of poison on each thorn point. The hold had come away from the horizon and stood blocky and powerful midway between the three of them and the skyline.

Before the Hold. The bricks of the wall were waist-high and man-long, starting to crumble at the corners. They'd been whitewashed once, long ago before the thornbush was planted, but the whitewash was cracking and flaking off in spots. High up, near the crenels, a frieze of skulls. At first she thought they were carved, then she saw they were bone, real bone, sunk halfway into the mud and left to stare from blank eyeholes at land they'd once ridden over, majilarn skulls gathered in the bloody warfare of the Raider's Moon.

The gate curved in a quarter-arc between two high walls with crenellation that would let defenders fire down, devastating any attackers foolish enough to break down the gate and ride through. When they turned into the hold, the sound struck her like a blow in the face—the high honking brays of rambuts, the howling of chini, the ring of metal against metal, the shouts of children and through it all, a hum of voices high and low, female and male. She winced. The soft thick mud bricks of the curtain wall absorbed sound so that from the outside there was little evidence of the sheer volume of noise contained within.

As they rounded the baffle curve they turned toward a large rectangular building two stories high, the top story half the width of the bottom, the setback, like the court beyond the corner, filled with working women and playing children. Lacy rails of molded polished cane were planted in the brick of the lower story, fired brick this, a pale ocher like thick cream. Behind the rails very young children (the older ones were set to work carding wool and chewing leather) played ancient games inherited from their elders, women young and

old sat in groups pounding grain, whirling spindles, sewing
leather into sandals, stabbing needles at cloth held taut in
tambour hoops, weaving in small hand looms, doing the thousand small things that kept the fenekeli clothed and fed. As
Hekatoro led them past the end of the structure, several
women came and leaned over the rail, exchanging low-voiced
comments, low-voices and inaudible to those below because
they were a polite people, these fenekeli. They looked quickly
at the strangers, looked quickly away, bright black eyes shining with curiosity quickly hooded—not at all polite to stare
even if your visitor has green skin and is for some reason riding the headman's favorite rambut.

They turned the corner of the crowded dwelling and
moved into a long rectangular court equally busy between the
first structure and a similar one on the far side and a third
square dwelling at the back only a single story high.
Stretching out into the open space, slanting down from near
the top of the first story, painted awnings provided a little
protection from the bright, small winter sun. Painted. Dusty
broad stripes, chartreuse and carmine, amber and azure laid
down thick on the heavy cloth whose fusty odor mingled with
the other smells—sweat and musk, cooking food, the pungent
oils of the sweetsop trees growing through the worn cream
bricks that paved the court, their leaves touched to a light
bright yellow by a few frosts but not yet starting to fall. Near
the front of the court a group of women in busy-patterned
robes congregated in a laughing, chattering group about the
waist-high coping of a broad well each waiting her turn to
dip her double-handled water jar.

The rambut's hooves clicked sharply on the bricks. Hekatoro led him past the well, dropped the leadrope and turned
to speak to her.

She heard him but the words were meaningless to her and
she ignored them, though she didn't like to appear rude, because there was something else that demanded her attention,
demanded it so imperiously that she had no mind left to give
to him. There was a trembling inside her, in her legs and in
her belly, like nothing she could remember except perhaps
the first night she and Tayyan made love and curled about
each other in her narrow bed, a fluttering as if the soul
within her trembled and prepared to yield to a pull—a pull,
yes, a line squeezed round her viscera, tugging, not painful
only insistent. She stood with her hand flattened on the
saddle, its leather warmed by her body, feeling that fugitive

warmth as the noise in the court swelled around her. Distantly she heard the old man say something to Hern, heard Hern reply, the sound only, not the words not any words.

She stepped away from the rambut, swayed. The beast stood watching her, ears pricking. She circled about a suddenly silent group of women seated in a rough circle about a flat basket heaped with linat wool, the redbrown spindles shiny with much handling and the oil from the wool, held quiet now in long-fingered hands of glistening umber, the women not-looking at her, not-looking at each other, graceful necks stiff under the elaborate braided loops of their coiffeurs.

She saw them in passing, brief vivid image, and left them, forgetting them.

She walked diagonally across the court, passing, with small note, crawling naked infants, old men coming out from the shade of the awning to look obliquely at her, line drawings cool blue shadows on skin like burnt honey with red honey lights. Small ragged dusty figure she moved across the court drawn toward a back corner where a dusty tree grew up past the end of the awning, an older tree than the others, a lacetree with fragile openwork leaves bleached fire red by the frosts. She felt age like a dry, sweet perfume coming out from it to shroud her—and another sweetish smell, not so pleasant, the smell of rotting flesh. Her feet dragging, she moved slowly into the shade of the tree and stopped before an ancient man, gnarled and hard like the tree he crouched beneath. His matte umber skin was dry, hard, a little dusty like the tight-grained satinbark of the tree. He squatted quiet beneath the tree, his not-quite-yet-dulled eyes shifting to show slices of their yellowed whites. Black flies walked on a stiff stained bandage wrapped around a forearm he laid across his thigh as if its stringy round was a tray for holding something he didn't want connected with himself. She smelled more strongly that sticky sweetness and felt the pull jerk her toward him.

Saying nothing, everything fading from before her but that ulcerated wound, she knelt and closed her hand as gently as she could about it.

Pain. It slides into her hands, into her arms, it is warm and strong like hot cha inside her. Slowly, tenderly, she strokes her other hand along his arm, moves fingers feather light about the oozing wound beneath the rag. Her touches are on the edge of pain now. He begins to sweat copiously.

She feels a tickling, he feels a tickling, as she weaves new flesh layer on layer, fiber by fiber, warm and clean. He smiles, opens a wide toothless mouth and laughs. She laughs. Both sweat. Both breathe fast and shallow. She strokes the knot of the soggy bandage and it comes loose under her fingers. She unwraps the wound. The ooze and pus are crusted on new clean skin supple and pale against the cracking dark umber skin on the rest of his arm. She sits back on her heels, dropping the filthy bandage beside her. He touches the healed wound, presses his thumb down hard, jumps to his feet, yelling, snapping his fingers, slapping his hands in a dance of jubilation.

Serroi sat back, dazed with weariness. She heard a cry from the watchers, then a woman thrust a child with a great lump distending its throat in front of her and the pull was back, demanding and inescapable. She reached out, flattened her palm against the lump. There is a wrenching wrongness in the flesh, it sickens her, she fights to set it right, dimly she feels wonder because her body seems to know more than it possibly could about this healing, and she feels a touch of fear because it is magic, magic she has fought against all the years of her adult life, and as she thinks all this, the thing in her that heals keeps working, the lump is absorbed back into the boy's body, the wrongness in him is corrected. She drops her hand and the pull is back, another child is laid on her knees, a scrawny sickly child with an obstruction in him that keeps him from swallowing solid food, she heals him, telling the body to absorb that obstruction, and another is set before her and she reaches out to him and the clamor in the court is unbearable, she is sick with exhaustion and the pulls keep coming. Then there is more noise and a shadow pools around her and the pulls retreat.

She looked up. Hern was standing over her, scowling at the others. She looked past him. The fenekeli had withdrawn, the noise smoothed out like pond water grown quiet once the wind has dropped. Hern reached down his hand. She took it. It was warm and strong and comforting in a way that disturbed her because it seemed to her she needed that comforting a bit too much. The thought of depending on him, on anyone, was not one she relished. With him half lifting her she got to her feet. He was worried. He felt her withdrawal though she hadn't actually tried to pull away from him; as she knew him, so now he knew her, from the inside out, *most unfair*, she thought, he could read the shift of muscle, the small tautenings of her body she couldn't even see, *unfair, unfair.* She freed her hand and pushed at her dirty hair. "What now?"

"You all right?"

"Tired. A little scared."

"Want to go on, get out of here?" He touched her cheek very gently; she felt the anxiety in him and the deep caring, reached up and touched his fingers with hers.

"I don't think it matters where I am, things won't change, not for a while." She looked down at her tattered sleeves. "And we need clothes."

He laughed then, dropped his arm around her shoulders and turned her toward the single-story building at the back of the court. "Hekatoro's got a room ready for us and water heating for baths."

"Baths, Maiden bless, right now my idea of bliss." Though the ailments of the fenekeli kept pulling at her, giving her a wobbly feel inside, Hern's strength gave her strength to break away from them. He walked her though the silent staring groups of people and took her into the cool darkness of Hekatoro's clan hive.

They stayed at HoldHek a tenday, living in a quiet corner of the big house. Because she was driven to, Serroi sat under the ancient lacetree and healed those that came to her or were brought to her. A strange and rather terrible time. When she came out in the morning the noise in the courtyard bit off, there was a subdued and strained silence, awe perhaps, more than a little fear, uneasiness and wariness as if she were a strange animal whose potential for danger was suspected but unknown. ClanHek was healthy in the main, but there were always accidents, a crushed foot to be straightened and reformed, an abcessed tooth, skin cancers, injured eyes, shingles, boils, rashes and a thousand other non-lethal but nagging disabilities. And some came to her without physical ailment, needing just to talk, their spirits trapped until the fragile wings tattered in the web of intense and unremitting communal living.

Because Serroi was driven to the healing, she hated it. It was as if a stranger had crept inside her body and taken over its functions. It wasn't the healing itself, it was the loss of control that troubled her. This brought back too many bitter memories, the Noris using her body to drive her beasts into exhaustion and death, using her for his drive to extend his rule into the realm of the living, making her do things that sickened her. As she had wrestled with Ser Noris, so she wrestled with the compulsion to heal, wanting nothing to do with anything that smelled of magic. When she wasn't healing she sat in somber silence staring at a wall of the room Hekatoro had given them. At night she joined herself to Hern, seeking in a frantic passion exhaustion and escape from the dreams that tormented her.

Hern came into the room carrying a tray. Serroi was sitting on a wooden bench in the corner by a window, her head and torso in shadow, her hands tight on her knees, the late afternoon sunlight painting gold patterns on the heavy white linen robe, picking out green-gold highlights on her small straining hands. Lips pinched tight together, he squatted beside the low table that occupied the center of the room and transferred the bowls and pots from the tray to the table. When he was finished, he put the tray on the tile floor behind one of the pillows drawn up to the table, sat back on his heels and gazed at her, his face troubled, a muscle jumping at the corner of his mouth. He watched her a while, then lit the wick of the white porcelain lamp in the center of the table. She glanced at him, looked away again. "Atoro was disappointed," he said. "You told him you'd join him for the evening meal."

"I changed my mind." She stared out the window at the darkening sky. "Besides, my absence is a lot more welcome than my presence." She unhooked cramped fingers from her knees and leaned back until her shoulders were pressed against the wall. "He was being polite, that's all."

"Polite!" The word exploded out of him, then he pressed his lips together, turned away from her and began uncovering the dishes, loosing warm spicy smells into the room. The light through the unglazed window was darkening to red, turning her skin black where it touched her. More calmly, he said, "He appreciates the healing and what it costs you. Show the grace, meie, to let him pay his debts."

"Cost me—hah! He hasn't the faintest notion. You either."

"It's difficult to sympathize when you spend your time sulking in corners." He stood. "Come over here and eat something."

"I'm not hungry." She drew her fingertips nervously across the front of her robe, glanced at him, looked quickly away.

"But you will eat. As a matter of grace and necessity." His voice was soft now, hardly more than a whisper.

"Necessity?"

"Right. Eat or I shove food down your little throat."

She slid around, stared at him. After a long tense moment, she laughed. "Hello, Dom. I recognize you now." She got slowly to her feet, smoothed the robe down over her hips and came across the tiles to the table. She settled herself on a pillow, bent over a bowl with meat chunks in a thick gravy. Rather surprised, she said, "I think I am hungry after all."

"Tst," he said. He kicked a pillow against the wall, lowered himself onto it and sat, watching her eat.

For several minutes the only sound in the room was the ting and scrape of tableware against fine porcelain.

"They have no vocabulary of swords here."

Serroi looked up startled, a skewered piece of meat halfway to her mouth. "What brought that up?"

He laced his fingers behind his head. "A little non-threatening conversation."

"Oh." She popped the chunk of meat into her mouth, patted her lips with a square of linen from the table. She chewed quickly, wanting to laugh at the teasing look on his face, a little irritated, knowing that he'd recognized her struggle and had wanted to help, hadn't known how to help, had raged against his helplessness, though now she realized even if he didn't that he'd given her what she needed, simply by being there to touch and care what happened to her. She smiled tentatively at him. "They live too close together. Swords would be more a danger to them than to their enemies."

"Their arrowpoints and spearpoints are porcelain, or something like that."

"The Nasri-fenekel ceramics are much prized. We have some of their work at the Biserica." She rubbed at her nose. "They glazed the walls of Skup."

"Mmm. They're expecting the majilarn raids at the end of the passage. They're unpacking and oiling their bowstaves. Seem to take better care of them than they do their children."

"Wood's scarce here." The food in her belly was warm and comforting, a weight to weigh her down; it tied her to the earth, brought her back to the smells, the textures, the colors and tastes, that she had a tendency to float free of when she wasn't healing. "Thanks, Dom."

"Hah. Hekatoro's got a cousin."

"I'd say he has a lot of cousins." She sipped at the hot herb-al infusion. It was rather bitter, but it had a cleansing effect on her mouth and a very faint aftertaste that was pleasant and rather minty.

"This cousin has a boat."

"Oh."

"Uh-huh. And he knows a way through the Kashinta marshes."

"Smuggler?"

"It was not mentioned."

"Mmmm." She glanced at the window. The sky outside had gone dark, all the color faded. "We could use a little luck."

"True."

"Shinka's a bitch to get through without money."

"Which we don't have."

"Too true." She broke a roll apart and sat holding the pieces in her hands. "A chance to avoid Shinka isn't something to pass up unless. . . ."

"Unless the price is too high?"

"Right. What is it?"

"I'm not quite sure." He frowned at the white-over-gold glow of the porcelain lamp. One corner of his mouth twisted up; he pulled his hands from behind his head, spread them quickly wide then dropped them into his lap. "Your services, I think." He shrugged. "Past and future." His eyes flicked over her and away; he was frowning, worried about her she knew, wondering perhaps if the mention of the healing would upset her since the healing seemed to be so disturbing to her for reasons he couldn't know.

She bit into the tough white bread, smiling as she chewed, letting the silence stretch out between them. He stared at her openly now, gravely at first then amused by her as he saw that she'd shifted out of that difficult neither-nor state of the past ten days. It was odd even to her that she'd come so suddenly from it, perhaps simply because she was tired of suffering. She laughed, put the bread down. "I'm tired of suffering."

"That's good." He leaned against the wall, his eyelids drooping over lazy grey eyes. "The Cousin is in Tuku-kul now, he'll be there another few days. Hekatoro says he can get us places on the boat." He yawned, patted the yawn. "Down the river, through the Marsh, across the Sinadeen to Low Yallor and the freeport market."

"As easy as that."

"It could happen."

"You think it's likely?"

He smiled suddenly; slitted grey eyes twinkled and invited her to share his amusement. "What's likely about any of this? Why not an easy glide along the river, a moonlight flit across the sea?"

She started tearing the bread apart and dropping the bits into congealed gravy. "Hern?"

"Mmm?"

"Do you want to go back to living in the Plaz?"

"What? No." He got to his feet and went to stand at the window, staring out at the patch of stars visible from that small square. She felt his withdrawal. He'd exposed more than he'd wanted to—to her and to himself. He reached out and closed his hand around the molded cane inset. "No," he repeated, his voice muffled. "Maiden's tits, I spent a lifetime there bored out of my mind. Doesn't matter what I want, I'm going back. Mijloc's mine. They're mine, my mijlockers, taroms, ties, traders, all of them. I won't let that bitch Floarin have them." He laughed suddenly, mocking himself, but she heard the truth in the words that he wouldn't admit to himself. "Not while I have blood in me," he said and thought he was joking.

"Then we leave tomorrow?"

"Like we came, a little cleaner and not so ragged. Atoro's taking us along with a packload of trade goods. He likes the thought of doing us a favor. Doing you a favor. I'm not quite sure what he thinks you are but he's sure a little propitiation couldn't hurt."

She stroked the nape of her neck, considering this. "You know him, I don't."

"Not his fault."

"I know. I know. You've spent the last nine days telling me." She threw her arms out, stretched them up over her head, pulled them down again, straining the muscles of shoulders and back. "I don't like losing control."

"What?" He turned, settled himself on the bench, shoving a pillow behind his back, stretching sturdy legs out before him. "Never happen."

"Hah! Much you know. You think I want to sit all day under that damn tree? Hunh. Wave a wound at me or a disease and bang! I'm locked to it. No choice. Listen, things get rough, you better plan on dropping me. Stick a spear in some idiot and first thing you know, there I'll be on my knees beside him, healing him."

"Come here."

"What?"

"You heard me."

"Since when do you give me orders?"

"I wouldn't dare. Come here."

She pushed away from the table and stood, a tingling warmth spreading up through her. She touched the ties at her neck, her fingers trembling, wanting him with a sudden urgency that rather startled her. She walked slowly to him, stretched out both hands and saw as he took them his composure was as false as hers. She pulled her hands free, touched his face with soft stroking circles, his clean-shaven face. She smiled, traced the chiseled curves of his wide mouth then drew her hands down his chest, feeling the hard flat muscle beneath the thin cloth of his fenekeln shirt; she slid her hands inside his shirt. He laughed, scooped her up and carried her across the room to their blankets and sleeping mat.

The night was shut down good and tight by the time they got close enough to smell the river and the effluvia of the many kilns. Clouds hung heavy over the town, and off-and-on wind swept cold and noisy along the road. She shivered, not from the cold but the boiling, seething clouds of foreboding that poured out of the city and settled around her. *Something waits*, she thought. She looked back at the lumbering vachai loaded high with trade goods, looked past him to the east at the plateau it was too dark to see. *I wonder, could they be waiting for us?*

Hern and Hekatoro walked ahead of her, talking now and then, unaware of the chill that shot through her. She rode the rambut again, the heavy material of her linen robe bunched up above her knees. She'd have preferred to walk but Hekatoro insisted and too much protest would have been a breach of courtesy so she yielded and consoled herself with the thought that Atoro could ride the beast back, the placid dehorned vachai pacing behind him, its load consigned to the Cousin. Sitting beneath the lacetree tending the endless stream of complaints, she'd seen from the corner of her eye a staccato series of still images—huddles of women, of men, excited children shouting lists, rapid calculations on long brown fingers. She hadn't understood then but it was clear now what was happening, had come clear when Hern told her about the Cousin and stirred her from her brooding, her morose rebellion against a fate that had swallowed her in spite of all her furious fighting.

Healwoman? No. Shawar? Who could say. Not me. Healwomen use herb-lore, not what works in me. She wiggled her shoulders, uncomfortable even out here away from the sick and the hurt and the needing; she felt a thousand phantom tugs from the town ahead as if she walked past a corral where flying spiders had pasted their silk, long strands drifting on the wind, brushing against her, trying to cling to her, neither painful nor individually irritating. It was the number of them, the number of the touches, the unremitting small tugs that tormented.

The gates of the town were open. It wasn't Raider's passage yet and the Heks of the Plain were coming in every day with their packs to meet the river captains in discreet back rooms of the many waterside taverns, nothing so blatant as to provoke fury in the Shinki ductors. No one disputed that they knew what was happening, it would be impolite to assume otherwise. And it would be both impolite and impolitick to conduct such illegal transactions within view, forcing the ductors to act against their own comfort, something equally discreet presents attempted to assure against.

A guard leaned in a lower window of one of the gate towers idly watching the stones sit, smoking a short clay pipe stuffed with duhanee, dreamy eyes now and then on the flat spurts of pale smoke he blew out into the chill air. When the three entered the baffle below him, he took the pipe from his mouth and called down, "Who goes?"

"Hekatoro, cousin, come a-visiting."

The guard chuckled, a slow drawn-out sound. "Ah," he said. "How could I be forgetting that Olambaro's galley be nuzzling a wharf this ten-day. Eh-Atoro, have a care to your feet, a new ductor's laying dung about. Got an itch he's looked to scratch on some blockhead's corners."

"Not me, o-eh cousin, not me." Hekatoro laughed and strolled on. The guard sucked on his pipe again and went back to contemplating the stones.

The old fenekel led them around the baffle wall and into a dark and empty street. They wound their way through other silent streets, past lamplit, noisy courts, the life inside shut away from the street by high mud-brick walls. Tuku-kul was a city of inner courts where no outsiders would be welcome or find anything but idleness and boredom. Serroi's sense of foreboding increased until she was sick with it. And sick with the healing compulsion. And glad now she rode the rambut, there was no way she could walk.

Light rose against the sky, a dim torchlight glow shining between the dark bulks of the walled houses. At every turn it seemed just a street or two ahead of them.

Foreboding blacker and blacker. Alert—a stabbing into her gut. Serroi gasps, dives off the rambut, shoves Hekatoro off his feet, slams into Hern, sending him staggering, hits the ground, rolls onto her feet in front of them, her hands outstretched as three Sleykynin come rushing round the corner, roaring a challenge, the leader with a sword, the other two holding whips loosely coiled. She is not-thinking, not-acting, seized by a sudden irresistible force that surges in great waves up through her shaking slight body. Green light pulses about her hands, pulses from her splayed-out fingers.

The light hammers at the assassins who freeze in midstride, their mouths gaping below the velater half-masks. They begin to change. Slowly, horribly, they change. Their bodies writhe, their skin hardens, turns papery, their heads elongate, bifurcate, the two portions spread apart and grow, up and up, divide again, grow up and up. Eyes, mouth, all features are absorbed, gone. Their arms strain upward, stretching, thinning, their fingers split into their palms and stretch outward from the wrists, whiplike branches spreading in a delicate fan. The velater hide is absorbed into their altered flesh but there is a short rain of metal objects, buckles and rivets, knives, swords, whips, a pouch of coins.

The green light dies. Her arms fall.

Hern came hesitantly around to stand in front of her. "Serroi?"

She dropped to her knees and began vomiting. He knelt beside her, held her. When she was finished, he wiped her face, lifted her onto her feet and held her until her shaking stopped, warning Hekatoro to silence with a glare and a shake of his head.

When she was calm again, he cupped his hand under her chin and lifted her head. "Serroi?"

"Yah, Dom." She moved her shoulder, worked her mouth. "Looks like I'm not such a dead loss after all."

He looked past her at the three twisted trees. "No," he said. "Looks like." He took his arms away, frowned thoughtfully at her. "You together again?" When she nodded, he went over to the trees and began poking about among the odds and ends of metal and accoutrements dropped about the new-made trunks.

Hekatoro sidled closer, his eyes rounded, irises ringed with white, mouth dropped open. He flattened himself on the ground by her feet. "Beiji-behandum," he said, his voice rumbling against the dirt.

"Oh get up," she said irritably, shoving at her hair, rubbing at her forearms. "Maiden bless, you don't think I meant to do that, do you? Stand up, Atoro-besri. Please."

Hern came back with sword, knife and whip—and a small heavy pouch that clinked. He shook it, "Repaying what they took from us," He pulled the pouch open and inspected the contents. "Well, well, repayed with interest."

"Enough to *buy* passage?"

He glanced at her, suddenly still, his outline bold and black against torchlight still a street or two away. "Possibly," he said.

Hekatoro was silent, looking from one to the other, sensing things unsaid behind the words. He read his own meaning into the exchange. "Favor for favor," he said, breaking the silence. He nodded, grinning, back on his trader's ground, much more comfortable there than on his face before mystery. He snapped his fingers. "Buy passage, no. I pay. You ride, no fuss. I get rid of obligation sitting on my head. Hah." His eyebrows wriggled wildly, then dragged down and together. He trotted off to round up the rambut and the vachai.

"Would it matter that much, being hired to heal?" He rubbed the back of his hand against her cheek. "If that thing in you makes you heal anyway?"

She leaned into his caress then moved away. "I suppose not. But I'd rather be compelled from inside than out, if you see what I mean." She swung round to stare at the gnarled and twisted trees. "That scares me, Hern." She ran trembling fingers through her hair. "What am I turning into?"

Hekatoro pushed open the door and stepped into the tavern, Hern and Serroi close behind him. The taproom was noisy, hot and dim, lit by thick crockery lamps with holes pierced in the sides to let light from the burning oil through, though not enough light to cut the thick shadow and smoke. The stench of hot oil was strong enough to overwhelm the other stinks in the room, the sweet stale mead, the clouds of rank duhanee, bitter ale, raw spirit, sweat, farts, body odor, particularly pungent because of the mix of races within the room. In a back corner of the room, surrounded by silence and space, two black clad men with the honey-gold faces of Shinka sat scowling at the others, at pale northards, amber shinkin a little nervous under the eyes of their countrymen, fenekeln dark as new-turned earth, scrawny unhappy majilarn brooding over kifals.

There was a shout. Another fenekel who might have been Hekatoro's twin was pushing through the crowd and in a minute was pounding him on the back and shouting extravagant compliments. A slight figure slipped out past them, a skinny whey-faced, bulge-eyed northard. "Mus'll take you beasts around back and see the packs brought up." The words were a gentle murmur flanked by Olambaro's more boisterous questions and answers. He led them across the room, a shoving circuitous path around busy tables through the noisy throng moving between the bar and the tables. After a word with the man behind the bar the four of them— Olambaro and Hekatoro trading stories in a dialect so thick and with allusions so personal they were incomprehensible, Hern and Serroi silent behind them—the four of them went through an inconspicuous door at the bar's end and up a narrow flight of stairs to a small tight room on the second floor.

Olambaro held the door open, waved them in, then stood waiting while two silent grinning men brought in the packs from the beasts and deposited them on the floor by a low table. As they left he walked round the table, stepping carefully among the scattered pillows, seated himself on a plump red silk cushion and waited till the others had seated themselves. Not-looking at Hern and Serroi with fenekeli politeness, he said, "Beginning to think you weren't coming, cousin."

"O-eh, a bit of this and that happening at the Hold."

"Yah, so l'il Ando said. To anybody'd listen. Full of funny stories he was, a couple ears looked pleased to hear 'em, strangers, mean looking, you know what I mean." He shrugged. "Long as they don't be ductors, I figure I keep hands off. L'il Ando got hisself one damn good drunk outta it." A knock on the door cut off what he was saying. "Who?"

"Silkar, Cap'n." Even muffled by the door the voice was harsh and unhuman.

"Come." Olambaro's eyes slid momentarily to Hern and Serroi, his teeth flashing in a broad grin then vanished immediately into a dignified gravity.

Serroi had to struggle not to stare at the man who came in. She'd grown accustomed to her own muted olive shade, but this one was scaled like a viper and green as the new leaves of spring. He wore a linked belt of beaten bronze with a needle-pointed bronze knife clipped to it, a short leather kilt and a heavy bronze medallion on a chain about his neck. Carrying a fat-bellied jug of wine, his long slender fingers hooked through the handles of four cups, he stepped around the pillows with a predator's lightness to set his burden on the table before Olambaro. When he straightened, he stared a long moment at Serroi, his glowing golden eyes moving from her face to her hands and back, then he left the room with the same silent glide.

The corners of his mouth twitching, Olambaro popped out the cork and poured wine in the cups. "The harvest, I hear, is beyond praise this year." He passed the cups to his guests, then sipped at the wine so they'd feel free to drink.

"True, yes true," Hekatoro murmured. He took a gulp of the wine then sat holding the cup at heart level. "Though the weather be some strange. I hope your passage down river did not prove too strenuous." He drank again, his dark eyes twinkling. There was mischief even in the back of his neck and his brows were prancing up and down in time with his breathing. The Cousins were gently teasing their guests and at the same time gently sparring with each other.

Serroi looked down at her hands. Her skin gleamed in the soft glow from the fine porcelain lamps bracketed about the walls: the glow also woke shimmers of green and red and blue from the cushion covers, kindled gleams in the hand-rubbed hardwood of the wall panels. In the comfortable warmth—in several senses—of that room Serroi was beginning to recover from the profound upheaval of mind and spirit brought on by the events in the street. It wasn't particularly pleasant to serve as conduit for such a terrible force. Her lips twitched. A force that disposed of attackers by transforming them into rooted vegetation. *Effective but drastic,* she thought, reached across and rested her hand on Hern's thigh. His eyes smiling at her, he covered her hand with his.

"One trusts the river is free of snags and vermin."

"Storm scours have disturbed the channels more than usual and there are always vermin." Olambaro tapped a thumbnail against the side of his cup making it ring like a porcelain windbell. "A healer is a useful thing to have on board."

His brows compressed into a brambly line, Hekatoro

snorted. "L'il Ando. Next time I send him looking, I sew his mouth shut."

"Should storm later this night. More wine?"

"Good Southron this." Hekatoro pushed the cup across the table with the tips of his fingers. "Might be you have a barrel or two for trade?"

"Might be." Olambaro filled both cups, brushed at his fiercely coiling moustache. "Millvad making more knives at that magic forge of his?"

"One or two. But this can wait a breath more. Got room for passengers to Low Yallor?"

"Could be, ah, could be. Working passengers."

"No."

"No?" For the first time Olambaro looked full into Serroi's face, his black eyes snapping with interest and curiosity. *L'il Ando must've achieved real eloquence,* she thought.

"If there happens to be need, the healing is free," she said quietly. "I will not be compelled."

"Ah!" Olambaro grinned at Hekatoro whose face contorted into a rueful grimace. The old fenekel spread his hands in disgust at this willful breach of the usages of bargaining. Olambaro looked from Hern to Serroi, back to Hern. "Two," he said. He examined Hern with the same lively curiosity, scratched at his broad flat nose. "Two. Food. Sleeping space. Deck space taken from cargo. Hmmm. Sleykynin hunting 'em. Hmmm. Two and two." He made a play of moving his lips and ticking whispered items off on his fingers.

"Two and two?" Hekatoro frowned.

"Got two already riding down river." He rubbed his thumb across the tips of three fingers. "Working passengers, these, meien, standing guard and killing vermin should the need arise."

"Meien." Serroi leaned forward eagerly. "Who?" Hern's hand tightened over hers. Impatiently she pulled free. "How are they called?"

Olambaro shrugged. "They didn't say."

"Where are they now?" As Olambaro hesitated, she said, "I'm of the Biserica myself, man, I'm no enemy of theirs."

"O-eh. I know you now." He slapped the table making the wine cups jump, gave a shout of laughter. "O-eh, l'il meie, four years gone in Dander market. Shieldmate twice you length and you standing ward while Marnhidda Vos she ground small the profits of Cadandar Merchants. You changed you calling since." He stroked a finger along his moustache, raised a bristling brow. "And found yourself some new enemies it seems." He eyed her a moment longer then jerked his head up and down in a decisive nod. "Yah. Healing free of charge, passage free of charge, you and you friend there. Mind you, should we be set on, I'll expect you both to mind my generosity. Hah! Now. You want to know about meien. They watch my boat for me, keep the vermin off." He grinned. "Always sticky fingers and snoopers hanging around my *Moonsprite*." Slipping two fingers into a sleeve pocket, he fished about then brought out a ceramic disc—on a crimson ground, a black circle with three curved lines inside, the fenekeli sign for moonsprite. "My flag's raised, lantern's lit and hanging on the mainmast. Out the front and to the right. Not hard to find." He rested his gnarled hands flat on either side of the disc. "We leave in two days."

"I have to talk to them. Maiden bless, Captain." She got to her feet. "Maiden bless, Hekatoro friend."

Hern came after her. He pulled the door shut and caught hold of her arm, his fingers digging into her flesh. "Why?"

"Why what?"

"You lit up like . . . like the green at Primavar."

She loooked at the hand on her arm. "Let me go."

He took his hand away. As she stood rubbing at the sore spots that would be bruises later, he gazed helplessly at her. She could feel a tightly controlled anger working in him. "A man I could fight," he said suddenly, "this. . . ."

"Don't be a fool, Dom."

"Fool. Your fool. Want to see me caper?"

Pain, anger, jealousy, need—they struggled in him and battered at her until they became too much for her to bear. She stretched her hand to him but before she could touch him, he jerked away. "Healer," he whispered, his mouth working as if the word had a foul taste. They stood frozen a moment, his shoulders jammed against the wall, her hands half-raised, reaching for him.

She sighed and lowered her hands.

"I thought things had changed between us," he said. "That there was more than . . . that we were friends as well as lovers. Lovers! Damn you, Serroi. As soon as they come, you leave me, run to them eagerly. Eagerly, Serroi. If you could have seen your face. . . ." He closed his eyes, sucked in a breath, let it explode out. "Forget it." He swung around, pulled the door open and stepped through it, slammed it in her face as she started after him.

"Ah-zhag," she breathed. She reached for the latch, pulled
her hand back. "Not the time. Not the place." Shaking her
head she moved quickly along the hall and started down the
stairs. "Why do people have to be so damn difficult? Nothing's simple, nothing's ever simple." Her booted feet clicked
on the stair tiles, the small sound cutting through the muted
roar coming from the taproom below. "Always making mistakes. Me. I'm always wrong about something. So easy to
make mistakes. Hurt and get hurt. Hunh!" She eased the
door open, winced at the noise, stepped out into the smoke
and smell. *Hern*, she thought, *Ser Noris. Both of them.
Touchy as a girl in the throes of her first crush. Who'd have
thought it? Hern! With all the women he's had. Maiden bless,
what does he think I am?* Perhaps because she was small
enough to be a child and because the light was too dim to
show her other peculiarities, no one bothered her as she
crossed the room. She pushed through the swinging door and
stepped into the street. The fog-laden air was cool on her
face, then cold. *Possessive bastard. Wants to own me. No,
that's not right, no, maybe a touch right. Old habits die hard.
His defenses melted with the fat. Yes, that's right, the fat was
a defense, yes that too, poor Hern, a crab without his shell.
Ai-ye, Maiden help us, I'm as bad, no shell for him no shell
for me. How we going to spend a tenday—more—cooped up
on a small boat?* Pulling the hood up over her head and
clutching it together under her chin to keep the brisk wind
from blowing it off again, she crossed the street, her bootsoles
slipping on the worn cobbles. *He's certainly old enough to
know how to deal with his weaknessess. I hope he is. Don't
be stupid, Serroi, of course he is. You threw him off balance
a moment. He's intelligent, you know that. You're belittling
him again. Woman, act your age. You're as bad as him.*

A number of broad-beamed riverboats were snugged
against the stone wharves, rocking with the wind that
whipped the nameflags about and plastered Serroi's heavy
linen robe against her back. It cut through the cloth as if
nothing were there and made her think wistfully of the heavy
wool cloak the Sleykynin had taken from her on the far side
of the plateau. The winter that was bypassing Valley and
mijloc was putting its foot down here. It was a bit far south
for snow, but unless she was much mistaken, there'd be frost
on the ground by morning. She shivered and walked faster.

The wide-bellied boats were much alike, deliberately so, it
seemed to her, to confuse the Shinki ductors. She watched the

flags as she walked along; color was hard to make out, some
of the patterns impossible to discern. Then she laughed.
Olambaro's flag was twice the size of the others and stiffened
with wooden battens at top and bottom so it wouldn't twist or
droop. A storm lantern hung from the mainmast but the boat
seemed deserted. She knew it couldn't be, no one but a fool
would leave a fire lit aboard a wooden boat with a strong
wind blowing. She walked around some boxes piled on the
wharf and saw two figures sitting on the end of the dock, legs
dangling over the side. She made no effort to walk quietly,
she knew they heard her in spite of the noise of the river and
the keening of the wind. She detoured around a solitary bale
and found herself looking down at inky fog-wreathed water.
She let the hood blow back and slid her hands up inside her
sleeves, hugged her arms tight against her ribs. "Vapro.
Nurii."

Vapro swung her legs, smiled up at her. "Serroi."

Nurii leaned out to look past Vapro. "Sit down and talk to
us."

Serroi eased herself down beside Vapro. "You got the
Call-in?"

Vapro: "Uh-huh. Finally."

Nurii: "Gila and Jankatt. They went on North after they
left us."

Serroi: "How's Marnhidda Vos?"

Vapro: "Mad. Ward had another year to run, you know."

Nurii: "Yah. Says we're the only ones she trusts not to
steal her back teeth and now this. She wants her money's
worth."

Vapro: "Yah. Says she paid for a full ward and a full
ward is what she's going to get. If our wars are over come
spring, we damn well better shove ass out her way or she'll
show us what war really is."

Serroi: "She hasn't changed."

Nurii: "Not a hair."

Vapro dropped a hand on Serroi's shoulder, squeezed
lightly, took her hand away. "Chak-may stopped in Govaritil
on her way north to the Sharr. Told us about Tayyan. Zhag's
curse on all Nor."

They wanted to ask her what she was doing so far from
the Valley, what she was doing in healer's white not meien
leather, Serroi knew that and knew also that they would not.
Agemates and friends, willing to take what she could give
and let the rest go. "Southport's closed," she said. "Kry thick

as sandfleas and twice as mean. And don't try getting through Skup. I ran into a mess there and made it worse."

Vapro snorted. "I take it Oras is a bad idea too."

"Last we heard, Floarin's collecting an army there." She kicked her feet, watching the heavy cloth pouch out. "Try the passes south of Sankoy. The Creasta Shurin are still free and willing to help."

Vapro frowned. "It's Decadra passage already. The passes should be closed till spring."

Serroi shook her head. "The Nearga-nor have cancelled winter. The Valley will be turning on a spit by now, the mijloc not much better." Her mouth twisted into a mirthless smile. "No snow."

"Oh zhag, and I hate the heat." Nurii sighed. "Sitting around and toasting slowly."

"Not much sitting around with Yael-mri running things." Vapro sighed. "Ah for the halcyon days when all we had to look out for was Marnhidda Vos."

"I'm on quest," Serroi said.

"Thought you might be. Ser Noris making a nuisance of himself?"

"Yah. Dom Hern's along with me. I tell you so you can forget it."

"Forgotten already."

"Right."

"Maiden bless the both of you."

"But you'll tell us the tale when we're old and grey, won't you?" Vapro chuckled. "Something to pass the long hours."

Nurii pinched her nose. "Or conjure ghosts by the Gorduufest fires."

Serroi laughed. "When we're old and grey," she said.

A bedroom on the third floor of the tavern. Serroi stands with arms crossed, shoulders pressed against the door. Hern is looking out the unglazed window at the fog dripping from the eaves.

"Talk to me," Serroi said, breaking into the painful silence.

"Why?"

"Afraid?"

"Bored."

"Liar."

"You got something to say, say it."

"You don't trust me enough to listen."

"Give me one reason why I should."

"Poor little man, got his feelings hurt."

He crossed the room with two long strides, reached for her to shove her away from the door.

"No!" She caught hold of his arm with both hands, held on when he tried to pull free. "Fight this out here. Now."

He swept his arm in a short vicious arc, whipping her away from him, breaking her hold and sending her tottering back until she came up against the bed.

"Run away then," she shouted. "Run, little man."

He swung round to glare at her.

"I'm not your mother, Hern. Look at me. I'm not Lobori or Floarin. Look at me. I'm stupid sometimes about people, but I don't lie, I'm honest, give me that."

"Honest?" His stiff face softened. "Better a little tactful hypocrisy." He opened hands clenched into fists. "Dammit, Serroi."

"Yah. I know."

He leaned against the door, folded his arms across his chest. "No guarantees?"

"No. Take it as it comes." She sank down on the bed, held out her hand. "Always friends. Nothing changes that. The other. . . ." She shrugged.

"Back to that, eh, Serroi?" He took her hand, turned it over, brushed his lips across her palm.

"Dammit, Hern."

"Yah, I know."

CHAPTER XIII:

THE MIJLOC
(AT THE BISERICA)

Tuli and Rane descended into heat. Tuli's eyes blurred and smarted. It was hard to see. Her lungs burned. It was difficult to breathe. The macain whined with every step as heat from the near-molten earth and rock struck up through their fibrous pads. There were no small lives rustling through the brush. There was no brush, only a few bits of twisted charred wood sitting in the ash of its one-time foliage. A wind blew down behind them, marginally cooler and denser air from the mountains creeping downhill into the oven blast. Now and then she glanced at Rane from the corners of watering blurring eyes. *How can anyone, anything, endure to live here?*

The morning passed with a stingy reluctance as they wound down the mountain and across the stretch of wasteland before the North Wall. When they finally reached it, they found the Great Gate standing open a crack, wide enough for a single rider to pass through. Rane pulled her macai to a complaining stop, cupped her hands about her mouth and shouted her name into the burning rustling silence. Without waiting for any answer, she rode through the gap. Bemused, Tuli followed her, wondering more and more if there was anything at all left alive in the Biserica Valley.

Rane let her catch up, her dark green eyes amused. "Only a little more," she said, her voice hoarse but cheerful.

Tuli grunted, unwilling to say what she was thinking.

A moment later they broke through a shimmer of heat haze into coolness.

Tuli straightened her back, stared at the bewildering confusion of large structures ahead, rising behind a moderately high wall with corbel-supported walkways extending out from the top. Windows winked cheerfully at her. She blinked. The only other building she'd seen with so much glass in the windows was the Plaz in Oras. She turned to Rane. "Glass?"

Rane shook her head. "Not such a luxury as you might think. We make glass, Moth. We can't tax like Floarin so we have to find things to sell or trade. We get a good price for our glass objects." She looked up at the swollen sun, visible through the bubble of coolness as a vague glow. "Used to get. I doubt the furnaces are lit right now."

Tuli giggled. "Yah, I bet they aren't." The first shock of coolness was passing; it wasn't really cold in here, only less hot to a degree that made living possible.

They rode through a pointed archway and around the end of the baffle wall, threaded through narrow ways between the lower walls of the inner courts. In a corral attached to a long low stable an old woman and a gaggle of young girls were sponging down a few wilted-looking macain. Rane edged her mount to the corral fence, leaned over the top pole and called, "Pria Melit."

The old woman looked up, grinned. She handed her sponge to a girl working beside her, gave her a few low-voiced instructions then came across the dry manure with an easy swinging stride that belied the age and suffering carved deep in her hardwood face. As she came up to them, a broad smile sank pale blue stenda eyes in nests of wrinkles. "Eh-you, Rane. Back so soon?" She looked past Rane at Tuli. "A new candidate?"

"Could be, could be not." Rane nodded at the dejected macain. "Those all you got now?"

"Yah. Took the others up into the Teeth couple days after you last left. Least there's water up there, And browse." She reached through the poles and scratched the nose of Rane's mount. "Those two look well enough. Mijloc suffering much?"

"Some. Starting to need rain. Winter planting's going slow, if it goes at all. Floarin's not helping much with her tithe."

"Silly idiot, cutting her own throat. Leave your gear here, I'll see it's sent over to Yael-mri's varou."

"Maiden bless, Melit." Rane swung down and waited as Tuli dismounted more stiffly, stamped her feet to get feeling back in her legs.

Tuli followed Rane for a few steps, looked back. A girl with long black braids and a honey-colored face was climbing over the poles. The girl saw her watching, grinned and waved, then jumped down and started leading the tired macain into the stable.

The little gesture stayed with Tuli as she followed Rane,

warmed her. She felt like laughing, really laughing, almost like she'd felt sometimes at night, running with Teras, when the air was silk against her skin and all the night smells invaded her and she laughed aloud with joy at being alive. It was not quite that yet here, but she felt the promise of it in the air. She hugged the feeling to her. A glance at Rane told her she couldn't speak of it to her. *Memories*, she thought. *I wonder what it's like to love someone a quarter of a century.* She rolled the words on her tongue. *Quarter of a century.* It sounded like forever. Twice as long, almost, as she'd been alive. She glanced at Rane again. *I wonder if it was worth it.*

They moved into a covered way that led into one of the courts of the many-courted building. There was a space of silence around Rane that kept Tuli from talking to her or touching her, a hard transparency between them like the unexpected glass in all the windows. She brushed a hand along the tight-fitted stone of the way. She hadn't really thought of it before, but there had to be somebody to cut stone, somebody to spin and weave and cook and work in the fields and do all the things ties did on the tars. *I could work in the fields here and no one would yell at me*, she thought. *Or tell me it's not women's work.* She suppressed a giggle, her hand pressed over her mouth, her eyes flicking to Rane and away.

They came out of the way near one end of a courtyard. At the other end six girls not much older than Tuli were gathered about a short, stocky woman. All seven wore light smocks and short loose trousers. The girls repeated over and over a series of four poses, moving smoothly from one to the other as the older woman called the numbers. Rane neither looked at them nor stopped, but went immediately into another covered way. Tuli watched a minute, fascinated, then ran after Rane.

Another court. Under a bright striped awning a dark-haired woman about her mother's age sat at a loom, her feet busy at the pedals, her shuttle doing a flickering dance among the threads. On pillows by her feet young girls worked awkwardly with spindles, trying to twist an even thread from wool that other girls teased with carding combs. The slap-thump of the loom, the soft spin song of the girls, the other small noises made a serene music that filled Tuli with a sense of peace even as she realized that more than a minute or two of such work would have her screaming with frustration and boredom.

They passed through several more courts. In one a woman

bent over a potter's wheel shaping a broad flat bowl while girls pounded vigorously at lumps of moist clay. In another there were more dancers, older than the first, young women, dancing to a more complex rhythm plucked for them from the round-bellied lute in the lap of a gentle-faced woman. In another court girls and women sat fletching arrows, the glue for the feathers thick and glassy in stoneware pots perched on small charcoal braziers. In another, woodworkers carved stocks for crossbows while others assembled the bows from the stocks and bits of steel and bronze and others set points on crossbow bolts and on short spears. Many of the women and girls in these courts hummed or sang worksongs, some were talking, laughing. The Biserica seemed to Tuli a busy, noisy, friendly place, filled with life and, in spite of the threat of war, filled with a cheerful tranquility.

Rane led Tuli into the tall central building. Most of the lamps on the walls of the long dark corridor were left unlit but the few that burned turned the air hot and added the stench of burning oil to the other odors that hung in the stale, lifeless air. Rane walked faster, her face and body tense, anger evident in the harsh rasping of her breath. She turned down a broad hall that crossed the one they were in, pushed open a door at the end of this with just a touch too much force. It crashed inward against the stop. Rane cursed under her breath, ran her fingers through her faded blond thatch then strode into the long narrow room with tall windows marching along one wall and a wooden, backless bench pushed against the other.

A door in the far end opened and a tall woman with a plain clever face looked out. She smiled. "Sand fleas chewing at you again, Rane?"

"Zhag's curses on the Nor. I hate to see. . . ." Rane finished the sentence with a nervous flowing circle of her hand.

"I know." Yael-mri looked past Rane at Tuli. "Another candidate?" There was a hint of weary exasperation in her voice. Tuli heard it and scowled at the floor.

Rane heard it and stiffened. "A friend," she said curtly. "As to the other, we'll see."

"Forgive my rudeness," Yael-mri said. Her mouth tilted into a rueful smile. "We're starting to feel a bit pressed." She pulled the door open wider. "Come then, we'll talk."

Rane didn't move. "With your permission, prieti-meien," she said with a cool formality that brought a slight frown to

Yael-mri's face. "If the Ammu Rin is not in the Shawar right now, we need her services."

Yael-mri's brows shot up. "I thought. . . ." She laughed. "Never mind, the heat's addling my brain. Yours too, my friend. You know anything in the valley is yours. Ammu Rin is teaching this tenday. Come see me when you're ready." She stepped back and closed the door.

Rane relaxed, sighed, drew the back of her hand across her eyes. She didn't speak as she moved across the aste varou to look through a window into the dead garden then up to the mountain peaks rising in the distance, their pale blue tips floating like ghosts above the outer wall. Hands clasped behind her, talking to the rounds of wavery glass set in lead strips, she said, "Yael-mri is . . . was . . . older sister to Merralis." Finally she turned, composed again, walked past Tuli, called over her shoulder, "Come."

Feeling confused and a bit annoyed, Tuli followed her through a further labyrinth of corridors, courts and covered ways until the ex-meie pushed open a lacy gate of molded cane filling a pointed arch and stepped through into a large open garden that must once have been a pleasant peaceful place. Now the grass was dying, the flowerbeds empty, dry soil raked into neat patterns and set with stones, low crooked shrubs bare of leaves but with sufficient grace left to show what they could be again with enough water and care. Rane dropped a hand on Tuli's shoulder, stopped her. "I hate this place."

Tuli stood quiet, wondering why—if that was so and the sudden subdued passion in Rane's voice suggested it was so—why if she hated it so, she didn't hurry across and leave it behind. "Before . . ." Rane said. "Before, they used to bring the sick out here to sit in the sun." She sucked in a long unsteady breath, shook her head, ran across the grass, stopped in the doorway of the small bright building to wait for Tuli. "Healhall," she said when Tuli came up to her.

A space that was either a very long but narrow room or an over-wide hallway stretched the length of the Healhall, lit by huge windows on the Southwall. The inner wall was faced with a white stone that had veins of gold and green rambling through it, the ceiling and the window wall were painted white. Rane and Tuli walked on Sankoy rugs of simple design and jewel-bright color, passed windowboxes filled with flourishing green plants, even a few fall blooms. Midway down the hall Rane opened a door without knocking and stepped into an anteroom with backless benches along its sides, a table at the far end.

A girl about Tuli's age was sitting at the table, frowning intently at a book open before her. Lips moving, fingers moving along the script, she was struggling to read whatever was written there. So intent was she that Rane and Tuli crossed the room and stopepd by the table without disturbing her concentration.

Rane rapped a knuckle on the table. The girl started, looked up. "Oh." She blushed. "Yes?"

"The Ammu Rin." The corners of Rane's wide mouth twitched; laughter danced in her dark green eyes.

The girl smiled, her own eyes the green-brown of a woodland pool, reflecting the silent laughter and lighting her face to a fugitive beauty. Tuli caught her breath, ducked behind Rane. She recognized the girl. *Da . . . Dani . . . no . . . Dee . . . Dina . . . yah, Dinafar. Going to the Gather with her brother . . . Jern . . . yah, that was his name. Wonder what happened to him. S'pose their old uncle wouldn't keep a girl so she came here. Wonder if she'll know me.*

Dinafar stood. She wore a simple white robe without sleeves that skimmed along the lines of her rather mature figure. "If you'll wait just a moment. . . ." She stopped, her heavy brows rising, her head tilted slightly, her whole body a question.

"Tell her Rane and a friend."

With another flashing smile the girl nodded then disappeared through the door beside the table.

Rane turned to Tuli. "You need me with you or would you prefer to talk for yourself?" Her long fingers tapped a nervous tune on her thigh.

Tuli looked away uncertain and a bit frightened. She wanted to cling to Rane, yet Rane had made it clear she was unhappy in this place and uncomfortable with Tuli's problem. Tuli swallowed. After a moment she said, "All I have to do is tell. . . . tell this Ammu Rin what's worrying me?"

"All you have to do is tell her. She won't bite." Rane's eyes flicked to the door. She'd already fled the place in her mind. Tuli saw that and swallowed a sigh.

"All right," she said. "I can do it by myself."

"Good girl, Moth." Rane took a step toward the door, looked at Tuli. "When you're finished here, ask someone to take you back to Yael-mri's varou." Then she was gone, the door shutting behind her with a controlled quietness.

Dinafar came back, looked surprised when she saw Tuli alone.

"Rane had to leave," Tuli said. "Anyway it's me has to see the healer."

"Oh." Dinafar stared at Tuli. "I know you. One of the terrible twins. Tuli Gradindaughter. Going to Oras."

"Yah. Been here long?"

" 'Bout a year now."

"You brother's still with your uncle?"

Dinafar screwed up her face. "That's a long story. Maybe if you stay I can tell it." She glanced over her shoulder at the door. "The Ammu's waiting. You better come." She stood to one side of the door waiting expectantly. Tuli walked slowly past her, feeling her stomach cramp, wishing she'd had the nerve to ask Rane to come with her. It was funny. She hadn't been near as bothered getting her father loose from the guards. They stepped into a room.

It was small and square and breathless—and empty of anyone. Tuli swung around.

Dinafar laughed and took hold of Tuli's hand. "Come. The Ammu Rin is out in a court just past the examining rooms. It's too hot in here." She squeezed Tuli's hand then she flitted on ahead, the hem of the white robe fluttering about her ankles. She vanished through a curtained arch.

Tuli followed her through three more rooms, nesting one against the others like cells in a honeycomb, rooms with narrow cots and backless armless chairs drawn up beside the cots. Each room, small and white, clean and stripped down, had a niche in one wall with a ceramic or wooden statue, glazed or painted in bright primary colors. After the fourth room they were in a short hall, and Dinafar was pulling Tuli with her through a round door, past a heavy curtain.

They stood at the edge of a small square court, a fountain playing musically beside a tree whose trunk disappeared into a hole in the canvas that covered the whole of the open space.

Tuli noted these things but paid little attention to them: the huge form of the old woman sitting beside the fountain dominated the court. Her face was round as Nijilic theDom at his fullest, a deep rich brown with fire-orange gleams where the light sat strongest. Her eyes were large and round and a milky white with no pupils and only a hint of irids. She was blind. Her nose was a great jutting beak, her mouth was delicately carved but big enough to match the rest of her. She sat in a vast armchair surrounded by small bright pillows. Her legs were stretched out before her, her feet propped on a low ottoman. At the moment Dinafar and Tuli pushed past the curtain she was discoursing sleepily to the young women seated on cushions beside her. She stopped speaking when Dinafar and Tuli stepped onto the grass, as if she'd somehow heard the faint rattle of the curtain rings, the brush of two bodies past the heavy cloth. Her head turned toward them and she sat waiting for one of them to speak.

"Ammu Rin, Rane's friend Tuli Gradindaughter." Dinafar spoke shyly, hesitantly. She tugged Tuli past her, gave her a tap in the small of her back, sending her out into the court. Tuli took a few steps, glanced back. Dinafar was gone, heading back to her book and her struggle to decipher it.

The Ammu Rin lifted an arm that seemed to Tuli as big as the hind leg of a macai, held out a large but shapely hand. "Give me your hand, Tuli Rane's friend."

With a mixture of reluctance and awe, Tuli laid her smaller hand on the warm pink palm.

"You're very young, child. How old are you?"

"Fourteen, almost fifteen, Ammu Rin."

"Almost fifteen?" There was amusement in the deep, rich voice.

"Well. . . ."

"Never mind. You are troubled about something?"

"Yah. I need to know. . . ." She swallowed, looked quickly at and away from the silent attendants. There was no way she could talk about such private things with all these strangers present.

The Ammu smiled. Tuli stiffened until she realized that the smile was gentle and filled with understanding. "Vesset," the old woman said.

"Yes, Ammu." One of the young women jumped to her feet. She was blonde and tall, a stenda, in her early twenties, a slim, vivid figure. She stood gracefully in front of the Ammu, stenda grace like Rane's.

"Take them." The Amma waved her free hand toward the seated attendants. "Go away till I ring. Go. Go." She waved her hand again.

Silently the white-robed girls laid their fans aside and got to their feet. They bowed silently and left quickly through the curtained arch, Vesset, equally silent, following with that restrained elegance that reminded Tuli so strongly of Rane. Watching her, Tuli sighed.

"Such a sad sound." The Ammu chuckled, warm laughter wrapping around Tuli and relaxing her. "Sit you down, child, tell me your sad tale. And we'll see, we'll see what we can do."

Hand still swallowed by the Ammu's, Tuli kicked a pillow closer to the chair and eased herself down. "I think. . . ." she licked her lips. "I think I could be pregnant."

"Ah. You think so."

"Yah. I'm . . . um . . . overdue by five days. Rane says that's a bad sign."

"Ah. A bad sign."

"Uh-huh. I don't want his baby. Phah!" She pressed her lips together, the breath hissing through her nostrils as she fought with the anger that threatened to drown her every time she thought of Fayd. The Ammu's hand held hers, warmed her, calmed her. The soft rustle of leaves hidden by the canvas, the squeak of the awning ropes, the rippling music of the water, all these small sounds combined with the enfolding warmth of the Ammu's presence to soothe away the last of her rage and she found herself retelling what happened the night Fayd forced her, why it happened. "I couldn't bear it if it looked like him," she said. "I get so angry at him it scares me. Makes me wonder what I might do to the baby. Sometimes I get so mad I don't think, I just hurt people. I could hurt it, even kill it. One time I told Teras I might like kids, but that was before. Now that I might, I don't, oh Ammu Rin, I don't want kids, not now." Tuli squeezed her eyes shut, pressed the back of her free hand against her mouth. After a minute she dropped her hand, gazed hopefully up at the Ammu. "Am I?"

The Ammu was silent a moment, then she sighed. "We'll see. Tuli child, I'm a Reader, not a Healer." Her mouth curled into a smile. "Just as well, healing is not what you need. Lean forward, child, set your forehead on my knee and be patient for a while."

At first Tuli was tense, a knot in her throat, another beneath her ribs, but the slow stroking of the big hand along her shoulders relaxed her until she nearly fell asleep. Finally the hand left her. "You can sit up now, child."

Tuli straightened, blinked up into the broad calm face. She thought of speaking but waited instead.

"It's very early to be sure, even for me, but there seems to be a possibility in you. Understand me well, Tuli, I can't be sure, I'm not sure."

"Oh." Tuli felt cold. "What can I do?"

"What do you want to do?"

"I want to stop it from happening," Tuli cried. "Oh Zhag eat him, I could kill Fayd. I told him I didn't want to do it, but he wouldn't stop, he wouldn't."

"Mmmmm. You're very young." The Ammu nodded slowly. "Young to learn we pay a price for all our acts, will-we, nill-we." She laughed, shaking the tight-curled white fleece clinging close to her head. "There's a bell somewhere about. Find it, will you, child? Ring it for me."

Tuli searched among the pillows, found the bell and shook it vigorously.

"Enough, enough, you'll wake the stones." The Ammu's voice quivered with laughter. "Do you do all things with such enthusiasm?"

Tuli set the bell down. "Everything except sewing and cleaning."

"Hah, never met a candidate who did."

"I'm not a candidate." She was getting tired of hearing that.

The Ammu Rin wasn't listening. She turned, leaning on her arm, fixed her unseeing eyes on the door.

Vesset elbowed the curtain aside and stepped into the court. She carried a heavy tray with a pot of cha, two cups and a number of small pots with pipe handles on the lids. She set the tray down beside Tuli on legs she deftly unfolded from beneath it, saw it was steady, then got to her feet with a quick ripple of her body, perhaps a touch of extra grace to put the visitor firmly in her place. "Would you have a cup of cha, Ammu Rin?"

"And don't you make it better than any. Yes, yes, Vesset, pour me a cup of cha."

Vesset flushed with pleasure. A small smile on her lips, she put a dollop of honey in a mug, added a grating of sim and a pinch of paer, poured in the steaming cha, the heat of the liquid releasing a sweet mix of scents to perfume the air around them. She put the cup in the Ammu's hand, waited until the old woman sipped and smiled, turned to Tuli and truly smiled. "Would you like the same?"

Tuli nodded. "Oh yes."

As Vesset prepared the second mug, the Ammu said, "When you're finished there, love, make an infusion for me of miska-pierdro and bring it here. This we won't speak of, please."

"Yes, Ammu Rin." Vesset handed Tuli the steaming cup. "Think of saving some of this to wash away the taste. You wouldn't believe how foul it is."

Tuli sipped at the sweet spicy liquid, watching Vesset disappear beyond the curtain.

The chair creaked as Ammu Rin settled back. "Miska-pierdro is a herb mix. Like Vesset said, it don't taste so good, but it's safe, quite safe. We've had a number of tie girls too young for marriage and unwilling to make lives here; they've returned to their homes, married later and produced healthy children in those marriages." She cradled the cup between her large hands. "If indeed you later change your mind, child, and want children, then know there will be no physical result from what you choose to do now."

Tuli nodded, forgetting the Ammu couldn't see, but the old woman smiled anyway seeming to know what she was thinking.

"When Vesset comes back. . . ." The Ammu shifted again, wiped sweat from her face. "She'll have the infusion with her. Swallow it now. You'll get another dose of it after supper and a third in the middle of the night. We'll wake you for that. You'll have to spend the night here in the Healhall. Come the dawn, you'll be feeling right miserable but on the way to recovering yourself, and without the burden you now carry. You will be riding out again when Rane leaves?"

"I meant to, I will if she'll wait the night for me. I've seen how little she likes to be here."

"Ah. A sad time, that. We did what we could, though it was little enough." She nodded her big head. "Pardon me an old woman's curiosity, child, but do you think you will be a candidate later?"

"I don't know."

"It doesn't matter. Don't let people push you into anything you don't want." She chuckled. "Not that I think you will."

Vesset came back carrying a small porcelain jar with a wide mouth and straight sides. She knelt beside the tray, took Tuli's mug, looked in it. "Empty. Well, thanks be, it's a big pot." She prepared another cup and handed it to Tuli. "Keep this awhile yet." She picked up the jar. "Open your throat, young Tuli, and throw this down. Try your best not to taste it."

Fingers trembling, the moment on her before she was ready for it though she thought she'd been preparing for it for near a passage now, Tuli took the jar. It was cool and slippery, the liquid inside rocked by the shaking of her hands. "Maiden bless," she said and threw the liquid down her throat as she'd been told. Even so she could hardly keep from gagging. Vesset took the jar from her and helped her lift the cha mug to her lips. "A couple of gulps of this and you'll feel better."

When she'd emptied the cup Tuli indeed felt better. She licked her lips and sighed. "Two more."

Vesset laughed and stood.

Ammu Rin leaned forward. "Send young Dinafar to me, she's labored long enough on her lessons."

"That I will." Vesset flicked her fingers at Tuli and went away.

Tuli watched the curtain sway and hang still again. "She's going to be a healer?"

"Vesset? She already is, Tuli. A healwoman, the best of my students. If times were other than they are, she'd be going out next summer on her first wanderyear."

"Oh. How long has she been studying?"

"Ten years." Once more the chair creaked as the Ammu shifted her weight.

"Ten years!" Tuli stared at the old woman. The milky blind eyes opened. Ammu Rin smiled and nodded. "Does it take that long to make a meie?"

"Some learn faster than others." Ammu Rin scratched the side of her nose. "Put you off, eh Tuli?"

"That's almost as long as I've been alive."

"It goes fast, yes, it goes." She turned her head to the door.

Dinafar pushed past the curtain. "Ammu Rin?"

"Ah. Dinafar. Take young Tuli here to the prieti-varou. And after that, if Rane is agreeable, show our visitor about. Take the afternoon free, Dina, you've studied enough for today."

Dinafar grinned, rubbed at her eyes. "Maiden bless, my head thanks you, Ammu Rin."

"So go, the two of you."

Tuli finished the last of the sweetened cha and put the mug on the tray. She scrambled to her feet, hesitated. "Should we take away the tray, Ammu Rin?"

"No. No. But you could ring the bell again. Gently, this time, gently, child."

Dinafar knocked on the varou's door.

Rane opened it and looked out, saw Tuli, raised a thin blond brow. "Did you get your answer?"

"Uh-huh." Tuli grimaced. "I got to stay overnight."

"I see. That's no problem. You'll be ready to leave early tomorrow morning?"

"That's what she said. Ammu Rin. And she said Dinafar could show me around if that's all right with you."

Rane grinned. "Enjoy yourselves, the two of you. You'll be sleeping in the Healhouse, Moth?"

"Yah."

"All right, you're set." She lifted a hand in one of her comprehensive gestures, stepped back and shut the door.

Dinafar danced across the aste-varou. "Come on, there's lots and lots to see. What shall I show you first? Oh I know, come on, come on."

The Watchhall magnified the sound of their feet. It was empty, no chairs or rugs on the floor, nothing, just a broad expanse of tile, black tile, dusky soft black like the sky on a cloudy night, a vast room, longer than it was wide, as high as it was wide, ceiling lost in shadow. On the walls also lost in shadow great tapestries stirred in the fugitive drafts that haunted the corners of the hall. At the far end a long rectangle bolted to the wall above a broad dais glowed in the light of a row of lamps, a brightly painted collection of shapes set on a field of blue.

Dinafar caught hold of Tuli's hand, pulled her across the tiles. "It's the whole world," she said, her voice booming in the emptiness.

"Ahh. Where are we?"

"See that green bit there on the middle chunk of land?"

"Yah."

"That's us. And the yellow bit just above, that's the mijloc." She pointed. "See that little red dot? That's Oras. If you go down the coast a little from that, see, where the blue goes in and out a lot, that's where the fishers live, you had to see some of them at the Gather, that's where I was born and grew up." She wrinkled her nose. "And, Maiden bless, I'll never see the stinking place again."

"That bad?"

"Tell you sometime."

"What're those black lines?"

"Roads, sort of. Caravan routes. The one there in the yellow, you should know that one, it's the Highroad." She jumped onto the dais and dipped her hand into a silver box attached to the wall beside the map, pulled out a handful of silver pegs and let them rattle back into the box. "These are the meien, each one is marked. Come on up, let me show you." She picked through the pegs while Tuli peered over her shoulder. "Trying to find someone's I know. Ah! Look."

A glyph was stamped on the thick round head of the peg. "That's for Leeaster, she's my dance teacher. When the pegs are in the box that means the meien are back in the valley. Look over here." She ran along the map, jumped up, touched a narrow violet strip dotted with red city spots. Two silver pegs were still in their holes. Back on her feet, she said, "Va-pro and Nurii. Far as we know the Call-in hasn't reached them yet. They're Serroi's agemates so she probably knows them."

"Serroi?"

Dinafar flushed uncomfortably. "Oh, a friend of mine."

"Oh." Tuli stared at the map, at all the black lines, the red dots that were cities, the silver pegs that marked the wards of all the meien still out of the Valley. She'd seen the Sutireh Sea for the first time at the Gather. She and Teras had climbed onto the city walls and looked out and out and out across water that didn't seem to end. Now she saw the Sea was only a little wider than the widest part of the Cimpia Plain. And there were more red city-dots on the unknown land on the far side of the Sea. She'd never thought of there being land out there, and people living on that land. She stared and stared at that patchwork of colors, appalled by the sheer size of the world, so much bigger than she'd had any idea, so many lands, so many different people. And she didn't even know much about how Stenda lived and they were almost close enough to spit on. And she didn't know anything at all about Dinafar's fisherfolk. "It's big," she said, awe trembling in her hushed voice.

"Yah." Dinafar patted her arm. "I remember the first time I saw this. Made me feel about so big." She held thumb and forefinger half an inch apart.

"And the meien go all over?"

"Yah. Healwomen too."

"You don't mark healwomen?"

"Healwomen wander, they don't have wards. No way to keep track of them."

All those places to go and see, all those places. . . . Tuli sighed. "Ten years," she said and brushed her hand back over her hair.

"Goes fast."

"So the Ammu said." She walked down to the end of the dais. Hundreds of small copper rectangles were tacked to the wall, names incised in each. "What's this?"

"The roll of the dead. All the women who've lived here, the meien and the healwomen and the craftswomen, everyone. When someone dies, we watch the night away in here, everyone in the Valley. If the woman dies in the Valley, we burn the body to ash and give the ash back to the earth." Dinafar's voice was very soft, her eyes shining. "We spread the ashes on the fields and in the orchard so the dear one returns to us in the fruits of the earth." She shook herself, laughed and jumped down from the dais. "That's enough solemn things." She danced away across the tiles and pushed the big door open. "Where you want to go next?"

"The glass place. I want to see how you make glass."

"Well, you won't, it's all closed down. Too hot."

"I'd like to see it anyway."

"All right, you won't see much."

A low blocky building. A big open box. High pointed windows with round bits of stained glass set in lead strips, painting colored rounds on the slick white floor. The melting furnace was a large square structure raised off the floor and backed against one wall. A charred wooden walkway passed in front of the round openings of the furnace, long blackened pipes and a hundred other enigmatic objects lay about haphazardly; she didn't know what they could be for and wished she could see the place when it was working. She sighed. "You're right, it isn't much interesting like this."

"One. Two. Three. Four," the stocky woman counted, echoing the count with beats of her hand. On near noiseless bare feet the girls moved in disciplined unison, one pose flowing into the next faster and faster until they were a blur of step-bend-turn.

"The Cane dance," Dinafar whispered. "Bend like bastocane before the wind."

"But why? What's it for?"

"Itself." Hand over her mouth to hold back a giggle, Dinafar danced across the court and into the covered way. She turned to wait for Tuli.

"Tchah!" Tuli said when she came up with her.

"Well, that's what they say. Actually, it's part of teaching us how to make any fool sorry he bothered us."

Pottery. Fires out under the kilns. Too hot.

Smithy. Women and girls sweating over spear points and arrowheads, the smell of hot iron and sweat, the clang of metal on metal, the hiss of metal quenched in cool water.

Weaving hall. The great looms silent, the huge chamber dark, silent. "It's usually full of noise," Dinafar said sadly. "The weavers have moved outside until the weather breaks."

Kitchen. Pots, steam, noise, girls everywhere, irritation, laughter, fussing—like a seething stew, different ingredients popping to the top in turn to give a whiff of their own particular flavor. They were quickly chased from this place.

Maiden Shrine. "Can't go in there now. The Shawar are working there and they don't like to be disturbed."

"Working?"

"Fighting the Nor, you know, trying to fix the sun so it's right again."

Smoking sheds. Posser haunches wreathed in pungent smoke, strips of dark almost black hauhau meat drying, black sausages dangling.

Storehouses. Barrel on barrel of salt fish, salt meat, crocks of preserves, bins of grain, sacks of tubers, strings of dry fruit and wax-coated cheeses.

Barns. Empty of stock except for some hauhau cows kept for their milk and a few macain. Stuffed with hay, more bins of grain. "Until the weather breaks," Dinafar said, "most of the stock is up in the mountains."

Girls everywhere, a flood of girls drowning the older women, girls chattering, laughing, silent, intent, impatient, sullen, cheerful, glowing, lazy, bubbling with nervous energy, tie girls, tarom's daughters, city girls from Sel-ma-carth and Oras, girls from distant places and distant peoples whose names and locations Tuli didn't know. A culling of girls, the rebellious, the restless, the pleasure-loving, the pious, some fleeing the repression of the Followers, some seeking whatever it was the Biserica seemed to promise them.

The promise of the Biserica. Tuli began to see how little anyone knew of the Valley, they knew the keepers, the meien, the healwomen, they knew nothing at all about the craftswomen, teachers, fieldworkers and all the rest. The promise of the Biserica. Whatever else it was, it meant hard work, accepting responsibility, and in the end a kind of freedom not found anywhere else in the world, not that she knew anyway, though she was forced over and over again to realize just how little she did know.

As the day wore on, Tuli grew silent and thoughtful. One moment she was sure this was what she wanted, that this was what she was born for. The next moment she missed Teras dreadfully, missed her mother and her father, Sanoni and the ties and all the familiar and comfortable things she'd grown up with.

A vague nausea floated under her ribs and the revolting taste of the infusion kept coming up into her throat.

In the middle of the night a hand shook her awake— Vesset, with the third dose of the miska-pierdro. Tuli sat up, scrubbed at her eyes.

"Come, little one, one last gulp." Vesset bent over her, stroked her tangled hair.

Tuli shuddered. "Must I?"

"Can't leave the job half done." Vesset's high-cheeked face was tender in the shadowed light from the porcelain lamp sitting on the bedside table.

Tuli sighed, took the small cylinder and tossed the liquid it held to the back of her throat. "Gahh, that's awful."

"Here." Vesset handed her a stoneware mug. "Juice. It'll cut the taste."

Tuli took the mug gratefully and gulped down half the juice before she lowered it again. "Maiden bless," she said.

Vesset chuckled. "Be you blessed. Listen. In a little while you might feel some cramps—or you might not. This takes different people different ways. Even if it gets really bad, don't worry. It'll pass. By morning you'll be sure enough you're going to live."

"Oh marvelous."

Vesset bent down, touched Tuli's cheek, then went quietly out, taking her lamp with her.

Tuli sat in the quiet darkness, sipping at the juice, aware even more than before that she was in a strange room in a strange bed. She felt on edge, uncertain. She touched the sheet beside her, stroked her hand along the blanket pulled over her knees. Strange smells. Strange feel. Alone. She shivered, missing the soft night breathing of her family, she'd

never slept in a room by herself before. Defying she didn't
know what, she tossed down the rest of the juice, fumbled the
mug onto the little table, wriggled and bounced herself out
flat on the bed, pulled the blanket up over her and lay staring
into the darkness. She was tired but the first hours of sleep
had taken away the urgency of her need. Sleep evaded her.
When she forced her eyes shut, they popped open again. She
yawned, stared up at the dark-lost ceiling and tried to relax.

I can put off deciding, she thought. *Maybe there won't
even be a Biserica when this is over. If I just knew, really
knew, what I want. I need to see Teras. I need to talk to
Mama.* But she knew even as she thought it that it wasn't
really so, that Teras wasn't a choice for her anymore, that
Rane was right, she had to let him go his own road, that her
Mama would make her choose for herself. *Still, I've got time
now.* She flattened her hand on her stomach. *I can make my
own choices, not have them forced on me. Mmmm. If I go
back to the mijloc I'll have to marry somebody, I wonder
who.* She made a face at the darkness. *Not Fayd, aghhh! not
that chinj.* She began turning over in her mind the boys she
knew from Cymbank and around, those her age or a little
older. As she drifted toward sleep, the many faces merged,
blurred, blended and oddly enough finished up as Dinafar's
laughing face.

About an hour later she woke as cramps like knife blades
stabbed into her.

Yael-mri and the stable pria Melit rode with Rane and
Tuli as far as the gate. Outside the protecting bubble, the air
was hot and dry though not quite so terrible as it would be
later on. The night's cloud cover was shredded and worn so
that the swollen sun was partly visible through rents near the
horizon. The dawn was quiet, the wind having dropped until
it was only a sometime pat on the face. The three women
spoke little until they reached the Great Gate.

Yael-mri held up a hand and pulled her mount to a stop.
She leaned over and touched Rane's arm. "Take care," she
said. "We need your news, you know that, but not at the ex-
pense of your life."

Tuli moved impatiently in the saddle. She wanted to leave
this place that demanded too much from her and she seethed
with impatience to get on with the ride north. She was excited, nervous and triumphant. When this was over she'd
have more adventures than Teras would. She wanted to go

back and show him he wasn't the only one to do exciting and important things. And all those tie girls with their giggles and hateful sly digs, she wanted to look at them with a face that said, *you're nothing, no one. Look what I've done while you sat around and gossiped.* She smiled at the pictures in her head, not quite able to believe they'd ever happen, she might be young like the Ammu Rin said but she was old enough to know the scenes you plotted in your head never worked out the way you thought they would.

She sighed. *Still talking.* She closed her eyes and thought about the morning. Dinafar had brought her breakfast—

She threw Dina the pillow, then settled herself cross-legged on the bed in front of the long-legged tray. Dina kicked the pillow against the wall and sat down on it, sat with her hands laced behind her head watching Tuli eat. "Wish I was going with you," she said.

Tuli didn't have an answer for that so she kept quiet and sipped at her cha.

"It gets boring here sometimes, all the studying and everyone so serious, well, that's not true, it's just we know bad times are coming fast, worse than now, I mean, and it just feels wrong to play and be lazy, though we do it anyway, you know, and they scold us some but they smile when they do it."

"Rane spent a lot of time talking with Yael-mri." Tuli heard the sourness in her voice and winced. *I sound jealous,* she thought. She sneaked a glance at Dinafar to see if she'd noticed. Dinafar was looking with exaggerated casualness at the door. Tuli sniffed.

"Oh, they got things to talk about, you know. There's people out in the mijloc, well, all over, but the mijloc is what's worrying us now. Anyway, they keep an eye on what's happening and Rane is one of them that bring us news." Having talked away her awkwardness, she gave Tuli one of her broad glowing grins.

"Yah, I know." Tuli emptied the cha mug and went to work on the porridge. Spoon halfway to her mouth, she said, "We're going on a swing around the Plains when we leave here."

Dinafar sighed, got to her feet and walked slowly to the door. In the doorway, she swung around, hesitated, said, "You'll come back, won't you? Please?" Without waiting for an answer she wheeled and fled down the hall.

Lost in memory, Tuli missed most of the conversation beside her until the pria Melit gave a sudden sharp exclamation and pointed.

The clouds in the east were breaking fast now, disappearing as if the sky absorbed them into itself. In a wide blue space the sun pulsed violently. Even as the four of them watched, there was a sound like a snapping lute string and the sun settled to a distant cool glow, its normal size and color in a sky that was suddenly a wintry blue without the distorting copper tinge they'd seen for passages.

"She did it," Yael-mri cried. "She pulled him off us." The three women laughed and wept together, and pounded their saddle ledges and threw back their heads, whooping. After a few moments, though, Yael-mri sobered. "I doubt he can reestablish the lens, not with the Shawar warned and ready to fight him. There's still Floarin and her army, but the army won't march until Spring now. We've won some time—no, Serroi won it for us. Time," she sighed. "Take care, Rane. You could have some stormy riding now the weather's broken."

Rane nodded. "Maiden bless," she said softly. "You and the Valley." She stretched, settled herself in the saddle, grinned at Tuli. "Let's go, Moth."

CHAPTER XIV:

THE QUEST

A dash down the river, tedium in the marches, chaos on the Sinadeen.

Low Yallor, loud, noisy, crowded, busy.

Behind them the sea.

Outside the breakwater the storm-prodded sea lashed at the stones as it had lashed at the *Moonsprite*.

In front of them, Yallor Market.

Around them, a confusion of ships.

Trading ships that hugged the southshore of the Sinadeen and went south along the west coast of Zemilsud, or north to stop at Trattona of Sankoy, Oras of the mijloc, nameless ports north where the ivory fishers lived. Tiny outriggers from a dozen swamp clans on the north shore of the Sinadeen. Ocean-goers from the Sutireh Sea. Noise, color, confusion. Land merchants, ship's captains on shore wandering about, examining merchandise piled high in market booths, bargaining in loud roars or near inaudible whispers. Local porters trotting along under huge burdens, shouted on by anxious buyers.

And everywhere, pulling at her—sickness, pain, needing. Sores. Deep-hid tumors. Syphilis and related ills. Burns. Cuts. Rotting teeth. Suppurating ulcers. Fever. Fever. Fever—the breath of the swamp breathing over the town. She clung to the low-slung guardrail, blind to the confusion swirling about her, to the corrupt and stinking water below her and fought to win some control of the compulsion that threatened to drain the strength out of her until she was hollow. Roots writhed within her feet, immaterial roots wanting to be real and plunge down and down into Earth's cool heart.

Someone touched her shoulder. Blinking and trembling she looked around. Hern was frowning down at her. His lips moved. After a moment, she realized he was speaking to her. ". . . .wrong?" he said.

"Hold me," she said.

293

"The healing?"

"Yes." She leaned against him, his strength shielding her from some but not all of the needing. His arms came around her. She clasped her hands over his.

Norii and Vapro swung overside. Standing in a water-taxi they waved at her, then sat and let the waterman row them to the shore. Hern's arm tightened about Serroi. She felt briefly like laughing, knowing his relief at seeing the back of them, though he'd said no more to her about them.

He murmured into her ear, "What can I do?"

"Get me through the market." With a quick round gesture she took in the noisy throng on the shore. "To someplace where there aren't too many people. I'll be all right then."

"You're sure? You know I have to see about transport and supplies for crossing the Dar."

"Hunh! I'm sure of nothing."

"Sounds better." He laughed. "Over the side then. You can do the rowing. I'll sit and watch."

"In a posser's fat eye you will."

"Then we better take a taxi." He scooped her up and swung her over the guard rail, lowered her into a boat nuzzling against the *Moonsprite,* startling the waterman seated in the stern.

The Dar stretched out to the horizon on all sides, a sheet of shallow water ruffled by the constant wind into painful glitters, broken by scattered clumps of feathery reeds twined about with blue-flowered vines. Day in, day out, always the same. Day in, day out, the wind blew, driving the double-hulled craft south and west toward the mountain range they could not yet see.

Swarms of small black biters rose at dawn in swaying swirls like dust devils in the Deadlands. Hern and Serroi were fresh blood for them, tender delicacies that called them from all over. At first they tried burning green reeds. Instead of driving the biters away, the choking black clouds seemed to entice more of them. They tried going overside and spending the worst of the day in the water, but the water had its own pests, small round leeches the size of Hern's thumbnail, boring worms that took only seconds to bury themselves in living flesh. Serroi had to spend an hour driving them out of Hern's body and out of her own.

On the ninth day out from Low Yallor, Serroi settled into a tense brood, stopped thinking and started trying to trust the new things working in her. She sank into a trance. The biters crawled over her, into her eyes, nose, ears, along her legs, into every crevice they could find.

She is aware that this is happening but it doesn't touch her.

She sees Hern staring at her. He stretches out on the narrow deck between the two hulls, reaches out to her and wipes the biters off her face. She thinks of telling him she is all right, that he doesn't need to be troubled about her, but she lets the impulse fade.

The sun moves from near the horizon until it is a double handspan above it.

The trance changes. Now she sees nothing. She sits in darkness, a profound nothingness that is wonderfully restful.

Now she sees a fire burning before her, what it burns is not clear at first, then she sees it is burning her body. She is no longer in that body, yet somehow she is in a body. She knows that because she stretches out a hand. She can see the hand. It is solid, small, green. Her hand. She puts her hand in the fire that is burning but not consuming her body. Her hand burns, the bones are black inside translucent, fire-colored flesh.

The burning hand moves.

It touches: a feather-headed reed. The reed crisps to ash.

It touches: the water. Steam rushes up about the hand. Red and yellow fish swim between the fire-colored fingers, swim unconcerned past blue-white billows of steam, evade the groping fingers with ease.

It touches: a trumpet-shaped bloom, a bright blue bloom with a golden throat. Smooth blue, cool blue. So cool it cools the fingers' fire, cools the fire to water, the water drips away. The hand is green and opaque again.

Green hand holding cool blue bloom.

A vine coils tender tendrils about the slim green wrist.

The slim green fingers stroke the vine, trace it down and down, into the water, into the mud. In black ooze green fingers close around a fat knobby root, feel the slick glassy skin, wrench the root free of the ooze.

The hand is out of the water. The tuber rests on its palm and begins to seethe and boil, reduces itself after a moment to a creamy white liquid. Black biters hover over the liquid, then dart away.

Serroi blinked. There were no longer any biters around

her. Hern was back in the other hull, free of biters also. The craft was skating along across the water, wind-driven, humming, hissing, creaking.

"So you're back."

"So I am." She rubbed at burning eyes with a hand that felt numb. Carefully she straightened her legs, began massaging her aching knees, first one, then the other as she looked about for any sign of the vine in her dream. Nothing. She wrinkled her nose. Yesterday nearly every clump of reeds seemed to sport the nodding blue blooms, right now she couldn't see a single one. She sighed, glanced at the sun. "Time to eat soon."

"Umph."

"You're grumpy today."

"Nipped to death, bite by bite."

"With a little luck no more of that."

"What?" He sat up; the boat lurched, water splashing over the sides.

"I think so." She patted a yawn. "Depending on if we can find one of those vines." She yawned again. "The ones with the blue flowers."

"Like that?" He pointed.

Beyond the edge of the sail she saw a touch of blue. "Right." She crawled forward and began uncleating the halyard. "You want to be helpful, you could toss the anchor overside when I get the sail down."

The juice from the crushed and simmered root spread over their skin kept off the biters but did nothing for the tedium.

Day in, day out, sitting or lying without moving because the boat answered to most movements, lurching, dipping, swaying. Air warm and moist, heavy and humming, the wind always blowing, day and night blowing inland. The boat skating over water three feet deep or less some of the time, blundering by chance into the channel of the river that rose in the mountains and emptied by Low Yallor into the Sinadeen, the channel they kept losing and finding again. One day melting into another, all the same, eternally the same. Sleeping at night, sail down, anchor overside, boat tugging at the anchor line, never sleeping well, never tired enough to rest without nightmare and constant waking. Picking through the diminishing supply of charcoal. Measuring out grudged handfuls of the herbs for the herb tea of the fenekeln. Endlessly netting fish to supplement meager trail rations.

Tedium, tedium, TEDIUM.

They fretted at each other and fretted at themselves. Hern began to brood about what was happening in the mijloc. For days he kept gnawing at it like a chini pup gnawing a boot, kept going over and over and over the same ground until Serroi felt like screaming. Did scream. A bitter shouting match relieved some of the tension but both began to wind tight again when day after day passed and the mountains were not even a hint on the horizon.

As he brooded, Hern grew steadily more certain that the whole quest was a mockery, there was no Coyote, no Mirror. All this was just to get them both out of Yael-mri's hair. He fussed with this idea, argued with Serroi and stared past the sail at the empty western sky.

Near sundown on a day that was like all the rest, they saw a jagged blue line etched into the cloudless blue of the sky. A ghostly guess at first, on the next day the line bloomed into a mountain range.

Each day the mountains were fractionally higher and clearer.

The wind began to grow erratic. One day it was only a pat against the cheek and the boat sat still in the water, the sail flapping idly against the mast. They unshipped the poles and tried moving the boat that way. And went from disaster to disaster, sending the boat in complicated caracoles, getting the poles stuck in the mud, left clinging to them while the boat slid gently from under their feet, nearly capsizing their craft more than once. By necessity, they learned finally how much pressure to apply and how to apply it together, and learning this earned an unasked-for bonus, a good night's sleep.

They woke stiff and sore to hear the wind blowing again, to feel the boat rocking under them as it fought the anchor.

The patches of reeds closed in around them and the water shallowed even more. On the tenth day after they sighted the mountains, the double bow knifed into a hump of mud and stuck there. Hern used his weight to rock the boat while Serroi shoved with the pole, trying to push them off the hump. The boat didn't budge. Cursing fervently Hern stripped, slid into the murky water. Rope biting into his shoulder he planted his feet in the ooze and hauled the boat free.

Half an hour later the craft was stuck again on a narrow mudbar that lay just beneath the surface of the water. This time they managed to pole it off. It grounded again and again

that day before they gave up and settled for the night. They
were slathered with stinking black mud, thumbnail leeches
plastered over legs and feet, borer worms coiled thick in their
flesh. They lay staring at the sky, too weary to attempt anything more strenuous than breathing.

Serroi twitched, gritted her teeth and rolled up onto her
knees.

Hern opened one bleary bloodshot eye, saw her grinning at
him. "You're no eye's delight yourself," he said.

"No." She dipped the waterbucket overside and brought it
up half full of water. She eased herself and the bucket onto
the mid-deck. "Get yourself up here if you can without sinking us."

"Hah." He crawled up beside her, stretched out flat.

Serroi washed the mud from his legs, set rag and bucket
aside and began stroking her fingertips down along the solid
flesh of his leg. As she moved from groin to toes, she felt
dozens of sharp twitches like minute fishhooks set into her
own flesh. Humming softly, she curled both hands about his
thigh, thumb to thumb, slid them slowly down over his knees,
along his sturdy calves and feet, driving out ahead of them
the borer worms, dislodging the grey and swollen leech discs,
healing the holes and sucker wounds. When she finished the
second leg, she sat up and rubbed at her back. "You're clean.
Be nice, Dom. Fetch me some more water."

He sat up, scratched at a knee. "Yes, mama."

"Fool."

"Your fool, love. Value me."

"Oh I do. More on dry land though."

"Hah. Hand me that bucket."

She flattened her legs on the deck, looked them over,
sighed "Done for now. I hate to think about tomorrow."

He grunted. When she looked over her shoulder, he was
pouring water through the strainer. He saw her watching.
"Thought we could use something hot."

"One of your better ideas." She swung around and eased
herself off the mid-deck into the other hull. "There's a round
of cheese and some waybread left. I don't feel up to fooling
with much more. You?"

"No." He gathered the ends of the straining cloth and
lifted it off the sooty cookpot. "We'll have to leave the boat
fairly soon. Be more trouble than it's worth." He reached
over the rail and sloshed the cloth about in the water.

"Shouldn't be too far to the edge of the Dar. I can already see the brush on the hillsides."

Serroi looked up from peeling wax off the cheese. "Dry land. You know how good that sounds?"

He chuckled, wrung the cloth out and draped it over the rail to dry. "I'm growing webs between my fingers and toes." On the mid-deck he opened the firebox, got the fire going and set the water on to boil. "Any idea where that damn river is now?"

"Not the faintest." She set the cheese on the cutting board and began slicing it into thick chunks. "I did try searching for it. All this water, it messes up my outreach." She pushed the hair off her face, closed her fingers about the small leather pouch that held the tajicho, ran her eyes along the line of mountain, stopped as she saw something she'd seen a hundred times before but hadn't taken in. "Hern, look." She waved the knife at the mountains.

"At what?"

"Didn't Yael-mri say we were to look for a dormant volcano?"

"Yael-mri, hunh!"

"Forget all that, isn't that a volcanic cone right there?" She waggled the knife. "Look at it."

A truncated triangle, it rose above the rest of the peaks, its elegant simplicity of form notably other than the jagged, irregular summits of the lower mountains. "Mount Santac," she said. "Coyote's Mirror."

Hern looked down at his feet, flexed his toes. "Zhag," he muttered.

Serroi laid the knife beside the cheese and began unwrapping the waybread. "I know. A long miserable walk and we can't even be sure he . . . it . . . will be there."

The next day was a repetition of that slow painful slogging through the marsh. And the next. Then they broke through a solid band of reeds into the river channel. With the help of the reeds they kept to the channel from then on, following the wide loops and twists of the river. The wind rose and died, rose again, blowing in the wrong direction. Foot by foot they fought the strengthening current until they left the reeds behind and with them the Dar.

Just before midday on the nineteenth day since they sighted the mountains they reached the first rapids. They beached the boat for the last time, assembled the things they would need for the trek to the mountain and set out walking along the riverbank.

By sundown they were some little way into the foothills, eating roasted fish and groundnuts beside a river now small and noisy. Serroi sipped at her herb tea as she watched the flames flicker above branches neatly layered within a ring of stones. She had a feeling of unfolding as if she'd been wrapped tight about herself for so long that she'd forgotten how to stretch out. The cool crispness in the air, the trees in spring bud here where the seasons mirrored those on the far side of the Sinadeen, the green smell of the spears of new grass pushing through the old, these things woke in her a lightness of the spirit and a feeling that the long troubling struggle was near its end. She smiled at the flames, the pungent tea warm inside her, looked up and met Hern's questioning gaze. He was rubbing thoughtfully at his calves, flexing his feet, working his ankles.

"Two days. Three maybe," she said. "If we hold out and the way doesn't get too bad."

He straightened, drew his thumb across his chin. "Coyote's Mirror," he murmured. "Hunh. Coyote's Mirage."

"Thought of what you might look for in that mirage if it's not."

He shrugged. "What are we fighting? Nearga-nor. Your Noris. Floarin and her army. Seems to me I'd better get something to fight the army and let you and your friends in the Biserica take care of the magic." His eyes narrowed. He stared past her, reached for the Sleykyn sword.

Serroi swung around. A small grey beast with a bushy tail, big ears, a pointed nose, hovered on the edge of the circle of firelight, slanted eyes glinting red. It had a raffish, jaunty look, an un-beastlike intelligence in its red eyes. She thrust her hand palm out at Hern. "Wait." Her eyes on the beast, she called, "Coyote?"

The beast canted his head to one side, ears pricking. He grinned at her, red tongue lolling, then swung around and trotted off, the last thing she saw the insolent waving of that scruffy tail.

For two days they followed the river, climbing laboriously

up the steeply canted bank, the perfect cone of the volcano hovering always over them, the grey beast scampering effortlessly before them. And he haunted the campfires each night. Though Serroi grew more certain with each appearance that the beast was indeed Coyote or at least had something to do with him, Hern watched it with angry eyes, convinced that she was fooling herself, that the wit she claimed to see in the beast was as much a mirage as the whole quest.

On the evening of the fifth day of the climb they reached the timberline. The snowclad slope stretched another quarter mile above them, steep, radiantly pure line. The stream they followed came from a high thin cut in the rim of the cone, fell in a foaming rush half the distance, smoothed out for the rest, flowed past them in a black glass slide. There was no sign anything lived here but coneys and rockhoppers.

"Camp here?" Serroi slipped cold hands into her sleeves. Her breath was a white cloud in the crackling cold air.

"Why not? Nothing up there. I'll get some wood." Hern disappeared into the twisted and weathered trees growing low over equally scrubby brush. Serroi kicked a few runnels of snow off the limp yellow grass in a small round clearing in the brush and hunted out small stones. She built a fire circle, unrolled her blankets, doubled one and spread it on the ground, sat on one end, pulled the other blanket about her shoulders. She was beginning to feel as grim and angry as Hern.

Chasing a mirage, she thought. *I think he's right. Chasing a figment of Yael-mri's imagination. Bait to pull my Noris off the Biserica, that's all she wanted.* She dragged the tajicho's pouch over her head. Through the thin leather she could feel the crystal warm and alive.

While she was holding it and nerving herself to act, Hern came back with a meager armload of wood. Without saying a word, he built a fire then came to sit beside her on the blanket.

"Looks like Yael-mri played us both damn well."

"Looks like." Serroi pulled open the neck of the pouch and shook out the tajicho. "So this isn't a total futility." She drew back her arm, preparing to hurl the crystal down the mountain.

"Hey, hey, not away, let me see, let me, give it to me." She swung around and saw a scrawny little man with wild grey

hair and a long pointed nose hopping from foot to foot. His
nose twitched, his pointed ears twitched, his greenish eyes
glowed with excitement and greed. He quieted immediately
and grinned at her, a sly look on his odd, ugly face. "You
don't want it, give it to me."

"I can't," she said with more patience than she thought she
could feel now. "It's patterned to me and me alone."

"Ah. Ah. Ah." His nose twitched again. His grin widened
until he seemed to have no chin. "Let me hold it, please-
please?" He tilted his head and put a comically ingratiating
look on his face. "I want to see it."

Hern was scowling. He dropped a hand on Serroi's shoulder. "Who are you?"

"Now, now, that's mine to ask. Who're you and what are
you doing on my mountain?"

"Your mountain." Serroi laid her free hand on Hern's. She
wouldn't look at him, not yet. "Then you are Coyote."

"Ah. Ah. Could be." He sidled a little closer but was careful to stay out of reach. "Could be."

She sucked in a breath, let it trickle out, trying to calm the
turmoil inside her, felt Hern stiffen, both of them not quite
daring to resurrect hope. "The prieti-meien Yael-mri asks that
you take a moment to listen to us. She told us to say favor
for favor, Coyote, bids you remember the debt you owe."

"Yael-mri." Coyote tittered, then guffawed, repeating the
name over and over, clutching at his little pot belly. Finally
he wiped streaming eyes. "Ah. Ah. Ah. A favor. A look in
Coyote's mirror." He tilted his head, gazed from Serroi to
Hern. "Maybe so." His long impossibly thin arms shot out. A
long impossibly thin finger jabbed at Serroi's fisted hand.
"Give it to me. I will see it, I will hold it. First or nothing."

"It might be dangerous to you," Serroi said slowly. "It kills
all magic but mine."

Coyote tittered. "Ah. Ah. Kind little green person, good
sweet tasty little one. Thinking to warn poor Coyote. Ah.
Ah." He closed his fingers into a bony fist and beat against
his bony chest. "Not magic, me, oh no. Not me. Give me."

Serroi shrugged. "Catch then." She tossed the tajicho to
him. The glow of the crystal died as it left her hand. It was a
dark pebble again when Coyote snatched it from the air. As
it touched his chalky fingers it seemed to change, to grow
translucent though the fire did not rewaken in its heart.

As soon as the tajicho left her hand, there was a shimmer
in the air and Ser Noris was there, a short distance from her,

his face paler and more worn than before. "Serroi, haven't you struggled enough? Make an end of this foolishness."

Hern's fingers tightened on her shoulder, but she slipped from his grip and rose to her feet. "Ser Noris."

Coyote laughed, a jarring sound like the bark of a hunting chini. "Favor. Yes. Come, I show you my house, get out of this cold. Come, I show you my Mirror. Ah!"

"No!" There was a driving urgency in Ser Noris's dark rich voice. "Don't trust that creature. You don't know what it is. Serroi, he's the Changer. Serroi, he'll change everything; you'll destroy everything you're trying to save. Fight me if you must, but not with that."

Serroi stared at him. He was frightened. She'd never thought to see that. She drew a dry tongue along dry lips. He stretched out his hands to her. "Come to me, come home." His voice shook with tenderness and fear.

She stared and the compulsion to heal stirred in her. Hern caught at her arm as she took a step toward the Nor, jerked his hand away as if touching her burned him. There was a wrongness in Ser Noris, she felt it, a sickness that went to the heart of him, she had to touch him, heal him. She took another step. Fire burned in her hands. She looked down at them. They shone with a clear green light, the bones were shadows in green glass. She stretched out her glowing hands and took a third step toward him.

At her first step triumph lit his face, at the second, when the light began to shine about her, the triumph faltered, at the third step, he stared at her appalled. Her hand brushed his. He screamed and jerked away, his flesh changing, melting. She took another step and reached for him. With a soft anguished sob, he whipped into nothingness, retreating she knew without knowing how she knew to his sanctuary in his tower.

Serroi blinked, felt a sudden dizziness as if the world was shifting under her. Hern caught her before she could fall.

Her body was boneless, strengthless. She felt him scoop her off her feet. She was shivering, so cold she could not even feel his hands on her.

"Have to get her inside." Hern was shouting at Coyote. *He shouldn't be doing that,* she thought. "You said you have a house. Where?" *A house and a fire,* she thought, waves of shivers passed over her, she could hear her teeth clicking together.

"Ah. Ah. Ah. You follow, yes? Follow." The little man

glided along the line of brush until he came to a sheer cliff poking through the snow. He knocked against the stone and it melted away from him. "Coyote's home on the mountain, in the mountain." He tittered and went trotting inside.

Hern hesitated, glanced at the sky. The sun was almost gone and the wind was blowing icy against them. "Coyote," he muttered, shook his head and followed Coyote into the mountain, Serroi cradled in his arms.

Two days later the first snow flakes fell on Tuli and Rane as they came out of the mountains onto the southern edge of Cimpia Plain.